BABY,

LET'S MAKE A BABY

PLUS TEN MORE STORIES

BABY,

LET'S MAKE A BABY

PLUS TEN MORE STORIES

by

KIRK CURNUTT

RIVER CITY PUBLISHING
Montgomery, Alabama

© 2003 by Kirk Curnutt
Published in the United States by River City Publishing,
1719 Mulberry St., Montgomery, AL 36106.

Printed in the United States
Designed by Nancy Stevens
Cover Photograph by Kip Curnutt

Library of Congress Cataloging-in-Publication Data:
Curnutt, Kirk, 1964-
  Baby, let's make a baby : plus ten more stories / by Kirk Curnutt.
     p. cm.
  ISBN 1-57966-036-3
  I. Title.
  PS3603.U76B33 2003
  813'.6--dc21

                                                          2003003920

First Edition

Always and Anon,
For Kip,
Le petit prince

CONTENTS

"A young French writer, who was asked by a publisher for a Life for a series of biographies, replied: 'Certainly, but I don't know any history. You choose a character. All I demand is that it shall be a man or woman who had a consistent desire to give a certain direction to his or her life and was always brought up against a closed door.' "
—André Maurois, *Aspects of Biography* (1929)

OVERPASS

Me and Stebbie's sittin' on a speed bump in the parkin' lot when up comes Monteiro and Nazz. Monteiro's ridin' in this shoppin' cart with Nazz behind him, pushin', Nazz's feet kickin' hard at the pavement so every five, six steps he can hop on the bottom crossbar and ride someways. They shouldn't be gettin' away with this. The cops don't like this sort of dickin' around. Usually they standin' outside the grocery to shoo away kids who're up to no good.

"Yo, Stebbie," Monteiro calls out. He's scrunched down on his haunches so his legs bulge like a pair of fresh packed Christmas hams. "You goin' to church with me tomorrow or what?"

"Shut up, Monteiro," I say. "You know you don't go to no church."

"Was I talkin' to you, futhermucker?" That's Monteiro's favorite word. He made it up hisself, he likes to brag. "I was talkin' to your brother. Right, Stebbie?"

Stebbie don't answer. He's got his head bent hard to one side like that's where the last gasp of air in the world is. His gray tongue is stuck out his mouth, and he's got a big string of drool unspoolin off it. As my pops says, Stebbie's a dumb ass. Don't talk, don't listen. Just makes faces and looks like he's tryin' to see things from under his eyelids, which never come higher than about halfway up his eyeballs.

"What church you claim you go to?" I ask.

Nazz stops the cart next to the speed bump where we're sittin', but Monteiro don't get out. "First Presbo," Monteiro tells me. "Don't I, Nazz?"

Nazz shrugs. A shrug's about as much as you gonna get from Nazz. Next to Stebbie, he's about the least talkin' person I know.

"First Presbo's a rich man's church," I say. I know this for fact. "You got to give up a wad of bills to get in the door."

"Maybe." Monteiro finally stands up and hops out the cart. He's a short kid, only about five foot plus some. Most of the time he looks even littler than that because he got a baby face and the

clothes he wears is always about three sizes more than they ought
to be. Stebbie's way taller—more than six. Big, too, since he's
twenty and so much older than the rest of us. Monteiro pulls a
pack of gum out his pocket and stuffs a bunch of sticks behind his
teeth. "Them rich people come and get me every Sunday morning, though. They give me a shirt and tie and food, and all I got
to do is sit around and listen to them go on about the Bible.
Sunday night they come get me again, and I sing in the choir.
Get a free dinner for that, too."

Nazz and me are smilin' at the idea of Monteiro singin' anythin', much less church songs. Stebbie's laughin', too, but not at
nothin' in particular. He's always laughin'.

"They said I could bring a friend tomorrow. Because of Easter
and all. You think I'd waste that on you or Nazz? No way. You
good boys already. I want Stebbie to go with me. You think he
understands it? Hey, Stebbie—Stebbie—" It takes Stebbie a few
seconds to recognize his name. He looks over at Monteiro, his
tongue lollin'. "You understand Passover?" Monteiro asks him.

"Shut up," I go. "You know he don't get none of that stuff."

"It ain't hard." Now Monteiro's voice is all spitted up from
chewin' the gum. His cheeks are fat, too. "See, Stebbie, they
killed Jesus, but Jesus come back to life. They buried him all up,
but he got out the tomb like it wasn't nothin' more but bed he
was getting out of. People heard him goin' over their houses in
the middle of the night. That's why they call it Passover."

Me and Nazz are bustin' laughin'.

"You got it all wrong as usual, dumb ass. Right, Nazz?" Nazz
don't say nothin', of course, but he's chuckled up. "Passover was
like Thanksgiving," I tell him. "The people got out the desert,
and they decide to have this big meal every year to celebrate. It
was a long time before Jesus even came around. They just happen to throw this party the same month that Jesus got hisself
killed."

Monteiro hacks his wad on the ground.

"What do you know anyway?" He's all snarly now. He's pretty thin-skinned. "It's not like you even go to church. And if you
do, I know you not gettin' no free meals out of the deal."

"Aw, who cares, anyway?" I go.

Then as we're just talkin', hangin' out, here comes the cop out the grocery doors. It's always same one every time we're here: a big dumb lookin' guy, his face white and bumpy like dried paste.

"Get out of the parking lot, you morons," he yells. There's nobody around, so he can talk to us like that.

"We're not doin' nothin'," Monteiro tells him. He and Nazz are leanin' up against this red truck.

"So go do nothing somewhere else," the cop says back. "And get off that vehicle this instant. You can't just go sprawl over somebody else's stuff if it's not yours."

Monteiro and Nazz snap up attention-like and step a ways away.

Monteiro goes, "Hey, mister, you know Bible stuff? You know what Passover means?"

"Sure, I know what it means. Don't you?"

"Sure. I know all the stories, back to front. What's your favorite part?"

The cop acts like he's thinkin'. Then he goes, "The bit where God wipes out all the little criminals. Makes my job a whole lot easier."

"Har har har," Monteiro says back. "That's real funny, mister. You know the story I like? The one where God says the last'll be first and the first'll be last. About time for that, dontcha think?"

The cop's smilin'. "Well, son, I hate to break it to you, but when that happens, you and me will be standing in line right next to each other."

"Yeah, right," Monteiro goes.

Me and Nazz shake our heads. Stebbie's lookin' toward the big bright sign up above the grocery. I don't know if that's exactly where he's lookin' or not. He's always starin' at somethin'. You can't ever quite figure out what, though.

"Now that we've got that established," the cop tell us, "feel free to get lost. You know the manager doesn't want you out here."

"So where you want us to go?" I say.

The cop looks a little spooked—I guess because I hadn't said nothin' yet.

"How about home," he snaps in a way that lets us know it's not a suggestion he's makin'. Before I can give him some talk back, he's gone inside the grocery again.

"So what we gonna do?" I go to Monteiro. He's pushin' the wad of gum around with the toe of his sneaker. Nazz's leanin' back against the truck, like he's cool with whatever. Truth is, there isn't much around to do.

"Hey, Nazz," Monteiro says. "Let's go up on the overpass." He looks at me, actin' like he's not sure whether I'm good enough to invite along. "You can come with us," he finally goes, "but if you're gonna, you gotta bring Stebbie."

Stebbie moans and slobbers again, hearin' hisself get talked about. I grab his arm and pull him to his feet, and then we all head off together.

A hundred miles to the northwest, a woman placed a valise in the trunk of her Honda Civic and slammed the lid shut.

"I'm not sure I'm ready for this."

With her was another woman, younger, perhaps by as much as ten or fifteen years. The first woman, who was named Mary-Angel, closed her eyes for a moment, as if trying to keep her balance. They were standing in the driveway of Mary-Angel's newly purchased garden home, which sat a few blocks from the campus of the small liberal arts college where she taught in the foreign language department.

"Oh, come on," her companion complained. "What are you afraid of?"

"I'm afraid of my parents," Mary-Angel admitted. "It was easy for you—that feel-good, enlightened Congregational stock of yours. I'm sure your parents ran right out and got themselves a PFLAG membership. Probably marched behind Larry Kramer in a parade with placards and power-to-the-people smiles. My folks aren't like that, Suz. They're Catholic, for God's sake."

Suz folded her arms disapprovingly. Her bag was already in the trunk. "And you're how old? You don't think even good, old apostolic Catholics get suspicious when their daughter's thirty-five and never had a"—she made a mocking pair of quotation marks with her fingers—" 'significant other'? Didn't you show them your dissertation?"

"Are you kidding?" Mary-Angel squeezed her keys in her palm. "I didn't want my advisor to read it, much less my parents. And just because I wrote about Colette, that's some kind of clue to something? Didn't I teach you better than that?"

"Get real, girlfriend. You know the word's out. We're quite the object of scrutiny. Ronnie Vasquez told me we were the hot topic at the last Scholar's Club mixer. Your esteemed colleagues aren't clueless, you know."

Mary-Angel started to cry. She didn't want to, but she felt her eyes water. By the time she realized she couldn't hold it back, a tear was already sliding from under her glasses. It ran alongside her nose.

"I'm up for tenure next year," she said as she sobbed.

Suz took her in an embrace. She felt Mary-Angel's thick frames press into her neck, but she held on anyway. "Why do you need to be embarrassed?" Suz whispered. "Let's just do it, get us out in the open. You'll feel so much better. I know you will."

"It's just—it's just—" Mary-Angel found it hard to speak through her gasps. "I've just hurt them in so many ways already. You don't know, but in so many ways."

"Shhh. Remember Sacher-Masoch." Suz recited a line from memory: " 'Pleasure alone lends value to existence; whoever enjoys does not easily part from life, whoever suffers or is needy meets death like a friend.' So relax. Relax and enjoy me."

Mary-Angel drew back, repulsed by the sudden inappropriateness of a quote she'd put on so many midterm examinations for her students to identify and interpret.

She said, "I remember the other part, the moral: 'Whoever allows himself to be whipped, deserves to be whipped.' " She laughed in a strained, awkward way, and the women formally stepped apart. "Why am I so weak?" Mary-Angel wondered aloud. "You make me feel hijacked sometimes. Your overtness, your directness—I wonder to what degree I'm being used for a higher cause, as though my privacy, my discretion have to be hoisted up to the level of an agenda for me to have you be happy. Why can't I love you, simply and ably, without having to declare it?" Out of nervousness, she jangled her keys. Their music chimed softly amid the evening quiet.

"Because there is no love if it's undeclared," Suz told her.

Mary-Angel smiled again, a forced pleasantry. "What a role reversal we've undergone. The student is now the master, the teacher the slave. Why is that?"

"Because there is no love if it's undeclared," Suz said again. "I really think I was brought into your life to show you that. That's my only ambition now."

Mary-Angel drew a deep breath and began unlocking the driver's side door. "You all peed out? It's a six-hour drive, you know."

Suz was across from her, plucking at the moussed spikes of her hair while she waited for the click of the passenger lock. "Yes, I'm fine. I'm looking forward to meeting your parents. I can't wait to look them in the eye and say, 'Mr. and Mrs. LeVot, I love your daughter to the depth and breadth of my soul.' "

"Oh, Jesus Christ," Mary-Angel swore. They got into the car and left for the interstate.

Somewhere to the south, a nervous man fiddled with a portable CD player in the darkened hollow of a 1969 Chevy which he himself had spent countless hours customizing.

"You like Springsteen?" he asked the woman beside him. She was mid-fifties and still attractive, a pretty widow who had been introduced to the man a few days earlier by friends of a friend. This was their first date.

"I'm on the road so much," the man went on, "I find myself playing songs about being on the road. Not Jan and Dean type stuff—not hot rods and deuce coupes and little GTOs. Sadder stuff, like Bob Dylan's 'Tangled Up in Blue.' Do you know that one?"

The widow shook her head so that the gray hair framing her cheeks swept her shoulders. The man liked the fact that she still wore her hair long. Most women her age cut theirs short.

"It's really beautiful, amazing words. But here, let me play you this one first." He pushed a CD onto the spindle, shut the case, and pressed the song-selection button. Slow, plaintive piano chords filled the idling car. "It's called 'Racing in the Streets.' I suppose I like it so much because I'm a grease monkey at heart. Here, listen to the first line."

The woman listened politely as the singing started.

"Did you catch the words?" the man asked, pushing the pause key. "He says he's got a '69 Chevy. In case you're wondering, I had the car long before I knew the song." He allowed the music to resume. "Hear that part? He's talking about a 396, which is an engine, with Fuelie heads and a Hurst on the floor. Isn't that amazing, to make poetry out of machinery? I suppose you've had to have torn an engine down to really identify with it. I mean, I try to not take the lyrics too literally, you know, but I think it's about indirection, about the problem of finding some sort of direction for your life that makes you feel like you're headed somewhere. Or maybe not; I don't know. I guess I like the music because it sounds sort of lonely, and that's a feeling that it's taken me a long time to be okay with. I mean, I don't mind being lonely." He suddenly laughed at himself. "I should just let you listen."

As the song played, the man maneuvered his vintage automobile along a thoroughfare of strip malls and fast-food restaurants. The clutter of the brightly lit signs created a thin halo around the caul of the night.

"My husband looked at cars as investments," the widow told him when the song was over. The man turned the CD player off while she spoke. In his mind he was trying to decide what song to share next with her. "He kept a log of the mileage. He'd list the dates when he had the tires rotated and balanced and when he'd changed the oil. Every year, he'd calculate what he thought he could get for re-sell against the blue-book value. I don't think he was ever really passionate about his cars. I just think he wanted to come out on top of his money."

The man said, "I get it from having to work the road. I was always into restoring cars from when I was a kid, but it wasn't until I started traveling so much for my job that I thought about what it means—the constant movement, the repetition of the constant movement as you go back and forth across the same space. Some guys at my company have huge territories, multi-state regions, and they rarely see the same stretch but once or twice a month. Mine's small, and I cover the same ground so often that it's messed with my sense of time. I mean, I don't think in days anymore. It never pops into my mind that it's Tuesday or Wednesday. To me it's just Exit 172 day, Exit 258 day."

"Allie said you work too hard. She said she and Terry are always begging you to go to the mountains with them."

Allie and Terry were the friends of the friend who'd introduced them.

"I guess the routine gives me security. And I like to be alone, most of the time. It's easier that way." He took a breath. "I'm sure they told you about the accident. It's certainly okay if they did. I won't be mad. It's sort of what I'm famous for."

"They didn't go into details," she assured him. "They just said you'd been hurt in a fall."

"Trimming limbs. You know how they say to stay off the top rung of a stepladder? Well, I'm living proof of that wisdom. Here's why." He held up his right hand. Through the moonlight, the woman saw that his fingers were pinched and crimped. "You'll see, too, when we get to the restaurant that I limp badly as well. My wife at the time was really into taking walks. I think she got married to have a walking companion. Once I couldn't keep up, she just kept on going."

"My husband didn't like going for walks either. He worked a lot, too, but he had a good sense of balance. He played basketball in the community center league, and he'd run on the treadmill at the gym a few times a week. I'm sure you've gotten the scoop on me, too. He's been gone six years now, and this is the very first time I've dated, or even been alone with a man. I have to admit that it feels very strange. We were together twenty-six years."

The man felt himself smile.

"That's great. I always imagined how wonderful it would be to wake up with someone with that much history between you. Just the feeling of security. As if time itself were watching you late at night, while you slept, saying to you, 'You're safe.' Or maybe, 'You're the one with whom I'm well pleased.' Well, as you know, it just never happened for me. I've been married three times, twice when I was younger, then this last time when I was in my fifties. I can't tell you what went wrong. Two of them had a good go. One was very short, because of the accident. I had books checked out of the library for longer than Cecilia and I were married."

The woman laughed politely at his humor. "I can't say I've not enjoyed living alone since he died," she told him. "There are a lot of ladies at work my age who are either divorced or wid-owed. One of them has never been married. We travel together a lot. We went to Ireland last spring for ten days. It was a nice time. The great thing is that no one's desperate for a man. That's the saddest thing to happen to women after fifty. They don't feel like they can survive the loneliness."

He said, "There's part of me that believes that loneliness—wait, that's not what I mean to say. Aloneness? But that's not even a word." He laughed again, nervously. "Being alone, there's part of me that believes that it's good for us to be alone. I don't know; maybe I'm just trying to convince myself of something. But when you're alone, you can get something done, you know? Accomplish something. I mean, yes, it's wonderful to be doing nothing with someone, lying on the couch and movie-watching and all, but shouldn't finishing some actual task you've started give you the same satisfaction? As you can probably guess, it drove my all of my wives nuts that I spent so much time listen-ing to music and rebuilding cars."

They grew silent as they arrived at Le Pont du Ciel, the French restaurant where the man had made dinner reservations.

"Well," he said. "I think everything's going good so far. You're having a good time, aren't you, Marcy?"

"Yes," the widow answered, and he could tell she was smil-ing. "But I feel like I have to say this up front, Joe, just so no one has hard feelings later on. I'm really not looking for a relation-ship. Do you know what I mean? I like having friends, but I like living alone. And I'm fifty-six. Do you understand that?"

"Terry and Allie said you'd say these things. To be honest, it almost scared me from asking you. But rest assured, I don't have any expectations. I would just like to be good to someone, you know? That and to share a conversation. Fair enough?"

"Fair enough," Marcy agreed.

"We're a few minutes early. Would you like to hear another song before we go in? It's one of my favorites."

Marcy rested back in her seat. She felt safe and comfortable with Joe. "I'd love to," she told him.

Not far away, Ray Dean Josephs placed the gun barrel to the back of his girlfriend Cheryl's head as they sat in the apartment from which, three days earlier, she'd thrown Ray Dean out. Both of them cried, their voices tangling loudly enough that their upstairs neighbor kicked his heel on the floor in annoyance. Also crying was the couple's fourteen-month-old son, whom they'd nicknamed Doobie. Doobie sat on the floor, naked except for a pair of oversized diapers that bunched up over his belly. His nose had run unwiped for nearly two hours, ever since Ray Dean broke out a rear window to reenter the apartment.

"I tried to tell you," Ray Dean said. As he always did when he was agitated, he was chewing at the ends of his bushy mustache. "I tried to tell you there's no way I can let you take him away from me. I'm a man, Cheryl. A man can't stand having his world taken away. Why couldn't you have just understood that, baby? Why couldn't you have just known me like you was supposed to?"

Cheryl felt the barrel resting at the spot where her skull became her neck. She was looking at her son. The baby's arms reached for her, as they had off and on through the entire ordeal. *He's going to kill me*, she thought. Cheryl's whole relationship with Ray Dean had been one long fight—fights over Ray Dean's drinking, Ray Dean's whoring, Ray Dean's not paying his fair share of the bills. Throughout their fights, though, he'd never laid a hand on her, and that fact made it incomprehensible to Cheryl that this was how her life should end. *I'm going to die, she thought, with my son whom I love more than anything in the world reaching for me and me unable to hold him.*

"Think about this, honey," she heard herself say. "You shoot me like this—my brains, my blood, they're going to get on the baby. You can't be that angry at me. You can't. Look at him, honey. We created him. Together. Us. How could you hurt him like that?"

"You're too strong-willed for your own good." Ray Dean stepped to her side, lifting the barrel away from her head to put it to his own. In her peripheral vision Cheryl watched the pistol cradle itself against the indentation where his hairline flared toward his right ear. Then, just as quickly, he pointed it back at her. He was measuring the distance his arm would have to travel between shooting her and himself. "Your daddy told me you was too high on yourself. You know that? He said you stared too long in the mirror when you were a girl." Tears began streaming out his eyes again. "I just can't believe you would take my boy from me."

"Ray Dean," Cheryl gulped, "you can't do this. You can't. It's just so crazy."

"Don't you believe in fate, baby doll? I believe we're together for a reason. We were supposed to come together, make a baby together, grow old and die together." He pulled the hammer back, locking a bullet in the chamber. "I guess now we just die together."

She screamed, and the baby screamed, but after a few seconds of staring at the end of the gun, waiting for the projectile to burst through the hole, she realized he hadn't fired. Ray Dean suddenly let the weapon fall to his side. He tapped furiously at his lips with the index finger of his other hand, shushing her.

Outside, someone pounded a fist on the apartment door.

"Don't say nothing," he whispered. She watched as he went to the apartment's foyer, the gun slid between his skinny shoulder blades by a bent-back arm. He yanked the door open. All Cheryl could see over Ray Dean's shoulder was the crown of a bald, wrinkled head. It was their upstairs neighbor. Ray Dean argued with him when the man threatened to call the police if the racket didn't stop. "Mind your own business, cowboy!" Ray Dean screamed, and he slammed the door so loud Cheryl thought he'd shot himself in the back by accident. When he turned around, Ray Dean's face was red and twisted from the exertion of thinking. He yanked his ball cap off his head and wiped at the grimy indentation the lining left in his hair. Then he grabbed Cheryl's arm and jerked her up.

"Where we going?"

"Out riding," he said, pulling the cap's bill over his eyes. He shoved her toward the back bedroom, back toward the broken window that he'd crawled through.

"Ray Dean, you can't leave Doobie here alone. You can't!"

His lips wrinkled like he was choking on a cherry pit. Then, without warning, his arm arced out, the gun butt clutched in his fist, slamming into the dry wall. It stuck there for a moment until Ray Dean yanked it out, leaving a toothy hole.

"Goddamn, Cheryl!" he yelled. "You always got to be nagging?"

He ran back and scooped Doobie in his free arm, then motioned for her to keep moving. She had to walk barefoot over the shards of broken glass. She felt her feet bleed as she lifted herself onto the sill and squeezed through the opening. Ray Dean didn't seem to notice. Once outside, he grabbed her by the elbow and dragged her to his Impala. He set the boy down and rifled the pockets of his Wranglers for his keys. Once he found them, he struggled to open the trunk with his left hand, his right still keeping the gun trained on Cheryl.

"Get in," he told her.

"You can't put Doobie in there, too," she said. Ray Dean shoved her as she tried to lift herself into the trunk. She fell into a pile of dank work clothes and boots, her shoulder cracking against the spare tire.

"I wouldn't put my son in no trunk," Ray Dean told her. He was shaking his head, his lips wrinkled again. The damp ends of his mustache were twisted. "You always got to think the worst of me, don't you?"

And he slammed the lid down, leaving Cheryl lying in darkness.

So after we get kicked out of the parkin' lot, we go sit for a while on the embankment of the cloverleaf by the interstate. It's pretty dark by this time of night, so nobody hassles us out here in the long weeds and wild flowers. Me and Nazz take turns with this lighter. It's kinda fun to watch the grass burn. You take one of the long spears, and you put the tip in the flame, and it just eats its way to the ground before sizzlin' out. Stebbie don't care nothin' about this, course. He's just stretched out, disappeared in the fronds and stalks. I only know he's still with us because of the mooin' he does. And Monteiro. Monteiro's latched onto him tonight somethin' fierce. They're off from me and Nazz but not far because I can hear every word Monteiro's sayin'.

"Last Sunday school, they talkin' about this guy who goes out in the woods. He's got this big decision to make so he wants

God to tell him what to do. He says, 'I'm throwin' this rock at that tree, and if it hits it, Lord, I'll go one way, and if it misses, Lord, that's you tellin' me to go the other.' So he throws the rock, and it hits the tree. And he does what he thinks he's supposed to, and it all works out okay. But you know what I'd have done, Stebbie?"

Stebbie blubbers a little.

Monteiro says, "I'd have made sure to pick me a thick-ass tree first. Har har har."

"Leave Stebbie alone," I tell him. "You're just makin' fun of him bein' dumb."

"I'm not either. I take better care of him than you. I'm takin' him to church tomorrow."

"You're not either," I say. "There's no point in him goin' and makin' a fool of hisself for stuff he don't get."

Monteiro rolls over onto his knees and stands up, lookin' at the concrete bridge that goes over the highway. He stuffs his shirt-tail back in his pants.

"Hey, let's go up there, Stebbie. We can talk in some peace there."

He scampers up the hill until he's on the pavement. All you can see is his silhouette. He calls down to Stebbie, who's lost in his own world until he hears his name. Then Stebbie goes up the embankment, too, his big arms swingin' like a monkey's. Me and Nazz play with the lighter some more, but then I decide I don't like Monteiro up there alone with my brother. So I climb up, too, and Nazz goes with me.

When we get up on the overpass we find them standin' at the concrete guardrail, lookin' down.

"What you doin' to him now?" I say.

"Nunya," Monteiro goes. "Shh. Here comes one." We look back and see headlights headin' south from the top of the incline, right towards us. Monteiro clears his throat and goes, "If I don't hit the car, I throw Stebbie over. If I hit it, I won't."

Before we can say anythin' else, he's got what looks like a big cotton wad comin' out of his lips. It hangs there for a second, dan-glin' and thinnin', stretchin' longways until it snaps right at his chin and falls. We rush to the rails and watch. Even though it's dark as hell, we can see Monteiro's goober, lit up white like a

Christmas bulb. It splats itself right square on the roof of the car
as it comes out from the girders.

"Someone's looking out for you, Stebbie," Monteiro says
with a big grin. "That's what they teach you at a rich man's
church. Everythin' happens for a reason."

"You just lucky," I tell him. I'm lookin' down at the highway,
thinkin' what a long fall it would be.

"Oh yeah?" His little head is all tight and cocky now. "Then
try this. Next car comes, it's Stebbie's turn. If he misses, he stays
with you tomorrow. If it hits, that's someone somewhere wantin'
him to go with me tomorrow. For Easter."

"You're wack," I go.

But Monteiro puts Stebbie at the railin' anyway, and he
mimics hockin', showin' Stebbie what to do. We don't have to
wait long for a car because it's a holiday and all. So another one
heads south at us. Monteiro cocks himself back, waitin' for the
rush of the tires to be sucked under the hollow of the overpass,
and then he smacks Stebbie on the back, yellin', "Go!" Sure
enough, Stebbie purses up and shoots a gob out his mouth. I'm
thinkin' I won the bet because he spits it in a high arc that's
gonna let its target get to the next town before it drops. But then,
as we watch, the gob shoots down and smacks on the trunk, drib-
blin' slow over the lock.

"Still don't believe me?"

"You're both lucky," I say. Nazz nods his head, too. He's still
with me.

So we go from spittin' goobers to tossin' pebbles. There's all
kinds of dinky bits of concrete and rock slivers we're chuckin'.
And we're sayin' crazy stuff like "If it hits, I'll lay flat dead in the
street" or "If it misses, I'll snake me a bag of candies from the grocery, right under that cop's nose." What a thing. Whatever we
want to happen, deep inside us, that's what does. I'm almost
startin' to believe Monteiro's got magic.

And then he goes, "Wait a minute," and he runs to the side
of the overpass where it meets the slope of the embankment. He
disappears for a minute or so, leavin' me, Stebbie, and Nazz just
lookin' at each other, wonderin' what he's doin' next. Then he
comes back, and that's when I see it. I see him with that chunk
of brick, all brittle and cracked. He's bouncin' it in his hands.

From inside the trunk, Cheryl could hear the baby bawling. Doobie wasn't far away at all; only a few inches of insulation and foam separated them. She placed her hand against the backside of the backseat and felt for the weight of his body. Ray Dean mustn't have lashed him in the car seat, though. She could tell when her son's feet were scampering across the cushions, and whenever the wheels took a corner too fast, she heard his body spill into the foot wells. She screamed for Ray Dean to stop and to put the boy down proper, but the only response she received was from the vibrating metal around her. It rattled anxiously as the car's velocity increased. When the speed finally steadied, she knew Ray Dean had reached the highway.

As she lay among the work-smelling clothes scattered on the trunk floor, she tried to make sense of the course of events that had delivered her to this point. She wondered what sin she'd committed to deserve it. She wondered if it were true that, as her old man had told Ray Dean, she was too high on herself. Maybe Ray Dean was her punishment. But that was a passing thought. The longer she inhaled the stink of Ray Dean's dirty laundry, the more she knew that there were two people who deserved blame for her being here—her and Ray Dean. Ray Dean because he was a disaster of a man whose only success in life was the absolute thoroughness with which he failed at everything he tried. And her because she'd allowed his instability to erode the order that she wanted for her own existence. She thought of all the times she'd been told she should leave him for good, all the times she'd known that she should. Of how ruthless that certainty sounded when she told it to herself. And of how weak those words proved when she found herself unable to do it. *I am weak*, she thought. *I have allowed this to happen to me. I am not to blame, but I have let it go on.*

Then she thought of a home she always believed she'd one day live in. It wasn't a mansion or even a big house, really, but it would be clean and well-organized. It would have made beds and scrubbed baseboards. There wouldn't be razor hairs stuck to the bathroom grout, and the shirts in the closets would hang straight from the hangers with their collar buttons buttoned. Cheryl imagined, too, the neatness of the silverware drawer she would keep, the soupspoons separated from the regular ones, the steak knives kept in a different tray than the butter spreaders. She asked herself what she had ever thought it was that would impose such orderliness upon her life. Was she waiting for a different man? Some money? A man with money? She couldn't say. All she knew was that for reasons she didn't understand she had left the task of putting everything in her world in its proper place to an outside force. Suddenly, Cheryl felt foolish for even day-dreaming of orderliness when her real life was a mess.

She twisted to her side and felt at the carpet, grasping for the lock. When she found the casing, she bent a finger around the T-bar, hoping to slip the clasp from its hold. The metal wouldn't budge. Her finger throbbed. Cheryl slid her palms along the decklid, up toward her face, until she found the wiring for the tail lamp. She wrapped the cord around her knuckles and yanked until she felt the socket assembly pop free. With the same finger as before, she jabbed through the bulb hole, trying to knock the reflector loose, but the plastic fasteners held. She arched her back, her head hitting the trunk lid, and she reached behind her for the crank of the tire jack. She dragged it from under her clav-icle and gripped it with both hands. Then she shoved the crank in the bulb hole. The housing split from the force. She shoved again until she heard the reflector crack in two and tumble onto the highway. Then she could see it: outside. Moonlight slanted down over the interstate, and the haze of other cars' headlights glistened in the distance. She pushed her finger through the bulb hole again, and this time, she felt air rushing around her skin. She knew then she would be okay. She was going to get her life straightened out.

After an enjoyable dinner, Joe asked Marcy if they might drive for a while and listen to music. They had just merged onto the interstate. When Marcy tightened in her seat, Joe realized the request had made her apprehensive, and he apologized pro-fusely.

"I guess I'm not good at this," he said. "It just seems so unnat-ural at our age to be jumping these hurdles. You know what Allie said when she told me I should ask you out? Maybe I shouldn't even say. We were having such a lovely time before I made it so

self-conscious for us. But she said it. She said that if any two people were made for each other, it'd be us. Isn't that an insane thing
to say about two strangers?"

"I'll have to have a talk with her about that," Marcy
answered, trying to lighten the mood.

"Do you even believe in that kind of thing?"

"What kind of thing?"

"Destiny, inevitability. The idea that two people are brought
together for a reason."

Marcy said, "I've never thought about it, I guess. My husband
and I, when we would go to retreats with our Sunday school
class, we would always say we were blessed because God had
given us each other. Is that what you mean?"

"Yes. That sort of thing. I've often heard people our age—
people who've been married for many years—wonder if they
hadn't settled in some small way by ending up with whom they
did. I always found that very sad, sad to think that after years
together one person could even want to imagine a different life."

Marcy watched a pair of taillights swerve onto the highway
from an entrance ramp.

"Whenever I want to feel sorry for myself," she told him, "I
think believing in purpose is even worse. The hardest part of losing my husband was coming to grips with the fact that he was not
my life but just a period in it. A huge period, to be sure, but there
I was, not even fifty with years to go, and suddenly, I had
nowhere to go. I couldn't see a future without him. Since then,
I've wondered if I'd spent my marriage thinking our togetherness
was by accident whether I'd have appreciated it more. I don't
mean I didn't appreciate it. Just that if I'd realized how easy it was
for us to be apart, I wouldn't have taken it for granted. Fragile
things have a certain beauty, you know. They're beautiful
because we know they won't last."

The man didn't say anything.

"Joe, are you listening?"

Joe hunched forward in his seat so his chin nearly rested on
the steering wheel.

"I could have sworn I just saw a finger come out of the back
of that car up there," he said.

So I'm sayin' to Monteiro again, "You ain't givin' him that."
I say it four or five times, much to Monteiro's delight. He likes it
that I'm tryin' to keep my brother out of trouble. He'll start to
hand Stebbie the brick chunk and then, without warnin', pull it
back, laughin' so hard I can see his gums, which are purple.
Futhermucker, he keeps callin' me.

"Nothin's gonna happen," he goes. "Stebbie's a good kid.
Bein' dumb, he don't got bad stuff in him. You think somebody's
gonna let somethin' bad happen to someone who don't understand what's bad?"

He gives Stebbie the brick finally. Stebbie's holdin' it,
lookin' at it, slobberin' on it. I see Monteiro laughin', motionin'
for him to hold it over the guard rail, and Nazz is sorta smilin',
too, like he wants to laugh but isn't gonna let hisself. That's
when I get mad. I shove Monteiro. It's not a big shove, but he
trips over his big floppy cuffs and falls back flat on the asphalt.
He's so skinny I think for a minute my one shove's made a pan-
cake out of him. But then Monteiro jumps up and comes at me,
and we start wrestlin'. We're rollin' around in the lanes, bringin'
up dust puffs. Nazz is yellin' at us to stop. And then I hear
Stebbie yellin', too. He's yellin' and smackin' his hands together,
and that's when me and Monteiro and Nazz realize it. We realize
he's gone and let go of that brick.

"Think about the people in these cars around us," Mary-
Angel was saying. "Are their lives really any different from ours?"

"They're very different," Suz answered. She was again pulling
at the tips of her hair. "They don't have to face half the things
we do. Nobody calls their love an abomination. Nobody turns
their love into porn. That car we passed a while back, that
souped-up Chevy, I bet those people have never known a day's
unhappiness. Minds far too fine to be penetrated by despair. I just
bet you."

"God, you know how to go on." Mary-Angel adjusted her
seat, her back throbbing from the ride. They were only ninety
miles into their trip. "I want to be comfortable in my own skin,"
she told her lover. "I really do. I'd like to believe that all this
you're making me do—all this 'coming out' that you demand of
me—I'm hoping that's the end result. At the end of the day, I'd

just like to be able to sit back and, no matter what, feel in control. Set my house in order. Get from point A to B without any mess."

"You will," Suz assured her. She, too, sat back. She let the seat tilt back until she was almost reclining. She put a hand over her eyes to keep out the overhead lights. "Getting from A to B's no big deal. What keeps those two points apart? Nothing but a straight line, that's all."

She felt Mary-Angel's hand stroke her cheek.

"You are good for me, you know that?" Mary-Angel spoke softly. "You give me confidence. I do believe that if we can just get past tonight, we'll be okay. Okay and in control. Don't you think?"

"I don't think, babe. I know."

Mary-Angel laughed at the braggadocio. Suz was smiling, too, humored by the exaggerated confidence in her voice. She felt good. She was twenty-one years old, and for the first time ever, she believed she'd contributed to another person's life. She had helped Mary-Angel, and that knowledge was intoxicating. It made Suz a little vain. *I have done this important thing for her*, she told herself. *I have helped her take charge. She will be a different person now because of me.*

"I really do believe, Mary-Angel," Suz said, looking over to her, "that I was given to you for a reason, you know?"

That was when the windshield shattered.

Afterward, Cheryl sat in the long grass of the interstate shoulder, a blanket draped over her shoulders. Against her chest rested Doobie, who'd finally exhausted himself to sleep after crying for so long. A few feet away, Ray Dean's Impala rested nose down in a muddy sprawl where the shoulder sloped forward into a field of weeds. Ahead of it was the Honda Civic, listing slightly, the broken glass on its hood sparkling like firefly tails. Farther up still was the old Chevy, calm and untouched. Through the moonlight, Cheryl could see the silhouette of the Honda's driver, her head arched back at an uncomfortable angle against the headrest. Cheryl knew she was dead. The woman hadn't once moved in the forty-five minutes that Cheryl had been sitting in the grass. She knew, too, because from the minute the Impala came to a stop in the ditch after Ray Dean slammed on the brakes and the car spun, she'd heard the screaming. It went on for several minutes until drowned out by the sirens, and it continued on until the passenger from the Honda was sedated and taken away in an ambulance.

"He'll rest well now," someone said. It was the woman from the Chevy. By all appearances she was the same age as Cheryl's mom. The first time Cheryl saw her, she was holding Doobie, patting his head while he gurgled and howled at the sight of his father's face split open on the steering wheel. "Are you okay? You're so quiet."

"I don't know," Cheryl answered. "I feel a little outside of myself right now."

"That's to be expected, I guess," the woman said. She squatted beside them.

"How long had you followed us?"

"Not far. A few miles. Joe over there saw you first, and then when we were sure that really was a finger he'd seen, we tried to keep up with you without him seeing us. Joe was so upset he didn't have his cell phone. We had no way of letting anyone know. We were going to have to pull off and find a phone for the police. That's when it happened."

Cheryl was looking at the Honda.

"It was the most terrifying thing I've ever seen," the woman told her. "I didn't know what was going on. I just saw her car swerve sideways. I thought she'd lost control. And this car, the one you were in, it tried to avoid hers, but it clipped the fender and spun itself out." She, too, was looking at the Honda. "We stopped, Joe and I, and we ran up. He limps badly, and I didn't want to embarrass him, so I let him go ahead of me. I'm glad I did. Part of me wishes I'd stayed behind completely."

"You saw her then?"

The woman put her face into her hands for a moment and was silent.

"I'm sorry," Cheryl said. "You've been so kind. But I can't get over the fact that there's a dead body ten feet from me."

Finally, the woman said, "I'm just glad about your baby. When Joe came over here and said there was a child on the floor—I couldn't have handled it if something had happened to your baby. Excuse me." She stood and walked away, sobbing.

Cheryl watched her go to the police car, where her friend, the man, was describing what had happened to a crowd of highway troopers. She thought of Ray Dean, who'd also been taken away in an ambulance, his nose and jaw broken. She thought of her son, who'd only suffered a cut on his forehead, even though the impact sent him flying over the front seat and onto the mats on the floorboard. He would be okay. Tomorrow she would apply a fresh bandage to the wound and dress him in his new Easter outfit, and they would go to church.

The man from the Chevy walked up. He was small and seemed somehow defeated. The first thing he did was to apologize for his limp.

"It was kids," the man told Cheryl. "Only ten or eleven, that trooper says. He caught them at a grocery down the road. One of boys is mentally handicapped. Of course, they're blaming him."

Cheryl didn't know what to say. She saw the man's attention wander to the Honda.

"It shouldn't be long. One of the troopers will take you home soon."

Doobie stirred, whimpering slightly as he swatted at his face with a bent thumb. The beauty of that unexpected movement startled and then pleased Cheryl. She thought of how she should have been home tonight, sitting in the rocking chair that she kept near her son's bed, waiting for just that sort of shudder of life to come over him. The child heaved with a deep breath, and his body relaxed into a heavy, sad stillness. In a weird way, it reminded her of the dead woman's stillness.

Cheryl looked at the misshapen outline of the woman's skull, barely visible in the darkness. She wondered about the invisible grid of time and space, the laws of motion and probability that had conspired to kill her. She understood that had that brick fallen a few seconds later, it would have struck Ray Dean or maybe even Doobie. She knew that the couple from the Chevy was probably thinking the same thing. She wondered why this night, why these lives, hers, the woman's, the couple's. Those kids'. She shut her eyes and tried to believe that it wasn't quirk or coincidence. She tried to convince herself that the wreck had to happen for her and Doobie to be saved. That woman had died so she and her son could live. Yes, Cheryl decided, that's what she would believe. It was just easier that way.

"Say," the man from the Chevy said suddenly. "I've got a CD player in my car. Would you like to listen to some music?"

At first the invitation seemed absurd and inappropriate, but then Cheryl asked what CDs he owned. The man named several titles that were meaningful to him: *Pet Sounds, The Philosopher's Stone, Darkness on the Edge of Town, Blood on the Tracks.*

"Oh, that's one of my favorites," Cheryl suddenly said. "Yes, I'd like that—to listen to it, if you don't think it's disrespectful. Thank you."

ETUDE AND BELL TOWER

So to join up you dropped your pants. It was that easy. You dropped them and then the block commander—that was his official rank, not "sector commander" or some such military designation, but "block commander," a title better suited for a neighborhood crime patrol—he squatted down so his face was level with your crotch, and you were either admitted to the ranks or you were killed. Of course, no one was ever killed. Everyone was always admitted to the ranks because if you weren't one of us, you had no business being there in the first place. In my case, "there" meant the bell tower of the cathedral on the southeastern side of the market district. I had an offer to go to the skytower closer to downtown, which was a hotbed of action. But I told the recruiter I was afraid of heights and that I didn't think I could lean out an open window seventeen stories high without vertigo getting the better of me.

The truth was I remembered the bell tower from a recital I once attended in the city in my youth. It was the only other time I'd ever been to the city. I remembered the fruit and vegetable stalls just up from where the cobblestone alleyway met the sidewalk. My thought was that at night I could sneak down through the tower and the cathedral sanctuary to pilfer a potato or an onion. That way I would be eating something other than the rations we were served. At home in the provinces I'd heard stories of boys going hungry from the insubstantial portions of jerky and tomato soup supplied to each outpost. I knew there were no sheep in the city like we shot and stewed at home. And, unlike the others, I never sank so low as to eat the grubs that were plentiful in the wood rot all around us. So to the bell tower I went, where the block commander was kind enough to remove the cigarette from his mouth before approving my cock.

"What did I tell you?" I said when he stood up. "I'm a garden spade, not a flat-head shovel."

33

"That's only the first test," he said, unsmiling. He appeared to be my age, twenty seven, with short-cropped hair and a carrot-colored nose. Later he told me his name, Oscar, and that he was raised a kilometer to the east in the city's outermost arrondissement. I once asked if he ever recognized anyone who happened into his crosshairs. He said no and that it bothered him more than if he had.

"You can shoot?" he asked me.

"I can shoot."

He wanted to know where I'd learned. I told him the name of my home province. It was Oscar's job to be suspicious of volunteers. He made some crack about the poppies rumored to be grown there and waited to see if I corrected him. So I did, but he didn't seem relieved. If anything, my answer only aggrieved him. He spat out his cigarette, not bothering to extinguish the lit tobacco, and poked a finger over his shoulder.

"That's Stéfan and the other's Hector." Our two comrades lay on stacked bales of hay at their assigned parapets. One looked over and jerked up his thumb in friendship. He was porcelain-faced and far too pretty for the army. The other refused to take his cheek off his gunstock and merely waved over his shoulder. Oscar bent his head forward in a confidential whisper. "Stéfan you won't find objectionable. He's a boy. But Hector aspires to his name. He's our ideologue." Oscar drew back and spoke openly now. "They take the south and west. I draw east, which leaves you north. You object?"

"What's to object to? No sunrise, no dusk. My fellow garden spades!"—I was trying to appear an enthusiast—"Being new here, I know there must be a downside to the north. Am I right?"

"You'll lose the humor, if you please," Oscar snapped. He looked at his watch. "You've got forty-five minutes before the pedestrian rush. Then you can show us what the provinces are made of. You understand the rules?"

"Yes."

"That should be yes, sir, because I am your commander. But since there are only four of us present we'll dispense with the obsequies, as long as you don't need a reminder of the rules. Recite, please."

I cleared my throat and tried to remember what the recruiter taught me.

"I'm not to hit anyone. I'm to hit the brick, cinder block, and pavement first. Windows are an option only if no one is within five yards. I should avoid storm drains and man-hole covers for fear a ricochet may strike a bystander."

Oscar was staring at me, trying to ferret out any possible sarcasm. Or maybe he was hoping for a trace of some.

"Your recruiter trained you well. Who was he?"

I said his name—a young man from my province, some years my junior, who'd left and returned home with promises of food, shelter, and revenge for the indignities of the centuries. Those were his actual words, the indignities of the centuries. When I told this to Oscar, his grim face cracked and he finally smiled.

"Him," he said with contempt. "He and Hector spring from the same stream. In all the times I've heard him speak I've yet to hear a word I would ever mistake for his own." Then, as if realizing he was a block commander, he resumed his seriousness. "Forty minutes." He tapped the face of his wristwatch. "Get some rest."

I stretched out on my bales and propped my chin on the parapet edge. The truth was I had no interest in avenging the centuries' indignities. I was here strictly for the money. In the past year my family's harvest yielded just enough to feed us. But then my wife's menstrual cycle failed to come round. When that happened my mother took me by the collar and gave me the business. "Now you've done it!" she said. "Another mouth! Now it's up to you if you want to make amends for this indulgence of yours. You have no choice but to enlist. You are likely to be shot the first day and then where will we be?"

I had no intention of taking a bullet. I knew there was a demand for snipers. I knew I could split a bird's heart from a soccer field away without mussing a feather. All I had to do was demonstrate this to the recruiter, and once he sent word up the chain of command, I was in. Provided I could pass the dropped-pants test.

From the parapet I saw my firing range. It was a block of business fronts, mostly shoesmiths, tailors, a pharmacy. There wasn't much foot traffic, only a brave few who scurried from doorway to doorway with bags of candles or kerosene for those nights when electricity was in short supply. I'd heard that shopkeeps had stopped accepting cash to barter their stock for foodstuffs. I thought of my wife and her protruding belly and I was glad she was in the sticks. There was a cellar beneath the cow stall in the barn that was big enough to accommodate her and my father in case a renegade division came upon our farm. My mother could deal with them. They wouldn't hurt an old woman. At least that's what we'd banked on earlier whenever the insurgencies arose. They would shoot the men and abduct women under forty, keeping them as indulgences until the next village promised a fresh bounty. As my mother told me, insurgents had a taste for pregnant women. "Because they're perverts!" she insisted when I questioned how she knew this for a fact.

Forty minutes passed and Oscar was screwing a scope onto the bridge of a beautiful new rifle. When he handed it to me, I smelled the barrel.

"Never been kissed," I said, and I hoisted the butt to my shoulder. Through the scope I saw the magnified concrete and pockmarked boughs lining the street—planted, I assumed, by the city fathers in better days. "What is it?"

"Mauser 86SR," Oscar answered. He stood at my back while I drew along the street.

"It's light. And I like a manual bolt. And what's this? The stock is ventilated. Fancy. I suppose it's Russian."

"German," he told me.

I was surprised. "How are they snuck past the embargo lines?"

"I couldn't say if I knew. Stéfan claims they're floated down the Danube, Hector believes they're trucked over the Carpathians. My guess, however, is that they're dropped from yankee planes. However they're financed, it's clear that our patrons have deep pockets."

"Then they won't feel it as they fill mine," I said. "Ammunition?"

He tossed a bale off a nearby stack and kicked open a crate with his boot. Inside were the magazines, the bullets resting in sweet, silent rows. Oscar passed me one of the clips.

"Nine rounds," he said when he caught me counting. He looked at his watch once more. "Just right for our needs. Too easy

otherwise to get carried away. You get carried away, you hit someone, then someone will try to hit us back. Our job is to instill panic,
keep the shop shelves empty, starve the unclean into leaving."

I snapped the magazine into place. Then I lay back on the
bale and waited. Within minutes pedestrians began to crowd the
doorways and peek out from under the overhangs. It was nearly
three o'clock, when the bravest of the fruit traders manned their
stalls. Maybe they weren't braver, just greedier. In return for their
stringy green onion stalks or meager cabbage heads they would
accept jewelry, baseball cards, dust ruffles and stolen hotel towels. All of these items they then sold for cash on the black market. That's why both sides, however much the one hated the
other, agreed to hate profiteers most of all.

"Whenever you're ready," Oscar said.

I caught a woman's prancing feet on the walkway. I waited
until she was out of my line of sight and then I worked the bolt
and pulled the trigger. There was less kickback than I expected—
just a short hammer pull and the burnt cartridge smell. I didn't
have time to see what I'd hit, but I could see the woman was
prostrate on the ground. I pulled the bolt and shot again. This
time a small chunk of curb several inches from her toes popped
up and dissolved into dust. I drew several degrees to the west,
behind her, and hit a window ledge. By this time those heading
for market had taken cover. They were prepared at any moment
to lurch behind trash cans and awnings. Because the streets were
fairly empty, I could fire without delay. I let several shots go in a
line that dotted the soiled facades of the buildings. Then, for a
finale, I aimed down one of the stalls and drilled three heads of
lettuce. When I looked up, I expected Oscar to be impressed. But
he was simply there, leaning along the tower wall.

"You'll do," he said. As he returned to his post, I was left
wondering whether he'd hoped I would fail the audition.

That was how things went over the next few weeks. Six
times a day, at six and nine A.M., at noon, and then at three, six,
and nine P.M., the four of us strafed our small territory, making
sure we hit no one while disrupting the lives of everyone. Across
the city, there were fourteen other sniper squads, some with as
many as ten men to a post. We weren't allowed to leave the bell

tower except for bathroom breaks. That left us with little to do
but sit and talk, except that no one talked. By night we slept to
the sound of church mice nibbling our bales. During the day
chugging trucks and cockroach-shaped Volkswagens provided a
constant parade that kept us from thinking about how rarely we
spoke. Every other week we were granted a night's leave. The
higher-ups didn't want us seen entering and exiting the cathedral, however. We were forced to take our holidays after dark,
which proved unfortunate since the cafés and cantinas closed at
dusk. All in all, city life was far less glamorous than what the
recruiter promised.

"My fellow garden spades," I said whenever the lack of conversation grew oppressive. "Why is it, do you suppose, that our
enemies should prefer the shape of a flat-head shovel?"

No one spoke at first. Then Hector, the more bellicose of my
companions, said, "They aren't circumcised because the blood in
their pricks fuels their barbarous souls."

Stéfan chuckled at this, but as I was lying on my back with
my head pillowed by my windbreaker, I could see the disgusted
look on Oscar's face.

"That's a wives' tale," I told the boy when Oscar chose not
to express his disdain. "For them, the abomination is disfiguring
the body. To cut the flesh is to wound the soul. We continue this
gruesomeness in the belief that it's cleanly and a precaution
against infection, but that is a medicinal folly."

"Professor," Oscar said softly. He was sitting up, twisting
some baling wire around his wrist, fashioning a makeshift
bracelet. "You talk too much. We aren't here to teach or learn.
We have a job. We do it and nothing more."

After that, I knew we were condemned to remain strangers
with nothing but the shape of our penises between us.

My time in the bell tower should have ended in this endless
tedium. Neither the block commanders nor our esteemed higher-ups wanted war, so we felt confident that we would never be
called upon to shoot at a moving target. That made our duty easier, for we didn't think of those we terrorized as real people. Of
course, I did at first. I'd never before seen a human body through
a scope. It was only natural in the beginning that I should

empathize with the housewife whose moldy loaf and lone tomato were spilled when I opened fire. I myself had suffered through
seasons of hunger, and I knew the ache of an empty stomach. But
such feelings stopped quickly. I reminded myself that I was a loyalist. If not to the cause, at least to my family.

Then one morning events occurred that brought a change to
our bell tower. We met our six A.M. quota of confusion, then
breakfasted. We were preparing for our mid-morning strike when
the sound of music found its way to our ears. I poked my head
over the wall. My first thought was that a traffic accident had
occurred. Down below, oddly angled, sat a baby grand piano.
Beneath the keyboard where a pianist would normally tuck his
legs was the bubbled front of a Volkswagen. It appeared as
though the car had nosed its way under the casing to nudge it
aside. But then I saw that several metal braces crudely attached
the piano to the Volkswagen; the protruding bolts brought to
mind Frankenstein and all those legends of body parts stitched
together. Adding to the strangeness was the fact that the top of
the little car had been sheered away and the seats removed,
replaced by a pair of two-by-fours that rested on the door frames.
A roly-poly man in a tuxedo sat atop the two-by-fours. He was
hunched over the baby grand, and his hands were dancing up
and down the keys. The sound he made was furious and violent,
a windstorm of noise that scratched the walls.

"What is that?" Stéfan asked. My station mates leaned along
my backside.

"It's noise," Hector complained, his face twisted in a groan.
"A screech, a caterwaul."

But it was Oscar, his head bent forward, who answered the
question. "It's Prokofiev," he told us. "The First Violin Sonata, I
believe. Of course, there is no violin, so you are only hearing the
melody as arranged for piano."

We looked at him, but there was no emotion, no hint of
another life he might have lived. There was just a sort of vague
familiarity in his eyes.

"You recognize that racket-maker?" Hector demanded. I
should mention that Hector suffered from an unflattering harelip, so that when he spoke with inflamed passion—which is to
say, whenever he spoke at all—the top of his mouth threatened

to unzip itself all the way up to his nose. The more he spoke the more his teeth pushed out from his rubbery gums until you wondered whether he might be trying to squeeze his entire jawbone through the rictus.

Oscar was nodding. "I know who he is. He was once affiliated with the conservatory, back when the conservatory was open. He used to teach technique there. Before that he was a professional. He's played his share of concert halls, if I'm not mistaken. Even if he didn't, he could have—listen to him. Do you hear those bass notes? They require a nimble brutality, if there is such a thing. It's too bad he doesn't have a violinist. The melody makes for an upsetting contrast; that contrast is what the whole mood of the sonata is about, I suppose. Prokofiev was capturing the discord between dream and nightmare." He shrugged, realizing that his words meant nothing to us. "It's a protest, of course. The man is making his point. But the selection is too obscure. Who cares about Prokofiev anymore?"

"What should I do?" I asked.

Oscar stood and straightened his flak jacket. He looked at his watch.

"It's almost time. We do our usual work, with accompaniment or not." The piano's noise rose again in another thick sledgehammer of sound. "It's a shame we can't wait for him to finish this particular figure. The third movement is more plangent, a wind in a graveyard." He stopped long enough to perk an ear out of the bell tower. "That'll have to wait for another time and place, unfortunately. To stations."

I stretched across my bale and sighted down the far end of the block, the usual starting point of my barrage. The corner facade had been hit so often that it appeared scarred by chainsaw serrations. Oscar began his countdown and gave the command. I wasn't surprised that the firing drowned out the music.

When the calamity settled, however, I was surprised to discover the tuxedoed man still sat atop the Volkswagen. His concentration was unbroken, despite the splattered eggs, overturned bicycles, and howling dogs that filled the street. I looked to Oscar's face, which flickered with enthusiasm.

"Ah, we're just in time for the finale," he said. "Listen—the bass part will rumble like a hollow belly!"

By the third day it became apparent that, however gifted the pianist might be, his repertoire was limited to this one piece. Each morning the ass end of the baby grand would poke slowly around the street corner, prodded along by the Volkswagen it was grafted to. The car never moved faster than ten miles an hour, presumably because the shaky wheels screwed to the piano legs couldn't be trusted on the irregularly laid cobblestones. The pianist would halt his contraption just a few yards beyond the fruit stalls, and then he would hoist himself onto the two-by-fours from the hole where the driver's seat had once been. Sometimes he played as long as five hours a day. On others, he would disappear after only two or three renditions of the sonata. We maintained our strafing schedule as commanded, but it was clear that the man was oblivious to our work. In the times we weren't firing, Oscar gathered us together to teach us about the music. He always whispered, as though our talk might distract the man in the way our bullets didn't.

"My guess is that he chooses Prokofiev for the statement the selection makes, not for the sake of the music itself. Because Prokofiev, you should know, began as a modernist, an innovator who desired to wrest music from the clash of sound. But Stalin denounced his atonality as unpatriotic, and he was forced not just to melody, but to the most insincere form of melody that there is—the national melody. Think of it! You as a composer have a world of scales and tones and techniques at your disposal, and yet every time your fingers stretch to make a chord you must worry whether the authorities will deem your efforts counterrevolutionary. After a time, how do you even decide what keys to press? How could you live with that dual loyalty, first to your imagination and then to the state?

"In the end Prokofiev did what any of us would in that situation. He compromised. He gave the higher-ups the patriotic themes they demanded. But he expressed his own imagination in the contrapuntal rhythms. That! Do you hear that? Three bass notes that seem to bully the melody, to taunt it with its flatfootedness. Much later they would call those bass figures 'Stalin motifs'—but that was long after Prokofiev, and long after Stalin. They died on the same day, didn't you even know that? Stalin was fat and bloated from the purges, which is quite the paradox

if you think about it. The paradox ate his brain—literally, I've
heard it said. And there was Prokofiev, impoverished and near
starving because he couldn't convince the bureaucrats that he
wasn't a formalist. Do you know their definition of a formalist?
Anyone who made art out of personal longing rather than patri-
otism. Imagine such a thing! As if you could take the personal
longing out of the art!"

The truth was I didn't care about this man Prokofiev or his
problems. I was more interested in Oscar himself. When I first
joined the bell tower he seemed to revel in his dourness, like a
man who peppers his food knowing full well the heartburn it will
give him. But now he was alive with eagerness, and the most
dangerous kind, too. When he spoke about the music he
betrayed the fact that there was something he cared about more
than fulfilling his immediate duty. His chattiness made Stéfan
nervous and displeased Hector. But I suppose I was guilty of
encouraging his talk. It took my mind off the boredom.

He talked about so many things, all of them having to do
with pianos. He insisted that the most beautiful part of the
instrument isn't the keyboard or the casing or even the action
but the wrest plank, the board that holds the tuning pins. "From
a distance the wrest plank looks like a map," he would say. "A
topography map—hills and mountains and the fine lines of flowing rivers." Oscar told us, too, that the fibers on the felt tips of
the hammer shanks should run parallel to the strings to avoid
gouging grooves in the fabric. He even taught us not to think of
grands and baby grands as more complicated than uprights just
because they're bigger. "Take your finger off a key on a baby
grand," he said, "and it's gravity that pulls the whippen and
damper back into place. But on an upright, all the levers and
jacks sit vertically, so you need a whole other series of springs to
return the parts to their proper place."

Of course, none of this made a bit of sense to us. But I kept
listening because I was enjoying those words of his. There were
so many, and they were all so odd, almost magical in their sound.
Hearing them was like holding a foreign coin, trying to decipher
the legends and the imagery. What were those words? I only
remember a few. Arpeggio—that was one. "An arpeggio is a swirl
of notes. Imagine spinning a color wheel. It's the same effect,

only in sound." Cantata: "From the Latin word meaning 'sing,' thus meaning, obviously enough, a composition with different types of singing, choruses and solos, recitatives and arias. . . . But now I must define these for you!" And one more: étude. "Very simple," he said. "A study. More correctly, a study designed to teach a specific technique, but the generic meaning will suffice: a study."

It was from this crazy quilt of words that I pieced together Oscar's story. As a child he had shown some proficiency at the piano, although he was never adept enough to become a concert performer. "To do that," he told me, "you must have what are called 'spatulate' hands." He stretched out one of his. "I have fork fingers. They won't spread farther than an average set of tines." To my eyes the span of his fingers didn't seem abnormally narrow, but I didn't argue because I didn't want to interrupt him.

Instead of performing, he concentrated on music theory, hoping to establish himself as a composer. It wasn't that absurd an ambition. In those days the government ran the conservatory, and it peopled it with young men who competed for pensions. Most of these positions involved teaching, but one in every six boys earned a composer's sinecure. With the money, the boys were obligated to produce one concerto and one sonata per year, no more and no less. And the compositions had to evoke patriotic themes.

"I should have been an ideal candidate for that position," Oscar said. "But I squabbled too much. In one of our first assignments, we were to compose a piece in the key of C major. You know why, don't you? Because in the key of C, you only have to use the white keys. But I was fond of accidentals, which they kept calling wrong notes, as if any note could be wrong if you heard it in your head. 'If it's so wrong,' I argued, 'why are the black keys here?' It was only one exercise, one étude, but I was bullheaded. Of course, that didn't endear me to them.

"You see, they were forced to teach us a very simple theory of harmony. They would tell us, 'You are to stick with diatonic intervals and avoid chromatics.' Why? Because diatonic intervals sound sweet and whole, while chromatics give off a sense of dissonance and confusion. The prejudice is written in the very names given to the arrangements of sound. You know what they call the first, fourth, and fifth of any scale? They're perfect. But if you move one of those notes down a semitone—from a white key to the black one below it, perhaps—it's no longer perfect, it's diminished. Then there was the other word they were fond of: resolve. 'If you must use a 7th,' they said, 'it must resolve into the tonic.' Why? Because resolution is what music is meant to give us: a sense of unity, completeness, order. Order was their most favorite idea of all. 'In all aspects of composition the effect must be to reassure the listener that there is an order that is pleasing because it reflects the natural structure of our way of living.' That was the golden rule.

"Of course, they weren't the first to invent such things. Had we been students in medieval times we would've been taught to avoid the tritone. That's any interval composed of three whole tones, and it was determined back then to be so injurious to the ears that it was demonized—literally demonized, too: they called it 'The Devil's Interval.' Now imagine for a moment working under such a restriction while trying to produce an etude in C. The tritone in that scale is the space between F and B. How do you avoid it? Why, you would be told to drop the B to a B-flat, and as probably even you know, B-flats are black keys. You see what I'm saying, don't you? Had our teachers for some arbitrary reason believed in the imperfection of the tritone we'd have had to move from a white note to the black one below it! Or, by the same token, had we known this history we might have been tempted to taunt our elders. We could have said to them, 'Yes, but, haven't you considered that your logic of resolution dooms us to go to the Devil?'"

It was because Oscar entertained such thoughts that he knew he'd be denied that composer's sinecure. He couldn't keep his fingers off the black keys, and he couldn't find it in himself to resolve his 7ths. "Oh, and yes," he added, "whenever I came within a measure's vicinity of a tritone, I couldn't help but smile—devilishly, as you might expect." When it came time for the conservatory to award his class their posts, he was relegated to a pair of part-time jobs intended as a rebuke and a humiliation. It would be his duty, he was told, to maintain the conservatory pianos. That meant tuning them, gluing cracks and loose joints, replacing snapped strings. The rest of his time he was to work in the listening library as curator of the school's phonograph collection. Each day he was to pick a shelf from an archive's worth of shelves, and he was to swab the dust from each disc, one by one, making sure that neither human oils nor static electricity interfered with the ability of subsequent composition students to appreciate the importance of harmony and order.

Oddly enough, Oscar didn't mind the work. Being stationed in the listening library allowed him to study from the conservatory's LPs, many of which reveled in the musical sins that the faculty denounced. It was through those albums, for example, that he became so familiar with Prokofiev. And there were others, too: Shostakovich, Schoenberg, Mussorgsky. He was ambivalent on the point of Stravinsky: "I considered myself a modern, but it struck me that I preferred *Firebird* to *Le Sacre du Printemps*. I mean, I could appreciate the historical value of *Sacre du Printemps*, but how could I be a modern if I didn't enjoy listening to it?"

It was a question I couldn't begin to answer.

As for tuning the pianos, it was here that Oscar exacted his revenge. "There is a phenomenon of sound called a beat," he said. "It's not a rhythmic beat, but more like a pulse. When strings vibrate at different frequencies, the faster ones take over the slower, and the tone will seem to bulge. You wouldn't think it, but for many notes on a piano, especially those in the treble, there's more than one string. There has to be, otherwise the sound wouldn't be loud at all. So when you tune a piano, there's three times the work for many of those keys, and the trick is to ensure that all the strings vibrate at the same frequency so the pulses evaporate. What I would do is monkey with the tension in those strings so the vibrations were out of synch, but just barely, just audibly. A player would come along to strike a chord, and the sound would expand and contract until the ringing would feel like a drill bit in a back tooth."

Of course, the faculty complained about his lack of tuning proficiency, but Oscar blamed the humidity. The conservatory furnaces were hard to regulate, so all he had to do was insist that the thick heat was drying out the soundboard and loosening the tuning pins, thus making the strings slacken and go flat. "Come summer, I would tell them they were hearing false beats. A false beat is when a pulse occurs in a single string, usually because of a rusty spring. I would tell them that if they wanted that pulsing to stop, they had to supply me with reliable parts. Of course, there was no money for replacing rusty springs, so they had no comeback."

He spent three years playing these kinds of mind games. The most entertaining times, he said, were the recitals. Whenever the conservatory threw open its doors to justify its existence to the authorities, the faculty would fret about whether their instruments were tuned or not, and they would insist that Oscar sit behind a curtain next to the school's prize concert grand. If a professor thought a certain note beat too blatantly, he would order Oscar to sneak his way to the pinblock to slip his tuning lever over the offending screw. Then Oscar would adjust the note while the student playing tried to maintain his concentration. "At those times I was as close to a performer as someone without spatulate hands can be," he said. "At the very least, I was duetting with those students."

He'd probably be in the middle of a duet, too, had this latest insurgency not arisen, forcing the government to close down the conservatory. Oscar understood the thinking. What good was music in a time of war, he'd ask me, even if war wasn't what we were supposed to call it? The conservatory doors were chained shut, and the faculty and students sent home. The ones with means learned to barter their belongings for food. Those who didn't, like Oscar, had only one recourse. They joined the army.

After four days of storytelling Oscar woke me during a midnight lull.

"The pianist is a fool if he goes on," he said. "He has made his point. The higher-ups won't permit it much longer. They can't tolerate his bravery. He's forcing things to a head."

Nine days into the music, Oscar again shook me from my slumber.

"It's been decided. A courier has been dispatched. He must stay home tomorrow. Should he come back, the consequences are his."

But the following morning saw the Volkswagen's return, and the playing went on uninterrupted. You could see the coloring in Oscar's face evaporate.

"He's being selfish. He thinks he's only putting himself at risk, but it's the piano that's going to suffer. They shoot him, they'll destroy that instrument." He was staring out over the rooftops. Some distance away was the gray outline of the skytower that loomed over the downtown district. "After the conservatory closed, it didn't take the foragers long at all to break in and haul off everything of value. I have no idea what the records might've fetched from a profiteer, but I'm sure that the pianos I kept tuned were worthless. At least, they were worthless when they were in one piece. I've heard rumors that the casings were broken down for firewood, the strings and pins sold for scrap."

He was shaking his head. "If we lose this campaign," he told me, "we will belong to an imaginary country. But you know what? If we win, we will as well. All we're fighting for is a fiction. But those pianos, they were real. And this one's real—for now at least. But he's put it in danger."

I didn't know what to say.

After that noon's strafing we broke for lunch. We were eating our jerky ration when a runner climbed the rope ladder that we kept dangling from the trapdoor. The courier was all of ten years old. The higher-ups used the sons of conscripts as messengers under the theory that a child could move through the arrondissements more easily than an adult. The boy handed his dispatch to Oscar. Stéfan gave the boy some chocolates sent him by his mother. When Oscar finished with the directives he folded the envelope and stuffed it into his back pocket.

"I'll be back after dinner," he told us. But since he wadded his bedroll into his backpack and grabbed an extra day's ration, we doubted it. Two days later, when Oscar still hadn't returned, we began betting on how long before a new block commander arrived. In the meantime, we did the work expected of us. And we listened to the music.

"Why do you think he left?" Stéfan asked the night a chill wind kept loose straw blowing in the air.

"For the only reason anyone would abandon his duty," Hector told him. "Oscar was a coward and a traitor."

"You should learn to speak for yourself," I said. "Maybe he found something to live for beyond the cause."

"There is only the cause," Hector spat back. He voice sounded empty and mechanical, so I turned over and tried to sleep.

The next morning we were greeted by the young runner's return. This time he demanded a treat before he handed over the envelope. Because Stéfan was the only one among us with enough chocolate for a bribe, the boy gave him the message.

Stéfan looked it over, looked at Hector, then looked at me.

"You better read it," he said, giving Hector the note. You could see the joy descend over Hector. It looked like a bee swarm. He snapped the paper taut between his fingers, displaying it to me.

"I'm the new block commander," he declared. "I've been promoted."

"Congratulations," I said with a shrug. "You'll serve well."

He folded the paper and tucked it into his shirt.

"Can you guess my first order? I'm sure you've been anticipating it. I'm to shoot him and destroy that instrument."

I felt Stéfan eyeing me.

"They certainly know how to choose a loyalist," I told him. It wasn't a good thing to say. The smile on Hector's face bled away, and that harelip unzipped itself further than usual until this time it resembled a wolf's snarl.

"You would do well to obey. Oscar tolerated your jokes because like you he was ambivalent. But I'm not."

And with that, he went to his bale, stretched out, and napped contentedly. Even in his sleep he was gloating.

Some time later I approached him.

"You're to kill him?"

Hector sat up, his palm caressing the cheek of his rifle.

"Of course not. That would undermine the strategy. I'll merely strike his left hand. The bullet will no doubt go straight through the bone and destroy the keys, too. I bet I can reduce it to kindling with three shots."

"And cripple him," I added.

Hector shrugged. "He had his warning."

Either oblivious or indifferent to his fate, the pianist didn't fail to disappoint. Shortly after the dawn strafing, we heard the now-familiar shriek of his worn brakes as the Volkswagen nudged the piano into place. A moment later we were serenaded by a cluster of tones we'd come to expect. Now more than ever, Prokofiev's third movement indeed sounded like a wind in a graveyard.

"You'll move voluntarily?" Hector demanded. He stood beside my station, his Mauser balanced against his chest so its long tripod legs poked at his kneecaps.

"And if I don't?"

Now it was his turn to shrug. "Then I'll have the honor of shooting two enemies. Just because you're a garden spade doesn't mean you can't be the enemy."

I rolled off my hay and acted out a matador's veronica to let him know the bale was his for the taking. All I had to do was retrieve my own Mauser. As soon as I'd cleared my weapon from the parapet, Hector laid belly down on the straw and began tightening the nuts on the leg stands. When the gun was steady he put his eye to the scope and began adjusting the focus. The entire time, the discordant sonata wafted up toward us, as it had for almost two weeks straight. For the first time I appreciated what Oscar had meant about the clash between the melody and the low bass notes pounded out by the pianist's left hand. There were two ways of looking at the world in that music.

Then the barrel of my Mauser made contact with the back of Hector's neck, and he shuddered. "You'll let him finish out this movement," I said.

I shut my eyes and gave myself to the twirling melody, which soared and then sank, pulling me along in anticipation of a resolution that, for all the dissonance in that sonata, I knew was imminent. Only when it finally came and the chord congealed in a tangled but stable complexity of tones would I open my eyes. When I did, I was relieved to see that the mess my trigger finger made hadn't disturbed the pianist's concentration.

At least that is how, awash in the aftermath, I imagine events having happened. The truth is that as my eyes were pinched shut I wasn't thinking about harmony and atonality or consonance and dissonance. I was thinking about me—or rather, I was thinking about what my mother would think of me were I executed for killing a block commander. "He died for what? For eighty-eight keys strapped onto four bald tires? What craziness is that?" The sound of her giving me the business was enough to make me realize how unlike either Oscar or Hector I was. Simple enough, I was a traitor, both to the cause and to art, for I was living in the name of nothing more than my own survival. That's a trait common to my people, the people of the provinces. Call us formalists if you like.

So now I spend my days on the seventeenth floor of the sky-tower downtown. It remains a hotbed of action, though my new commander insists I'll soon be reassigned to a field platoon if my aim doesn't improve. He doesn't believe me when I tell him about the vertigo.

In the hours between strafes I lie on my side and try to catch hold of the sense of imbalance that twists my stomach. To ease my dizziness I imagine Oscar out there, somewhere, in a room with newspaper covering the windows, perhaps, or in a wine cellar with a lone candle for illumination. I can hear him saying those words of his, arpeggio, cantata, étude and all the others, speaking each as if its music could substitute for the music that, in all likelihood, he'll never hear again. In those few patches of time I call sleep I dream of him describing how the felt threads on a hammer shank should run parallel to a string and how a wrest plate of tuning pins resembles a topography map. How the insides of an upright are actually more complicated than the insides of a baby grand—I never would've guessed that.

And Hector? Oh yes, I know all about him. For maiming the pianist and destroying an octave's stretch of keys with only three pulls of his gun bolt, he was made a lieutenant. That means he has his own squadron of thirty-five garden spades who rout the countryside to avenge the indignities of the centuries. From time to time rumors come my way. I've heard it said that he's an intolerable hothead in conversation and is prone to bloodlust and perversion, particularly with pregnant women.

Reports from the field are that he's much despised by his men.

FALL OF THE
HOUSE OF
OXLEY

Two weeks after signing his first home mortgage, Oxley discovered a crack in the top of his kitchen doorframe. He was cleaning the walls, scrubbing away the fingerprints of the previous owners, when he spotted the thin, shoot-like zigzag. Running his fingers over the little barbels of wallboard whiskering out of the slit, he told himself they were just cobwebs, or maybe pencil smears left by the carpenters when they'd squared the trim. But then the crack refused to disappear, and by the end of the day's cleaning, he discovered several more capillaries veining out of the windowsills, feeding into corner floorboards, creasing the paint in some places. Tracing those spots, Oxley grew aware of his breath: a wheezy breeze trapped in the belfries of his nostrils. He feared an asthma attack, something he tried to guard against by wearing a filter over his mouth whenever he dusted blinds or swept out the track lighting. He wore that filter even though he knew how silly it made him look—like a mad scientist besieged by a deadly virus.

The cracks weren't the worst, however. One night as he lay sleepless, his insomnia as bad as his asthma, he heard a soft snap, like a finger flicking quickly off a cheek or a loud drip in a rusty bucket. Then, a little later, another. Naked (he was sensitive to the humidity and thought he might rest better if his armpits and groin weren't soggy) he squatted over the floor and rested his ear to his newly polished hardwood. He didn't hear anything, yet the drip haunted him until four o'clock, when he finally dissolved into an uncomfortable sleep. Over the next weeks, the pops and cracks caught him off-guard as he read the paper, sat on the pot, daydreamed in his recliner. They always occurred just after he'd convinced himself that he was paranoid. Finally, when he found a windowpane slivering without explanation, he had to accept that he'd perched on shaky ground.

"It's the prairie soil," his realtor said when he called to question her about the cracks. Her name was Henrietta. She'd turned to selling houses when her retired husband, a lieutenant colonel formerly stationed at nearby air base, ran off with a master sergeant. "I'll tell you, it's the curse of this county. There's not a house around here without some settling. You ever been out to Grenadier Lane? Those are $400,000 homes, and they've got cracks in the walls that look like vaginas. Just get a patch kit—it's the same principle as hair plugs. You fill in the spot, repaint it, and nobody ever knows anything was wrong."

"But that won't stop the shifting . . ." and then, hoping, he added, "will it?"

Truth be told, Henrietta intimidated him. They'd met at a tennis club shortly after Oxley relocated to the Deep South to manage his ad agency's forty-seventh most profitable district. Over fruit juice, after she swatted three matches' worth of serves down his throat, he admitted he was in the market for a house—his first house. She volleyed back with a business card. It all happened so quickly that he might as well have been a virgin slipped a Mickey Finn by the town smoothie. Henrietta escorted him to open houses and showered him in estimates. She lavished him in friendly lunches at which, after saying, "This is on me, of course," she twirled her fork tines in vermicelli while inviting him to describe his dream home. Oxley always drew a blank and covered with the same lame joke: "Well, for starters, it's got four walls. . . ."

Now Henrietta was laboring through a pregnant pause. "You did sign off on the structural report, didn't you?"

"I think so," he fumbled, "because you said it wasn't covered in the closing costs, right?"

"I'd have to look at the papers, but that sounds right." In the background he heard a ringing beeper, and he wondered if Henrietta had motioned for a colleague to page her. "Can I call you back? I've another client waiting at a closing. Late as usual—take care."

And with a dial tone for accompaniment, Oxley felt his innards go to stone. The slab groaned, the joists creaked, loose shingles slapped the roof. He imagined the floor giving way beneath his feet as the entire lot tumbled into a fissure.

He hadn't even wanted a house, he reminded himself. Shortly after his promotion, his regional manager took him aside and told him in no uncertain terms that he needed to put down roots. Oxley was thirty-three, after all. He'd never been married, and he was pale and wan in a way that made most doubt he ever would. Besides, clients weren't comfortable dealing with apartment people. A house was key to a career. The idea did have its appeal: Oxley knew he wouldn't miss the noisy nights when upstairs neighbors practiced their line dancing before hitting the bubba bars. But a house was a burden, too—2,200 square feet of responsibility. So many things could go wrong, and Oxley was cursed when it came to ownership. He believed he had a reputation for frying alternators, popping tires, overflowing toilets. At least in an apartment you could leave when the handyman came to snake the shower drain.

Despite the dread that Henrietta's words aroused in him, Oxley girded up his loins and set about doing what a real home-owner would. He made a list and spent an hour wandering the canyonesque aisles of the local hardware franchise, astonished that nails could come in so many sizes and extension cords in such varying lengths. Back home he emptied his purchases on the back porch. Then he treated the neighborhood to a ballet of caulked soffits, sandpapered fascia boards, and spray-washed fungi. He even hammered eight feet of fresh privacy fence between his house and the brick fence that ran along the western edge of his property line, shellacking it with weather-beater to ward off the rain and termites.

This sudden burst of industry startled the block. At first neighbors peeked through their blinds; then they began changing their sprinklers more frequently to soak up the unexpected sight. Oxley understood their curiosity. His first day in his house he found himself at a loss for words when the couple kitty-corner to him uttered the word *girlfriend*. Since then, rumors circulated. Oxley was a single man, after all, with no visible woman in his life, no demonstrable interest in hiking, biking, or any such "out-doorsy" activity.

Not that this inquiring couple was exactly holy. They weren't married for starters; they made a point of mentioning that in their opening salutation, introducing each other as "life partners." They'd lived on the street nearly fifteen years, having purchased the local Gold's Gym franchise back in the mid-1980s, when the fitness craze was booming. Now they were up to three locations. Oxley wasn't surprised to learn of their profession. Both sported the souped-up, flagrant athleticism of eight-cylinder engines stuffed into four-cylinder chassis. They had a propensity for talking in unison, and they wore matching Lycra tights. Never discrete dark colors, either, but flesh tones with spots that could have been measles as easily as polka dots. Her name, of all things, was Happy. She swore it so, and Oxley felt bad for her. That was a burdensome name to live up to.

"You're quite the housewife," Happy's companion said that morning as he tramped over an oblong brown spot in the grass. It had cropped up in Oxley's front yard when his lawn-care service overdosed the zoysia with fertilizer.

"Just doing my part for property values," Oxley answered. He'd nicknamed his neighbor Brick. Happy's last name was Breck, and her companion's artificial tan radiated a rubicund glaze that suggested he'd just been yanked from a kiln. Brick 'n' Breck—Oxley liked the alliteration.

"With a house, you know," Brick was informing him, "there's always something. And it's never less than $500."

Nearly everyone Oxley spoke to since he signed his mortgage had said exactly those words.

"Hey, now that's some nice stockade fence there. What kind of wood is it?"

Oxley felt weak, nervous, identified. He didn't want to admit he couldn't tell one sort of wood from another. To him, it was all . . . wood.

"It's oak." He said the first thing that came into his mind. And to prove he knew what he was talking about, Oxley whacked a nail into a plank. The nail quivered briefly, then dropped into the grass.

"Oak? No . . . really?" Now Brick was peeking over the planks, curious about the secrets his neighbor needed to hide. "A little pale for oak, I think?" He palmed the grain. "Rough, too," he said. "They told you you were buying oak?" Before Oxley could answer, his neighbor squatted beside the fence and poked his fingers through the slender space between the slat bottoms and the shoots of zoysia. "At least you kept a half-inch here from the ground. Subterranean mites are a big deal in this area. They nearly ate the Bourjailys next to us out of house and home a few years back. Darn near $15K in damage."

Oxley swallowed hard, imagining his timbers whittled to toothpicks.

"Hey," Brick went on surveying the property, "This your crawlspace?" He was fiddling with a little gated trellis hidden between two puffy shrubs. "You checked your pipes lately? I know the Le Bons who used to live here installed plastic ones a few years back. Your man was afraid of lead poisoning. He was a little paranoid, to say the least. He listened to that Chuck Harder guy, you know, sans irony."

Brick's shoulders were submerged in the entry now. Behind him, Oxley imagined taking aim with his surf mocs; one good kick and his neighbor would be entombed in the sinking prairie soil, crushed, maybe, like a dry walnut by the three-core stretcher blocks shouldering the foundation.

"Whoa," the neighbor said. His voice rumbled through the underbelly of the house.

"What?" Oxley dropped his hammer, fearing a chasm in the floorboards.

"You don't have a vapor mat." As Brick pulled out of the crawlspace, the coiffured erection of his hair ruffled briefly on the frame before springing back to stiffness. "Your floor's soaking up the humidity."

"That's bad?"

Brick's lips tightened; he looked grim.

"Your house, it can't air itself out naturally because . . ." he paused. "Your bottom's soggy."

Oxley felt his sphincter contract.

"So a vapor mat . . . it'll stop it?"

"It traps the moisture in the ground, keeps it from rising. I guess I'm not surprised the Le Bons didn't have one. They weren't the smartest people. Or the cleanest for that matter."

"They must have had lots of kids. The walls were crawling with fingerprints."

"P.W.T. You know what that is? Poor white trash. They collected kids the way they collected aluminum cans—by the tonnage. Sort of sad, though."

"What?"

Oxley felt a twinge of breathless suspense; for the first time, he wasn't the object of block gossip. He was sharing in it.

"Their older kid ran away. It was right before we bought our place, maybe sixteen, seventeen years ago. It's the closest I ever came to knowing a real runaway. It's weird. Every time I hear about one, I think of that kid, what he's doing now, if he was ever tempted to call his folks."

"He's probably better off," Oxley decided.

"Oh, that's for sure." And then Brick's eyes took fire, glowing anew with amphetamine enthusiasm. "Hey, we're running a special at the gym this week, a twenty dollar membership fee that regularly goes for thirty. Just last night Happy was saying she'd love to get hold of your cardiovascular system."

"Well," Oxley stalled, "a lot of people would like that."

Brick didn't get the hint.

"Think about it, though, will you? Life—it's precious." And with that bumper-sticker certainty, he marched off across the lawn, his shorts hoisted so high that his buttocks were molded in the shape of a smiley face.

Oxley squatted in front of the crawlspace and peeked. The underside of the house was dark. All he could see was the uneven earth, pockmarked in spots by clumps of clay. He thought of the thirty years' worth of moisture absorbed by the beams, and without putting away his tools, he rushed into the house to test the floor. Sure enough, in several spots the boards creaked and dipped beneath his weight.

Two hours later he was unfolding a newly purchased tarp, hoping the house didn't collapse before he could smooth out the crawlspace. He laid the plastic across the lawn within easy reach of the hole and then, armed with a flashlight, a rake, and a ball-peen hammer to break up the dirt clumps, he crawled inside. On his stomach, with joists and pipes striping his back and legs, he felt pinned down, vulnerable to attack. The flashlight beam broke through silvery cobwebs, floating dust, and fat bugs who didn't live under the threat of an oncoming swat. Oxley tossed the rake ahead of him and tried to drag the ground flat. The plastic teeth barely scratched the soil.

A dozen strokes later his shoulder muscles felt as if dowels had been drilled through his blades. He was smacking a clump flat with the ball-peen when the head struck something too hard to be clay. Oxley whacked it again, just to let it know nothing could survive his brutality, and this time he heard a satisfying crack. With his fingers, he fanned away the loosened dirt to discover a yellow chip of what he figured was some sort of obsidian rock. Yet when he brushed more soil aside he found the object curved in an oddly familiar profile, its crevices complicated and detailed. It made him a little sad to think that he'd destroyed some natural art that had lain undisturbed as long as the house stood over it. Scraping at it with his fingernails, Oxley committed himself to excavating the relic; he'd glue the chip back in place, hang it on his wall in a gilt frame. But the rock was splintering, and he pulled loose a popcorn kernel.

Only when he held the kernel up to the beam of his flashlight did Oxley realize that his fingers held a rotting incisor. When he rotated the beam so the light fell to the soil, he was greeted by the idiot death grin of a chipped mandible.

After that things happened so fast that only several hours later, his knees unstable, his hands shaking, did Oxley realize he hadn't eaten all day. He stood at the periphery of his lawn, restrained by a strip of yellow plastic that the police strung around the front of his house. Officers swarmed at the womb of his property. To accommodate them, the police had torn down the trellis gate and jackhammered a wider entryway. Then several disappeared into the hole with huge lights, drills, and shovels, leaving behind only extension cords that tangled their way to the surge protectors outfitted to Oxley's overtaxed outlets. When Oxley asked one officer assigned to crowd control why they needed all the gadgets, he learned that they hadn't come just to remove the body. That ground was a potential minefield of evidence. Then it hit Oxley that a corpse tenanted the underside of his house.

"What they're doing," the cop explained, "is digging around the object." He was careful not to say skeleton. "They'll be removing sections of ground to sift through them."

"You can get sections of ground out of that hole?"

The officer shrugged.

"They'll open it however big they need to, I 'spect."

It didn't take long for the neighborhood to gather. Mercifully, Brick 'n' Breck were teaching an aerobics class when the first squad cars rolled in. But the rest of the block, most of whom Oxley only knew by sight, crept across their yards, collecting like the run-off of their gutters. They surrounded him, inching him toward the yellow tape until the crowd-control cop had to hold up his palms and say, "Folks, you need to stay back, just stay back, please." Oxley felt their breath on his back, the accumulated weight of their curiosity. Yet no one asked him why the police were stuffed in his crawlspace. Instead, they whispered amongst themselves. The guy known for wearing black socks with his sandals said he'd been expecting this for years. The old woman who could talk without taking the cigarette out of the side of her mouth repeated, "I knew it," as a tobacco plume rose and frosted her locks. Another neighbor reached across the tape to confide the secret the street apparently shared; the officer blinked, scribbled something in his notepad, and then passed the information to the detective in charge.

"What's going on?" Oxley asked the cigarette lady. Her ash dropped an inch from his toe. She'd asked him roughly the same question twenty minutes earlier and had been rudely rebuffed, so she took a certain pleasure in hesitating to answer.

"What you've unearthed is that Le Bon boy," she said loudly. A few feet away, a mother told her children to run home. "Nobody believed that business of him running off. The boy couldn't look over his shoulder without getting turned around."

"You mean . . ." Oxley panned the faces of his neighbors, none of whom looked shocked, just grim and tired, as though they'd been anticipating this day for years, "everybody knew?"

The woman puckered instead of answered, her cigarette rising until the stalk threatened to burn her rounded bulb of a nose. Before Oxley realized what he was saying, the words were already out of his mouth: "You think my realtor knew?" he asked.

It wasn't a conscious thought, but the entire time Oxley stood watching the police wiggle in and out from under his house he assumed that things would return to normal once the bones were gone. Relief was the first sensation he felt when the soiled men emerged pink-eyed from the hole, body bag in hand. No more jackhammer rattling his bedroom curtains; no more standard-issue boots stomping his Impatiens. No more neighbors standing for hours at the edge of his property line, disappearing at dinnertime only to return a while later with greasy faces and smelling conspicuously of chicken fried steak. All he wanted, Oxley told himself, was to go in his house and use his bathroom in peace.

The first clue that normalcy was a ways away: the police told him he'd have to relocate for a while. Brick 'n' Breck offered the use of their guest room, which he accepted only because it was moderately more appealing than being marooned at a Motel 6. His ad agency was generous and granted him a week's leave. For two days he watched from his neighbors' kitchen window as the police cut footpaths across his zoysia. When they asked to search the attic, he noticed they didn't bother to wipe their feet in the foyer. They left the hand towels wadded on the toilet tank after they flushed. Oxley couldn't understand why they rolled studfinders across his walls and dragged metal detector-type machines along his floors. As his anxiety steepened, he began noticing scuffmarks on the hardwood, uneven picture frames, cabinet doors left unlatched. The police were intent on destroying his house right before his eyes.

Finally, when he witnessed one officer tapping his ceiling with what looked like a stethoscope, he demanded an explanation.

"Mrs. Le Bon let something slip about a videotape," the policeman said. He spoke low, as though he were violating the confidentiality of the case. "We get hold of that tape, and if it's as incriminating as we suspect it is, we file this job under *finito*."

"What if you don't find it?"

"Oh, we will," the officer assured him. He put the listening sensor back against the ceiling. "We'll find it if we have to strip this place down to the nail holes."

Oxley went white.

"If I were you," the cop said, "I'd be calling my insurance agent, lickety split."

But on the third day the officer in charge returned possession of the home.

"You found the tape?" Oxley asked.

"No, no tape," he said with a grimace. The officer was a hurly burly sort who looked like a perfect candidate for Brick 'n' Breck's health plan. Then the man caught himself. "Hey, wait. Who the hell told you about the tape?" He shook his head. "These damn detectives gossip worse than a women's sewing circle. Of course, if you come across it, you'll let us know, right?"

"You think it's still here, somewhere in the house?"

The cop shrugged and left Oxley to his speculation. Oxley spent his first few hours alone walking the rooms, trying to locate the unchecked cranny that only he, as the house's rightful owner, would know about. He came up empty, however. As he tried to sleep that night, the groans and pops seemed a whispered code he couldn't quite crack. When he finally slipped into a dream, it was set in the last apartment in which he'd lived—a small but cozy one bedroomer with absolutely no place to hide anything, not even a videotape.

The morning that followed presented a new concern. Oxley was luxuriating over his morning dump when the doorbell sounded. He quickly dropped the lid, deliberating over whether he should flush. Oxley's sewage pipes were the old concrete ones that gargle when toilet water floods their throat. Whoever stood on his porch would surely know they'd interrupted him. He finally decided not to tip the handle. He drew his pajama bottoms up to his hips and went to the door.

"Catch you at a bad time?" Brick asked. He was shirtless, his muscles and veins bulging against the hairless expanse of his chest.

"Not at all," Oxley lied.

"Well, how's it feel?"

"How's what feel?"

"How's it feel," Brick's eyebrows arched over his eyes, "to be a tourist attraction?"

"I don't know what you mean."

"Just watch."

Brick drew his finger to his lip, shushing Oxley as a car approached. Traffic in the neighborhood was always busy in the morning because Oxley's street served as a shortcut to the thoroughfare that fed the downtown business district. Sure enough, the car slowed just as it passed Oxley's property line. Although the window was rolled up, Oxley could see the occupants' faces. They were taut with fascinated repulsion, like those of young children who happen upon their parents' lovemaking. When the driver realized she was being watched, she turned her head, embarrassed, and sent the car shooting forward with a sudden jolt of speed. Her wheels whined as she took the corner along the north side of Oxley's property. The back right tire rolled over the curb and ripped a treaded swath through his zoysia.

"That's what we in the South call rubbernecking," Brick said. "This is the first you've noticed of it?"

It was, but it certainly wasn't the last. Later that day, as Oxley cut his overgrown grass, he counted twelve cars that slowed to stare. And that was after lunch, before the dinner rush. That evening, as he set his garbage cans out for the next day's trash pick-up, he spotted just as many. And it kept happening, over and over. Even when Oxley stepped dripping naked from the shower he caught them peeking. He wondered just how far through his half-drawn blinds they could see.

On Sunday morning he was reading a weekly wrap-up of the Le Bon case in the newspaper when he heard a crash. He stepped outside and saw two cars parked along the curb opposite his driveway. One was the Saturn that the cigarette woman kept on the street so her son could come and go. The other was a spiffy Nissan Maxima. When Oxley saw Henrietta stooping over the front bumper, he realized why that car looked so familiar.

"Does your neighbor always park in the street, or was today just my luck?"

As Oxley approached the Saturn he saw that the passenger door was crunched in. The paint was stripped as well in long jagged streaks.

"A lot of people park in the street. They're not moving, you know, so they're supposed to be easy to avoid."

Henrietta lit a cigarette and motioned him over to the open driver's door.

"I need you to do me a favor," she said. She pointed to the floor beneath the passenger's seat, where two empty beer bottles lay on their sides. "Get rid of those for me, will you—before the police show up."

"You've been drinking? This morning?"

"Oh, no. Of course not. They're from hours ago. That counts as last night, doesn't it? I mean, it's only about eight morning-wise. Just run them over to your trash real quick."

"I can't do that." Oxley had his palms stretched up at her. "That would make me an accomplice."

"Oh, for Christ's sake." Henrietta leaned into the car and set the bottles on the ground, kicking them down the sewer drain. "There's a city ordinance about parking in the street. It says your wheels have to be less than five inches from the curb. Hers clearly aren't."

Oxley eyeballed the distance between the curb and the Saturn's tires. It was maybe three inches.

"You were staring at the house," he said suddenly.

"What?"

"My house—you were staring at it, not paying attention to the road. That's why you hit her car, isn't it? You were probably thanking the Lord you'd gotten your commission before that body turned up."

Henrietta frowned.

"Now, that's not very nice, not nice at all. But okay. I have to admit. I was curious. Everybody is. You may not know it, but every realtor in a thirty-mile radius has driven by your place. They're putting a mental picture in their permanent files. Because they want to make sure that if they ever get a feeler for a listing from you they'll know to run the other way."

She sucked deep on her cigarette and blew an almost perfect oval out of her nostrils.

"You know, there was a house on the market down in the Cloverdale district, about four, five years ago. The realtor was using it for his . . . um . . . assignations. He picked up the wrong hunk bunny and ended up . . . well, you can guess. That one's still for sale. How do you think your Amityville Horror will fare?" Another smoky circle shot from her nose. "I hope you like it here, because I have a feeling that you're going to be staying for a long, long while."

The old woman came stumbling down her drive. When she saw her battered car her jaw dropped and the cigarette fell end over end. Oxley watched it hit the concrete and roll to the gutter.

"It's that house!" she yelled at Henrietta. And then she turned on Oxley. "Goddamn those Le Bons! If it was so important to keep those bones they should've taken them like they took the furniture!"

Oxley couldn't argue with her reasoning. As he watched the traffic cop struggle to keep the women separated over the next half-hour he wondered why the Le Bons had left their son's body behind. Were they afraid of stirring up some vengeful spirit that hadn't bothered them for fifteen years? Or had they forgotten he was there, only a few feet below their bed? He tried to imagine them sleeping in that new home, wrapped in their mutually blubbery embrace. Could they snore in peace? Could they have sex? Was living easier on another street, or had it never been hard?

After a time, Oxley stopped noticing the stares. He allowed himself to go shirtless again when he mowed the yard. The humidity brought out too deep a sweat, and he didn't like the way his T-shirt stuck to his back. He trimmed his magnolias and raked the pine bark that the squirrels gnawed off his trunks. Slowly he began cataloguing the imperfections of his neighbors' homes, taking a certain pride in his taste when it told him he could never live with mildewed mortar and faded trim. When he saw Brick 'n' Breck pulling weeds or blowing grass clippings off their driveway, he felt that his property could easily outshine theirs—if only his hadn't been a mausoleum for so long.

Then one morning as he cut across the zoysia for his paper he sank ankle-deep in water. It gathered in a long uneven pool from his sprinkler spigot to the magnolia that anchored the yard. When the plumber arrived he needed only scratch his teeth a few times with his matchstick before confirming Oxley's fear: the waterline had rusted. As he signed the labor contract Oxley realized he was paying $800 for the privilege of watching this doughy man shovel up his sod. Even worse, every twenty minutes or so the man asked to use his toilet. When the man was done and back at work, Oxley slipped into the restroom to disinfect the bowl and sink. Then he hung the hand towels back on the rack. The plumber had left them wadded on the tank.

"You sure get a lot of traffic on this street," the man said when Oxley went outside for his mail.

"A lot of houses around here for sale," Oxley answered. "They draw a crowd."

The plumber rested his elbow on the shovel handle.

"This place of yours looks familiar. I'm sure I've seen it before. I musta done a job here once. But I sure can't remember that part of it."

"You ever watch the nightly news?"

"Nope. Don't even own a TV. But hey now—I bet you got you plastic sink pipes, don't you? Sure, it's clear as a bell now. Had to get down in that crawlspace and everything."

Oxley stopped, his arm in the craw of his mailbox.

"You've been in that crawlspace?"

"Oh, hell, yes." He kept wiping his forehead with a red bandana he kept crumpled in his fist. "Whole place gave me the heebie jeebies. I'm not too kind for tight spaces, and she's a tight one in there."

"Tell me about it." Oxley pretended to go through his correspondence. "You didn't see anything . . . unusual?"

"Plenty of turds, I'll tell you that. Had them all in my hair and everything by day's end. But unusual? No, nothing extryordinary."

"No?"

"But I'll tell you what unnerved the hell out of me. That fellow that owned it then—that old boy stood there by the crawlspace opening while I was working. I seen his chicken legs there

in the entryway the whole time. The wife would come out and
I'd hear them arguing about him going inside, but he wouldn't
budge. Can't stand it when a man thinks I'm trying to skunk
him. Sure enough, the bastard tried to jew me down. And he'd
already signed the contract."

The plumber went back to digging, laughing at his own story.

"Two things I can't stand: a crooked Jew and a straight-up
nig—"

Oxley dashed into his house so he didn't have to hear the
rest. Hours later the plumber cranked his T-stick on the waterline shut-off valve, and the faucets sang again with running
water. After he waved the old man away, Oxley stood at his door
staring at the long strip of unearthed lawn. His zoysia looked as
though a mole had tunneled a subterranean catacomb under it.
But then he looked at the cigarette woman's dusty windows, and
the dying pine growing up against the side of Brick 'n' Breck's,
and the forsaken landscaping of the raisin-headed Bourjailys
next to them. And he didn't feel so bad—until he remembered
his crawlspace.

Then it was a few days before Halloween. Oxley carved two
pumpkins, which he sat on the outer corners of his porch. In
their hollowed heads he stuck two fat candles and a pair of small
speakers connected to a handheld tape recorder hidden behind a
nearby planter. When plugged in, the recorder played a tape loop
that said "touch me and die" every few seconds, just in case mis-
chievous teenagers attempted to mess with his decorations.
When Halloween was over, Oxley planned to return to the novelty shop and purchase a decorative sign he'd seen: "Forget the
dog; beware of owner." He liked that one a lot. In the meantime,
he taped a black cardboard witch to his front door and dangling
spiders to his windows. He even fashioned a scarecrow out of an
old broom handle and an oily ensemble of lawn-mowing clothes.

He was hammering the broom handle into a few stacked
bales of hay he'd ordered from a local farmer when he noticed
Brick observing him from his driveway.

"Fancy, fancy," the neighbor said. As usual, Brick's tight
shorts outlined his pelvic features with codpiece clarity. "I don't
know that we've ever seen anything this elaborate around here."

He folded his arms. "But you really think kids will come to your door? You don't think they'll be scared away by . . . well, you know."

He stuck his tongue out of the corner of his mouth and drew an invisible slash along his throat.

"Have you chosen your Halloween costume yet?" Oxley asked.

"Well, as a matter of fact, we're debating whether to go as—"

Oxley interrupted him. "Here's what you should do. Get yourself a skeleton suit, and sprinkle your vacuum bag on it, and, voila! You can tell everyone you're Timmy Le Bon."

Brick stared.

"That's about the sickest thing I ever heard," he said, and he got into his car to go work out. Oxley was delighted—as he figured, he'd never have to be invited to the gym again.

He was so pleased with himself that after finishing the scarecrow he treated himself to a cup of spiced apple cider. He had just heated a mug's worth in the microwave and was preparing for the dash of ginger he liked in it when the doorbell rang. He snuck a quick sip anyway; the cider was hot and burned the roof of his mouth. He was tonguing the coming blister when he opened his front door.

It was a plump man in a crisp blue suit with heavily pomaded hair that left greasy streaks on the sides of his ears. Oxley pegged him for a lawyer before he even introduced himself as Julius McElvoy, local attorney. The woman behind him was frumpy and plain, with creases in her face that resembled a heavily tilled terrain. Her loose floral dress bunched at her waist, leaving exposed a pair of thick calves crisscrossed with varicose veins. She looked vaguely familiar.

McElvoy was saying, "This is—"

"Mrs. Le Bon."

The woman allowed herself a faint smile and then dropped her eyes to the brick walkway.

"I almost didn't recognize you," Oxley said without thinking. "You look so different."

McElvoy stepped between them. "Yes, well, I'm sure you know about Mrs. Le Bon's current legal problems."

Oxley was still looking to the woman. He couldn't decide if the snow-white cowlick crowning her forehead was naturally pointy or if she hadn't yet brushed her hair this morning. "Sure, but I thought you were arres—"

"Bail," the lawyer intervened. "Mr. Oxley, you're undoubtedly aware that the police were searching for a tape. Our understanding is that they failed to obtain it. Is that your understanding?"

"That's what they told me," Oxley answered. The lawyer squeezed his client's hand reassuringly.

"Sir, Mrs. Le Bon is here to retrieve that tape. Now, from a legal perspective, you are the homeowner, so of course we need your permission to get it. I would tell you that, technically, that tape is still Mrs. Le Bon's, so we hope you'll be kind and allow us into your master bathroom."

"The bathroom? But shouldn't the police get the tape?"

The lawyer's face puckered. "One thing you should know about the police, sir: conclusions are something they like nothing more than to leap to. I'm sure in their minds that tape is a key piece of crime-solving evidence, but I can assure you that it's not. It really has nothing at all to do with this . . ." He paused to choose the right word. " . . . *situation*. Mrs. Le Bon would just like it returned. As I hope you can appreciate, she's suffered an inordinate amount of stress these past weeks, and the tape will do her immeasurable good. So perhaps we could pretend we're here for nothing more than a Christmas ornament or bronzed baby shoe inadvertently left behind. All we're asking is for the opportunity to claim what's ours."

"I guess—"

"Good then," McElvoy said, and he slipped into the foyer. "This way I assume?"

Oxley followed the lawyer through the hall to the beds and baths; Mrs. Le Bon trailed behind him. It made Oxley nervous to be sandwiched between the two.

In the bathroom, McElvoy stood on the toilet lid and rapped his knuckles at the ceiling vent cover. He looked at his client, and she nodded and then lowered her eyes again. The creases on her face drew taut.

"You wouldn't happen to have a screwdriver we might use, would you?"

Oxley went to his outside laundry room and rifled his meager assortment of tools for the one screwdriver he possessed. It was a cheap, thin-handled thing he'd bought at a pharmacy. Next paycheck, he'd been planning on buying himself one of those deluxe Craftsman sets he'd seen advertised on the Home & Garden network.

When he offered McElvoy the screwdriver, the lawyer massaged the knuckles of his right hand. "Would you mind loosening those screws for me, son? My arthritis has been kicking in this week."

Oxley slipped the Philips head bit into the screw grooves and tried to twist. The screws had been painted over at least once, probably twice, and they didn't seem interested in budging. The effort to turn them brought an embarrassing grunt from deep in Oxley's throat. He knew those screws would have pirouetted obligingly if only he owned a battery-powered driver.

When he was finally able to pull the screws out and lower the fan cover, McElroy nudged him out of the way with a brisk "Best if I handle it from here." The lawyer stuck his arm through the hole in the ceiling, his lips twisting wryly when he caught grip of his catch. Getting the object out the hole proved a difficult matter, however. McElvoy had to yank several times. Oxley thought for sure the lawyer would pull the entire ceiling down on their heads.

"This is all?" he asked Mrs. Le Bon. A dusty, rumpled pillowcase dangled from his hand.

"The tape's inside. Inside the pillow, I mean. The stitching should be torn out on the bottom end."

Brows wrinkled, McElvoy shoved his fist in the case, burrowing deep in search of the hole in the pillow. When he finally pulled his hand free, he held an unlabeled tape, along with a fistful of stuffing. "This should end our imposition upon you, Mr. Oxley," McElvoy said with a satisfied nod. "We can go now, Esther."

Mrs. Le Bon closed her eyes, her face balled by a troubled sigh. "I want to watch it," she said softly.

"You want to watch it . . . here?" Oxley said with shock.

McElvoy drummed his fingers on the tape. "That's not a good idea, not a good one at all. I don't recommend it."

Mrs. Le Bon ignored her lawyer. She was looking, pleadingly, to Oxley. "Please," she begged.

Oxley pointed past the hall to the living room. "In there," he said, and this time, he brought up the rear.

He stayed in the hallway, out of the television's line of sight. The lawyer stuck the tape in the player and fiddled with Oxley's remote before sitting back in the leather recliner. There was a shot of static, then the sound of voices, their words obscured by a loud tape hiss. Oxley didn't need to know the words, however. The tone was revealing enough. It was revealing because it was so surprising. The sounds were festive, joyous even. Oxley heard laughing, clapping, singing: *Happy birthday to you, happy birthday to you, happy birthday our dear Timothy . . .*

"He turned 15 on August 15th," Mrs. Le Bon said, hypnotized by the television. "So I made sure he had fifteen presents. My husband, Denton, he was very angry with me because he thought fifteen presents would cost a lot, and we've never had money. But I was always thrifty when it came to my spending. Denton should have appreciated that more."

Oxley leaned along the hallway wall. "I don't understand why you would hide this tape. The police think—"

"Esther," McElvoy cut in. "You shouldn't be talking, especially not to a stranger."

"I want to tell my story to someone!" Mrs. Le Bon screamed. Oxley recoiled at the sudden explosion. The lawyer merely scowled harder, squeezing his eyes into thin slits so only part of what played out on the television screen made it past his lids. Meanwhile, the woman said, "You should see this part, the upcoming part. The look on his face when he opens the little portable radio I gave him. He loved music, you see. He talked all the time about running off to become a rock star."

A moment later, McElvoy thumbed the stop button on the remote. "We'll be leaving you now, Mr. Oxley," he said, much to Oxley's relief. McElvoy held the crease of his trousers as he stood.

"Oh, my baby," Mrs. Le Bon moaned. She put her face in her hands and began howling fiercely. She rocked back and forth in her chair. "Oh, my baby."

McElvoy said, "It's best for all if we go, Esther. We'll get you something to eat and then a nap. You'll feel better rested."

But Mrs. Le Bon wasn't paying attention. She was staring through her slobbery fingers at Oxley. "You're judging me," she said. "I can tell you're judging me."

Oxley trembled at the accusation. "Me?"

"You have no right, no right unless you know what I've been through all these years."

And then, with a sudden gust, the woman was on her feet, dashing through the foyer with a speed that defied her girth. Before either Oxley or McElvoy knew what had happened, she was out the door. The two men stared at each other for a second and then launched into pursuit.

They weren't sure where she'd disappeared to until Oxley saw her feet slipping into the crawlspace. He and McElvoy tripped over themselves as they ran to the hedges. A sour expression crossed the lawyer's face when he saw the mud around the hole.

"Do you mind?" he asked Oxley. His hands rode up and down his clothes. "This suit—the retainer wouldn't even cover the dry cleaning, if you know what I mean."

Oxley squatted at the crawlspace entry. From under his house he could hear the woman's sobs as she called out the boy's name. Oxley laid on his knees and palms and pushed himself through the hole. It was dark inside, and within inches he was blind. He moved toward the crying until he felt toes brush his forehead.

"I want you to know," Mrs. Le Bon said, gulping. "It was me. I kept him here all those years. So many times Denton threatened to sneak down in the middle of the night and get rid of the bones."

Oxley swallowed hard. "You—you came down here? To hold him?"

"Every night. I did it every night as if I were tucking him in."

"This whole time? The whole fifteen years?"

"Yes, yes." Her words were slurred. "Every night for fifteen years. After a while I couldn't touch him because . . . because . . ." Oxley could barely make out the words. "He started to fall apart."

Oxley's heart thumped. With his ear to the ground, he swore he could feel its vibrations throb through the turned-up dirt.

"Denton said he would take the bones away for me. But I told him it was his fault, that in so many ways he took the boy from me even before my boy was taken. I wouldn't let him do it again. I said I'd turn him in the first time I came down here and couldn't hold my baby."

Oxley wasn't sure what to say. "It's good you did turn him in. Because now they've got him. He can't hurt you or anyone else again."

"No," she sighed. "I can't tell you what it was that made the two of them go at each other so hard. There was nothing the one said that didn't set the other off. They fought all the time. Maybe they were too much alike. They were both bullheaded. They hit each other all the time. I wanted my baby to be safe, to get away, but I couldn't let him go. Don't you see? I did the only thing I could."

"What? What are you saying?" Then Oxley realized exactly what she was saying. "You? *You?*"

"It wasn't any different from putting him to bed. No different from what I'd done for him all his life. He liked me to fluff his pillow, and I told myself that's all I was doing. I was making sure he could rest better, that his rest would be peaceful."

Oxley thought of the pillow McElvoy struggled so hard to yank from the bathroom vent. "Oh, God! How did you ever get out on bail?" And then it hit him. "Wait. You're letting them think it was your husband, aren't you? You're letting him take the blame!"

"Denton sold the house without asking me. He said it was time to move. It'd been long enough, he said. He kept the house money and moved us in with his mother in Chisholm. The first night I found my way into her crawlspace. I just couldn't stop. I knew he wasn't there, but I pretended he was. I pretended for three months. I was just so relieved when you found him. I thought I'd be able to hold him again. But the police won't let me. They've got his bones stashed away, and they won't let me touch him. Denton should have known that's all I wanted, that that's all I ever wanted . . . to hold him. I blame Denton. Oh—" And her voice broke off again in sobs.

Oxley felt his throat tighten. "Why are you telling me this?" he demanded, angrily. "Why me?"

Mrs. Le Bon remained silent for a long time except for an occasional heave. When she finally consented to answer him, Oxley wondered if she stayed quiet because to her the question was so obvious that it didn't need asking.

"I want to tell my story to someone," she said.

The only words Mrs. Le Bon said after that, however, were "My baby, my baby."

Her crying felt like nails in Oxley's palms. It pinned him down. He wanted so badly to slither away, to slip from the house, these events, this skin. But he stayed there, and as his eyes slowly grew accustomed to the dark, he made out the shape of Mrs. Le Bon's body. She lay on her side, one arm extended as if in an invisible embrace, the other tapping at a mound of dirt next to her belly. Oxley tried to imagine her going through this nightly routine as if it were perfectly banal—brush teeth, comb hair, pat dead son's fleshless corpse. The crying grew louder now, thundering through the floor beams. It was so loud Oxley was afraid she'd shake the house right off its foundation, entombing them together for eternity. He remembered how his home had groaned and creaked for so long, and he wondered if it was an echo of mother love that gave voice to those ghastly, ghostly noises. He didn't know, couldn't begin to answer. All he knew was that a few inches from him a woman lay crying. He realized that he ought to try to comfort her, so Oxley reached out consolingly, but the crawlspace was cramped, and his hand only made it as far as the pudge of Mrs. Le Bon's thigh.

SLEEPING BEAR

He says, "Hey, check these out," and he pulls his shirt up to his throat. A few feet away, tamping a tent stake with a rubber mallet, his six-year-old son looks up and is unimpressed.

"This is five hundred sit-ups a day you're ignoring," Baby Doc tells the boy. He pats at his belly, which houses a faint set of rippled knots. "Crossovers, bicycles, leg lifts, squats, twists—" He goes on even after his son resumes his work. "Crunches are the best. They hurt the most." He lets his shirt down. "Tomorrow we get up early and do some together. How's that sound?"

"Okay." The boy is indifferent, but at least his average is up: every third swing or so, he's actually making contact with the stake. Baby Doc twists together one of the two flexible poles that support the tent and threads it through the toe line. A halo of evergreens shelters the campsite, giving it a deceptively isolated feel. Past the overgrown ferns is a county highway where car tires squeal when they take the nearby bend too fast. Thirty years ago, when Baby Doc and his father took to the woods here around Empire and Glen Arbor, camping meant state-park plots of cleared land—no electrical outlets, soda machines only at the ranger station, an outhouse for a shitter. At night you might hear card-game talk from parked RVs drifting across the heather and pigweed, but the early mornings were silent and austere. Now Baby Doc brings his boy to a place called Jellystone, a franchise park named for the home of a cartoon character. Should father and son run out of things to do, there is a pool and an activities area just up the gravel roadway that the tents encircle. There's a scavenger hunt scheduled for this afternoon.

"Anthony," Baby Doc says when he realizes the boy has nearly driven the tamp under the dirt. "That's probably enough. We need to leave the tine above ground to hook the rope through."

Together, they raise the tent. It is just a two-man, nothing fancy, but still bigger than a pup. They drape the rain guard over the top and stretch the elastic lines to secure it. Then they lay their bedding inside, where it is hot and stuffy. On the picnic table is the ten-gallon cooler. Anthony fishes through it for cheese crackers, his third pack this morning.

"My stepdad says he's gonna take me camping someday."

Baby Doc has begun chopping branches with a hatchet. He tosses the branches in the fire pit for tonight when they'll roast marshmallows and make s'mores.

"Your stepdad, is it? Is that what he likes you to call him?"

"I guess so."

"Well, if he's your stepdad, I guess that means you're supposed to step on him."

Baby Doc doesn't mind that Anthony doesn't laugh. He knows his son is obligated to appreciate this other man. This is Baby Doc and Anthony's first weekend together in almost a year, after all. Baby Doc hasn't spent much time with him lately. At least not sober time.

"So why do you think he's called a stepdad if not to step on him?"

Baby Doc can't help drawing out the joke. The boy shrugs, his lips powdered with cracker crumbs.

"Maybe it means he's your stepping stone. Or your stepladder. Or maybe it means that he's just a step away from being your real dad."

Anthony doesn't worry about what words mean. Baby Doc has to laugh at himself. Here he is, baiting his boy to make fun of a guy who houses and feeds him, who pays his health insurance. Baby Doc gives little more than the occasional check, which these past months his mom in Saginaw has taken to cutting for him. She's been footing the bills since he had to take his leave of absence.

"Can we start the fire now?"

"Sure," Baby Doc says. "Let me show you how not to start one."

He throws a birch log into the fire pit and wads newspaper under the peeling white bark. Then he soaks the newsprint with lighter fluid.

"You bring the matches?" he asks the boy. Anthony looks at him, blinks, says no—seriously, as though he'd meant to, but forgot.

"Go punch in the cigarette lighter and bring it to me."

The boy returns from their truck with the glowing lighter coil. Baby Doc touches it to the paper and the flame eats through the ink to the log.

"Here's something your mom will never want you to do." Baby Doc squeezes the can of fluid so a steady stream teases the flames taller. "She'll tell you it can climb back to the bottle and explode in your hands, but I've never seen that happen."

For the first time today, something intrigues Anthony. Leave it to fire, Baby Doc thinks. Maybe the boy doesn't understand why hot dogs and baked beans need that thick a flame. Or maybe he wonders why they don't just drive to a fast-food place.

When the fire settles, Baby Doc and Anthony hammer a grate over the pit and arrange their lunch. Baby Doc slices an orange in half and lets the boy suck at the pulp while the hot dogs thicken and blister. When the beans begin to bubble, he stirs them so they won't stick to the skillet.

"So what do you think of Anthony as a name?" Baby Doc asks as he works. "Do you like it?"

"I don't know," the boy says with yet another shrug.

"I think it's a pretty good name. But I think we ought to come up with a nickname for you, too, one like I have. They call me Baby Doc because they called my dad Papa Doc. Did you know that?"

"No."

"It was your mom's idea to call you Anthony. She didn't like my suggestions. I wanted to name you Rufus. Or Ivory. I think my favorite was Egbert. So maybe we can come up with a nickname from that, something like . . . Egg Doc. What do you think of that?"

"I think that's pretty dumb," Anthony says, disinterestedly.

Baby Doc agrees. Fortunately, the food is ready. Baby Doc wraps a bun around one of the hot dogs and doctors it with condiments from the cooler. But when he hands the plate to Anthony, the boy looks aggrieved.

"What's the matter?"

"I don't like mustard," he says.

"Since when?"

But Baby Doc doesn't wait for an answer. The boy is teary, and Baby Doc knows that since when was a long time ago. He serves the other hot dog plain. Neither of them are hungry, but they start in on the food because it's noontime, and they have driven three hours to be here, and because there is really nothing else to do.

After a second bite, Anthony's face twists in pain. The hot dog spills from his mouth back onto the paper plate, chewed and spitty.

"What's the matter now?"

"It's too hot."

"Jesus Christ." Baby Doc wipes the boy's lips. "If it's too hot keep it out of your mouth."

He wipes his own forehead with the kid's napkin. It is unseasonably humid this summer in Michigan, especially for as far north as Traverse City. He sweats harder now than he ever did when he was liquored up.

"Take a sip," he says, motioning toward an open water bottle. "And eat slower. You burn yourself when you want it too much. Rushing ruins it. You've got to feel it's earned, not given."

Anthony drinks and spits and spits again to get the scald off his tongue. This is okay, Baby Doc thinks. He can dislike the food and my jokes everything will still be okay. As Anthony cautiously tries the beans, Baby Doc hears his own talk about earning instead of taking. He wonders if the nonsense that he spouts isn't a way of getting another sort of bad taste out of his mouth. Baby Doc knows he's never earned his hungers.

"So what do we do now?" Anthony asks after finishing two-thirds of his plate.

Baby Doc has been watching his son, looking for a hint of himself in his gestures and expressions. He isn't surprised they aren't there.

"Good question." Baby Doc tosses his plate onto the still-burning birch, where it collapses into ash. Off in the distance he hears the whistle of the campground staff organizing the children for an arts and crafts activity. Paper-bag puppets, he thinks, or potato printing. A diversion while the parents lounge in folding chairs and read paperback novels. "I say we hit the dunes," Baby Doc says. "So we can start earning dinner."

Baby Doc is six weeks out of rehab, where he exchanged an addiction to alcohol for one to sit-ups. That's his explanation of events, anyway. More than the talk and the drying out, he's discovered how not to want to drink by doing twenty sets of twenty-five exercises. Whatever moved him to boozehound has been replaced by the folding and stretching of his muscles. He knows all their names, too: the rectus and transversive abdominis, the internal and external obliques. Baby Doc learned about them from the workout book that his girlfriend gave him while he was at the clinic. At forty, Baby Doc is young and vain enough to think that within another few months he can parade without a shirt like the topless boys who skateboard the Bay City streets.

For now he's content with the order that the sit-ups bring to his life. They are a form of discipline, just as his drinking used to be. He was always a very disciplined alcoholic. He drank the same amount at the same time each day consistently for years. He was never really drunk, he likes to think, just—*enlivened*. And then, later, when things at home went bad and his wife decided she deserved someone better, the divorce gave him the time and space to practice that discipline. Now sit-ups do the job. They're the caulk that holds together the leaky ship of the day. He can count them off as enthusiastically as he used to count off Jägermeister shots.

In the car on the road to the dunes, Baby Doc asks Anthony if he likes stories.

"I don't know," the boy says. "I guess so."

Baby Doc has a story to tell. In three days he'll return to the company whose insurance plan paid for his clinic stay. His boss hopes he's smart enough not to botch a second chance at selling prescription pharmaceuticals, for Baby Doc's good at the job. He was once salesman of the year, and he holds the all-time record in his mid-Michigan region for the most units pushed in a fiscal quarter. Even with the mess that is his personal life, the boss says, he still has a shot at a marketing-manager position. Baby Doc's ex and his girlfriend both want him to take it, for the work will get him off the road and stabilize him. They all want him to make it up to Anthony.

Baby Doc doesn't hope for much one way or another. His only ambition is for good stories. He'd like to tell his son about the girl in Ann Arbor whose navel he paid to have pierced. That was after several three-dollar pitchers and assorted hooter shooters. The girl was wild. She made out with Baby Doc in the parking lot within an hour of knowing him. She even let him cop a feel. But the minute she sat in the chair she changed. She squeezed Baby Doc's hand hard and screamed so loud the kid piercing her got scared and dropped his needle gun. That story cracked Baby Doc up. Then there was the time he and Steve Smith cut out of the reps meeting in Detroit. They had an incredible argument over something that seemed important at the time. It ended with Baby Doc tossing a bottle at Smitty, which bounced off his forehead and shattered next to the chair leg. Smitty looked dazed for a moment and said, "Did you just do what I think you did?" Baby Doc liked that line so much that he adopted it as his personal refrain. For a couple of years he indulged himself in whatever outrage came to mind. Whenever he managed to shock those around him, he'd slip into his faux naif voice and sing it out: Did I just do what I think I did? That was how he'd ended up with so many stories.

"Here's a good one for you," Baby Doc tells his son. "You know why they call it Sleeping Bear Dune?"

Anthony has started to fall asleep as they drive west of Traverse City toward Glen Lake.

"According to Indian legend there was this father bear." Actually, it was a mother bear, but Baby Doc is tired of mothers who claim to have their children's best interest at heart. "His little cubs drowned in Lake Michigan, and he was so full of grief at their loss that the Great Spirit—God, you know—put him to sleep to ease his pain. So just remember as we're going over the dunes: under the sand there's a sleeping bear, and if you step down too hard, you'll scare him awake."

"Dad," Anthony says, having long grown bored of such sweet tales.

"I'm telling the truth. We'll ask."

In family court, Baby Doc told a story he wasn't sure was really his. He had to fudge the plot if he was going to get to spend time with Anthony, away from his ex. Before this weekend, their hour-long visits took place in her basement, where father and son played video games or made watercolor rainbows. The whole time, Baby Doc had to listen to the overhead beams vibrate to the sound of the stepdad, upstairs, giving piano lessons.

"Do you remember what you were feeling that night?" the judge asked him.

"I remember being drunk."

"That's not all, I hope."

"No, it's not. I guess I felt anger."

"You guess?"

"I was feeling anger. Yes. I was hurt, but I was in the wrong. It was my fault. I shouldn't have done what I did. But I'm better now."

The truth was he wasn't angry at all. The night things really fell apart—the night that landed him in the clink and got him remanded to the clinic—was just like every other, a long look for fun. Baby Doc had always been good at fun. That night he'd gone out after work. The ex paged him, demanding her support check. That was the only time he heard from her. It was never, "Take the boy for a while," but always, "You're late." He went to her place and was juiced just enough to tell her how he planned to scotch the whole $500. Then the stepdad stepped onto the lawn to lecture him. The stepdad taught sixth grade. He enjoyed nothing better in life than talking to grownups as if they were sitting in the little desks that filled his classroom.

"You've got a responsibility," the stepdad kept saying. That was when Baby Doc demanded a paternity test. To this day he can't believe he did this, but he did. And it was funny, too, but it sure set his ex off. She threatened to call the cops. He dared her to. The neighbors came onto their porches. While they watched, Baby Doc urinated in her shrubs and kicked out the headlights on the stepdad's Volvo. Then he drove away, fell asleep, drove some more, was pulled over and got busted. Whether he got busted for driving under the influence or for vandalism he never knew until it was too late to call it fun.

"You recognize now that your son is your responsibility?" the judge asked him.

"Yes, I do."

That affirmation still in his ear, Baby Doc looks at the boy: a bundle of black hair, two arms and legs of responsibility. Other memories come back to him. The ex, the girlfriend, the boss. He remembers all the times people have told him about his responsibilities.

"You're ready to assume that obligation?"

His AA sponsor has asked him that. So has his lawyer, his mom, several friends. Through it all he lies and says yes. Or maybe he isn't lying. He knows he's capable, and he's willing. He just wants it to be fun.

"Hold on," he warns Anthony. "Hard left."

He almost misses the turn into the old bait shop where the highway bends along the lake. Once out of the truck, he hoists the boy onto his shoulders and steps into the store, where he is greeted by a row of wine bottles and the smell of air-conditioned grubs. The counter is unattended. From somewhere there is the low, muffled buzz of a radio. "Billy," he calls out. He's surprised the shop is still open. Nowadays when they fish the lake, most tourists buy their worms and beer from a supermarket.

An old man appears between the aisles pushing a broom. He is orange from the summer, and he stoops forward, as though his body were trying to catch up to the cigarette that hangs from his lips.

"You Billy?"

"Sure," the man says.

"I'm Papa Doc Canfield's boy."

The man draws a blank. "Damn," he says suddenly. "It's been a while. How long?"

They shake hands.

"Fifteen, sixteen years, I suppose. Don't know exactly, but a while. This is my boy." He pulls Anthony off his shoulders to speak to him. "Billy here was a friend of your grandpa's. You don't remember your grandpa, but this is his friend."

"Pleasure, son," Billy tells the boy. All the time Billy talks the cigarette bounces up and down like a maestro's baton. "Ain't been long enough for you to grow like this. How long since your daddy been gone?"

"Eleven years this March."

"Damn," Billy says again. He shuffles to the counter where he pulls out a bottle and a thermos top. "You want a drink? To celebrate?"

"I don't drink anymore. I'm into physical fitness now. We're heading over to climb the dune. I thought we'd stop in and see how many old timers are still around."

"Some of us is," Billy reports, downing a gulp. "My lease is up next year, though. The government's trying to push me out. But we got a lawyer who's doing them a good fight."

The old timers are folks who owned homes around Sleeping Bear before it was first organized into a state park back in '75. When the government appropriated the land, some of the locals sold out and left. Others like Billy and Papa Doc Canfield signed leases that, for a dollar a year, allowed them to stay. Now the leases are expiring. When their time is up, the old timers are supposed to sell their land to the park authorities who will level their homes and return the area to wilderness.

"Thing that burns me up," Billy is saying, "is that they want me out of my place and yet they've got all kinds of shacks and lean-tos already abandoned that nobody's yet tore down. I say when the government's done their end, then I'll think about doing mine."

"I'm with you," Baby Doc tells him. He realizes Billy is drunk. Midway through his sentence the cigarette falls out of his mouth and he goes on talking as if he didn't know it'd ever been there in the first place. "Hey," Baby Doc tugs at Anthony's shirt. "Go get us some bottled water for the climb."

The boy heads down an aisle.

"Your Pop," Billy says, "I once saw him deliver a calf dead serious after we'd played poker all night. Damnedest thing I ever saw. He drunk probably six scotches and when the time came to work, he just turned it off. Never understood it. Wished I could but never did."

Anthony returns with two waters.

"You get you some gum," Billy says, wagging his finger at the boy. "Compliments of the house."

"Go ahead," Baby Doc says. Anthony fishes the racks for his favorite flavor, grape.

"And you," Billy goes on. "You get something too." He sets a pint of vodka on the counter. "This'll build up your stamina. Get you up there with your daddy."

"I told you, I don't drink anymore."

Billy doesn't believe him. "Never heard such a thing," he says. The ex, the girlfriend, the boss, the judge, the mom—Baby Doc wonders how many of them are as incredulous as Billy, who slips the pint in a brown bag, folding over the edge. As Baby Doc says goodbye, he takes the bottle. He figures he can pitch it once he's out of Billy's sight.

From the bait shop they drive north to Pierce Stocking Drive, which takes them over a porcupine-gnawed covered bridge to the dune overlook. There Baby Doc leaves the truck, and they begin hiking the sand. The tourists around them carry small coolers and backpacks with snack bars and sandwiches. They sport Lycra shorts and long-beaked caps and noses smeared with sun cream. Baby Doc despises these things. He and his father knew the bluffs before 1967. That was when the local lumberman Pierce Stocking laid the first roadway between Glen Lake and the pine plantation that lies southeast of the bear's wind-scrubbed hump back. The road made it possible for the dunes to become a state park eight years later. Before then, one could make it past the cottonwood thatches over the sand without needing a drink, even in the August humidity. You knew that Lake Michigan was on the other side, its always cold water waiting to shock the hot out of you.

Now, as Baby Doc and Anthony make their way up the first slope, there are signs warning you to stay hydrated, to stay on the designated pathways, to turn back if you're feeling tired. Even though this is as close to nature as Baby Doc's been in a long time, he likes to believe that he experiences the dunes differently than the tourists. For them, the hike is about endurance. But for him, it's about humility. He wants to see the landscape as it shows off the most natural of natural processes, the slow grind of time. A glacier took centuries to carve Lake Michigan; now its waves eat away at the shore while the wind spills the loose sand until the juniper and the soft grasses can no longer take root. The piles that the water once built thrust by thrust are whittled away into bald mounds that resemble overturned bowls. Maybe that's why Baby Doc was such a fan of the good times: he wanted to believe that he could escape the grind. But now he knows that the land holds the truth of his own puniness in the order of things. It will show him that he isn't immune to erosion.

When they reach the top of the overlook, Baby Doc tells Anthony to look around. Behind them is the blue crescent of Glen Lake, ahead the slightly grayer churn of Lake Michigan, broken only by the steepled juts of the Manitou Islands. The distances impress the boy. He seems amazed that the world is this big. "Enjoy seeing water while you can," Baby Doc tells him. "Once we head down the trail, we might as well be lost in the Mojave Desert. You ready?"

Anthony nods. They start down the first slope, but the boy doesn't make it far. The sand burns the tops of his feet, which his rubber flip-flops leave exposed. It doesn't anger Baby Doc. He's glad. He scoops Anthony into the air and sets him on his shoulders. The extra weight upsets Baby Doc's balance, and he has to stab his feet deep in the dune to keep upright. His feet also burn, but in a good way. By the bottom of the first descent, they are amid tufts of sand cherry and puccoon. Their names come back swiftly to Baby Doc. He remembers how his own father would call out them out to Baby Doc on their walks to the lake, both in English and Latin, and then quiz him on the way back. He thinks about how overwhelmed he felt as a child to learn that a plant was more than just a plant, that the fauna could come in so many shapes and colors. As he and Anthony follow the trail, Baby Doc spares the boy those kinds of specifics. He wants him to enjoy the ride.

The lake is two miles from the overlook. As they mount and descend the dunes' steep grades, they pass the ghost forests formed by the skeletal remains of old hemlock and basswood trees. The dead limbs stick out of the sand like paralyzed fingers, their insides hollowed by the wind's sandpapering. Occasionally, Baby Doc comes across a paw print. He points them out and fibs about bears snacking on the tourists. Anthony is silent. From time to time, he seems to wobble on his father's shoulders, so Baby Doc lowers him and carries him at his chest. Despite the sun, the child soon falls asleep.

Baby Doc wakes him up when they reach the overlook to
Sleeping Bear Dune. The hundred-foot hump hasn't looked like
a bear for years now. More than a third of the altitude of its
broad, arched back has withered away, and time has weeded out
the trees that old explorers used to call its fur coat. Pretty soon—
maybe his own lifetime, Baby Doc thinks, maybe the boy's—the
dune will disappear completely.

The hump is so unimpressive anymore that Baby Doc does-
n't even point it out to Anthony. Instead, he sets his son down
and leads him by the hand along the trail to the lake bluff where
the dunes end in a thin cluster of beeches and maples bedded by
ferns and wild flowers. The bluff has steepened over the years
because the waves scoop out its base. Baby Doc asks Anthony if
he needs to ride down or if he can drop the incline by himself.
The boy chooses to go it alone. Baby Doc sits him on his rump
on the bluff's edge and lets him wiggle over the side. He falls
about four feet, his legs plunging up to his ankles in the sand. He
walks a few paces and tumbles forward. Baby Doc jumps the bluff
and rushes to him, almost spilling over himself. He pulls
Anthony upright, and together they make their way to the shore.

The lake is as cold as he remembered. At first Anthony
wants to nothing to do with it, but as the father wades up to his
knees, the child tentatively approaches the foamy waterline. The
waves are rough today; Baby Doc is barely up to his thighs when
one rushes forward and douses his chest. The chill brings a grimace to his face. It's frigid enough to burn, just like Baby Doc's
sit-ups. The boy laughs.

Baby Doc can't stay in long. When he was a child he was
immune to the cold. Once it numbed his skin, he would play for
upwards of twenty minutes until his father called him out, fearing hypothermia. Papa Doc always told the same joke: Go in
with nuts, come out with cubes. It seemed oh-so hilarious back
then.

As Baby Doc sits on the sand, toweling himself with his
shirt, Anthony is drawn closer to the waves. Soon he is up to his
knees. As each swell approaches, the child braces himself by
squatting and hunching slightly forward, like a defensive tackle
waiting for a running back to rush him. When the waves plow
into his torso, he is thrust backward, but he doesn't fall. Anthony

never falls. The water does its best to knock him down, but he holds himself steady. It doesn't take long for the boy to begin laughing, his giggles drowning out the crash of the breaks. Baby Doc understands why. There's a certain thrill to being engulfed by those waves. When they can't slap you on your back, they suck your footing out from under you. That moment of lost control is intoxicating. Baby Doc knows it well. A couple of months ago, there was nothing he loved better than the fun of being lost in that loss of control.

After one especially strong wave bowls into him, Anthony spins around, water streaming from his hair and fingers. His head is cracked in half with a wide smile, the kind you have to be six to let fill your face. And Baby Doc thinks, This is it. This is what it should be. It should be possible to have this fun and, like the boy, stay upright.

That night, at camp, they cook and eat their dinner, having earned a ferocious hunger from their hike. After cleaning the skillet, they roast marshmallows for the s'mores. Baby Doc likes to burn the ones he won't eat. He sticks a trio of them on his spit, placing them in the thick of the fire. When the marshmallows ignite, he waves the blackening mess in the air like a warrior's sword. Anthony thinks it's pretty funny. Baby Doc squishes one of the boy's marshmallows between a pair of graham crackers sandwiching a chocolate square. Then he makes himself one. The s'mores are sickly sweet and sating in an uncomfortable way. Baby Doc looks forward to waking up early and doing his sit-ups.

When they finish the treats, they lie against a log and let their sleepiness overtake them. It is only a little after nine o'clock, the earliest Baby Doc has felt drowsy in years. Nine used to be the hour that the night first came to life. Around them, throughout the campground, there is the low chatter of things winding down. "We'll rest well tonight," he tells Anthony. "We've earned a good sleep."

But it's too late. The boy's eyes are closed, and his body goes slack.

Baby Doc lays him in the tent in a sleeping bag. Then he sits back at the fire's side, watching the flames retreat into embers. The heat brings beads of sweat to his brows. He is thinking of his father, and of Billy. He wonders how that generation could drink all the time, be drunks, and still function. Baby Doc never saw his father kick out headlights or piss in the bushes. If anything, alcohol gave Papa Doc a fluid grace. Like Billy said, he could turn it off. That's the part Baby Doc never understood, keeping it under control. Keeping control seemed to undermine the whole point.

Then, without warning, Baby Doc hears a blast of music from another campsite. It startles him, but he expects it to die down as soon as the owners of the CD player realize that they've cranked their volume too high. Only the sound doesn't go away. It gets to him pretty quick. He can't understand why anyone would want to shatter the night quiet. He hops up and tracks the noise to its source. It's two teenagers, ball caps pulled low to their eyes, friendship bracelets covering their wrists.

"What the hell are you doing?" Baby Doc demands.

One kid cuts off the music.

"We're just having fun, man," the kid says. "Sorry."

But Baby Doc can tell that he's not. "I got a kid trying sleep over there. Can it, will you?"

Yeah, man. Sure, man. Sorry, man.

Baby Doc barely leaves their plot before the music kicks back on. The kids are laughing at him. Baby Doc knows it. He curses to himself as he jogs the circular drive back to his site. At the picnic table next to his tent he fishes for his hatchet. Then he runs back to where the teenagers are sitting. Their eyes bulge when they see him peel into their firelight bearing an axe. With a crazy, menacing slice of his arms, Baby Doc pantomimes hacking the boys. Then he stares them down as he struts over to the extension cord that connects their jam box to the power outlet. With one quick chuck, he plants the hatchet in the ground. The blade severs the cord. All is quiet suddenly except for the pops and buzzing that accompany a short shower of sparks. The teenagers aren't sure what just happened was real. Baby Doc tries to think of something smart to say, but before he can, one of the boys lets out a scream that sends Baby Doc running toward his own tent.

By the time he slips next to Anthony to stretch face down in the empty sleeping bag, he can feel his heart pounding almost as loud as that music. One thing circulates in his thinking: Did I just do what I think I did? Only he knows it's not funny. Either that scream has awakened park security, or the teenagers themselves will call the authorities, and Baby Doc will be taken in, and that will end his time with his boy. He can't understand what that anger was that made him threaten the teenagers, to actually cut their cord. He can't figure out where it came from. He can't believe that it's something that's been inside him, all this time, even after his rehab, something inside of him now, hibernating. If he'd been drinking, there'd be the buzz to blame. But that excuse isn't any good anymore.

He flips on his back. Moonlight spills through the tarp, silhouetting everything in the tent. Baby Doc remembers that he never threw away Billy's gift pint. He recalls all the good times he used to have, back when nothing was too serious. It hits him suddenly: he knows he won't not drink again. It won't be tonight. It may not be for a long time. But the immensity of things, their consequences, they're just too heavy, and all Baby Doc wants out of life are the good stories to tell.

With the night silence crawling all around him, Baby Doc waits for the park security to come, if they're coming. In the meantime, he watches the hump of his son's back rise and fall to the rhythm of his breathing.

COMPLICITY

The moment the elevator began to lift Darby realized she had stepped into the perfect metaphor for what she'd felt since the news broke. Being stuck in what amounted to a shoebox dangling from a shoestring forced her to appreciate anew the complete lack of choice she faced. She felt, too, the intensity of her isolation, the confinement that suffocated and benumbed her. More complex yet was the sensation of simultaneously rising and falling, of being pulled toward something she couldn't avoid while something else, a part of her, dropped behind. Of course, the part of her that dropped didn't fall far enough to be forgotten—it merely lagged beneath her a little, just far enough to sow a seed of unease in her belly.

To relieve her discomfort she tried to remind herself that the ride to the tenth floor was a short one. So would the appointment to which she was running minutes late and, with any luck, the rest of the day. But Darby also understood that this counsel was self-deceiving. However brief this morning might prove in the overall scheme of things, there'd always be the compulsion to revisit and relive the experience. She never before thought that reality had to be true, but events were circling back upon her to prove otherwise. And the more she accepted that fact the less appropriate this metaphor now seemed. The whole point of an elevator, after all, was to elevate. To rise above, as the word implied. Yet uplift no longer struck her as likely. That part of her that sank within her even as the elevator drew upward, that something that cradled itself in the gully of her hips, wasn't going to let her forget. What was that something? Darby knew exactly what it was.

It was memory.

Some inches to Darby's right stood her husband Matt, who poked repeatedly at the 10 button on the control panel. "Are you thinking," she asked him, "that the more you push the faster we'll get there?"

His finger froze mid-jab. Darby saw a reflexive glower of annoyance overtake his face. Yes, it was a mean thing to say, she decided, but wasn't it her right, today of all days, to say mean things? But then Matt's glare softened, as she knew it would. He hid the offending hand in a coat pocket, and his cheeks plumped with compassion. Darby knew that expression well. It was her husband's sympathetic face, at once earnest and rehearsed.

"Don't be this way," he said with a twinge of a beg.

"What way would you like me to be?"

"I'd like you to be yourself."

Aha, she thought. Therein lies the problem. Because from the moment that her OB-GYN's brow wrinkled as he rolled the ultrasound sensor over her jellied abdomen she had the sensation of being cleaved in two and made to live twice at once. There was the her of the here and now, of course, the one who endured the glib consolation of the hospital staff as it performed the battery of tests that confirmed what she intuited from the doctor's sudden change of demeanor. Then there was the her of the past, someone Darby had confidently come to believe no longer existed but who had actually been trailing her all along. She knew that now. The past never haunted her in any substantial form, never anything like a physical presence; it was (and would always be) a mere phantom breath, something vague but ominous that loitered at her shoulder.

What the OB-GYN told her when she inquired about the similarities didn't matter: "It's the same basic procedure, yes," he said, "but not the same situation. For obvious reasons." It didn't matter that this basic procedure had two names. One was sterilized by clinical formality (dilation & curettage, or "D&C" as they referred to it, a name that better befit a drug-store chain), while the other was so laden with emotion that Darby couldn't bring herself to say it outright. "Rhymes with contortion," she thought. "Distortion, extortion, proportion." It didn't matter either that the differences were so defining that these procedures took place in different facilities. The one required nothing more than a quick trip to the hospital, while the other usually meant a longer ride to a vaguely named building in a shabby part of town—or, in Darby's case, a whole other town, since there had been no such thing as a "women's reproductive health center" where she lived all those years ago. Yes, the OB-GYN did his best to reassure her that different names and different places denote different things, not knowing, of course, why she needed that reassurance. Yet Darby spent the week that separated the bad news and the first available D&C appointment baiting Matt with the similarities.

"What if I don't go through with it?" she asked. "What's it going to do? Kill me back?"

"Don't use that word, for God's sake," he would snap. And then, as always, he restrained himself by draping himself in a holy shroud of concern: "You didn't do anything to make this happen. It's a freak of nature. It happens to a lot of people for a lot of reasons, medical reasons. There's nothing we could've done differently to prevent it. Sometimes things just aren't meant to be. You have to know that, deep down. You have to."

"And back then? That was just something, too, that wasn't meant to be?"

She picked at him because she wanted him to broach the subject first. She wanted him to question, out loud, what she was secretly wondering, what she needed to believe he was wondering as well: whether the past was to blame for the present. But Matt was obstinate. He had a closet's worth of clichés to dress his aversion in. The past is the past, don't cry over spilt milk, let sleeping dogs lie. In more generous moods Darby credited her husband with enough savvy to not respond to her prodding with a platitude. No, he was a sweet, articulate man whose only ambition was for the two of them to be happy. So what if in his mind happiness meant not bringing up the what was, not ever, not directly, at any rate?

Darby knew it was Matt's guilt, his sense of once having wounded her by nothing more malicious than having loved her that made him suffer the past week so magnanimously. He endured her sarcasm and her anger and her crying with saintly patience. If he'd had bangs instead of a receding hairline she could have called him Prince Valiant. Could he have brought himself to talk about it, he probably would have said something designed to reassure her, something along the lines of, "I understand. I understand completely. You have a right to feel what you feel. Let's work through this." But he never said that. Their conversations, all of them begun, bent, and broken off to accommodate the demands of the workaday world, involved little more than him letting the smart remarks slide by, him changing the subject, him outright ignoring her. It galled Darby so bad she began to think of their exchanges as an implicit dare, a child's game of "who'll blink first?"

So there you go, she told herself the afternoon she heard herself say the words "back then." Congratulations. We have a winner.

Only Matt didn't seem to enjoy the victory. He cast his eyes across his knees, his shoes, the kitchen floor. Everywhere but in the general vicinity of his wife.

"Back then," he answered, softly and limply, "was a long time ago."

And it had been, she realized. More than a decade. Enough time, one would think, that she could approach the memory coldly and dispassionately, with her doctor's professional detachment or Matt's determined aloofness. For most of those intervening years Darby had been able to forget. Or if not exactly forget at least push it off to a sufficient distance that it no longer seemed a scene from her own life but something borrowed from an external source—the television, maybe, a chapter in a book she'd read, or a story passed along by someone else. Something, at any rate, that didn't belong to her.

Darby had learned to live with the memory because on those rare occasions it came back to her it did so only in bits and pieces, in shards of associations that were too fragmented to force themselves upon her with any degree of immediacy. A certain shade of blue sometimes seen in fabric swatch books or on paint samples reminded her of the clinic, for instance. That color stayed in her mind because it seemed such an odd choice for a building in an otherwise abandoned warehouse district. Darby could remember asking herself that morning as she and Matt made their way through the gravel parking lot—a morning begun a hundred miles away from home (home being a dorm room back then), in a dilapidated motel that only amplified the sordid grimness of it all—whether the shade might be a subtle rebuke, a taunt meant to tell her and women like her that they'd never feel that light or that airy again.

(But she had, many times, often even, and that fact discon-
certed Darby, too).

Then there were random times she stretched out in a den-
tist's chair, and the possibility of being splayed and vulnerable
excited an anxiety that not even the nitrous oxide could anes-
thetize. Yet these were remote, fleeting recollections, their significance dwarfed by the moments of great joy she had known: her
marriage, the birth of a daughter, the general contentment and
peace that she wanted to take for granted. She should be grateful, she supposed, that she'd been able to bury that slender bit of
her past so deep in the boneyard of her mind. But she was afraid,
too, that the medical necessity of removing this object within
her that had refused fruition would tear away something vital to
her own survival, the thing that had made it possible to love
Matt, to stay with him. What was that thing? She knew exactly
what it was.

It was the ability to avoid thinking about it.

You see, she wished she could tell her husband, whenever I've
thought of you all these years of ours together I've not been allowed to
remember you as you were at first, when we first met. I can't imagine the
boy who used to cut across University Avenue toward William Street in a
pair of black high-top tennis shoes, the one who always insisted on growing
his hair long even though it never grew long, just out, the one who pocket-
ed the leftover croissants and tubs of peanut butter from the cafeteria
where he bussed tables. I can't roll my eyes to laugh at the sight of you
pulling money from a bank envelope instead of your wallet as you went to
pay the check for our first flashy dinner together, back when flashy dinners
seemed a coy way of playing grownup. (I was eighteen; you had just turned
twenty). I can't tell myself the story of the time I packed a Styrofoam cup's
worth of bleach to take to the Laundromat and you took a gulp because
you assumed it was Mountain Dew.

I can't even bring up the first time we made love, which was in your
dorm room on a Saturday night after a block party when we were intoxi-
cated by the newness of it all. You had the radio playing and a favorite
song came on and you stopped kissing me just long enough to say, "This is
a favorite song and if you like me you should like it." No, none of these
moments are memories I can enjoy for the way they should be enjoyed,
which is to say for their being frivolous, for their having happened when we
were young and all things seemed possible as long as we didn't take too

much too seriously too soon. I can't go back there and access those memo-
ries because I can't ever pry them loose from context, from the lockstep pro-
gression of what comes next. All those scenes are stones on a road that
leads only to one place, and as you're so fond of saying in the heat of an
argument (any argument, about anything), "Let's not go there." So we
never do, and, as a result, time for us is halved into irreconcilable oppo-
sites, into the before and the after. And when and if we ever are able to sit
down and open ourselves up to the truth, we will have to confront the fact
that our love has been born twice and has lived twice, that it's been
through both B.C. and A.D. How did we miss out on the redemption that
the latter wrung from the neck of the former?

Once and only once before this miscarriage had Darby even
come close to breaking the unspoken vow to not talk about it. A
few years earlier she and Matt commemorated their third
anniversary by trading their two-bedroom condo for a four-bed-
room house. The number four struck Darby and Matt as a good,
manageable number—a family number. It meant, in addition to
their room and a study where Matt could keep up with work, two
rooms for the two children they planned to have. At the time
Darby was in her second trimester with the first of these children, and she found herself prone to bouts of estrogenated emotions that sometimes got the better of her. She would wake in the
middle of the night terrified that a random pang or throb in her
body was a danger signal she shouldn't ignore. Then, other times,
she would press at her swollen belly, gripped by the fear that she
was merely an inflated balloon, her skin stretched to hold nothing more than an abscess of air. Her OB-GYN, her mother, the
few women her age she knew who were already mothers—they
all kindly let her know that such feelings were perfectly normal.
She didn't include Matt in her circle of confidants, however. To
share those anxieties with him would have come too close to
reminding him of the fevered days before the decision was made,
back when she had demanded of him, relentlessly, "What are we
going to do?"

Darby didn't want to recall those tortured conversations
because she didn't want to remember the ambivalence they
brought out in Matt. He was stubbornly reticent, deferring to her
with the same hollow words: "It's up to you." Only Darby knew
from the way he mumbled those words that he really wasn't sin-

cere. Matt didn't really mean the decision was hers. He wanted her to infer what he was feeling so he didn't have to risk saying it out loud. No, Darby could never confess her fears to her husband as she came to term with their daughter because she knew he could only perceive them as a demand, as yet another test by which he was supposed to prove himself.

But then one Saturday shortly after taking possession of their new home they were decorating the living room with family pictures. Frames were strewn over the coffee table and fireplace mantel, and littering the floor were stacks of photographs they'd accumulated throughout their time together. Matt sat Indian style amid those stacks, thumbing through the various stages of their lives. "What about this one?" he would ask, holding up a shot of them taken at some friend's wedding reception or at a Christmas gathering of relatives.

There were any number of reasons for not displaying a particular picture: awkward angles, too much/too little light, unflattering red eye. But the more they went through this ritual the more Darby realized what they were actually up to. Unconsciously and yet deliberately, they were constructing their story for anyone who happened through their house. Darby could imagine hosting parties where people would slink along the walls studying the images to piece together the bigger picture that was them. And Darby knew that she or Matt, or she *and* Matt, would be right at their guests' side, narrating for them. Here's us at the wedding, they would say, slicing the groom's cake. And here's us at Disney World; we're still paying that trip off, we think. And us on the porch, just after we hung the swing where we'll sit on Sunday mornings to read the paper. And the goofy Olan Mills studio portrait we only posed for because his parents pushed us for something formal to put on their grand piano. Don't you see? What a happy, happy world is ours.

"We have two histories, you know," Darby suddenly blurted out when thoughts of what the photos didn't show proved overwhelming. "This is just the official version. Where to store the other, the secret one? If we had a cellar we could hide it behind the retaining wall."

Matt stared at her, disbelieving, as if she'd slipped into a foreign tongue he couldn't quite understand. "Where did that come

from?" he asked. Then the surprise hardened into opaque defer-
ence. He assumed the same inscrutable submissiveness he always
retreated to whenever he feared getting entangled in one of her
trickier moods. Darby didn't know how she had wanted Matt to
respond. Maybe she craved a flash of anger, some sign of exasperation. It would have been perfectly legitimate for him to say,
"Aren't you over that yet? It's been long enough." But Matt was-
n't that hot under the collar. He wasn't that callous. He simply
gathered the photo stacks together. "We can finish this later," he
said, and he ran off to unpack boxes in another room.

Here's the story they told friends and family, the one they
fleshed out from the photos hung in their home. They'd met in
college, yes, but they hadn't fallen in love. At least not the
durable kind of love. They were just kids, after all, and after a few
inconsequential months of going out, they both began to chomp
at the bit of being tied down. Depending on who inquired about
how they'd come together they cited different reasons for their
breakup. Matt was too immature then, Darby would say. His
main concerns were scoring good arena seats during basketball
season and rounding up a gang for dollar-pitcher night at the one
brewery where you could pass off a fake I.D. He played intramu-
ral softball, jogged and lifted weights, but his driving ambition in
those days was to hang out. As for Darby, well, Matt would play-
fully chide, she was too serious. She liked to read more than go
out, and she worried openly about what a bad exam might do to
her GPA. She wasn't the kind to argue with their football team's
ranking in the AP polls or to play quarters on a Wednesday
night. If all else failed they brought up the bout of mononucleo-
sis that waylaid her for a half semester. That excuse seemed as
good as any because just about every girl Darby knew in college
suffered at least a round of mono. All in all they'd found each
other nice enough but unremarkable during that first period.
They drifted apart with genial indifference, no hard feelings, no
big deal.

Then came the part of the story that people ate up. It's two
years down the road, and on the verge of graduation Darby lands
a job interview for a copywriter's position in an ad agency a few
towns away. She shows up for the interview, summa cum laude,

with an impressive portfolio from an internship the previous summer, only to discover that one of the members of the hiring committee is none other than Matt. Unbeknownst to Darby, he's been the agency's human resources rep since getting his degree a few terms back. Right away, each realizes how much the other's changed.

"She's actually got a sense of humor," Matt would say. "I can tell she's not such a cold fish anymore."

"And he's finally sober," Darby always added, much to the entertainment of whoever was hearing the story. They had these punch lines down pat. So pat, in fact, that the repartee inevitably reminded guests of a romantic comedy, one of those tart, brittle films where two opposites (think Clark Gable and Claudette Colbert in *It Happened One Night*) realize that the source of their steamy bickering is a boiling attraction. Matt and Darby could even add a bit of intrigue to the story to spice it up. Because this ad agency's small (less than fifty employees), fraternization among the staff is frowned upon. That means they have to see each other on the sly. And that means quick whispers at the snack machine, mash notes passed through the interoffice mail, winks and knowing nods during tedious meetings. Darby often recounted for people the kisses they'd steal during elevator rides. "So one time he looks at me and he goes, 'Why don't these damn elevators ever break down when you want them to?' That's when I really knew." It was sweet enough, guests said, to be a movie.

Darby agreed. Just like in the movies, their love story was built around moments of orchestrated serendipity designed to create an illusion of inevitability. And just like in the movies, too, she and Matt called upon all kinds of sleight of hand and trickery to make that inevitability—their marriage, their founding a family—seem the most natural thing on earth. What did it matter that the truth had to be edited because it was more complex? Don't all love stories, if you test their veracity hard enough, turn out to be lies?

In the aftermath of telling their story Darby sometimes wondered how people would react to the unexpurgated version. Could they deal with the fact that, more than inevitable, Matt and Darby's marriage was improbable? How to explain that after

the initial shock of seeing him again she'd actually found herself
drawn to him, and him to her? How weird was it that for all the
icy embarrassment that at first had them keeping their distance
they nevertheless sought each other out? What could they want
from each other? What could they give? Some recognition of
respect, perhaps, for their mutual suffering and sorrow. Or maybe
just the security of knowing that neither had ever taken what
had happened lightly, that each had learned from it, been
improved by it, if that was possible. Maybe it was reassuring to
know that in the aftermath the other no longer possessed the
capacity to be careless or flippant or self-indulgent. They had
learned the hard way the high cost of such things, after all.
Maybe, Darby thought on certain occasions, she ended up with
Matt for the simple reason that no one else could ever have
known her so thoroughly.

At times when the real story struck her as too incredible she
tried to explain it to herself by outlining what she believed were
certain statements of fact.

We could start over because we were different people.

*We were different people because we were in a different place and the
past seemed a figment of imagination.*

*We were different people, too, because we had been with different peo-
ple. In the interim you slept with other women to assure yourself you could
enjoy a woman's body without dread. And I slept with another man (only
one, don't worry) so at moments when I most resented you I could blame
somebody else.*

*And yet the past has always been here between us, determining our
choices and actions in ways we've never known. The fact, for example, that
we never made love until the first night we were wed. To not wait, I suppose, would have made the past all too real. And even after we were married I could tell it remained in your mind, however locked away. Because
for a long time each time you touched me you would ask, "Are you sure
this is okay?"*

It wasn't anything as obvious or transparent as morality that
made her feel these things. Darby could square her shoulders and
say that the decision they'd made (she'd made?) was at the time
the best one for everyone involved. What she regretted was
something at once simpler and yet more abstract. Darby just
would have liked to have a story she could tell—not to anyone

else, just to herself—that wasn't riddled with caesuras and ellipses.

But that wasn't an option because events were circling back upon themselves. As the elevator doors opened Darby was once again taken by the sensation of living twice at once. She tried to do as her OB-GYN did and remind herself of the differences. The hospital wasn't humid with the thickened air of fallibility, for instance. That was the memory Darby now recalled, the sight of young women (even the older ones seemed young) clustered in chairs, some with partners, some with friends, heads slung low as they signed release forms to avoid eye contact.

Darby remembered wondering back then what their stories were, how they compared to hers, where she fit in among them. She recalled how you could tell how those women coped by how they dressed. Some were primped to the nines, hair lacquered and curled as if by submersing themselves in formalities they could insulate themselves. Or maybe they just thought nobody would think the worse of them if they appeared presentable. Then there were others in sweatpants and pajama bottoms, more practical but more slovenly, too. Those women looked as if they'd just rolled out of bed. The memories led Darby to wonder what had become of them. Most, she felt reasonably sure, had gone on to become mothers, some of them many times over. They probably lived much as Darby had before this week, secure in the belief that distance excused them from the past, that they'd moved on and were over it. She figured she was probably the only one of the lot to marry the first man to impregnate her.

What I remember most, she then thought, is you. How you dealt with it. So young yourself and yet so determined to be there for me. Why? Any other twenty-year-old boy would have forked over a few hundred dollars and headed for the hills. But you not only insisted on accompanying me, you made the arrangements. Not the appointment itself, I mean, but the motel room, the car we had to borrow to get there. You had to pawn your stereo to pay for it all. You held my hand as I endured the rigmarole of the counseling staff. You held it as I waited to be called into the room and then you held it for the hour we had to wait to make sure there was no bleeding. I wanted so badly to believe you stayed with me because you loved me, and not because you felt as if you had to, because you felt it was right. I wanted something more from you than duty.

What if you'd loved me then in the way I needed?

You would have let me talk. You would have listened without worrying if I was blaming you. You wouldn't have done me the disservice of waiting until you thought I was asleep to slink off to the shower to scrub away the dirty feeling of complicity.

Most of all, you would have known that not every problem looks to you for a solution, that some things not even you with your dogged, dogmatic belief in getting through things can fix. You would have accepted the fact that there may have been a feeling or a worry or something I couldn't even name for you that I needed to voice if for no other reason than to get it out of me.

But now you're different. I know. So am I. The people who went through what we did aren't around anymore. And so you say, "Talk to me. Tell me what you're feeling." You want me to know that it's your concern for me that has you stroking my hair at night, patting my shoulder. And I know you are concerned. But you can't say you're selfless. Because you know as well as I do that you really don't want the truth. You know that what you really want is reassurance from me. You want to know that I can get over this so we can just get back to the business of being happy.

If I could tell you what's been going through my mind, what went through my mind then, this is what I'd say:

"Good fucking Christ, I feel I'm the mother of death."

But don't worry, I won't.

Because I know you couldn't handle it.

"You know what I want?" Darby asked Matt. They were in the waiting room. Matt's left arm stretched around his wife's shoulder, protectively. His right palm lay hard and heavy as a handcuff across the wrists wrapping her knees.

"What?"

"I want you to go buy me something to make me forget."

Out the corner of her eye she saw his face wrinkle. "Wouldn't it be better for me to stay? I think I should."

She shook her head. "I don't want that. Because if you do I know I'll end up hating you. I'm sorry. I can't help it. It's just better if you go."

Matt dropped his elbows to his sides with a long, bewildered sigh. Finally, he stood.

"Is there anything in particular you want?"

"You mean anything that will make it all better?"

He squatted at her knees so she couldn't avoid him anymore. "I'm doing my best," he said. "Please, do yours."

He spoke more sternly than she'd ever heard him speak. Then, knowing a response wasn't coming, Matt stood again and made his way through the maze of chairs. Darby tried her best not to look his direction, but her resolve failed and she glanced over her shoulder. Just as she expected. Matt's eyes remained fixed on her even as he tried to sidestep the outstretched legs of the ball-bellied women waiting their turn with the doctor. Nobody in the room spying on them would have guessed anything was askew, but because she was married to Matt, Darby was sensitive to the faint way his features curdled when he implored her. It struck her suddenly that for all his well-intentioned silence Matt was communicating loudly enough that his head might as well have been an illumined globe casting his thoughts across the walls.

We put history behind us once, the look on his face said. Is it really so impossible to believe we can't do it again?

BABY,
LET'S MAKE A BABY

—And then his wife says, "I think it's time."

Only the woman who lies curled against him amid an evening mess of sheets isn't his wife. Not yet, anyway. Their wedding is three weeks from today, and though she's made a vow not to spend the night with him until their union is official, they're too accustomed to intimacy after two years' time together to abstain. To him her body feels familiar in a way that makes them already wed, but he grants her this prim indulgence and doesn't complain when, at eleven-thirty several times a week, she dresses herself from the clothes piled on the floor and scurries to her apartment. As if to complete the illusion that there remains something between them as of yet unshared, they don't discuss the skirts and tops already claiming closet space in the house he buys for them, and they ignore the feminine toiletries that crowd the lavatory tank.

"What do you think?" she asks.

"I think I've been in this movie before," he answers.

And he has. Years ago, when he was twenty-one, he lay with another woman on the verge of becoming his wife. She was blond, not brunette, and a world apart from this fiancée in temperament. Yet he can't help but marvel at how similar they are in at least one desire: they both want to be pregnant, right now, right away.

"It's crazy," he continues. "You've never been in this deal before. You don't know what the pressure's like. And to throw a baby into the mix, right off the bat."

He allows the clichés to trail off when her body goes slack; he's made his point a little too insistently. But he feels he has a right. Years ago, when the proposition arose with the first wife, he gave in, and now he's father to a teenage girl with whom he remains estranged because having a child right away did more to destroy than preserve that marriage. He remembers how his ex-wife posed her intent to conceive as a dare. Do you love me enough, she was asking, to do this, right now, a trimester before we're allowed, even if it means embarrassing our families?

He understands now that he relented more out of passivity than desire. A vague fear of disappointing her motivated several weeks of conscientious lovemaking, sometimes twice a day, with no birth control while they bickered about floral arrangements and cummerbund colors. He remembers the shocked faces of his family when the bride-to-be showed up at the rehearsal dinner in a dress that accentuated the convexity of her belly. He can still recite verbatim the tortured, post-honeymoon phone call when he tried to convince a quartet of incredulous parents that they knew what they were doing, that in the white heat of their love they just couldn't wait to create a child. To this day his mother refuses to accept that her granddaughter is the intentional fruit of a cockamamie plan. It is much easier to believe in careless accidents.

He likes to think, too, of how much smarter the subsequent decade and a half has made him. He has spent the last ten years single to better himself. He has amassed a respectable savings account, diversified his portfolio, paid off credit cards, thumbed through stacks of self-help books in an earnest effort to overcome his failings. He has cut off flirtations when they became too serious, avoided most one-night stands, moderated his drinking and smoking, all in a priestly effort to prepare himself for a marriage in which he can do things right this time.

"You know," he hears this fiancée saying. She has propped herself up by her elbows so the freckles that cover her shoulders and chest are visible. In lighter moments of nakedness, he likes to connect those dots with a tickling draw of his index finger. "I know it's a crazy idea, and you know I'm not really serious. But I don't want you to tell me it's crazy. I just want to know that you love me so much that you would give me a baby. Do you know what I mean?"

"I know," he assures her, and he pulls her into an embrace meant to make her stay until morning. "And you know I love you that much. You know I do. Don't you know that?"

She doesn't speak.

"Don't you?"

Sometimes they argue about their age difference. He claims he's only ten years older than her because he likes the symmetry of the decade that separates their lives' milestones. They graduated high school ten years apart, college, too, so if she tries to remember, say, the specific year she was in eighth grade, for whatever reason, he can calculate the date just by adding a digit in the tens column of the timeline he maintains in his mind. That sort of tidiness at once humors and annoys her, for it's not true, and she can prove it by doing her own math. His birth year ends with an 8, hers with a 9. That to her equals eleven. Whenever she corrects him on this matter, he wonders why she insists on putting the additional distance between them.

"Because it's the truth," she answers. "You can't change facts."

"I think you want me older in your mind," he teases her. "It's your father complex. You want me *in loco parentis*. You know, to take care of you and all. To tame you, make you settle down."

She always rolls her eyes at this point in the conversation.

"That's what your parents like best about me," he continues. "I'm old enough to provide for you. Not that I'm moral or intelligent or upright, but that I'm older."

She knows he kids, but she's also aware of a certain fixity of judgment in what he says. So she counters: "Please. Your age is the one thing they don't like. They think you're going to decide you're too old for kids. My mom's afraid you'll wake up and realize that you've done your time, and you'll sneak off for a vasectomy. You are getting up there, you know. Only five years to forty."

"That's not old at all. You hear all the time about men having kids in their fifties and sixties. Nowadays even guys in their eighties make babies."

"That's obscene. But seriously, I want three kids by the time I'm thirty. That means we've got to get cracking, right after the wedding."

"Baby," he always tells her. "You know we can't do that. Remember the two-year rule."

The two-year rule is something that he read in a book about relationships, the idea being that marriages need time to solidify and take root before the pressure of children. That's the word he always uses: pressure. She knows why he's so insistent on following somebody's rule. She understands what he's been through, but she can't help but resent how quickly he speaks of dangers and pitfalls that must be eluded, as if their love were an unstable chemical compound that will stay together only under controlled laboratory conditions.

"God, please, stop with the two-year thing," she begs him. He pulls her into a conciliatory hug. Whenever he embraces her, she feels his belt buckle press against the pooch of her belly, and she is aware of the emptiness there. Sometimes when alone she presses her fingers against her stomach and imagines the loose skin pulled taut into a pulsing bubble. The entire process of childbearing mystifies her. At bookstores she likes to leaf through maternity guides, awed by the tangerine-tinged photos of blossoming embryos, all curled up except for the one finger or toe that seems to point, frailly, to the outside. Since she was a girl she has imagined the sensation of giving birth, not the pain of splitting flesh but the wonder of cradling that infant in its first pinking moment. She knows that her impulse will be to seek in the pinched, misshapen features what part of that life owes itself to her and what to him. She can think of nothing more wonderful than an opportunity to hold a baby and say, "I made this."

"Hey, I know," he tells her one afternoon when the two-year rule again creeps into their talk. "You have one in a couple years when you're twenty-seven and then two years later when you're twenty-nine, we have twins. Voilá, there's your three. How's that for a plan?"

She smiles and rests her chin against his neck. She feels him pat her back, a gesture of reassurance that she dislikes. Five pats, always five light taps on the same button of her spine. It strikes her as a gesture learned from a book. Everything, she realizes, everything according to a plan.

—And then they're married. At first she loves the snuggling comfort of her domestic routine. She takes pleasure in stacking her new skillets and pans on the bottom shelf beside the stove and arranging drinking glasses in the cupboard. She'll spend a half-hour bringing order to the canned goods and cereal boxes clogging the pantry. Each time she goes to the grocery, she makes sure to purchase differently designed party napkins, which she keeps in an antique sideboard for when friends drop by. He kids her about the fastidiousness and takes her upbraiding with good humor when, while unloading the dishwasher, he fails to return the spatulas and pizza cutters to their proper place.

Only a few weeks after their wedding, he grants her the indulgence of a dinner party designed to impress co-workers. He's not sure the crowds will mix well, for her office mates are khaki casual, and his are button-down reserved. Nevertheless, he splurges for a half-case of wine whose name he's not sure how to pronounce and then takes deep pleasure when the inebriated guests gush about her sherry chicken. After the party breaks up, the two of them gather the wine goblets from the living room and rinse the china. Later, still buzzing, they make love in the leather recliner occupied only a short time earlier by his boss. She whispers for him to stay inside her. He jokes about her having gotten him drunk so he'll let his guard down and impregnate her. She puts a finger to his lips and assures him there is no need to remove himself, for she's just started her period. He nods appreciatively because her cycle doesn't clash with his two-year plan, and he rocks his way against her in a rhythm that is at once intense and caring, sated with the certainty that they are in love and that all is well—

—And it is, at least until a Friday happy hour at a river-front marina when, after five or six Mexican beers, she discovers another man's tongue in her mouth. It's only a half-year into her marriage, and she has taken to attending these after-work excursions for the innocently illicit pleasure of gossiping away from home. She sees no harm in this. A few times a month he must entertain clients, and she has seen the rounds of margaritas and whisky sours itemized on his expense account. Besides, her co-workers are also married, and their going out seems a harmless way to stave off the looming drudgery of weekend chores.

This Friday night, however, a project manager with a fondness for fish and chips escorts her to her car and, without warning, kisses her before she can get behind the wheel. Initially, she registers the overwhelming taste of Tartar sauce, but as this foreign tongue squeezes past her teeth, she feels the unexpected adrenaline of spontaneity. It is the rush of being wanted, of being taken, of giving in to some stronger force. She thinks of the wrongness of what she's doing, but she can't stop. She remembers the first time her husband kissed her. It was like this—sudden, surprising, unsettling. When the man retracts his tongue and sheepishly begins to apologize, she places her index finger to his lip before driving home, intent on making love to her husband.

Over the next months, she and the other man trade covert, coded e-mails, laced with secret nicknames. They go to out-of-the way diners for lunch and drink together at bars where the neon signage casts an illicit glow over their indiscretion. Only vaguely will she admit the dangers of what she does, but she assures herself she can control her feelings. Besides, she justifies it all by believing that this is more for her than about her. This man wants her, she knows this. She's aware of the longing in the way he looks at her. Sometimes she even smiles at his fumbling attempts at flattery. She accepts his compliments because she understands that his sort of desire evaporates when the intimacy is consummated. It is the lust for the unfamiliar, and it is something her husband can no longer supply her. What harm can it be, she wonders? After all, it's a secret that he'll never know—

—And he is never supposed to know, until one Saturday evening she finds herself and the friend at an out-of-town restaurant after an afternoon of platonic shopping. She has talked constantly of a camping trip she and her husband took the previous weekend. The temperature had dropped below forty, and they had ended up sleeping in the backseat of their friends' Suburban for warmth.

"Let me ask you something," the friend suddenly interrupts, a dab of beer broth above his lip. "If you're so happy with him, why are you here?"

"What do you mean?" she asks, knowing full well what he means.

"I mean, don't you think it's a symptom? Don't you think it means something that you're here with me and not with him?"

"He's working this weekend. It's his season."

"It wasn't his season two months ago."

She doesn't answer. She has dreaded this moment.

"You know why I'm asking this," he tells her. He takes another steep swallow of his pale ale, and the spume mustache thickens before his brown tongue licks it away. "I'm asking this because I think I've fallen in love with you."

She doesn't speak. The friend's eyes broaden in anticipation, and she is afraid to disappoint him. So she says it.

"I think I love you, too," she says.

Her husband's first words when he finds out:

"I've been in this movie before."

And he has. When his daughter was barely three, he and the first wife turned to infidelity to stave off the banality of duplex life. He did it first, and it is a shameful secret he's kept from both women, partly for fear of losing the moral upper hand. Part of him has always wondered whether the first wife didn't deduce his guilt. He finds it easy to believe that she avenged herself by entering a flagrant relationship with a former high school friend. When they separated, he moved into the guest house of one of his professors, and for months they went back and forth, each threatening divorce, each attempting to seduce the other into a reconciliation. In the meantime, out of pique, he worked his way through an anonymous procession of undergraduate inebriates, one of whom, a waitress, herself married, banged on his cottage door one morning in a T and sweats to announce she was pregnant—only she didn't know by whom. Nine months passed before he could submit to the blood test that would decide his future. In that time, he lost twenty pounds, took up smoking and suffered from insomnia. When he learned he wasn't the father, he made a vow to never again get shoestrung by that kind of chaos.

Thus his first sensation as this wife lies crying across the bedspread is to feel ten years of maturity evaporate in an instant's confession. He wants to yell, strike out, berate her for allowing this to happen, but all he can do is sit back upon the pillows piled against the headboard and marvel at the perfect circularity of it all. There is only one saving grace to this situation: this time, there's no child involved.

A day or so later she piles clothes in the back of her car and announces she needs time to figure out her life. When she's gone he programs the stereo to play his favorite blue tunes. He contemplates going out for a pack of cigarettes, or some breakfast, or a wildly irresponsible affair of his own. But he is still in his pajamas, so instead he picks up the phone to dial a number he rarely calls.

His first wife, he tells himself, won't believe what's happened.

Over the weeks that follow she calls constantly, e-mails him at work, asks him to lunch. She is staying with a girlfriend, but he knows there are nights that she and this other man are meeting up. Come three A.M, when he can't sleep, he finds himself in his car gliding along the girlfriend's street, staring at unfamiliar houses. He prays he'll happen upon her car, and when he does find it snugly parked along the curb, he returns home, fixes himself a screwdriver, and sits alone in the dark. Those times that her car is gone, he lets his engine idle on a side street as he tries to see through passing headlights. He only does this twice. The second time a nearby dog takes to howling, and the porch lights that pop on scare him away.

Some afternoons they sit on the terrace of a local bar drinking. He has taken vacation time and surprises himself at how pleasant wine can taste before lunch. On the surface, she is more reserved, but only because she's better at hiding the turmoil. For him, the only compensation for his life going out of control is the pleasure of his newfound irresponsibility.

"What are we going to do?" she asks.

"It's not what we're going to do," he corrects her. "It's what you're going to do."

She never says anything at this point.

"Six months," he reminds her, a bitter burp on his breath.

"I know how long it was. You don't have to tell me."

"But you can't tell me why. You can't even say why you were unhappy."

"I wasn't unhappy."

"But you weren't happy, either. Go figure."

"I'm sorry. You've got to know that if I could take it back, I would."

"But you can't."

"No, I can't."

This makes him mad. So he says, "Well, I can explain it. It happened because mediocrity's like mercury. It rolls toward its own."

No one speaks.

"So what are you going to do?" he asks after a while's silence.

"Please don't ask me that. Just please don't."

He takes a long swallow and retreats into the tingle of inebriation. He closes his eyes and pretends his mind is a liquid paperweight, slightly shaken. The little flakes of sensation twirl as they fall backward and settle, snowing over his consciousness. He enjoys that feeling. He only opens his eyes to call the waitress to order another round.

At her family's insistence, she sees a counselor. Actually, she will see four different counselors, two in a single week, before she finds one that won't pucker in disapproval as she tells her story. This therapist is a woman.

"What did you like about him?" the woman asks.

"The attention. That's all it was, is. I mean, I'd walk into a restaurant or a bar, and his eyes would just light up. Nobody's ever wanted me like that. Except one other, I guess."

"Your husband."

"Yes. But that changed, as I suppose I knew it would. I mean, his wanting me—at some point, he became content, and our togetherness, it was having, not wanting."

"What does it tell you that you were married to someone who loved you, who wanted you, and yet that wasn't enough?"

"I don't know. I really don't. When I was with my husband, I'd be thinking about this other man. And you know the sick part? When I was with this other person, I wanted my husband. And not out of guilt, either, not totally. I mean, I love him. I love them. Both."

"Because they both want you."

"I guess."

And then it comes. She's been waiting the entire session for the words now tumbling off the therapist's lips. *Self-esteem.* Rhymes with green bean, she thinks. *Crisp and crackly with a but-*

ter sheen. Each counselor preaches the same gospel. Their theory is that she fell into this infatuation because there is a void inside her that only attention fills. But she doesn't buy it. She feels it's too pat, that it reduces what she believes is her complexity, her poetry, into a plain, predictable formula. At times like this, despite her confusion, she continues to enjoy the sweet assurance her vanity affords. It convinces her that she is special. And the truth is she doesn't want to have to explain herself. She likes it that her motives are a mystery. She doesn't want to have to sort through her feelings because she knows that if she does they'll lose their luster, and she will lose the allure that she wishes to possess. Why must she relinquish the riddle of herself?

"Let's try a different approach," this counselor says. She is a vaguely attractive woman, but too clinical. Her hair is combed into a neat bun at the back of her head, and her stiff collar circles her neck formidably, like a moat guarding a castle. There is nothing epic about her. "What attracted you to your husband? What made you fall for him in the first place?"

"We could talk. About everything. I'd never met someone who was so easy to be with, somebody I could talk to about anything."

"And this other man, the friend. What did you have in common with him?"

She thinks a moment. When she gives her answer, it hardly seems as momentous as when she heard herself say it in her head, before it was demanded of her.

"What we had in common," she tells the counselor, "is me. We were both interested in me."

—At some point, he's not sure when, he finds the equilibrium that lets him function. Maybe it's when insomnia loses its vampiric thrill, or when the sugary buzz of the screwdrivers he drinks gives way to a sourer glut. Or maybe it's just that he grows accustomed to the awkward circumstances of his life. Whereas he once avoided acquaintances who might not know about his wife's infidelity, he can now confess the situation with minimal embarrassment. He knows men and women who've let go of philandering spouses but can't let go their need to talk about it. They unleash their bitterness without hesitation, reciting the lies and slights to any stranger in earshot. He refuses to be like this. He knows that cuckold stories—his story—are a dime a dozen. And he also knows that when the walking wounded walk away from a conversation, their audience rolls its eyes and pouts with supreme certainty that it will never have to go through anything so melodramatic and messy.

So he keeps up appearances. He works hard to seem unfazed. He shrugs off sympathetic hugs and learns to steel himself when someone says, "You can do better." Which is what they all begin to say.

The only part he can't abide are the lovers. He sees them everywhere he goes now, in the meadows along the thorough-fares where they picnic, their baskets overflowing with cheese and crackers and fluted wine glasses, at the movies where they rest their heads on each other's shoulders, whispering and laugh-ing at the flickering images. The grocery is the worst. There they unassumingly brush arms and hips with the casual grace of mutu-al possession. He remembers that feeling, the simple ease of a touch or a tickle. He thinks about the nights—only six months' worth of them—when he was most aware of it. He would sleep on his left side, and she would lie curled along his back, and he would take the breath that steadily flushed upon his neck as the rhythm of contentment. Alone now, he chastises himself for his sentimentality, and he consoles himself by thinking that these couples are too foolish to understand that there will be a time when they will have to walk a mile in his shoes.

"They're not real people. They're characters."

So says his best friend's sister on the nights he visits the loft she maintains in the one part of town that passes for a boho dis-trict. Coming here is a way of stoking his vanity. He's fairly cer-tain that if he wished to he could sleep with this woman. Why else would she invite him over, ply him with scented candles and soft music and imported beer? But he won't test his theory. Doing so would only knot further the complications that rope his life, and if there's one thing that he knows he wants now, it's to not have to deal with any other complications. So instead they stretch out at a discrete distance from each other on her hand-wove carpet, and when she removes a joint from under the music box on her coffee table, he's more than happy to smoke along, not because the pot does anything for him, but only because the brown coat that it gives his tongue and teeth proves a bitter complement to his mood.

"I know how it feels to see them," she says. "These kind of couples, their perfection is intimidating. You can't image them ever suffering a day's discontent. But you know what? They're playing a part, living up to a lifestyle. They all date two years, marry, start having kids two years after that. Most of them could have ended up with someone else and never have been the wiser. And you know why? Because they're married to their milestones, that's all."

As grateful as he is for the conversation, he knows what she's saying is bullshit. And he doesn't just feel this way because he once believed that two-year intervals were commonsensical. He silently dismisses her talk because he knows that here in the boho district it's obligatory to put down home-buying, home-building young marrieds. This is a part of town that thrives on being different. So much so that the aromas spilling out of the open windows aren't anything as jejune as potpourri or citrus-scented aerosol, but patchouli and raspberry incense, and the chimes that accompany the smells aren't from guitar or piano lessons but from strummed mandolins, dulcimers, autoharps. His friend likes to believe she's equally exotic.

"You want my theory about you two?" she'll ask him on the nights she's particularly emboldened by dope. Not really, he tells her, but she always assumes he's kidding.

"You'll appreciate it. See, for her, getting married was the last great prom. It was all about pomp and circumstance, all about ceremony. So she gets to be toasted at bridal showers, fitted at the dressmaker's, treated to a wedding and reception. But then it's a month later, and suddenly she's asking herself why nobody's paying any more attention, why everybody all of a sudden assumes she has to be content to be bored just because she's settled down.

"That's all adultery is, you know. One more circus tent of attention. And you know why adulterous relationships don't last? Haven't you ever read *Madame Bovary*? Because, at the end of the day, adultery turns out to be as boring as marriage."

As his lungs burn from the toke he's holding in, he can't help but be impressed by the ease with which she dismisses his life. But she's got it all wrong. Life's been anything but boring lately.

Of course, this entire time he's fucking the wayward wife. It happens most often when she stops by to pick up the mail that piles up, unforwarded, on the credenza. Or when she comes to reclaim a book or photo album that hasn't been opened since she left. Once they even do it in the backseat of his car after meeting for drinks at a microbrewery. Flushed with Grolsch (his first drunk in a long time), he slips a hand under her skirt, and when she doesn't object, his twitching finger crumbles the distance between them until she finally grabs his wrist and tells him to get the check. On that night, in those minutes, their lovemaking is quick but intense, almost adolescently sloppy. For her, intimacy is evidence that he still wants her. It's proof that for all the hurt she's caused him, he can't resist her or her body, and if that's so, then he must truly love her, without judgment or prejudice. What do they call it? Oh, yes. Unconditional.

For him it's about power. As she tightens under the weight of his body, one hand grasping his shoulder, the other balled into a fist that she beats red against his hip, he flexes and grunts at her submissiveness, believing that with each gasp he can dominate her just enough to break whatever stubborn bone it is that makes her unable to settle. In the heat of his vanity he always imagines her other man watching, forced to his knees by the reality of her husband's command over her. Then, as his resistance erodes and he feels a shudder eat through his loins, it strikes him how easily he could really make her his. Should he pull out a second late, she would have to return to him. She would have to stay. But this is a line he can't cross. At the last moment, he withdraws and spills across her hipbone.

At home when this happens, he will hop up right away to fetch a towel, embarrassed by the messiness of his love. But tonight, in the backseat of his car, half-drunk, he relishes the sight of his jit on her skin. He wants to stretch out a finger and write his name with it. When she asks to be cleaned, he strips off his T-shirt and obliges, content to believe that even though the residue is gone, she's his. Because she's branded.

It goes on like this—

—Until one afternoon she calls his cell phone as he noses along a congested highway on his way to meet a client. Her voice sounds as it has throughout the past several months: nasal, choked, clogged with spit. She's crying again. For some time now he's taken pleasure in that sound, for it's proof that she's suffering, as he feels she deserves to be. But now there's a new quality to her words, edgier, more desperate. She insists she must see him. When he tells her he can't get out of this meeting, she gulps and mewls. He yells for her to tell him what's happened. When she finally says it again, clearly, he's so stunned he asks her to repeat it, but she hangs up.

She's pregnant, of course.

So he skips his meeting after all. He telephones the office to feign stomach flu. Then he turns his phone off and drives. He sets the cruise control at eighty and lets the wires strung along the highway lead him forward. The interstate empties as soon as he hits the city limits, so in no time the outlying subdivisions fall behind him, and he passes the little hamlets and county seats and the farms, and then on to a new set of cities.

As he moves he thinks how easy this forward motion is. With hardly a twist or bend in the road, he can just sit back, two fingers at six o'clock, and let the speed carry him. In the few moments that he's not feeling sorry for himself, he thinks that this motion is what his life should have been—the steady pace, the straight line, the easy ride from point A to B. He wishes he could muster the self-deceit to believe he's not at fault, that he's the victim of this circumstance. But he can't. The memories of remaining in her are too clear. So instead he recounts all his two-year rules. He thinks of how for a decade he's deluded himself by equating control with the cold measuring of time, as if an accumulation of hours relieved him of risk, as if the rote passing of a moment were a dispensation of grace. As if people ever actually crossed out the calendar squares until the day they could say to someone, "Time to make a baby."

So to outrun his anger at her failures and at his own he keeps going until he's nearly out of gas. It's nightfall when he finally has to pull over for a refill. Sixteen messages await him at his telephone answering service, one from his boss and fifteen from her. He wonders if he were younger if he would just go on and escape into another life, but he has a house, a daughter, a job, and, yes, a wife—sort of. There are places where he's expected. As he claims his credit-card receipt from the automated gas pump, he leans against the hood of his car. The sensation of suddenly not moving after so long is unsettling. In the clarity of that awkwardness he wonders how it can be that, having traveled this far, he's yet to get anywhere. But then he crumples the receipt and slips back behind the wheel to return to her. The feeling doesn't leave him. Within a few miles, he's accustomed to it. He even shrugs it off. As he tells himself, he's got nine months to get used to it—

—And then those months have passed, and it's the night of his child's birth, and the setting is straight out of a gothic novel: thundershowers punctuated by lightning, heaving winds that send the trees stooping. The corridor leading to the maternity ward is bathed in a castle's dimness, allowing only the faintest of shadows to flutter along the walls. In the delivery room itself he watches as his wife struggles to hoist herself onto the birthing table. As she grunts to lift her weight her paper gown pulls away from her thighs so she exposes herself to the entire room. Their obstetrician is unfazed by the sight; the nurses are too busy mopping her brow to notice. But for him it's a sign of how indiscreet their lives have become. Their reconciliation has been a procession of ambivalent scenes: they've sat through baby showers with friends who couldn't quite hide their incredulity as they presented their gifts, weekends with in-laws who let snide comments slip as they sliced their breakfast melons. Maybe strangest of all is what's happened between the two of them. There have been arguments and accusations, of course, but also interludes of intimacy and long stretches of peaceful coexistence. Once he took their togetherness for granted because he had no reason to doubt what lay ahead of them. Now he finds it disconcerting that he's grown complacent with its uncertainty. He sleeps with this wife, eats with her, but he measures their future in trimesters, not lifetimes.

"Push."

The room is alive with motion. The doctor bobs his head above the drapery that hangs over his wife's stirruped legs, cracking jokes. Only the fetal monitor responds with the predictable tap of its laugh track. Nurses are busy passing instruments back and forth; interns traipse about, reading dials and checking the fluids flowing in and out of tubes. As his wife bucks up on her elbows to begin huffing, he slips two fingers into her fist so she can squeeze them to the beat of her breathing. This gives him something to do, something to make him feel a part of things.

Throughout the night he's wondered whether the hospital staff is aware of his ambivalence. He's tried to mask it, tried to fake the giddy overemphasis he's heard in prospective parents' voices. When he stretches his vowels out to imitate their exclamation-point talk, his insincerity strikes him as obvious, transparent. He can't figure out how to seem eager instead of resigned.

"Push," the doctor says again. "Almost crowning now."

There's another contraction, another scream. The doctor's head disappears under the draping, giving her instruction. The nurses crouch down in anticipation. Everyone shouts encouragement except him. His wife squeezes so hard he wonders if her grip will snap off his fingers. He watches her back arch again as her face twists in pain. The staff keeps telling her she's doing fine, that she's almost there, but the sounds of her grunts and stooling embarrass him. He wishes he could stretch the moment out to hold off the consequences. But he can't. It's too late. He knows because he's been in this movie before.

The doctor swings upright and passes the child over her outstretched legs, laying it on its mother's chest. The baby's blue, pasty, and alive. A nurse aspirates it, its eyes breaking open as it squalls with discomfort. The crying saddens him; the baby saddens him. He wonders if it senses that it's been born more out of anger than love. But still, he thinks, there had to be some love, didn't there?

He realizes that it's time now for him to touch the child, to comfort it as a tiny finger tentatively uncurls and its lungs expand with the novelty of life. He pushes out a hand, but before he can make contact he realizes his wife is looking to him, not the child.

"We made a baby," she says, expectantly.

Yes, he thinks.

Now what?

In a Baby Orchard

"You like sweet tea, baby? If you're going to come south of Huntsville, you know, you'll have to learn to."

As Mrs. Felder spoke she stooped, the way adults are apt to do when talking to small children. The gesture made her head bigger than the thin stem of her body so she resembled a dandelion bent by wind.

"I don't think you've ever tried sweet tea, have you, Kiki?" the girl's mother asked.

Kiki pressed her face to the side of her mother's dress, which gave off a newly laundered scent. Mrs. Felder scared her a little; the woman had big bug eyes, like a cricket's. Kiki's mother could sense the girl's hesitation, so she curled an arm around her shoulder and did her talking for her.

"I tried to keep her away from sugar for a long time, but there's a point where that's not only not practical but plain impossible. The first time she slept over at a friend's house, for instance. The girl's parents fed them breakfast cereal as a bedtime snack. Once that happened, I knew we were done for. She was hooked."

"I went through the same thing with my children," Mrs. Felder said back. She was tall and red-haired, with the red as unnatural a color as what Kiki had seen before on passing cars. As the woman spoke she piled plastic cups from her pantry on a kitchen counter. Also there was a platter with a ball of cheese surrounded by odd-shaped crackers arranged in perfectly straight rows. "For a long while I refused to let my first ones have soda in the house. I have four kids, you see. Two are grown and gone, one just likes to think she is, and then there's Bo, who's not but six. With the oldest pair, I only let them drink milk and juice, but different kinds of juice, mind you, so they couldn't complain about a lack of variety. Then I found out they were stockpiling quarters to run to the pack-n-sack up by the bend. They were buying Cokes on the sly. My husband was letting them store the cans in the mini-fridge he keeps in his work shed, behind my back. That was when I realized I was outnumbered."

By this time Mrs. Felder had poured tea from a carafe into a small glass, which she then handed Kiki. Kiki had tried tea once before, but it was the hot kind, and it not only burned her gums but tasted thin and flat, reminding her of the river water she swallowed the time her stepfather tipped the family canoe on a float trip. This was different, though. This tea wasn't bitter. It was so sweetened it felt thick and heavy. Even after she swallowed Kiki could feel its stickiness on her teeth. She liked that feeling so much she downed the glassful in a few gulps.

"I guess that answers the question," her mother said through an embarrassed laugh. She gave the glass back to Mrs. Felder. "Kiki likes sweet tea."

Beeping interrupted the conversation. Mrs. Felder stepped to one corner of the kitchen counter and flipped open the lid of an electric breadmaker. Immediately the air filled with the dense smell of warmth. Mrs. Felder slipped an oven mitt over her hand and pulled what looked like a pail from inside the machine. She turned the pail upside down and shook it until a loaf slid onto the counter.

"We're big on fresh bread, too," Kiki's mother told her. "There's a little bakery we'll eat at, she and I, two or three mornings a week. They let you sample the really unusual grains, so I make her try them all, just so I can hear her say the names. They serve zucchini, proscuitto and cheese, cardamom. Hey, Kik, I want you to say pumpernickel for Mrs. Felder. It's the cutest thing you've ever seen. It comes out something like *pimpleknuckle*."

Kiki didn't want to talk. Fortunately, a second breadmaker beeped.

"I have to have two machines to make two loaves," Mrs. Felder told them. "Not because we attract that many guests. We really don't, as you'll see—usually only about ten or fifteen at the most. But I started making two at once because I kept catching folks wanting to nibble off the crust. It would drive my husband crazy. He'd go to break the bread and it would look as though the raccoons had beaten us to the chancel."

Mrs. Felder shook the second loaf onto the counter. It smelled differently than the first. Kiki wasn't sure what the aroma was until she recognized it. The second one smelled of peanut butter.

"When it cools down a bit," Mrs. Felder told Kiki, stooping toward the girl again, "you can pull off a bite. Just make sure you don't pull it off the wrong one. The communion bread's the sliced one, okay?" She took a long-bladed knife from the drawer under the breadmakers and began sawing the first loaf in half. Kiki kept looking at her cricket eyes.

"Why do you cut the communion bread?" Kiki's mother asked.

Mrs. Felder smiled. "Oh, that's my husband's idea. He's a stickler. At least he was. It's been a couple years now since Gary stepped down, but old habits die hard. We've been doing it this way since he was called to his first church, a long time back. I think he felt self-conscious. Because some Sunday mornings, depending on how old a loaf it was, he'd half to wrestle with the bread. Some services he'd say it was like trying to tear a telephone book in two. So we started cheating, just a little. That way, he could concentrate on the words of institution."

Mrs. Felder lifted each half-loaf in her hands, joining and separating the serrated ends, over and over. "Presto," she said. "Pre-broken bread. Or already-been-broken-in bread, maybe." She laughed as she returned the brown-shelled crusts to the counter. Then she gathered the crumbs into her palm and brushed them into the sink.

"You give communion each time . . . at each service, I mean?"

"Yes, at each service, although I'm not sure that's how I'd say we regard it. It's not a formal service, after all. It just so happens I married a minister, so when I began all this I had help close at hand. Gary's officiating makes things more somber and, I guess, more real, which, if there's a point to this, that's it. Plus I doubt we could have persuaded someone still in the pulpit to lead us. It's a little weird, after all. A congregation would think its pastor had gone loopy. No, we don't have a name for what we do, not really. What would you call it? It's just a gathering, I guess."

Kiki watched her mother's face shrink into an expression that had been a familiar sight for a time now. It wasn't a sleepy look but something more complicated. Her face was hardened and sad. Kiki always thought of her mother as young–her skin was smooth and soft and even if she kept her hair cut short above her ears its blackness was still as shiny as a doll's. When Kiki's mother was sad, though, she looked old. The look on her face said that she was tired but that she knew she'd be staying awake for some while to come.

"I have to apologize again for dropping in on you like this," Kiki's mother told Mrs. Felder. "It's just . . . well, when I heard that story on the radio, like I said, something in me insisted we be here. It's four hours from Murfreesboro, but it's straight down I-65 almost all the way, so it doesn't feel long. We probably never would've been listening to the radio if we hadn't gone to the sunrise service this year. We were on our way home, and the story wasn't half done when I said to my husband, 'I want to go.' We didn't even run by the house to change. That's why we're all dolled up. We came straight from church. I never expected to keep Kiki in her Easter dress this long."

"It's a very pretty dress," Mrs. Felder said. She'd spoken those exact words when Kiki's family first arrived at the farm, not twenty minutes earlier. Kiki's stepfather had barely pulled the girl from the backseat of the car before Mrs. Felder came down off the porch to stroke at the long drape of taffeta that hung from the girl's shoulders. It was indeed a fancy dress, periwinkle-colored and replete with soft yellow piping, puff sleeves, a scalloped collar, pearl buttons, and a ribbon tied in the shape of the Presbyterian triune.

Now Mrs. Felder was talking over her shoulder because she was squatting down in front of an open cabinet, rummaging. "We're happy to have you. You see you're not alone. Whenever the radio interviews me, people come. Everyone has his own reasons, and some even travel farther than from Tennessee. Once one of the big news shows did a piece on us, and a few days after the broadcast a woman from Portland was knocking on our door. Unfortunately—or fortunately, maybe—nothing was scheduled for that day. She was fine with that, relieved even. I just let her walk the orchard for a few hours, and she flew home."

Mrs. Felder only stood up when she located her best salver, over which she spread a purple cloth. She set the cut bread on top of the cloth.

"There's probably no surprise then in what I'm doing here." As she spoke, Kiki's mother started picking at the skin of a thumb with the fingers of her other hand. It made Kiki feel a little vulnerable to no longer be held by her mother. "Something happened to me, it's that simple. It's been a year now, and I can't not think about it. I won't go into details because I expect you know the story. From what I gathered from the radio, it's along the lines of what you yourself went through. What everyone who's here has known the joy of."

Kiki didn't know how long a year was, but she could remember when her mother was sick. It was the last time Kiki was supposed to have worn a new Easter dress. That morning when her stepfather woke her, though, the dress wasn't anywhere to be found. Instead, bibs and a pullover shirt lay at the end of her bed. After she was in her clothes her stepfather put her in the car and then, without saying any more, he drove her to the hospital. The first thing her mother said when he and Kiki walked in the room was, "Of all the days." Then she started crying. Kiki's stepfather went to her side to put out a hand to stroke her hair, but then without warning he pulled it back and sat in a nearby chair, crying himself.

Kiki's mother was still talking to Mrs. Felder. "Bringing up the subject drives my husband nuts. He'll tell you he doesn't like to go on about what can't be undone. Truth be told, I think he's a little jealous, because it was so easy for my first husband and me. With Kiki, I mean. We weren't married a calendar year before we had her. As you can guess, my first husband wasn't just a talker—he was a smooth talker." Kiki felt her mother's palm fall at the nape of her neck. "That one talked his way right out of our lives, didn't he, baby?"

"Yes, well," Mrs. Felder agreed. Her lips were pulled tight as she looked to Kiki. "We all have stories to tell."

Mrs. Felder hadn't stopped working. Now she was stripping the plastic safety cap off a big bottle of grape juice. She unscrewed the top to pour the juice into a green ceramic pitcher she'd set on the salver. Some of the juice splashed out of the pitcher's top, staining the purple cloth. When the bottle was empty she stuffed it into a garbage can as tall as Kiki and put her hands on her hips.

"There. I think we're all set. Why don't we take your daughter upstairs? We can introduce her to Bo. They can enter-tain each other while we go to the orchard."

Kiki felt her mother take her hand as Mrs. Felder led them from the kitchen past a breakfast alcove into a gathering room. There grownups stood in twos and threes snacking on pastries and cookies that looked too fancy to be homemade. Kiki knew that these people were strangers. They not only kept saying their names to each other but the names of their hometowns, too. Halfway through the room Kiki's eyes caught sight of her stepfather's suited leg. He was sitting sideways in a folding chair next to a couch occupied by Mrs. Felder's husband. They looked funny sitting next to each other: Kiki's stepfather was short and thin, but Mr. Felder had a belly that covered his lap. It jiggled when he talked.

"That's the name of the game in the Presbytery," Mr. Felder was saying. "According to the Book of Order, you take com-munion however often it feels right, just so long as you do it with some regularity. Most churches, you'll see it happen the first Sunday of the month. But when I was called I made a deci-sion to not only do it every Sunday, which threw people off, but to do it every time the congregation got together, which really threw them off. I'm talking Advent, Easter, confirmation, elder installation, every which event. Funerals even." Kiki's stepdad nodded.

"Nicholas, honey," Kiki's mother interrupted. "She's going to be with their boy while we're outside."

Kiki knew the news wasn't going to please her stepfather. He hadn't looked happy since they left church. "You're going to let her horse around in a $300 dress?" he asked.

"Would you rather have her in the orchard? Did you see how wet the ground is?"

Mr. Felder said, "Back of the house is worse. I laid out some plywood and a few carpet squares so nobody's shoes get mud-

died, but the trail itself's a mess. It hasn't rained like we've had
it lately in I don't know how long."

Mrs. Felder was smiling at Nicholas. "My daughter's
upstairs," she assured him. "She'll keep them from getting in
too much trouble."

Nicholas shrugged and then leaned forward far enough to
pull Kiki's hem taut between his thumbs. "This dress is a
month's overtime," he told her. "I don't want you ruining it. No
wrinkles in my periwinkle, alrighty, Aphrodite?"

Kiki nodded at the silly rhymes before her mother led her
to the opposite end of the gathering room. There a door
opened onto the foyer of the house. At the back of the foyer
was a large staircase with a carpet as long and red as a tongue
running down its middle. When they made it up the stairs Mrs.
Felder ushered them past a pair of closed doors into the first
open room. The first thing Kiki saw was the bed. It was tall and
long and unmade, with opened books and even a plate of the
same cookies served downstairs lying on the bunched duvet. A
boy sat there, too, his back flat to the headboard as his thumbs
tapped the buttons of a video-game remote control. Directly in
front of the boy, tucked deep in an armoire, was a television
whose screen exploded with bright colors. The boy was black.

"It's okay," Mrs. Felder told Kiki's mother. "You're allowed
to be surprised. Bo's adopted. We had him first as a foster child
and then we made him our own. Bo, this is Kiki. She's going to
stay here this afternoon with you."

The boy was too busy with his game to acknowledge them.
Mrs. Felder shook her head.

"Really, he's only anti-social when the Play Station's on.
Let me get Ronnie." She leaned out the door and called that
name. It took a few seconds, but then a girl came into the bedroom. She wasn't quite a grownup, Kiki decided, because there
were clips in her hair that made pigtails dangle at the sides of
her head, and the cuffs of her jeans completely swallowed her
feet. She also had headphones the size of buttons in her ears.
When she pulled them out tinny bits of music went spinning
through the air.

"Ronnie, I want you to watch Bo and Kiki this afternoon.
You'll be doing Mrs. Parker from Murfreesboro here a favor."

The teenager didn't say anything to Kiki's mother. She just said, "What about Em?"

Mrs. Felder's cricket eyes bulged a little. "You can watch all three, dear. It'll only be for an hour or so. Go get Emily and bring her in here."

When the girl left Kiki's mother said, "Emily's another daughter?"

"My granddaughter." Mrs. Felder's lips folded into each other for a moment. "Ronnie's the reason Gary retired from the ministry. She's a classic case of the pastor's daughter. Every time I get upset thinking about her just turning eighteen and having a two-year-old already, I remind myself that I was barely twenty when I had my oldest. Of course, I was married."

Ronnie returned just as her mother finished talking. With her was a littler girl than Kiki. The girl's skin was snow-colored and she had yellow hair that fell in thin threads from the diamond-shaped part on the crown of her head. "I wanted to get married," Ronnie said to Mrs. Felder. "But you wouldn't let me."

Mrs. Felder smiled at Kiki's mother again before squatting beside the smaller girl. The girl didn't seem interested in being introduced, though. She was staring at the colored patterns that the video game made on the television screen.

"You be good now, Kik," Kiki's mother said as she and Mrs. Felder began to leave. "You listen to Ronnie here. And Ronnie, if she doesn't listen, you come get me, okay?"

Ronnie nodded so that the music from her earphones seemed to pulse. When the older women were gone she rested her weight against the bed's edge. Em raised her arms and waited to be lifted. Ronnie pretended to ignore her until the girl began whining. "Calm down, calm down," Ronnie said as she hoisted and then dropped the girl, not a little roughly, beside Bo. Em bounced once but was too intrigued by the way the boy worked the remote control's buttons to complain.

"What's your name again?" Ronnie asked.

"Kiki."

"Kinky?"

"Ki-ki."

"Why'd they name you Kiwi?"

"That's not what I said."

Ronnie was laughing. "Don't get huffy about it. I know what your name is. My ears work just fine. But what I don't know is why you got that name."

"My dad gave it to me," Kiki told her. "He had a picture of this girl, and her back was a violin. Her name was Kiki."

"What do you mean her back was a violin?"

Kiki was nodding. "She had lines painted on her back that made her look like a violin. I forget the word."

"Strings?"

"No, not strings." Kiki drew her index fingers up and down her back, just above her hips. "The things that are holes, that let the sound out. They look like *f*. They've got a name, but it's hard to say."

"I'll take your word for it." Ronnie stood up. "You want up here? I know you're not allowed to do anything fun in that getup."

Kiki felt the girl's hands under her armpits as she was placed to Bo's right. The taffeta was long enough that as she rested on the mattress it made her legs disappear. The bird-beaked tips of her shoes were the only evidence that she even had legs.

"So how old are you, anyway, Kreaky?"

The names annoyed her, but Kiki didn't say anything other than what she was asked to. "Four," she told Ronnie.

"Cool. That's very cool. Because Em's two and Bo's six, so we've got two, four, six. If we had someone who was eight, we could appreciate." Kiki wasn't listening. Like Bo and Em she was watching television. "All right," Ronnie told them. "Since everybody's settled in nice and comfy, I'm gonna let y'all stay just like this. You're in charge of each other, got it?" She pushed the earphones back in her ears. "I've got some stuff I've got to do."

A little bit after Ronnie left Kiki realized that her eyes weren't on the screen any more. She was looking instead at Bo, whose face wasn't more than four inches away. When Kiki couldn't resist any longer she pushed out a hand and stuck her fingers in the spongy curls of his hair. Bo tried to jerk away, but Kiki didn't stop. She was patting his head.

"Quit," Bo finally told her, but without diverting his attention from the TV. He was winning the game, even as Kiki distracted him. The springy feeling his hair made on her palm reminded her of the time at school when she'd gotten in trouble for touching another boy. He was black, too, but not as much as Bo.

"I said quit," Bo told her again. His voice was louder this time, so she stopped because she didn't want Ronnie to come back. Then the screen froze a second before starting to blink. Bo squeezed the remote between his hands and said, "I lost."

Kiki pointed at Em. "She's falling."

It was true. The girl had slid her back down from the headboard so her head lay flat on the sheets. Her legs were up in the air, bent just enough to hold them by the ankles. She was rocking from side to side, almost imperceptibly at first, but then in an arc that widened until it seemed she'd lose her balance and roll off the mattress.

"She falls all the time," Bo said, unconcerned. "She can't get hurt."

He pushed himself onto all fours and crawled over Kiki's legs. When she felt his kneecaps crunching her bones she let out a pained yell and swatted at his hip. Bo toppled shoulder first onto the floor. "Ronnie's always in her room," he said when he was back on his feet. "She's got her own baby and she still gets in trouble. She's grounded right now."

He looked at Kiki, waiting for her to talk. When she didn't, he said, "What do you want to do?"

"I want to go to the orchard."

Bo frowned. "We're not supposed to. It's too muddy. Gary took me last night when they were digging the hole, but I had to stay on the tractor seat. He didn't want me to ruin my shoes. He only got off the tractor because he had to show the men how big to make the hole." They looked at each other for a minute. Then, without warning, Bo went, "Let's eat something."

"They said stay with Ronnie."

"Ronnie won't care. Look here. See what she does all day in her room."

Kiki lay on her belly and slid until her shoes came to the floor. She was almost out the door, following Bo, when she remembered Em. She made him get the girl. Bo went to the far side of the bed and scooped the child in his arms so her belly was squeezed at his chest. Em squealed but then laughed as she slipped down his front side to the ground. Bo took her hand, and they all went to Ronnie's room.

Ronnie couldn't see them watching her because her back was to the door. She had her feet propped on an open windowsill, and she was still playing music, Kiki thought, because faraway sounds drifted backwards over her shoulder. Then Ronnie dropped and rested her elbows at the sill. A smoke puff rose around her head.

Bo whispered: "She's not allowed to have cigarettes in the house. She's gonna get in trouble all over again."

Then he grabbed Em's hand and pulled her farther down the hall. Kiki followed. The hall ended at another set of steps, which were concrete with peeling paint instead of carpet like the ones at the front of the house. This stairwell led to a little mudroom with a back door and a bench tucked along a side wall. A row of dirty boots sat atop a newspaper spread under the bench. Kiki peeked through the curtain covering the backdoor window, hoping to spy the orchard. The only thing she could see was a metal shed with a tractor parked inside. When she turned away she realized Bo had left her and Em behind.

She found him in the next room, which just happened to be the kitchen where Kiki and her mother had spoken with Mrs. Felder. Bo was sitting on the counter in front of the breadmakers, the backs of his shoes knocking at a cabinet door. Kiki wondered why Mrs. Felder had made them walk all the way through the gathering room to the front stairs when the back ones were just a few steps away. Then she saw the big tuft of bread in Bo's fist. "Ruth always makes me my own loaf," he announced. "But I don't like the crust, so I just eat the insides."

"She said I could have some, too, if I wanted," Kiki told him.

The boy shrugged and reached behind his back for a small plug, which he squeezed in his fist before throwing it to Kiki. The bite was still warm as she stuck it under her tongue. Kiki decided she wouldn't swallow it but would let it dissolve so it lasted longer. Only the more the bread stayed there the blander it started to taste. Kiki didn't know why she expected it would be better. Then Bo dropped himself to the floor. He, too, had a swallow in his mouth. Kiki could tell because he'd stuffed it in front of his upper gums so his top lip bulged. She was going to tell him what a monkey his lip made him look like, but she remembered how a boy at school had gotten in trouble for calling a black boy a monkey, so she just chewed in silence.

"I'll show you the orchard if you really want," Bo said as he strutted back to the mudroom. He was ignoring Em, who was reaching out for her own bite of bread because nobody offered her any. It was only after Kiki swallowed that she realized why the bread was bland. There was supposed to be peanut butter in it, she remembered.

She didn't say anything to Bo, though, because she wanted to see the orchard. Throughout their trip down from Murfreesboro that morning her mother and stepfather had talked about it. Kiki hadn't been able to make sense of the conversation; she just knew her parents were using unfamiliar words the way adults always did when they wanted to talk without children understanding them. What she did know was that Mr. and Mrs. Felder had an orchard behind their house and that an orchard (as her mother explained to her) was nothing more than a yard with lots of trees planted in it. Kiki had decided the Felders' trees must be new ones because her parents kept saying that the Felders owned a baby orchard.

"I can't go outside because of my dress," Kiki said back in the mudroom. Bo sat on a step, his sneakers piled on the floor as he tried to jerk a duck-billed boot over his heel. Before the boot was even on Kiki saw him lunge forward at her hem. The next thing she knew she was covered in a cloud of periwinkle. She heard Bo going, "Just take it off," and she knew he was on his feet trying to yank the dress over her head because she could feel his arms batting at her shoulders. She threw her hands out against the taffeta until she felt a forearm hit something solid, which she shoved at. When her dress floated down from her face Kiki found Bo stretched backward across the staircase, his face wrinkled in pain as he said, "That hurt." One arm was behind his back.

"I'll get in trouble," she told him as he sat up.

"You can't get in trouble if you take off the dress. You can leave it here and nobody will know. The orchard's little and it doesn't take time to see it."

Kiki wasn't sure what would make her stepfather angrier, going outside in the dress or going outside without it. She finally decided it was better to take it off. She had on an undershirt, after all, and nobody would see her panties because they were hidden by tights that covered her up to her bellybutton. She turned and told Bo to unclasp the pearl button hidden at the back of her neck by her hair. After that it took only a pull of one arm and she was out of the dress.

"I need boots, too," Kiki said as she undid her shoe buckles. She moved Em off the bench so she could spread the dress across it. Meanwhile, Bo pulled a pair of cowboy boots off the newspaper. Even though they were sized for a little boy, they felt big enough to swallow Kiki's legs. When she tried a step, the toe slid off the bridge of her foot so the heel dragged across the floor. But by that point Bo had already yanked the backdoor open. He was picking Em up by the waist, setting her square in the muck that lay beyond the threshold.

When Kiki stepped outside she realized how the dress had insulated her. She hadn't thought it a cold day, just a cool one, but now she felt an after-rain chill rub at her elbows and neck. She could hear wind, too, blowing hard against the tin walls of the tractor shed. From the shed to the Felders' back door lay about a dozen steppingstones. Bo was already halfway across them, swiveling his hips stiffly so he went from one to another without bending his legs. Kiki herself had to hop, which was hard work in big boots. Each time she leapt she curled her toes up, hoping her feet wouldn't slide straight out. As for Em, keeping to the stones didn't concern her. She simply splashed her way to the shed.

"I'll show you the tractor," Bo offered Kiki when she finally made it to the concrete lip of the shed floor.

"I want to see the orchard," she told him, with more force this time. Bo looked annoyed, but he led her around a corner wall anyway. From there Kiki saw a patch of tilled ground choked with weeds and dead leaves. A few steps from the garden a tall pen circled a clapboard box. A pair of calf eyes peeked from inside the box. Just past the pen was a burnt-out trash barrel that marked the entrance to a narrow trail shouldered by trees on both sides. Without warning Bo squatted and leapt to clear the puddle that formed alongside the foundation. Em followed suit, but one heel hit water, splashing her sweat pants. Bo laughed.

"I can't jump," Kiki said, exasperated. "The boots are too big."

"Take them off," Bo answered. With a kick of one leg and then the other, Kiki flicked the boots from her legs. She felt the concrete's cold rise through her soles as she bent her knees. When she jumped she made it past the puddle, but the grass didn't seem any less wet. She could feel mud seep through the tights to squeeze between her toes.

But she didn't have time to worry about that because Bo and Em were already crouched behind the first big tree at the start of the trail. Kiki gathered the cowboy boots and put them back on. She was scrambling to catch up, but every few steps her feet would slip from under her. It wasn't because of the ground's being saturated. When Kiki looked down she realized the yard was littered with apples in various states of rotting to mush.

"There's the orchard," Bo said when Kiki made it to the trunk. He was squatting like an animal going to the bathroom. Leaning over his back, Kiki looked down the trail. At first there didn't seem much to see other than trampled grass, more apples, and fat old trees whose limbs threw checkerboards of shade over everything below. But then, where the trail ended forty or fifty yards away, she spotted the rows of folding chairs and the people sitting somberly in them. In front was a hip-high TV tray. A shape Kiki assumed was Mr. Felder stood behind it, lifting something in his hands. Beside him was what looked like a box, and then farther out, spread among the trees, were crosses. They stood straight up in the ground, reminding Kiki of the ones she sometimes saw from the backseat when her parents took the car onto the interstate. "I bet I can hear Gary," Bo was saying. "I bet he's telling them about breaking bread."

"Where are the baby trees?" Kiki asked.

She saw Bo frown. Before he could say anything, a scream broke the silence that camouflaged their spying. Kiki and Bo twisted sideways toward its source. There, at the pen, stood Em, her eyes squeezed tight and her mouth cracked wide, crying. At first Kiki thought the girl was screaming for something she couldn't get hold of because her arm was stuck into the pen. But then Kiki realized she couldn't see Em's hand because her entire fist had disappeared behind the rubbery lips of the calf, which had crept from its hut in order to suck greedily at the girls' fingers.

The minute Bo saw what was happening he shot away from the tree in an all-out sprint. He didn't run to his niece but headed instead toward the sliver of open space between the house and the shed. Kiki found herself running as well. She was unsure whether it would be better to follow him or help Em, who was still wailing away. Before Kiki could decide anything, however, one flopping boot came down awkwardly on a hardened apple that knocked her out of her stride, throwing her off balance.

She tried to steady herself, but her footing gave way and she knew the only question was how hard a fall she would take. Instinctively she slapped her arms at her hips, thinking her palms could blunt the impact. Then she knew she had landed, and her first thought as she felt wet grass in her fingers was that she was okay because nothing hurt. But then a moist sensation rose through her underside, burning its way past her tights and panties into the skin of her buttocks. The soiled sensation let Kiki know she had landed rump-down in the mud.

"Beauregard Vincent Felder! Down here, right now!"

Kiki had thrown herself down on Bo's bed not a minute earlier, so when Mr. Felder's voice boomed up the stairs her heart hardly had time to stop its pounding. The thump in her chest was made all the more suffocating by the weight of Bo, who sat astride her back as his fingers fumbled to clasp her pearl nape button. When Mr. Felder yelled again Kiki sat up, throwing the boy to one side. He didn't say anything, but Bo's face was kinked with dread in a way that let Kiki know they had little choice but to proceed down to the grownups.

In the hallway they saw Ronnie emerge from her room, fast, in a cloud of confusion and anger. "What did you do?" she demanded. And then: "Where's Em at?" Neither Bo or Kiki answered, so all Ronnie could do was follow.

That was when they saw Mr. Felder standing on the third step of the staircase, his right foot resting on the fourth as if he were threatening to come after them. Between his hands, resting atop his big belly was the salver, which still carried the communion loaf. A step or two behind him was Kiki's stepfather, the banister gripped in his fist. Mrs. Felder and Kiki's mother on the foyer floor, Em straddled on Mrs. Felder's hip. The girl's face was red and slick with tears and spittle.

That sight so startled Ronnie that she called out her daughter's name as she elbowed her way past Bo and Kiki. "You were supposed to watch her," she snapped as she went by.

"You were supposed to watch *them*," Mrs. Felder corrected her. For a moment Kiki thought the women were going to have a tug of war. Finally, Ronnie grabbed Em out of Mrs. Felder's arms.

"I only left them alone a minute."

"To go smoke!" Bo blurted out. Kiki saw Mr. and Mrs. Felder shoot the teenager a mean look. Then Ronnie's father turned his attention back to Bo.

"What I'd like to know," he was saying, sternly, "is where my loaf went."

He let the salver rest in one hand as the other took one of the bread halves and held it to Bo and Kiki's faces. All Kiki could see was a cave of crust.

"I hope you can understand my concern when I go to break the bread only to discover that the Body of Christ has been hollowed out."

"The loaf's my fault," Mrs. Felder said. "I made two of them just so this wouldn't happen, but I left both loaves sitting on the counter, side-by-side. I thought it was enough to tell them to snack on the peanut butter one, but I should've set it out for them. And when I came to get the communion loaf for the service, well, I should've looked more closely. I just never imagined they'd eat the poor thing inside out." As she spoke the lids on her cricket eyes kept opening and closing.

Mr. Felder was shaking his head. "I'd still like to think, Bo, that you'd have a little more common sense. And what's more, to ditch Emily because you're afraid of getting caught where you three aren't supposed to be. It's just not very gallant of you, not at all. You're lucky that the worst that happened was that that calf gave her a good thumb washing."

Kiki could feel her stepfather eyeing her. She tried to avoid his displeasure by focusing on the red carpet under his feet, but she made the mistake of assuming her mother would sympathize with her, and so she let herself look up. Her mother wasn't sympathetic at all, though. Her face was frozen with the same hard, worn expression she'd had for a long time now.

"Did you take that dress outside?" her stepfather asked. He stooped down in front of her so Kiki couldn't look anywhere but in his eyes.

"No," she said, and she hoped he believed her, because it was true–she hadn't taken the dress outside.

"You're sure about that?"

"Yes, sir."

"Let it go already, Nicholas," Kiki's mother said. "We should be heading home, anyway. The Felders have been very kind, and we've seen what we came to see."

She motioned for Kiki to join her. Kiki felt Nicholas stand as she went by. She thought that was the end of things because everyone had turned to go back to the gathering room. But Kiki didn't take more than three steps before Nicholas commanded everyone to stop.

"Just a damn minute," he said, and Kiki felt him grab the bottom of the dress, pulling it straight out from her back. "Angie, come here. It's just what I told you would happen. She's gotten something on the dress. It's stained back here." Then he pulled the dress higher to see Kiki's bottom. "Oh, for God's sake," he declared, and he spun Kiki around so her rear faced not only her mother but the Felders and Bo, too. "She looks like she's messed herself, like she went right in her tights."

And then it was later, and Kiki and her family were finally in the car, making their way home. In the backseat the girl felt the warmth of her newly dried undies and tights wrapping her legs and hips. That had been Mrs. Felder's idea. Before she would allow her guests to return to Murfreesboro she had insisted on cleaning the soiled clothes. Kiki had to strip down in a guest bathroom and then stuff herself into one of Em's sweatsuits, which was too small. Kiki still had pinch marks across her belly from the tight elastic waistband. While her underclothes went from washer to dryer Kiki watched her mother and Mrs. Felder attempt to blot away the faint streaks of brown that had seeped through the periwinkle. Nicholas spent most of that time on the porch with Mr. Felder, complaining about irresponsible children.

"This has definitely been a day for the history books," Kiki's stepfather said as soon as the car was on the interstate. Kiki's mother didn't respond. Kiki couldn't see, but she guessed that her mother's eyes were clamped shut. Ever since the mud on Kiki's rump had been discovered, she had shut them whenever her husband said anything.

"Really, Kik," Nicholas kept going. "I don't understand what you were thinking. I told you not to get dirty. But now I'm not sure which is worse, you outside running around in a $300 dress or you outside horsing around in nothing but your skivvies."

"You've made her feel bad enough," her mother said.

They drove for a little bit without anybody talking. Finally, Kiki answered her stepfather's question.

"I wanted to see the baby trees."

That brought a funny look to her mother's face, which Kiki saw in profile as her mother stared at her husband. "What are you talking about, honey?" she asked, still looking to Nicholas.

"The baby trees," Kiki told them again. "In the baby orchard."

Kiki's mother seemed to be waiting for Nicholas to speak, but he didn't, so she curled all the way around in Kiki's direction.

"Oh, Kik," she said, "there's no baby trees in that orchard. They call it that because—"

"Angie," Nicholas broke in. Apparently, now was his turn to talk. "She doesn't need to hear any of that. You'll give her nightmares."

"Will you calm down? She's my daughter."

"Oh, yes, she's your daughter. I'm just here to make the overtime."

Kiki's mother twisted even farther so she didn't have to see him. She was looking squarely at Kiki. "Honey, I'm going to tell you what it was we came down here to see. And after I tell you what's in the orchard, if you have a question, I want you to ask it, all right? Because you know you can ask me anything you want, right?"

Kiki nodded.

"Okay, good." She took a breath. "It's not baby trees that are in that orchard, sweetie. It's babies, the graves of babies, I mean. You see, sometimes a girl will have a baby, and maybe she and the boy who helped her make it aren't ready for that responsibility, and they're afraid of being parents and so–," She kept stopping and starting.

"They'll leave it somewhere, hoping somebody will do for it what they can't. And sometimes those babies are found in time and everything's okay. But sometimes not. Sometimes the babies go away naturally, and then there's other times when the boy and girl will . . . do something to the baby to make it go away. No matter why the baby goes away, Mrs. Felder will bring it, the body I mean, to her farm, and she'll give it a proper burial. She's just like your mommy, you see; she lost a baby once, too, and so this way she gets to mother all those motherless children. Her husband used to be a minister so he knows how to say prayers, and that helps the babies rest in peace there under all that shade. People like me, people who can't have babies anymore, we come to see the orchard because . . . well . . . that part of it I can't explain because I'm not sure myself." She stopped again. "Does any of that make sense?"

Kiki said yes, but inside she wasn't sure. She felt a little foolish about not understanding.

Then Nicholas decided to talk some more. "Why not explain to her why it's weird? Why not tell her that the way to get over losing something isn't to plant it right there in your yard, not fifty feet from the house you live in so that every day when you're out and about that loss is right there in your face, reminding you? Why not tell Kiki that part of it? Tell her how screwed up that Bo's going to be when he realizes how gruesome it is to have bones littered under the very trees he climbs for fun. The older girl, Ronnie, it's obvious what it's done to her."

The whole time he spoke Kiki's mother stared at him, meanly, her nose so pointed at the cheek not a half-foot from her own face that Kiki thought she hovered like a bird waiting to peck at a worm. But then the woman simply squared herself in the passenger seat so she stared straight outside.

"Nicholas," she said in a pinprick voice. "Nickety Nick Nick Nick. Did you know your name is another word for asshole?"

The stepfather clucked. "That's really, truly wonderful. Maybe the next time your daughter's dancing around in her underpants with some boy she'll remember to use that word. Won't you be proud?"

But by then Kiki had stopped listening. She had settled the back of her head against the seat, her chin pointed up a little so she could see out the window. She was tired. She knew that it took four hours to get home, but she wasn't sure how long that was. To pass the time she stared at the limbs that made up the tree line along the highway shoulder.

She thought of how she'd been told that trees came from seeds, but now she wasn't so sure. She wished she could stop the car long enough to look those trunks over, close up, to see if she could make out faces among the dimpled skins of bark. She'd once been told a story, after all, about a boy and girl who were turned into trees when they got into trouble. But Kiki knew the car wouldn't be stopping. It kept accelerating, in fact, as if trying to catch up to the rapid bursts of words her mother and stepfather exchanged. The quickening speed only made the girl drowsier, and even though she didn't wish a nap right now, it coaxed a yawn out of her. Kiki shook her head and stretched her eyes wide, determined not to miss any detail that might suddenly reveal itself in the long blur passing outside.

It was no good, though. The car's pace hardened into an insistent lullaby, and some miles on, before she even knew it, Kiki was asleep.

DOWN IN THE FLOOD

for Pete Rainwater

A dead man's face tells you all you need to know about his life.

That's what my dad told me the first time I was around to see the Chattahoochee bust the levee and drown up my hometown. I was maybe twelve, I think. I know I wasn't older, because I was still young enough to think that a flood could be a four-square thing. For starters, it freed us from junior high. It was Easter time then, and all the churches in town took on water, but nowhere near as bad as our school. The flood slicked over the hallways with red mud and made the gym smell like wet crackers. There was no place to hold classes in all that mess, so as soon as the fellowship halls of the churches were drained and dried, they sat us down in folding chairs, and, for the rest of the year, we studied with our books on our knees. But it was worth it, because for those two weeks when they were deciding where to stick us, I got to ride around in a skiff with my dad and fish for bodies.

See, my dad was a volunteer fireman; that's how I was able to go out in the flood with him. Volunteers back in those days, the sixties, worked under fewer restrictions than they do now. If my dad'd been a real fireman with the city, I know I'd never end up seeing the things I did. And it was those things that brought me to my current line of work. I'm a paramedic stationed at one of our three full-time firehouses. Before Dad passed away last fall he'd drop by the station to check out our trucks. "Nothing more fancy than what we ever had," he'd say. I think he was a little jealous. He was a cotton farmer, so about the only excitement he had was when a call for the volunteers came over the shortwave.

If I remember it right, the flood was a few days old the first time he took me out in the skiff. At first, the water only rose knee-high, so the public safety people could wade through the streets in their hip-huggers, checking on folks. But then on the third day the levee broke, and the river flushed up past the second story of the storefronts. Even though our downtown sits at a lower elevation than the rest of the city, a second-story waterline still meant that the rich folks up the hill would be up to their friezes in flood, with all kinds of muck dirtying up their colonnades and porticos and belvederes. It also meant that the lean-tos and trailers on the outskirts would be completely submerged. Most of those living on the outskirts were poor blacks who either picked cotton or worked as domestics for the few wealthy families in the east part of the county. If there were Red Cross shelters back then (I can't remember), people from the outskirts didn't go to them. They wouldn't leave their homes for fear that they'd get looted. So as soon as the levee busted and the rain showed no sign of letting up, the county called in the volunteers. A lot of those old boys, my dad included, owned either a rowboat or canoe, and one or two had bass boats, so it was their job to trawl the outskirts and pick the stragglers off their rooftops. I'm sure doing their part by saving folks made those volunteers feel real good, but I'm also pretty certain that each of them was wanting to haul out at least one corpse, just so they could say they had.

For a lot of years, I reckoned my dad carried me with him because he thought he was teaching me some sort of lesson. Then when I came to be an adult I realized I was there for a more practical reason: he needed my help pulling the dead weight from the water. See, a flood looks steady enough when it's sat for a while. It usually lies flat like it's sleeping, but then, when there's quiet, you can hear a gurgling rumble from deep down in its belly, sort of like vibrations from a faraway train. The runoff has all kinds of crosscurrents shoving and tugging each other, so if you try to stand or squat in a boat—even a flat-bottom boat—you're a fool to trust your balance. There was no way Dad could yank his bloated cargo portside without a counterweight to keep from spilling. He was nervous about me being there, I know, even though he'd never confess it outright. We wouldn't even make it past the gravel roadway that led to our house before he'd have me trussed up in a life preserver.

The volunteers put their boats in the water at a makeshift landing where a canteen had been set up under a long awning of tent. We barely made it out of the truck when the rich smell of coffee hit us. It was almost strong enough to drown out the gas from the diesel generators that doused the landing in light. The light cast eerie shadows on the men while they struggled to keep from slipping in the muck as they lugged their skiffs to the bank. Just a few yards out from shore, though, the beams dissipated so nothing could be seen but an occasional flicker from a kerosene lamp. Dad was a big coffee drinker, so as soon as we got the boat to the landing (which was nothing but a jerry-built ramp of plywood) he knotted the gunwale to a cypress trunk and tramped to the tent to fill two thermoses. The most I ever drank was maybe a half-cap's worth, enough to keep me awake. But Dad would down and down that coffee until, when he had to, he'd lean his knees against the backseat to take a long piss over the stern.

With a small outboard motor it took maybe a half-hour to make it to the outskirts. We'd set out in a formation with three or four other skiffs, but pretty soon each of us would be out of the others' sight, and only the churn of a wake or the throttle of an engine a few yards away told us we weren't alone. I don't remember any talk going on. Dad and I didn't even speak until the time came for him to get out the grappling hook, and he'd order me to the outboard's tiller. All that silence meant that as we rode there was nothing to do but watch as scum and flotsam slid past the prow. Mainly the water was choked with twigs and tree limbs, but every once in a while, a shoe bobbed by, or a baseball cap. Once I saw what I thought was a long cattail slither along with the current, but I wasn't certain. Sights like that made you wonder what'd never made it to the surface.

It was the sound of the animals that told you you were nearing the outskirts. The air was thick with the anxious squabble of chickens, their feet tapping on the corrugated tin roofs, and dogs howling for their masters. But the worst were the cows. They let out this unholy moan, their pitch starting low and then wrenching itself up in a high shriek that boomed over the leafless trees. One night as we rode through a pocket of silence, one of them cried out from nowhere, and because I was steering at that moment, I saw the unexpectedness of the bellow bring a shiver out in my dad. His shoulders rippled, and he immediately shot his eyes in the direction of the noise, thinking, maybe, we were about to plow right into the cow's flank. A second later he was looking over his back at me, his stiff expression telling me not to speak of what I'd seen.

Here's another odd thing about a flood: people rarely get stranded in one by themselves. They end up clutching chimneys and peeking out haylofts in groups of four or five. Most of these groups are composed of family members. Every so often, we came across a cluster of neighbors who'd made their way to the nearest tall structure when their one-story went under. Another strange thing is that people always insist on carrying one personal possession with them when they flee rising water. They weigh themselves down with the family Bible, or with a pile of quilts, or with photograph albums—almost never practical things such as flashlights or radios. Dad's skiff wasn't big enough to rescue more than two at a time, so when we came upon some people, Dad would call for reinforcements with a bullhorn he kept stashed under the bow seat. We carried a little throw light that we'd send over the brown slosh, and slowly the tips of the other skiffs would ride into sight, manned by silhouettes whose shadows evaporated as they pulled into the arc of our illumination. As they approached, the motors would cut off, and the skiffs drifted up to the roofline as though they were lining up for gas. One by one, the boats' drafts deepened as the exhausted bodies loaded themselves onboard by gripping the prams and lowering themselves to the wet floorboards. But loading up the living was the easy part. It was much harder when we came across a body.

The first one Dad and I retrieved belonged to a black pastor. He was minister to a little country church, one of those that's more shanty than cathedral. He'd gotten his wife and kids out of harm's way by breaking through an attic wall with a ball-peen hammer, but the water shot up into the attic entry too quick for him to hoist himself onto the slippery shingles, and he'd been sucked back into the murk. We put the wife and her babies—she had two, one a toddler and the other an infant that she held tight to her breast—in a separate skiff and headed them back toward the landing before we began looking for him. When the family was out of sight, Dad slipped the grappling hook into the water and began poling through the hole. My job was to keep the skiff steady by holding fast to a dangling fascia board, but with each thrust of the hook, the boat curled from side to side until I was sure we'd tump over. I figured Dad was crazy to think he could catch more than a floating hymnal or broken pew, but when the pole struck something that seemed to strike right back, I knew we had the man. Dad drew the hook to the surface, and we saw that it'd caught the shoulder of a black frock coat. We let the skiff drift away from the church so our floating towed the body out of the wall hole. Then Dad took the shoulders and I grabbed the legs, and we jerked the body up and over the side, dumping it without delicacy onto the ribbed boat bottom. Then we sat for a time, not talking again, staring at the pastor's open eyes.

"This boy had a lot of redemption on his mind," Dad eventually said. This was back when a lot of Civil Rights problems were going on up in Montgomery and Birmingham, and over in Selma, too, and I'd be dishonest if I didn't admit that my dad wasn't too fond of the blacks. At the time I wasn't aware enough to know what it meant to call a black man a boy. All I knew was that I was looking into a pair of vacated eyes. That and that I couldn't look away. The pastor's mouth was frozen open as well. Water drooled out his lips, streaming down both cheeks to puddle at the back of his ears. I was aware enough to understand that there did indeed seem something desperate in the man's expression. It wasn't at all what you'd expect from a minister, who you'd think would be jubilant to be heading heaven's way. Staring at the corpse was what made Dad come out with that line: a dead man's face tells you all you need to know about his life.

"Now a boy like this . . ." It was a minute later, and we were trawling slowly, so the motor barely let out a hum. "He's always got him a woman on the side. Even when he fancies himself close to Jesus. That's why you'll need to keep your conscience clean. Because the first person that sees you dead'll be privy to your secrets."

As we approached the landing, I could see the wife silhouetted by the lights in the tent. She was standing ankle deep in the water, the toddler at her hip, the infant braced against her shoulder blade. The whole family was motionless; they might have been a set of stumpy bridge spiles if it weren't for the aura of anticipation that they radiated. As we slid up to the bank, I cut the motor and then jumped behind the stern to shove the skiff onto the shore. I hadn't even gotten the bow out of the water before the woman was leaning into the boat, screaming and clutching at her dead husband. She laid the baby on the pastor's stomach as she pressed herself to his chest. All I could do was hold the stern steady while her heaving rolled the skiff side to side. Dad jumped to the shore, not looking. "Need a leak," he said over his shoulder. "When she's done you tie up the boat and come get you some eats." The woman was wailing now, the sound scarier than any animal I'd heard. For the first time since we'd found the pastor, I couldn't bear to look.

Eventually, some of the Red Cross men tiptoed into the water and took the woman by the arms. One led her to the medic station; the other carried the infant a few steps behind. The toddler followed on its own, not sure what else to do. I guided the boat to the bank and knotted the line just as Dad said. When I made my way to the tent, I poured some sweet tea from a pitcher in a cooler and started in on a sandwich from a donated tray of food. I was sitting in a folding chair, drying my feet by a campfire, when I heard one of the Red Cross people talking to my dad.

"You couldn't have covered him up with something?"

"I didn't think to pack a tarp or a blanket," Dad answered. "I coulda pulled that frock coat over him to hide his face, but I figured the woman'd be mad if I'd been wrestling with him."

"He was a minister, you know."

"He wasn't nothing but dead when I met him."

From the corner of my eye, I saw the man park his hands on his hips.

"Just make you sure you've got some sort of wrap before you head back out. We got enough problems with them these days without giving them reason to say we been disrespecting their dead."

So before we took to the water again Dad borrowed a wide sheet of plastic pool liner from another volunteer and wadded it under a middle seat. We didn't unroll the liner that night, nor, if I remember right, for the next couple of days. But then one afternoon we came across a woman—a white woman—hanging upside down from a tree limb. One leg poked straight in the air, while the other dangled at a crooked angle over a fat branch. It was the oddest sight; she reminded me of how kids'll stand on their hands and walk the shallow ends of pools. Her calves came out of the water just above the kneecaps, and it scared me a little to think that if the water were just a bit shallower her most private part'd be exposed to anyone riding by.

We guided the skiff up to the tree trunk, and Dad started snapping off branches to free her. When the body came loose, it slid under the surface and probably would've disappeared if Dad hadn't grabbed an ankle and tipped the woman sideways so she floated horizontal along the starboard. When we first hauled her in the boat, she lay face down. We decided it was more respectful to turn her.

"What are you thinking?"

We were halfway back to the landing, and neither of us had yet spoken.

Dad said, "I'm thinking we better get her covered up so we don't get chewed out some more." I unfurled the liner and tucked it as far up as her chin. That left her face still exposed.

"Tell me what you're thinking about her—about what her face says. Tell me her story."

Through the moonlight I could see his eyes draw across her corpse and settle on her head. Her features were bloated and distorted from being under the water for so long.

"I s'pect this one was wanting to live. She don't look scared or worried—just determined. I figure she'd a baby she was trying to hold fast to. Maybe she thought she could save it if she couldn't save herself. Can't tell that part. But she had something she was fighting the current for. I'm sure there's a husband somewhere out there looking for her. When you get right down to it, there's not that many different stories to separate folk. There's the love and there's the hurt, and everything else is a shade of inbetween." His jaws worked the gum that popped between his teeth. "Best get her face under that tarp, now."

So it became something of a game, something to kill the time. My dad and I only found maybe two more bodies, but each time I pushed him to guess for me just where in that space between love and hurt the faces told him those people'd lived. It was a game I kept playing long after the flood receded and I grew up to join the paramedics. My partner Carl and I, we've been teamed together nine years now, and we know each other well enough that, when we get called to a fatality, one of us is sure to pop the question. Over the years we've come up with some pretty far-fetched stuff—the heart-attack victim who died believing a lost letter would turn up in the mail, the woman in the car wreck who ran the stop sign racing to confront her husband's mistress, the old man who was relieved to die because his wife had gone before him. No matter what the circumstance, though, what Dad said rang true: those faces, however frozen their expression, were at least in some small part alive with story.

So last summer the Chattahoochee came over the levee again, the first time in thirty-six years. The water crested at forty-seven feet, which meant my hometown got swallowed up even more than it had in the spring of '65. Carl and I were assigned a city skiff, and this time we weren't allowed to go out at night unless an emergency call came in—the insurance liability's too high. But even though the flood rose taller than before, the town was evacuated early this time, and we were left trawling for stranded pets, not people. The chickens still tapped their claws on the corrugated rooftops, and the abandoned cows still let out their unholy moans, but in the daylight, the animals sounded more sad than spooky. For the better part of a week, I didn't think we were going to have any opportunity to guess a few secrets. But then we got sent to look for this woman on the outskirts who was said to run a puppy mill, and let me tell you, it turned out to be one hell of a story.

Our skiff had a bigger motor this time, so me and Carl made it to the outskirts in about half the time. It wasn't too easy to find our way around because the road signs were all underwater, and landmarks were few and far between unless you happened to know the patterns that the shingles on the tallest barn tops made. Still, we managed to get to what we assumed was the general vicinity of her address, thanks to a helicopter that circled over our heads. We did our own circling, too—around the trees that could reach the surface, the gables and roof lines poking up, even around the drifting clusters of wood. We were looking for anything buoyant enough to keep someone afloat. Something thick enough, at any rate, to hold a corpse steady against the current.

It took a few hours, but we found her. The water had shoved her along the overhang of a shed, where she'd gotten caught up on a protruding nail that kept her bobbing face first in the flood's lapping. Carl ripped the nail out of a knot in her jacket shoulder, but when he tried to hoist her torso up, he realized something under the surface had hold of her, too. Carl dipped over the port far as he could while I kept the boat balanced, but it was no good. "Whatever's got her," Carl said, "is too fond'a her to let go."

"So which of us is going in?" I asked. I was smiling at him; the sleeves of his shirt were sopping from his arms going into the water. He rolled his eyes and started unlacing his shoes.

A second later he was stripped down to his trousers. We tied a line through a back belt loop just in case the current was stronger than what it looked. The water was cold, but there was no easing himself in. Old Carl had to jump over all at once. He let out a yell when the water hit his chest.

He stayed under less than twenty seconds. We didn't have goggles with us, and Carl wears contacts, so he wanted as much as possible to keep his eyes closed. When his head broke the surface, his lids were pinched tight.

"You're not gonna believe this," he said. "She's got her fingers jammed in some kinda crate. One of those kenneling crates, I guess. They're shoved clean through the bars. They're not coming out."

"Well, let's just bring the crate in with her."

"Can't. It's either weighted down or wedged against something. Whatever the cause, it ain't budging."

"She got those fingers between them bars. There's gotta be a way to get them out."

Carl exhaled loudly so the water under his nostrils rippled. We both knew what it'd take to get her free. We'd worked enough accident scenes to know that you often gotta break bones to get a body loose.

Carl went down and then came up a few times. He was having to dislodge the woman finger by finger, and it was taking all his strength to yank at her hands and to frog kick to keep his place beside her. Finally, the woman bounced a little, and the hump of her back rose high out of the water. I knew then Carl'd busted her loose.

Once I helped my partner pull himself back in the skiff, we took the woman by the wrists and ankles to lift her up. This time it was my arms underwater. I had to shove them in and feel around because her legs were tucked up as if she were kneeling. "Jesus," I said. "She's stiff as starch. Rigor's got her already." Now it was Carl's turn to laugh at me. I had to lean so far over to find her feet I could have been washing my face in the water.

"She looks like she's praying," Carl said. It was true. Even though we had her on her side, her bent knees had her looking like she was bowing at an altar, and her arms met in front of her chest as if she were trying to clasp her hands. There was no way she could, of course. The tips of her blue, creased fingers jutted at awkward angles from her knuckles from where Carl'd had to break them. "You know the only way her hands coulda gotten jammed in that crate, don't you?" he asked me.

"Sure." We were both staring at her. I took a deep breath that seemed to drop my lungs into my stomach. "She shoved them between those bars. She was holding herself under."

Carl started drying his back with his wadded shirt, but I still couldn't take my eyes off that marble-gray face. "That's the god-damnedest," he said. He was pulling his socks over his ankles now. "Why would she do that?"

"I couldn't say."

"Well, shit. Look at her face. Take a stab."

"I don't know."

But that was a lie. Or at least close to one. I honestly could-n't answer Carl's question, but I probably should have been able to. See, I knew the woman. I didn't recognize her at first because of how badly the water drained away her coloring and matted her hair together into a thick mess. But I recognized her all right. I mean, I couldn't tell you her name, but I knew her all right. I'd slept with her once.

It'd been a couple of years. At the time, I was going through a bad divorce, and I ended up in this bar over on Jackson Street. It's one of those peanut-shells-on-the-floor places. I normally avoid them, but my wife had started telling me how this new boyfriend of hers had made her feel alive again after twenty years of me, and I suppose I was hoping to show her that payback's hell. I don't know how often this lady went to this place. Pretty often, I guess. I guess I didn't care to know. I just happened to be ordering a shot of bourbon when she started showing the bartender pictures of this new Weimaraner she'd gotten. I told her I had a rat terrier—or, rather, I told her that I used to have a rat terrier before my wife gave me the boot. I let it slip that the boyfriend was taking care of my dog now, figuring that if you mention your wife's boyfriend to another woman in a bar she'll take pity on you and be a little easier game. Soon enough, I was buying her drinks and telling her my sob story. One thing led to another, and I took her home.

Only I think she could tell I was regretting it the whole time. I clammed up pretty tight when we got to my place, and after we'd done our business, I let her think I'd gone straight to sleep. I don't know why. I guess I was afraid she'd want something from me, and I didn't know how to explain that there wasn't anything left to give. The bank had gone bust. Come first light, she got up, got dressed, and got out. I was sitting up against the headboard, watching her, not really sure, still, what I should say. On her way to the door, she gave me a half-smile and said, "See you." I don't think she figured she ever would.

So as I headed the skiff back to our paramedic post, I had to remind myself to keep my eyes on the water, not on her face. There was just something so exposed about her, though; I couldn't help myself. I mean, I couldn't get over the fact that here was someone I'd twice touched, once in life and once in death, and she'd brought out more in me now than she had then. I couldn't figure why. Maybe death, even after you're dead, can still strip you down one more layer of vulnerability.

It sure felt that way when we got her body back to land. Old Carl couldn't shut up about the suicide we'd retrieved, and soon enough, all the volunteers and the rescue squads that'd come from other towns to work the flood were wanting to know what I thought could drive someone to shove her fingers through the bars of a weighted-down dog crate and hold her head underwater. Whenever they asked me, I played dumb and blamed it on the Chattahoochee.

Not long after that the flood crested. The water retreated to its proper place, leaving the folks in the wealthier part of town to spend the next few weeks scrubbing mud off their colonnades and porticos and belvederes. Those on the outskirts hosed down the corrugated tin and scavenged the drainage ditches for washed-away soffits and fascia boards. Me and Carl stayed partnered up, and we still play our game whenever we're called to a fatality. But more and more I'm loath to invent too many specifics from those faces. I guess I figure that there was somebody in those people's lives, somebody as I was to that woman, who should have been reading the signs when the dead were still around.

Some nights, the ones when I can't sleep, I find myself wondering what expression I'll be wearing when I go. I even go so far as to practice. Silly as it sounds, I'll purse my lips together and clamp my eyes shut, real stone like, or I'll just lie back and try to let the most peaceful, relaxed feeling I know stretch out my skin. I do it, I guess, because I want to believe that whatever I've been through in my life can't be summed up in a sentence or two. I want to think there's a mystery to me that's beyond observation, a meaning that can't be reduced by a glance from a stranger's eye. Maybe there's not, I don't know. But for now I'll assume that there is, just so I don't have to deal with knowing somebody's going to claim to read me as I've claimed to have read so many others.

My story's mine, after all, and I'm taking my secrets with me.

CALL HER IEMANJÁ, BUT NOT IN CHURCH

I. She Sells Seashells

Little Conception turns the crank that feeds the trouser leg through the rubber wringers of the laundry tub. The trousers belong to Eduardo, as does the house in which Little Conception lives and works. Does that mean Little Conception belongs to him as well? This is a question that, inasmuch as she ponders questions, she finds hard to answer. Dr. Eduardo is a client who twice a week drops off his laundry in a knotted sheet on his way to the indigent hospital he supervises. Like many of Little Conception's clients, he is particular about how his slacks and undershorts and guayaberas are to be scrubbed. Yet compared to others' demands Eduardo's aren't so difficult to satisfy. The old doctor only wants homemade soap used in his tub water. Eduardo insists on this indulgence because he's an elderly man who remembers the days when laundresses cleaned clothes with a mixture of pork fat, wood ashes, and salt. This was long before the first supermarkets came to Brasil and his wardrobe began to smell of phosphorous and cardboard. The odor of detergent is something he can't abide, Eduardo tells Little Conception. So for a paltry sum he finances the mortgage on a home that's a real home and not a rattletrap, and after deducting the expense of the monthly payment, he splits with Little Conception the money that he browbeats various men in town to pay him for the luxury of having their clothes hand-washed and pressed by a compliant woman.

Only occasionally will Eduardo beg for things that have nothing to do with laundry. He tells Little Conception not to pray to the African gods, for instance. For Little Conception this demand is tolerable, too, because it's still less tedious than what other clients ask of her. Those men invariably come to claim their socks and pants expecting kisses, embraces, all that follows. When they proposition her, always with promises of additional money, a half-back of bacon, or a weekend's freedom from what they presume is her drudgery, she must remind them of how unhappy it would make Eduardo to learn of their offers. The men don't really fear the old doctor, but they don't care to suffer his displeasure, either. Eduardo's sphere of influence extends throughout this little *cidade* known as Fronteira Encantada, or Enchanted Frontier. His enemies have many enemies. Little Conception's even heard it claimed that Eduardo is so important that he could own this city if he wished.

After the trouser leg passes through the wringers she pulls the pants free and gives them a quick snap to shake out the wrinkles. Then she drapes them over a clothesline with clothespins she keeps in a rusted coffee tin. She only uses clothespins with forked legs, not the kind with the spring. Little Conception doesn't use those because they're dangerous for the baby.

The thought of her child brings a halt to her work as she turns an ear to the interior of the house. The laundress has a bad tendency to leave her child be, forgetting that, now, as a toddler, Nobrega can wander away on her own. When Little Conception hears the reassuring knock of a toy from inside she resumes her labor. She dumps Eduardo's garments onto the ground and begins sorting. Because the old man's soap only partially masks the acridity of his heavy perspiration, Little Conception must let the ones that smell most offensive soak longer. The only way to tell which articles most need soaking is to sniff them, so she brings fistfuls to her nose and then divides them according to their sourness. Little Conception has two piles heaped high when she realizes that the knocking in the house has stopped.

"Nobrega!" she yells as she leaps to her feet. She passes through the verandah door into a tiny kitchen where a steam plume curls from a skillet of simmering dende oil. Once past the stove Little Conception heads to the bedroom she and her daughter share. Even though little daylight slips through the blinds, she knows immediately her baby isn't there, so she rushes to her sitting room, where a hand-me-down television given to her by Eduardo sits on a fruit crate in front of a frayed couch. The laundress reprimands herself for not thinking as she makes her way to the front door. In the past Eduardo has told her: You must think now that you have a baby. You must. But she hasn't been, not at all. She continues to rebuke herself even after she discovers her daughter sitting in the dirt courtyard that separates her house from the street. The child is tracing lines and half-circles on the red ground.

Yes, Nobrega, Little Conception thinks as she hops from the porch to the ground to scoop the child in her arms. You are almost three now. Old enough to undo locks, old enough to unlatch doors. Maybe a fastener higher on the lintel will keep you inside. She makes a note in her mind to ask Eduardo about that. Then Little Conception spots what it was that enticed the girl outside in the first place.

It's a boy named Wilson de Sousa. He stands in front of the fence rattling a long stick of jacaranda wood against the iron rails. "The American comes today!" he yells to her. "You go see?"

Little Conception tries to shoo him away, but Wilson is thirteen, and he likes to think he's brave enough not to be chased off by a mulatto only seven years older than he is. A mulatto, what's more, who's mother to a bastard. That's what Wilson's father calls Nobrega, so the name's good enough for the boy.

"Come with us!" Wilson says. He makes his desire dramatic by jumping up and down on the dirt path outside the fence. "My brother goes, too! We all go see the arrival of the American!"

"No, no, no," Little Conception answers. The invitation angers her. Every August an American comes to live in the city for a year, and every year—at least for the past three, anyway—townspeople ask if she intends to introduce herself to the stranger. Lots of people go to meet each new American who comes to tutor classes in English in exchange for room and board at the Hotel Paulista. Most of these Americans are aspiring painters or writers who spend their off-hours honing their craft. But Little Conception has never much concerned herself with the foreigners, except for the one who is the reason that boys like this taunt and tease her. "Go home, Wilson de Sousa," she yells back. "Go home and tell your brother no."

Then she takes her child inside, slamming the door.

In the kitchen the dende oil now boils, so the laundress allows her daughter to play with a wooden spoon as she attends to the sea bass and shrimp that cackle in the skillet. A poke of a long fork lets her know that the fish bits are soft to the touch, that the diced tomato and onion squares dotted with malaguenta pepper have sautéed sufficiently. She scoops them with a ladle onto a plate, catching as much of the oil as she can. She lifts the skillet off her front burner, adjusting the flame so its blue-gold crown pokes higher through the ironwork, and then sets a saucepan atop the stove.

The saucepan holds grated flakes of coconut and peanut, which, when combined with the fish, will make a dish called vatapa. But this isn't Little Conception's dinner. She cooks this meal for a man named Diogenes who pays her once a week for the privilege of dining on her verandah. Little Conception knows he would pay for more than a meal if she allowed him to, but she doesn't. So Diogenes will sit for his dinner, and by the first bite of the vatapa his flattering remarks will be drowned out by the silence of his sulking. It's a ritual he and the laundress have shared for nearly a year now, and yet Diogenes shows no signs of relenting.

As for Little Conception, she long ago became inured to his presence, as well as the inevitable presence of Diogenes's wife, Dona Teresa. When Dona Teresa can no longer tolerate her husband's ambition to philander she will appear outside Little Conception's fence to accuse the girl of enchanting him with café mandingueiro, or witches' coffee. Café mandingueiro is an old Macumba potion in which a drop of menstrual blood is placed in a man's coffee. It's a white-magic spell cast by Brasileira women who pray to African gods. But as Little Conception cooks she doesn't think of Diogenes or the tedium that rebuffing him entails. Instead, she finds herself daydreaming of the new American, of what he will look like. She wonders whether he will at all resemble Kentucky.

Kentucky is the guest no one in Enchanted Frontier remembers fondly. Gossips still speak of him as a layabout who drank too much rum and talked impolitely about the girls who feed popcorn to the pet crocodile in the tiled pit of the city square. Little Conception remembers Eduardo's wife, Dona Betina, calling him the worst American ever sent to the city. She said it even before Kentucky left, his year only half over. "Why send us only men?" Dona Betina demanded. "The whole world knows what men want!"

And yet Kentucky was always kind to Little Conception.
Kind and solicitous at once. The mornings after she cooked a
meal served to him in Eduardo's home, Kentucky would appear
at her fence with a little book, begging to record her recipes. He
wanted to eat that well when he returned home, he told her.
When he was especially homesick he would ask her to cook him
something American. That meant a plateful of batata frita.
Except Kentucky always used the American word, French fries,
which he would then beg Little Conception to say as well, just
so he could relieve his loneliness. Then, when the laundress's
pronunciation rendered those words unrecognizable, Kentucky
would laugh until the food in his mouth showed.

What Little Conception would most like to remember about
Kentucky is his curiosity toward the African gods. He wanted to
know how in this day and age–a secular age, he would say,
although she didn't know what that meant–a teenage girl could
give herself to spirits. Little Conception tried to explain that
spirits were inseparable from the material world. She spoke of
how a good day could be guaranteed by something as simple as
leaving a lit candle at an intersection, or by laying a platter of
rice beside a doorsill. This was because most of the time the
African gods were attentive to the despacho, the offering. It was
Little Conception's mae de santo, the chief macumbeira who ran
the shrine where the girl attended white-magic services, who
taught her that African gods cared more than Catholic saints
about people. One might pray and pray to a Catholic saint without ever knowing the fate of one's petition. But African gods
were sociable gods who liked to visit and interact with devotees.
Yes, they could be vengeful and vindictive, but wasn't that mis-
chief better than indifference? African gods came to inhabit you,
to borrow your body to enjoy a smoke or a drink, to dance. "You
see," she told Kentucky many times, "African gods are homeless.
They're guests in search of a body's shelter. In that way they need
us, and that's the difference. Catholic saints are remote because
they have no need for any living thing."

Kentucky always wanted to know the gods' stories. He liked
to record them in his notebook, too. He would write down
recipes in the first half, then turn the book over to make space
for the gods in the second.

"First there is Olorum," the laundress would explain. "He originates all things but is too old and infirm to bother with us anymore. So he sends one of his many begotten sons, Oxalá, who provides the sky, prefers white doves, and avoids oil, salt, and spices. Then there is Oxalá's son Xangô who is a hothead with a face of copper and an ax in his hand. Xangô's counterpart is Oxum, whose femininity instills the power to charm but also the weakness of envy. She chases away Xangô's many concubines by tricking them into cutting off their ears and boiling them in tribute to her husband. And most important of all—most important to me—is Iemanjá. Iemanjá is the goddess of the sea. She provides for seafarers as well as all those who have been cast out of their homes, which is to say everyone. She's the mother of everyone."

"These stories sound suspiciously familiar," Kentucky teased her. "Are you sure you haven't pinched them from some other source? From the Vulgate, perhaps?"

"You think so? Well, then, yes, it's true. Because when the African gods accompanied the first slaves to Brasil they found it easy to hide their presence from Europeans by painting their faces white. Oxalá hid within the robes of Jesus Christ. Another deity is Ogum, the master of iron who forged the first cutlass to clear the forest. He recreated himself as St. George the Dragonslayer. And Iemanjá, well, she is Mother Mary. To this day there are many Brasileiros, proud Brasileiros, who believe the African gods are impoverished spirits next to the Catholic saints. Eduardo, for instance. He believes that if you pray to an impoverished god, you remain impoverished, and so he refuses to make offerings. But that's also why he's never happy. Instead he wants me to attend Mass. 'You can call her Iemanjá,' he will tell me. 'But not in church. There the priests insist you call her Mary.' Mind you, he doesn't attend Mass, but he wants me to."

Thinking of the afternoons Kentucky would sit on her verandah absorbing these tales saddens Little Conception. The heat of steam and the constricted space of this kitchen conspire to impress upon her a momentary sense of imprisonment. It is only a few hours from now, she thinks, that she must entertain Diogenes. She adds rice flour to the peanut and coconut flakes and waits fifteen minutes for the mixture to thicken into white sauce. All the while Nobrega beats the floor with her wooden spoon. When Little Conception is finally able to remove the saucepan from the stove she decides she deserves a break from her labors. She dresses Nobrega and then locks her door with the one key that she owns, which she keeps tied to her neck with a ribbon. She barely makes it past the gate of her fence when she realizes she must go back because she's forgotten her money. This occurs regularly because she's not yet accustomed to carrying coins and bills; she's only had money to spend on herself since Eduardo took her in. If the old doctor found out how often she left home without it, he would sit her down and reprimand her. You must think now, he would say. You are a mother.

With a few cruzeiros tucked to a breast, Little Conception leads her child to the city supermarket that sells inexpensive ice-cream cones. To get there they must cut through the public garden that is the city square. There bougainvillea walls keep out the sound of speeding traffic. Bordering the brick pathways are nasturtiums and begonias with trumpeting bulbs. At the tile pit, Little Conception loiters long enough for Nobrega to throw a chip of palm bark at the crusty plates on the old croc's back. Off to a side, through the trees, Little Conception can see the bus station where townspeople await the new American. She wonders if he will spend his time the way Kentucky did, answering questions about American things. Garages, fireplaces, basements, pizza, hamburgers, and, yes, French fries.

"They don't understand," Kentucky always complained in a mixture of English and Portuguese. "Talking about that stuff only makes the homesickness worse!" That was why, he told her, he didn't enjoy teaching his students English. Saying the words made him long for the things that those words stood for.

It was because he longed to escape the memories of those things that Kentucky begged Little Conception to travel to Rio de Janeiro for that year's Festa de Iemanjá, which most people call New Year's Eve. At least that was Kentucky's excuse for wanting to go. Little Conception was wary. She was just sixteen then and not once in those sixteen years had she been outside of Enchanted Frontier. Running off with anyone, much less that year's American, would anger Eduardo to the point of hiring a new laundress. But Kentucky was relentless. He said Iemanjá herself had informed him that she approved. He said he had set a candle outside his hotel room during a downpour as a prayer for guidance. Should the candle remain lit despite the rain, he told Iemanjá, that was her sign that it was okay for them to go. Of course, the candle's flame didn't go out. Little Conception remained suspicious, so she consulted her mae de santo. The old woman, her age scored in her skin from decades of lending her body to the gods, assured the girl that a candle burning in a rainstorm was indeed a sign of divine intent.

And so she went with Kentucky, riding twenty-six hours on a bus to the Rio seaboard where a towering statue of a beckoning Christ stands over a city of shantytowns and tourist beaches. As the bus carved through the hours he asked her to tell him the true story of Iemanjá, the one Little Conception hinted at whenever he would tease her by saying that Iemanjá was just another name for the Virgin Mary.

"What grief did the Virgin Mary ever know?" she asked him. "She simply lost a son that was never hers in the first place. No, Iemanjá has known true suffering, which is why compassion is her nature."

And then she told him the story:

"Iemanjá was made to bear a son to her brother Aganjú because she was the second woman on earth and there was a limited choice of lovers. She was a loving mother to this son, whom she named Orungan. But Orungan misunderstood the nature of his mother's affection, and one day in the woods as she walked along a trail he fell upon her in a fury of passion. Iemanjá tried to escape, but her son was too strong. When Orungan was finished he fled, afraid of his father. Iemanjá rose and tried to make her bloodied way through the forest, but she was too weak and fell, again and again. The final time she fell her breasts tore open and her milk spilled out to form two rivers that created the world's oceans. That's the volume of the grief Iemanjá felt. Her suffering filled oceans."

By that point, the laundress was aware of the ocean of grief rising in her own breasts, for Kentucky's hand had slipped beneath her dress. Kentucky spent most of that bus ride sliding his hand back and forth between the girl's thighs.

It went on after the bus ride, too. For the two days preceding the Festa de Iemanjá that they were in Rio they would rise in the morning and hike to the beach. There Kentucky would spread a towel over the sand as he told Little Conception to lie on her stomach so he could rub her legs with sun cream. She gave in to his touch and complied when he asked her to rub the cream on him because she believed Iemanjá was protecting her. The rain shower hadn't extinguished the candle, after all. Then at night Kentucky would take her to dinner, treating her to expensive meals that she'd never before eaten in a restaurant. Usually when she enjoyed a fancy dish Little Conception had cooked it herself in the kitchen of a rich man's house. And whatever portion of a plate she might save for herself was never consumed at a table. Whenever she ate in a rich man's house she ate standing up.

After dinner Kentucky would touch her more, often throughout the night until she would be so exhausted she would drift off to sleep even as he lay atop or behind her. And when it was over he would sit at the side of the bed, heaving to catch his breath as long beads of sweat rained down his chest and back. Occasionally he might stroke Little Conception's hair, but for the most part he stared into the darkness, talking to himself in English.

"My little Leda," he said one of those nights. "How was that for interacting with a god?"

But Little Conception, her belly and buttocks greased with his perspiration, hadn't understood his words.

Then came the night of the festival. Little Conception was worried because winning Iemanjá's favor required cowrie shells that could only be obtained in shops that specialized in Macumba accessories, and today of all days there would be a mad rush for such trinkets. But Kentucky wouldn't let her rise from the motel bed. "No, no, there's plenty of shells on the beach," he told her. "We'll scoop up a few of those." It was nearly evening before he relented. By that point he was drunk on rum and was perspiring through the white shirt attendees to the ceremony were required to wear. As they made their way to the beach, Kentucky pulling her along in a quick trot, Little Conception was aware that the chafed pain in her loins would burn even more when she entered the salt water. But she believed Iemanjá was protecting her, that the pain would be alleviated. So as they found a place among the thousands of worshipers gathered on the sand, she arranged her tribute from knickknacks she'd packed in her purse: a soap cake, a small perfume bottle, two white flowers, cigarettes, a straight comb, and a hand mirror, all placed in a silver-painted boat decorated with blue and white satin ribbons.

For hours they danced and drank until the time came to line up at the ocean's edge. At the stroke of midnight they then rushed into the surf, Little Conception with her boat in her hands. Kentucky had merely thrashed about in a drunken stupor, but the girl had waded until her shoulders were covered. She let her gift loose in the current, praying that Iemanjá would pull it farther out to sea. She stepped slowly backwards, the retreating waves drawing the sand out from under her soles, until the boat disappeared and she was reasonably sure it had been swallowed amid the dark splashes of the tide. Just to make sure she hadn't deceived herself about her standing with Iemanjá, she waited waterside for an hour to see if her gift would return to shore. When it didn't, she located Kentucky, who had passed out on a wooden bench, and they returned to their room. Except for the occasional intrusion of Kentucky's snoring, that was the one night Little Conception slept without interruption.

Back in Enchanted Frontier, Kentucky tried to justify the afternoons he visited Little Conception's house to distract her from her work by claiming she had placed a drop of menstrual blood in his coffee. Lying on a blanket in her bedroom, naked except for the splotches of red that his hip bones rubbed into her skin, Little Conception stared at the ceiling, trying to decide how to tell him it wasn't true. Because by that point there had been no menstrual blood to enchant him with.

After Little Conception and Nobrega share a cone at the supermarket, a smeared bit of sherbet drying on the little girl's cheek, they retrace their steps through the park. As they pass the crocodile pit Little Conception hears an excited murmur rising from the crowd at the bus station. The new American has arrived, she thinks. Through the gaps in the bougainvillea she can see the dust cloud kicked up by the crowd's enthusiastic clustering. She and Nobrega pause just for a moment, then resume walking.

At home she pours the contents of the saucepan atop the sautéed sea bass and shrimp, finishing the vatapa. She is about to return to the verandah and her work when she hears the familiar sound of jacaranda wood raking her fence rails. "Little Conception! Little Conception!" Wilson de Sousa yells. "I speak with the American! He wishes to meet you! It's the truth!" Little Conception turns a deaf ear to the boy's racket.

On the verandah she stares at the piles of Eduardo's unfinished laundry. She will need to heat water to complete the work. Although she must rush her efforts if she's to shower before Diogenes's arrival, she doesn't resent her labor. Little Conception never pines for a different life. The only thought that occupies her mind as she scrubs clothes is how to procure the blessings of Iemanjá and Oxalá.

That was the question she had had to ask herself when her menstrual blood no longer came. Why had Iemanjá refused the despacho she had so carefully set loose in the ocean? The laundress's bafflement hadn't been relieved until some months later, long after Kentucky disappeared only halfway into his year in Enchanted Frontier and her own body had been stretched and misshapen by the child she carried.

"Iemanjá is a loving but exacting mother," the mae de santo told her. "She has very specific requirements for maintaining her affection, and you failed at least one. Because Iemanjá demands that those attending the festival who truly wish her blessing abstain the night before they enter the water."

No one had ever informed Little Conception of this rule. In the years since learning of it she has wondered whether that knowledge would have mattered. Because in the end, she understands, Kentucky was no son of the water goddess. His devotion laid instead with Orungan, the boy whose passion drove him to fall upon his mother.

Kentucky remains in her thoughts minutes later as she soaks a guayabera in a tub of scalding water. She remembers washing a pair of Kentucky's trousers one afternoon shortly after he stopped visiting her. She found the pants under the basket she stores her own laundry in, left there, apparently, during one of the unending afternoons when he would shove deep at her thighs with a force that sent his hot breath wheeling across her shoulders. For some time she let those trousers lay rumpled, not wishing to acknowledge their presence because to do so was to acknowledge his presence in her life. But that afternoon she broke her resolve and in a gesture of reconciliation she decided to do what it was her lot to do for all men—scrub their clothes. And then, as she cranked the winch, she heard a cracking noise that had her fearing she may have broken a pocket watch or medallion. Only when she felt at those pockets what she discovered were seashells, the cowries they collected on the beach the night of the Festa de Iemanjá. The memory the shells recalled was of a drunken Kentucky handing them to her, commanding her, "Say this. I want you to say this, in English: 'She sells seashells.' " And when Little Conception complied, her pronunciation rendering those words a slur of "sh's," he fell on his back in the sand, laughing at her.

Little Conception held those crushed shells in her palm with a sense of irrevocable exile from the gods' favor. In Macumba to divine you must break a cowrie, but only into halves. One half stands for masculine principle, the other the female. The gods' will is made manifest according to the combinations that arise when the shells are thrown. Yet Little Conception's shells were reduced to shards and splinters. There was no way to tell which was male and which was female, no way to even begin to guess what the spirits might want.

It's like that with the African gods sometimes, the girl decides as she rubs Eduardo's laundry along the washboard. Despite what the mae de santo teaches, they can be as fickle as Catholic saints when they want to be. On occasion they speak to you directly and intimately. They make their love known by occupying your body. In the security of such moments Little Conception can call upon certain truths to pillar her world: *Gods need us; men want; the oceans are rivers of milk that flow from burst breasts*. In other times the gods retreat until their intent is no more visible than a wave washing along a horizon. And it is then that Little Conception prays most fervently. Oh my mother Iemanjá, queen of the salt sea, she will repeat. Oh my mother Iemanjá, descend and counsel me.

Worse than the silence that sometimes greets this prayer is the impatience it arouses in the spirits. Because Little Conception can imagine Iemanjá speaking to her as Eduardo often does, in a voice that is gruff and reprimanding. You are a woman now. And a mother, Iemanjá tells her. You must be smarter. And then when Little Conception begs for clarification, the answer won't come in the form of words at all, only in a sound that makes her feel as if she's a bauble cast to the sea. It's the sound that fills her thoughts now as she comes to grips with the fact that, thanks to Wilson de Sousa, the new American will seek her out. She will hear that sound this evening as Diogenes quiets her when, as is his custom, he will clutch her hips as she serves him his vatapa. It's the sound she remembers that Kentucky made, too, whenever she objected to his fingers prying at her thighs.

It's the sound that gods make when they grow weary of human pleading: *shhh shhh shhh.*

II. Shoeshine Boy

American music drifted toward the new American from a pair of loudspeakers that hung from a nearby streetlight. The music flowed slowly thanks to the stiff humidity that for days straight kept the young man sweating through his shirts. The fermented sugarcane didn't help matters. After two hours of sitting at a sidewalk bar, the American regretted downing the four shots of pinga that now burned a stripe down his throat. Flashes of heat erupted along his arms, and he was aware as well of a certain weight gathering at the back of his neck that threatened to push him face down into the pile of bottles and coasters littering the tabletop. But what really made his intoxication unreal was the sound of American words. After only two weeks in Brasil the new American had grown accustomed to hearing little beyond a language that made no sense to him. To suddenly comprehend the meaning of a wafting phrase was disconcerting because it made him realize he had forgotten he ever had the power to understand words in the first place.

"More beer?" Luis Roberto asked him. The American nodded and held his glass under the nozzle of the longneck bottle of
Antartica cerveja. Luis Roberto was his sponsor, charged with
taking care of him. The man knew bits and phrases of English,
enough to make the American feel welcomed.

Joining them were two other men, friends of Luis Roberto's.
The gray-haired man called Carlitão could say "Thank you very
much, please" in English, and when he was drunk he took the
American into his embrace and said these words over and over.
The other man, Valdir, was a medico like Luis Roberto. They
both worked at the hospital run by Dr. Eduardo. Valdir's skin was
much paler than the other Brasileiros'; he was whiter than the
American, in fact. His milky face was accentuated by a wild red
beard that collected in long tangles under his chin, and he wore
glasses that sunk so low on his nose that the lenses magnified his
eyes until they appeared three times too big for his head.

Valdir spoke as Luis Roberto poured the American's beer, his
hands slicing the air in arcs that came dangerously close to upsetting his own glass.

"What's he saying?" the American asked. Luis Roberto set
the emptied bottle beside his feet and then put his elbows on the
table. It rocked a little on the uneven sidewalk.

"Tomorrow is a holiday," he said. His English wasn't perfect,
but he was more fluent than anyone else in Enchanted Frontier,
other than Dr. Eduardo. He was particularly adept at American
syntax, almost never putting a plural verb with a singular subject
as many of his colleagues did. "What day is tomorrow?"

"September 7," the American said.

"Em português, favor."

The American stopped to think. He knew very little of the
language. He could say obrigado (thank you) and até logo (until
soon) and a few other things, but mostly he was inarticulate. The
day before Luis Roberto gave him a list of the months and cardi-
nal numbers from one to ten, and the American had tried to
memorize them.

"Sete de Setembro," the American answered before adding,
"I think."

Luis Roberto's brown face split into a wide, white smile. He
said "very good" in Portuguese before giving his guest a pair of

swift, masculine pats on the back. Meanwhile, Valdir had yet to stop talking. His face had gone so red it nearly matched the red of his dangling beard.

"Tomorrow we celebrate independence," Luis Roberto said, and he sipped from his own glass. "Valdir, elé é um . . ." Luis Roberto rolled his hands in the night trying to find the right word. "Elé é um Alemão."

The American didn't understand.

"De Alemanha," his sponsor elaborated. The American shook his head. Luis Roberto rolled his eyes as if looking to the American music to deliver the right word. Then he pressed a fin-gertip to the indentation above his wet lip while his other arm knifed straight in the air. "Heil Hitler!" he said.

"Germany," the American told him with a nod. Luis Roberto tried to repeat the word but his *g* and his *r* were weak. The American said the word in Portuguese, and the brown man smiled at his success. "We learn together," Luis Roberto declared, and he lifted his glass for yet another toast.

The American felt something grab him. He looked to the other side of the table. Carlitão wanted his attention. The man's hand was large and rough and felt like a baseball glove.

"Porque vocé vem ão Brasil?" Carlitão demanded in what seemed a stern voice.

The American didn't understand.

"Why you come to Brasil," Luis Roberto translated. But a song now spilling from the speakers distracted the American. He recognized it; the song had been very popular the previous spring. He had danced to it one night in a college bar with a girl whose name he didn't know, and when it was over he had kissed her, right there on the dance floor in front of a hundred strangers. The memory saddened him because he didn't want to be reminded either of home or that girl.

"Elé é jornalista?" the American heard Valdir ask Luis Roberto. He understood only because of the last word. On his first day in Enchanted Frontier he had told Luis Roberto that he was studying to be a travel writer and that Brasil would be the subject of his first book. He called the book a travelogue but Luis Roberto didn't understand and the American didn't know how to express the precise meaning. He didn't say more but he guessed Luis Roberto thought he was a real journalist with a book contract instead of a college junior with a Rotary Club scholarship that required him to teach English for a year.

Luis Roberto was nodding at Valdir and Carlitão, a wry smile pushing his lips flat. "Vai escrever de nossa vida," he said. "Vai falar que o Brasil é uma bagunça."

That made the three men laugh. The American joined in. He didn't know what was said; he just recognized the sarcasm. Then Carlitão put his hand on the American's arm again. His eyes were half open from mixing pinga and beer, and a cigarette hung from one corner of his mouth. When Carlitão finished his sentence, the American looked to Luis Roberto.

"He asks if Eduardo has yet read what you write."

"No," the American admitted. "But he has asked me to bring him a sample. He wants to read and discuss it."

Luis Roberto told his friends this, and the men all laughed. Then Valdir spoke.

"You will benefit from a tutorial from Eduardo," Luis Roberto translated. "He will sit you in a chair as he reads what you write. Then he will say, 'More adjectives!' Or perhaps his opinion will be 'Less adverbs!' " He stopped to catch more of Valdir's rambling. "If you were a painter like those who stay with us in the past, he would prescribe for you a color scheme. He would say, 'Yes, ocean is blue, but yours is an unreal blue. I would prefer some green for verity.' Or if you were to paint a mountain, he would tell you, 'Mountains are brown only in the imagination. Real mountains are gray.' And then he would try to tell you the appropriate density of the pigments. But you are a writer, so you will only have to contend with his advice to the writers: Mais ajectivos, advérbios demais!"

"Is that true?" the American asked.

Luis Roberto shrugged. "Eduardo, he is our—como fala?—paterfamilias." The American didn't understand that word, not even in English. "To each in this city he likes to say, 'Here is your life. Do what I say.' And so we do. Why? Who knows? But the Americans he brings here—you Americans—they dislike his advice. It frustrates Eduardo to no end, and by July as each American prepares to return home, Eduardo insists he will decline to invite another. But he always relents because he believes that some coming year there will be at least one who will consent to his control."

"He'll like what I give him."

This made Luis Roberto smile more. "He will? Yes, of course, he will. Why not? As long as you show the truth of Brasil, he will like."

"That's what I've done. I've worked hard to be faithful."

Carlitão said something. Luis Roberto waited patiently before rephrasing the words in English: "What is your subject?"

"I've only been here two weeks, so I haven't seen as much as there is to see. But I do have something, a descriptive thing, about this laundress I was introduced to. She tells me all about Macumba."

The sound of that word made Valdir and Carlitão stiffen in their chairs. They looked to each other for a second before Valdir shot out a slew of incomprehensible words. Luis Roberto wiped his forehead on his shirtsleeve as he listened.

"Valdir says not to write about that. He says that is too much the cliché. The world all over already considers us simple-headed, and we are not. He wishes for you to renounce the exotic. Otherwise you will not write of us as we are in reality."

The American didn't know what to say. He was just trying to make sense of what the laundry girl told him. When he visited her he recorded her talking and then, back at his room at the hotel, he would sit with his dictionary to translate what she said. It was hard because most of the names she used—Oxalá, Iemanjá, Xangô—weren't listed in his book.

Now Carlitão spoke. Luis Roberto laughed.

"He has a story for you to tell. It is about four friends who get drunk one night. He will even contribute his own dialogue to you."

Across the table Carlitão held up his palms. He was quieting everyone in order to build up suspense. He took a deep breath and then, after looking back and forth among the other men, he said, "Thank you very much, please" in English. The three Brasileiros howled. Valdir took his beer bottle and began tapping its bottom on the table in glee.

"I love you, please," Carlitão went on, and the men laughed some more. It made the American feel a little lonely and isolated to realize they teased him. Then the end of Carlitão's unfiltered cigarette burnt through the paper and singed his lips. He spat the wet paper on the ground and pushed it into the sidewalk with his sandal toe. The American poured himself a fifth shot of pinga to relieve his sadness. The taste was so distracting that it slipped his mind his friends were laughing at him.

Carlitão, however, hadn't forgotten. "I would very much like to enjoy more beer," he said with stately exaggeration. There were tobacco grains in his teeth. "Mister Garçon, I would like more beer to enjoy if you will, please!"

The waiter appeared on the sidewalk. He wore a tuxedo shirt and a bow tie, as did all the waiters in the city, despite the heaviness that saddled the air. "Precisamos mais cerveja," Carlitão demanded, a new cigarette already plucked from his breast pocket and planted between his teeth.

Another song emerged from the speakers. This one was also familiar, but it had no special meaning for the American, and he was glad. Weeks earlier it might have uncovered some hidden memory, but now it didn't need to. He was no longer that person. In a funny way he didn't even feel particularly American. Perhaps the fermented sugarcane made him vain, but the American kept telling himself that if his life had changed so much in such a short time then he, too, must be different in some or even many ways. The only thing that stood in his way was the language. As he poured a sixth shot, the American promised himself that he would work hard on his Portuguese until he could pass for a Brasileiro.

From the direction of the drifting music he could see the entrance to the city square. Over the past two weeks he had walked through it every afternoon. There was a knoll where the bougainvillea was thin enough to provide a view of the city courthouse across the street. After each day's lunch the American would sit on the knoll with a notebook. He had finished three stories in two weeks. They were good stories, he thought, ones that he started in his head many times in America but could never get on paper. The stories felt so good he hoped that his teaching duties wouldn't sap the energy and concentration he would need to finish more.

As he turned his attention back to the table he smelled the smoke of Carlitão's cigarette. The scent was sweet and pure. A few days earlier Luis Roberto had taken him to the little plot of land that Carlitão owned outside the city, and the three of them walked, their feet hot against the red soil, through the rows of tobacco that Carlitão grew to help support his family. The smell reminded the American of why he could finish three stories in two weeks. There was a purity of experience here he had never known. He felt it in the long nights when he sat with Luis Roberto and his wife and friends on their patio and they would all sing together until overtaken by sleep. He could smell the purity in the morning when he walked the market district and the fragrance of the freshly baked bread hung like mist. The purity revealed itself in the taste of coffee ground early each morning by Zina, the cook, as she rose to begin her work at the Hotel Paulista where he now lived. The American inhaled deeply and felt his drunkenness ripple along his nerves. He would do many things in Brasil, he thought, and they, too, would be pure.

Something touched his elbow. He thought it was Carlitão again, ready to butcher a new phrase in his comedian's English, but then he realized the texture wasn't heavy or rough like the big Brasileiro's hand. The touch belonged instead to a boy who had intruded upon their celebration. He was a mulatto, the color of coffee and cream, and his hair was short but uncombed so the bristles arranged themselves in knots and tufts. The boy looked young, perhaps as young as twelve, but he held a wooden box by the handle as someone older might hold a briefcase. Poking out of the box was a spoon-shaped brush. The boy said something that, of course, the American didn't understand. Once more he had to ask Luis Roberto the meaning.

"He shines your shoes," his sponsor told him. The American faced the boy. He pointed to the ground and pulled his foot from beneath the table so the boy could see he wore tennis shoes. The boy dropped his eyes only for a moment. When he raised them again the American thought the boy's eyes could have been two chips of plywood.

"Tem dinheiro?" the boy asked.

"He will settle for money," Luis Roberto explained. The American reached into his pocket and felt for some of the currency he carried. Days earlier he had sold a hundred American dollars for nearly thirty thousand cruzeiros to a friend of Luis Roberto's wife. The exchange made him a profit of nearly three hundred percent, so he felt generous. He put a dollar's worth of currency on the table. The boy eyed it suspiciously. The American pushed the money toward him but suddenly a hand came down and yanked the bill from his fingers.

"Too much, too much," Luis Roberto said. He held the American's cruzeiros in his knuckles. "Too much," he said again, and with his free hand he pulled a coin from his own pocket and tossed it to the boy. "Vai, moleque, vai," he told the mulatto, fanning his hands. The boy didn't budge, however. He looked to Carlitão, offering to shine his shoes. But the big Brasileiro wore sandals, so he just lifted a hand from the table and motioned the boy away without so much as making eye contact.

The boy didn't bother anyone else at the bar. Instead he crossed the street and disappeared among the carnauba palms at the garden's entryway. The American watched until there was nothing left to look at. He picked up his shot glass and wished for one last shot, his seventh.

Luis Roberto gave the American his money back. He said, "You give some. But not big. Give five cruzeiros. It is enough."

The American returned the bill to his shirt pocket. The alcohol he had consumed forced a yawn from his lips. Tomorrow he would be hung over, he knew, but it was a holiday. They would all sleep late and when they awoke, Luis Roberto said they would go swimming at the doctor's club that he, Eduardo, and Valdir all belonged to. An afternoon barbecue was scheduled there, and Luis Roberto promised the new American the richest meat he had ever tasted in his life. As long as he was with Luis Roberto, the American thought, he would be all right. All he wanted to do now was sleep.

"Vamos," Valdir announced. "Vamos dormir. E amanha, vamos bebir de novo."

It would be a few months before the American could understand what the pale man had said: We go. We sleep. And tomorrow, we drink again.

The four of them finished their drinks, their silence broken only by the American music. When the bill arrived they divided it three ways because Luis Roberto wouldn't let his guest pay for drinks. "You are friend, meu filho," the man said. The American knew meu filho meant "my son." "When I come to the United States, you pay."

They left money with the garçon as they tucked their folding chairs beneath the table. Valdir and Carlitão walked in front of the American and his sponsor. They led the way across the street toward the carnauba palms and the garden they would cut through on their way to sleep.

"You are sad," Luis Roberto said to the American as they walked.

"I'm drunk," he confessed instead, and they both laughed. "How do you say drunk?"

"Tomar fogo. It means literally 'to take fire' in English. Tonight we take fire. And tomorrow we take fire again. Tomorrow is day of independence."

In the garden, courtship games were in play. Dark girls walked the brick footpaths, their arms held gently in the palms of lovers. The unattached sat on benches, boys on one side, girls on the other. The music seemed very loud and unromantic to the American. He couldn't understand why the volume was so high.

"Tell me," he said to his host. Ahead of them Valdir and Carlitão shuffled along the bricks, arms around each other. They had taken to singing along with the American music, in English. Every other word they sang was "please" in long, untuned voices that stressed the e. "What was Valdir saying when his face got so red?"

He saw Luis Roberto smile. "Valdir has the blood of a German"—and his g and r were still very weak—"He is impassioned for Brasil. Sentimental, too. He says the Brasileiro is a very happy creature. Felicidade demais no Brasil. There is too much happiness in Brasil. That is the problem. As long as Brasileiro has pinga, he remains happy, and nothing more."

They passed the center of the garden where a baby crocodile swam in a pit of water gone green with algae. Around the perimeter of the pit two dark and beautiful girls threw popcorn to the scaly animal. They were very attractive to the American and when he passed the two girls he swore he could smell their perfume. He followed his friends down one of the lanes of the

garden where the trees thinned and the courthouse became visible. No lovers were around. Carlitão and Valdir continued
singing, their bodies now tumbling into each other. To the side
of the lane the American saw something move in the darkness.
When he looked closer he saw it was the moleque who had
begged his money. The mulatto sat on his box, the shoe brush
beside his naked feet as he fed himself a handful of popcorn from
his fist. The American suddenly felt nervous that the boy might
approach him again, and he was glad when he and his friends
had passed by without incident.

When he was safely away, the American tried to imagine the
boy asking the girls feeding the crocodile for that handful of popcorn. He must have smelled their perfume as he pushed his
brown hands toward them. It was too powerful a scent to ignore.
The boy probably even touched the girls, the American decided.
Their fingers must have met as the girls let the popcorn fall into
his open palms. The American felt a reviving breeze whirl
through the garden, and he wished he could have been touched
the way the shoeshine boy had been touched by two beautiful
girls framed by bougainvillea. For a romantic moment he wished
he were that boy.

"I am going to write a story," the American told his sponsor
as they came to the end of the footpath. The street ahead of
them was brightly lit, and thick, happy voices danced above the
lights on the porches. The music was behind them and wasn't
loud anymore. "It will be about three Brasileiros and an
American who take fire on a hot night and talk about the happiness of Brasil. I will write this story very soon, but not tomorrow. Tomorrow is a holiday."

III. TB

Eduardo was standing at the edge of the hospital portico finishing a Carlton cigarette when, without warning, the old
woman and her grandson appeared amid a shower of street-lamp
light.

"Doutor!" the bandana-headed grandmother yelled as she lugged her avoirdupois his direction. "I bring you the boy! I bring him back for you!"

Out of anger Eduardo feigned deafness. He clenched his jaws and trained his eyes upon the intersection beside the hospital. On a normal night, in a time of normalcy, Eduardo would be speeding through that intersection in his Alpha Roméo as he made his way home to his wife.

"Doutor! You must take the boy back! The spirits have refused him health!"

"Bastante," Eduardo growled when the woman's pleading grew irksome. "And no nearer. You haven't done enough already? Now it's me you want to infect?"

The grandmother and the child halted, still several feet away.

"But doutor, he passes blood now in his phlegm. You said you would help."

"I said I would try to help. That was before. You didn't do as I told you. I told you the boy must be quarantined, and what do you do? You steal him away. Now it's too late. There's no telling how many you will have harmed with your recklessness."

Eduardo had yet to face the pair, although he could certainly sense their presence. The grandmother's distorted shadow lay under his feet, thrown there by the street lamp. As for the dim-witted half-mute who was forever following her by a militarily precise half step, the deep rasp of his labored breathing was telling enough.

"But doutor, the spirits—we needed a blessing. The mae de santo, she said to bring the boy to receive her prescription."

"Ah," Eduardo went, the nicotine adding a scratch to his sarcasm. "A macumbeira will prescribe a regiment for a spot on a lung. Let me guess the treatment. First she drapes the boy in a linen shroud. Then she rubs him up and down with a squawking rooster. Then she wraps the shroud tight. Then she reaches up under the linen to decorate his chest with chalk crosses. And yet, you say, he's not yet cured?"

The old woman didn't answer. Her silence heightened Eduardo's annoyance. Given the volume of work and worry she was creating for him, he felt the grandmother owed him some small renunciation of superstition. In anger Eduardo flicked his cigarette ash in their general direction.

"What about work? Are you going to tell me that you've not had him panhandling this entire time he's been outside the ward?"

As he spoke the doctor finally deigned to look their way. Against the backdrop of the street lamp the grandmother's grimy white skirt glowed like an explosion of starlight. All Eduardo could see of the woman herself was the thick hand of cracked skin that brushed at her left cheek. At her side the boy stood motionless, his swollen belly bulging past the edges of an unbuttoned shirt that was several sizes too small. The moleque's face was blank except for the two churning pools of his eyes.

"Forgive me, doutor," the old woman said, "but the boy brings money. He's my moneymaker. If he's not there to sweep a sidewalk, to shine shoes, I have no food."

"How will he make your money when he's too sick to stand? What good will he be to you then?"

"Those are future questions. The present won't allow their asking. Please, doutor, you must take him. He's sick."

Eduardo threw his cigarette to the ground. "Stop asking. You already know the answer. What else can I do? Let you take him off to infect the rest of the city? I have no choice. But if you remove him from the ward again, I'll send the police after you. And for your mae de santo and every single macumbeira who thinks a squawking rooster can rid a boy of tuberculosis. Now, follow me."

He led them beneath the portico to the freshly scrubbed glass doors of the hospital. Inside, exposed ceiling bulbs dumped harsh light over the hallway. During the day the hall was crowded with poor seeking to have their broken bones set, their cuts stitched, their babies birthed. At night, after the staff stopped accepting appointments, the hospital emptied except for the lonely groan of inpatients awaiting death.

As he led the grandmother and the boy down a set of stairs to the makeshift tubercular ward, Eduardo found himself thinking about what the old woman had said: future questions. What had his life been but one long attempt to anticipate them? For forty-five years Eduardo had worked for the future of this city, the

city of his mother's birth more than a century earlier. He did so
in the belief that one man through service and caretaking and
not a little bullying could impose order upon a neglected patch
of soil. Yes, he had helped build this place, reinforcing its foundation and walls with the mortar of his devotion. And even if his
ambition had been taller rather than broader (Enchanted
Frontier was only one city, after all, and a small one at that: only
thirty-five thousand occupants) he had been successful. By any
measure one chose, he had succeeded.

When Eduardo arrived here all those years ago—young,
newly credentialed, just released from the army after two years of
obligatory service—Enchanted Frontier was little more than a
train stop wedged between the tobacco and coffee farms of the
upper reaches of the state of São Paulo. It was home back then
to saloon dwellers and whores and procurers trafficking in
untaxed rum and cocoa, the rest of the population a transient
wash of laborers who came and went seasonally from the farms.
Eduardo had never suffered any delusions about the city's eco-
nomic prospects. Enchanted Frontier might never be prosperous
in the way cities with industry and manufacturing were. Yet it
could at least be presentable, crisscrossed with clean streets and
schools and restaurants where the patrons outnumbered the
insects. A city had to be presentable if it hoped to cultivate a
middle class. And it was a middle class that Eduardo knew he
had to attract and appease if he were to raise this place from the
dust.

Finding the population itself had been easy. In those days the
state was eager to stretch its bureaucratic tentacles into the
region to regulate its unruly agricultural practices. There was a
ready supply of inspectors, supervisors, and functionaries of all
types, along with wives and children, available for relocation.
All they required was an outpost that promised an acceptable
quality of life. Eduardo had been the man to cajole local interests
to invest in that quality. Along the way he had made many people rich from state and municipal contracts, and he had enriched
himself, too. But the old doctor rarely thought about the rewards
he'd reaped. It was what he'd given that preoccupied him. And
what he'd given was forty-five years of sweat that made this city

a city. It was his sweat's salt that gave the city its crystalline sheen.

"Doutor," the grandmother was asking. "What can you do for the boy? How will you cure him?"

Eduardo could feel the woman just inches from his back as he slid a stethoscope along the child's bare chest. They were in the tubercular ward now, a windowless basement room with negative air pressure to prevent droplet nuclei from seeping through the cracks around the doorsill. The boy sat on one of the room's six beds, his heels tucked behind a bar on the metal bed frame. As Eduardo listened to the rales of the child's breathing, he was forced to stare at the dirt-encrusted toes left exposed by the boy's ratty flip-flops.

"I told you before," he told the grandmother. "There is a drug called isoniazid. With any luck it will inhibit the bacilli from reproducing. But that is only if his strain isn't resistant. That was what I had intended to test for before you disappeared with him."

"The drug—it won't make him sicker?"

"It shouldn't. And it can be taken orally, so he won't have to worry about injections."

Eduardo caught the boy staring at him. The child's face was perplexing. It was remote and emptied of expression, and yet the old doctor couldn't help but sense something there, a flicker of hauteur, as if the boy presumed the favor of Eduardo's services without the return expectation of gratitude.

"So," he said to the moleque, taunting him, "a shot wouldn't scare you? Not even after six months? Because when you administer shot after shot, the scar tissue builds up, and it takes more force to push the needle and pierce the vein. Knowing that should make you happy you only need drink your medicine from a cup."

The boy didn't answer.

"There is an additional risk," Eduardo informed the grandmother. He removed his stethoscope from his neck and placed it in the pocket of his lab coat. "Isoniazid depletes pyridoxine stores. That normally would not be a problem, but when malnutrition has already depleted pyridoxine levels, well, then—"

"Please, doutor, I don't understand."

The grandmother's voice was corkscrewed with concern. Her chafed hands kept batting at the air, as if she had no other way of expressing her agitation. Eduardo regretted trying to scare the boy because he'd only succeeded in frightening the old woman.

"It's not a great concern," he admitted with a sigh. "Pyridoxine is just another name for vitamin B_6. I will prescribe a vitamin supplement." The doctor rubbed his eyes before addressing the woman paternally. "You'll have to stay as well, you know. And I will have to collect a sample for a sputum smear from you. That can wait until morning. Tonight you'll have to list for me everyone the boy has been in contact with, before and after you stole him away, with addresses. Because they, too, will have to be tested."

Eduardo made his way to the ward door.

"You'll forgive me," he said, pulling a chain of keys from his pocket, "but you'll be locked in at night until I'm certain you won't run off. I can't risk an epidemic on account of the few cruzeiros his panhandling might bring." He inserted the appropriate key into the door lock as he stepped past the threshold. "There is a button by the bed to call a nurse if you require anything. But you shouldn't expect food tonight. Meal service won't begin again until morning."

The last Eduardo saw of the grandmother and the boy that night, they were staring at the backside of the door as it closed upon them, the old woman's face fat with wonder at what she was expected to do to pass the time. As Eduardo scaled the stairs to return to his work, he found himself wishing he'd taken the time to answer the question. Pray to your gods, he would have told her.

Back in his office, the doctor started the ceiling fan and opened the Venetian blinds as he lit another Carlton. Since it was his rule that there should be no smoking in the hospital, he felt entitled to break it. Once at his desk he sat meditatively for a short time before pressing an intercom buzzer. Seconds later the night shift's chief nurse leaned into the room.

"Yes, sir?" the nurse asked. Although the woman had worked at Eduardo's hospital for going on twenty years, he knew little about her beyond her name and reliable reputation. Somewhere in the back of his mind he thought he'd heard she'd recently become a grandmother for the first time.

"How long has it been, Lenia, since we last heard from our friend Rui de Silva?"

"Rui, doutor? It's been some time, yes. My guess is he's been retired."

"Been retired?" Eduardo smiled. "I like your phrasing. What about Ximbico? He's been retired also?"

Lenia nodded. "I know that he has. He's been retired to prison for some years now."

The news surprised Eduardo. "Some years now? It's been that long then?" He emptied his chest of air and folded his hands over his stomach. "I hadn't realized we hadn't needed those sorts of friends recently."

"No, sir," the nurse answered. "The supply system has run quite well since the governor came into office. No shortages to speak of. Whether that remains so after his term ends, who can know?"

But Eduardo had already raised his hand to wave away questions about the future. Normally that gesture was Lenia's cue to leave the doctor alone, but tonight she remained stationed in the doorway.

"You'll telephone in the morning then, sir? Now that the boy's back?"

"What choice do I have? All of our real friends have been retired."

"And what will happen?"

Eduardo's eyebrows rose on his forehead. "We'll be overrun, naturally. Because the program is nothing if not thoroughly organized. We'll have field agents to canvas the slums and managers to collate their information and supervisors to implement the treatment. It's all determined according to a model divided into stages. There is even a flow chart to illustrate the process. I'm sure you'll have occasion to see it for yourself. The process dictates, of course, that we be briefed. Not consulted, mind you, but briefed. You'll see, Lenia. It won't take long at all for us to be shunted aside. It won't take long for us to be retired."

Eduardo realized suddenly that Lenia couldn't look him in the eye. Her gaze wouldn't rise higher than his desktop.

"I have to ask, doutor," she began to say. Eduardo detected a new nervousness in her voice. Lenia wasn't accustomed to questioning him. "When the representatives of the program arrive, you won't . . . with the woman and the boy in the isolation room, you won't be . . ."

"No, I won't be locking them in the ward. How can I? There's not even a provision for a ward in the program. The sickest ones will be sent to sanatoriums in São Paulo. As for the rest, they'll have the drugs distributed to them. I know because I've seen the flow chart. Making sure the infected adhere to treatment falls under what's called education. That means when the program administrators give out a dosage they will say, 'Take this, and make sure you come back for the next one'—never imagining, of course, that the infected ones wouldn't come back. As I'm sure we'll be privileged to see, the program is built upon a great many assumptions."

Eduardo fell silent when he realized the extent to which he'd exposed his bitterness. He rose from his chair and stared through the slats of the blinds to hide his embarrassment.

"We'll telephone the authorities in the morning," he told her. "It shouldn't take the health department more than a day to send a team here. Nothing worse can happen in the interim. For now I'd like some time to myself. I should be home; my wife will worry that I'm unfaithful. But I'd rather be alone for a while."

When Eduardo heard the office door close he relaxed his shoulders, hoping to drain his rib cage of the tension coiling there. In his solitude he couldn't decide what disgusted him more, the grandmother's irredeemable ignorance or his own humbled vanity. Ridding Enchanted Frontier of the poor had never been Eduardo's aim. It was Christ, after all, who said that the poor would always be with us. Who was Eduardo to argue? No, his goal over the long stretch of his working life had been to contain them, to contain the threat of blight that the poor posed, both for the sake of his city and the sake of its middle class. Containing them meant many things, only some of which involved Eduardo's professional expertise. Yes, he had built a hospital where the poor received immunizations, where they were taught the rudiments of sanitation, hygiene, and childcare to lessen the danger of contagion. But he had also had a hand in upholding the zoning laws that kept slums from sprouting up anywhere other than in Enchanted Frontier's northernmost quadrant, far from the sight of the highways that fed commerce to the city. Nor was Eduardo above conspiring with city leaders when mugging and prostitution rates rose. At those times he would raise money to supplement underpaid police with private security fleets who targeted the glue-sniffers and gang lords. He had no moral qualms about pressuring the archdiocese to baptize the macumbeiras out of their white-magic beliefs. Hadn't the grandmother's willingness to start an epidemic for the sake of a ridiculous ritual demonstrated that spirituality and illness shared the common etiology of idiocy? No, Eduardo did not—would not—regret his actions toward the poor. If their carelessness outraged him, he could also say with certainty that he had served them, just as he had served this city.

What Eduardo regretted was his mistaken belief that four decades of hard work should spare his city future crises. That he could take every one of those forty-five years and stack them into a bulwark to ward off any threat that might arise in this, the twilight of his career. Before old age got the best of him the doctor had confronted any number of health crises: meningitis, HIV, and yes, tuberculosis, often. He had harangued the federal and state health systems for medicine and instruments in the flush times when those systems ran with a modicum of efficiency. And when the systems were in disarray, gutted by the reality of budget deficits and rendered impotent by the bureaucratic ineptitude that was the Brasileiro way, he could turn to men like Rui de Silva and Ximbico, profiteers who knew how to conjure truckloads of scarcities out of air. Of course, they only did so for the promise of an exorbitant payoff, but Eduardo always managed to finagle needed moneys from farm owners in whose interest it was to curb infectious diseases. In all instances the doctor who'd given his life to Enchanted Frontier attacked threats to his city with a determination born of his single-minded conviction that, medically speaking, he and he alone knew what was best for this place. It had long been tradition that when out-of-town administrators dared to enter his hospital Eduardo would pinpoint the

weaknesses of their treatment plans, identifying lapses of logic
and impracticalities. More important, the doctor knew how to
intimidate functionaries into relinquishing their authority, into
ceding their power by brandishing the saber of his will. It didn't
matter to Eduardo that behind his back those administrators
denounced him as power hungry and Napoleonic. Such men
weren't from here, and they inevitably quit in frustration or fled
back to their regional headquarters to justify their failures to
superiors needing excuses to mollify their superiors. The presence of such men was no more permanent than a footprint on
wet grass. Eduardo's presence, by contrast, was the very ground
from which that grass sprouted.

But that was then, for the campaigns had exacted their cost.
Eduardo hadn't realized it until this tubercular boy entered his
life, but bit by bit, his work had depleted the reserve of strength
that, in his pride, he had assumed inexhaustible. The current
tuberculosis program shouldn't have been any more formidable a
foe than any other governmental boondoggle that the doctor
had strong-armed and out-foxed. As they all were, it was founded on the dunderheaded notion that the poor could comprehend
the potential death growing in their throats and nostrils. That
the poor were rational. That they could be trusted. That they
wanted to be cured. And yet Eduardo had become aware that he
no longer possessed the fortitude required to dominate administrators and contain the infected.

Sitting back at his desk he scratched at the base of his neck
with an unclipped thumbnail. A spike of irritation rode across
his skin, awakening him to the different discomforts inhabiting
his body: the glut of a heavy feijoada dinner, an ache in a knee
from a weekend walk on a treadmill, the general weariness that
thinned his blood and softened his muscles. There was only one
word to adequately explain these pains: old. Eduardo could
accept the fact that at seventy he was an old man. What he
couldn't accept was the idea that forty-five years of effort could
erode a man to the point where he could no longer trust his
instincts.

It was a failure of judgment on the night of the moleque's initial diagnosis that first made Eduardo aware of his weakened
resources. The doctor had guessed at first glance that bacilli grew

unchecked in at least one of the child's lungs, perhaps both. The boy was emaciated, shivering, remote in a way that suggested malaise. Immediately Eduardo administered a Mantoux skin test, which required forty-eight hours for a reliable reading, and then a chest radiograph. He collected a saliva sample to identify the specific strain of TB. With those procedures completed he took the old woman and the boy to the isolation room, ordering them to stay until the laboratory could process the cultures he'd collected. The doctor tried to return to his rounds as if untroubled by the enormousness of what lay ahead of him, but a migraine forced a retreat to a cot he maintained in the doctors' lounge. When Eduardo felt well enough to rise again it was already dusk, and the hospital was empty except for the skeleton staff. He descended again to the basement to make sure he hadn't been dreaming. There he stood over the slumbering child, whose every breath rattled like a shaken maraca.

Some minutes later Eduardo realized he gripped something between his fists: a pillow from one of the empty beds. How easy it would be, he thought, to simply suffocate this threat. But it was too late for that. The damage was no doubt done. In no time there would be dozens more from the slum wrestling for breath in the same fashion. Some of the slum rattletraps, after all, housed as many as twenty people. The opportunity for infection was incalculable. That fact weighing his thoughts, Eduardo returned the pillow to its place on the unoccupied mattress. He made sure to remove any evidence of his temptation by smoothing out the wrinkles on the pillowcase. He decided both he and the boy deserved to rest easy that night.

It was when the doctor returned in the morning to check the moleque's vitals that he discovered the old woman had stolen him away.

From then on Eduardo found himself plagued by something that had never before ailed him: self-doubt. There wasn't a time within the seventeen days that the boy had gone missing that the doctor hadn't been haunted by the image of himself standing over that bed. He couldn't decide which was worse, to have failed to anticipate the old woman's stealing the child or to have taken hold of that pillow in the first place. In unguarded moments the brutal pragmatism behind the impulse to smother the moleque would poleax Eduardo with its full inhumanity, and he would be forced to question the legitimacy of the syllogism that for forty-five years had sanctioned his actions:

He had worked hard for his city.

The poor were part of his city.

Therefore, the doctor told himself, he had worked hard for the poor, too.

Lost in the labyrinth of his confusion, Eduardo didn't realize Lenia once again stood in his doorway.

"Doutor," she said. "Again, forgive the intrusion, but the new American has come. He says you wish to see him."

Eduardo reclined in his chair, more saddened than surprised to realize that this scheduled meeting had slipped his mind. He motioned for the nurse to send the young man in. To mark the occasion as a social event, the doctor set his open pack of Carltons at the guest edge of the desk. Custom dictated that the new American be invited á fumar, even though Eduardo knew the young man wasn't a smoker, at least not while sober. Once or twice over the past month the doctor had spotted this latest guest to his city loitering in this or that bar, brandishing a cigarette borrowed from this or that newfound friend.

"Olá, senhor," the young man said upon entering the office. He was dressed in an oversized T-shirt emblazoned with American slang, long shorts, and eccentric red tennis shoes. On his back was the blue hump of a book bag. This had been the new American's uniform since his arrival. Only two things made the visitor seem any less foreign: his skin had darkened and his português had improved.

"My friend," Eduardo responded with a formal handshake. "You finally visit. It's been all this time since your arrival and you don't come to talk with me. I was beginning to feel neglected."

A confused look clouded the American's face. Eduardo wasn't sure if it was the playful kidding or the words themselves that the young man didn't understand.

"I joke," the doctor finally assured the stranger as he pointed toward a chair. "You'll forgive us. We Brasileiros like to laugh, both at our expense and at others'." He stroked the edges of his mustache. "Now, you've brought me something of yours to read?"

"Sure," the American let slip in English. He zipped open his book bag and flipped through several notebooks before finding a pair of loose-leaf sheets of onionskin paper, which he then handed Eduardo. "I'm sorry," he continued in his own language. "I'm used to writing on a computer. I wasn't even sure I would have something typed for you, but Luis Roberto, he lent me a—como fala?"

"Maquina à escriver."

"Yes, a machine to write. That should've been obvious. I'll remember it, I promise. At home I've heard writing called a five-finger exercise, but this is the work of just two."

Eduardo held one sheet in each hand, uncertain he could muster the concentration to make his way through all the American words.

"Tell me what subject you write about. This"—the doctor said, holding up the papers—"this is about Brasil?"

"Yes." The American tried to formulate a sentence em português. "I speak with the girl, Little Conception. She tells me about her religion—Macumba. I write of it."

The news didn't please the doctor. "Perhaps it's best to leave the girl alone," he said. "She's lightheaded. It's easy for her to become lightheaded over an estrangeiro. I wouldn't wish you the problems some of our past guests have had with her. Do you understand?"

The American apparently didn't until Eduardo's expression enlightened him.

"You joke anew," the young man answered in Portuguese. And then in English: "I didn't come here for anything so simple as a girlfriend, lightheaded or not." To the doctor he now seemed defensive, almost offended. "I don't know what kind of students you've hosted before, but I'm not one of them. (And back to Portuguese) I just listen to her, that's all. And then I work."

"Naturally," Eduardo answered, and he heard himself chuckling, inwardly and inadvertently. He enjoyed the sensation because it was so unexpected. "You work, and I read. That is what our little international exchange is all about."

He laid the two sheets on the top of his desk and adjusted the lamp so the light brought out the formal texture of the paper.

The first two lines read: *Call her Iemanjá, but not in church. There priests insist you call her Mary.*

Eduardo looked up at the American. "It has a familiar ring," he said with a wink.

"She said you are always telling her that. In America, we don't call it plagiarism. We call it a tribute."

Eduardo chuckled again, out loud this time, and returned his attention to the typed lines.

Call her Iemanjá, but not in church. There priests insist you call her Mary, but in the darkness of ocean, in the spume of her salt surge, she is Iemanjá, the name the Africans knew her by long before their shackles and manacles. Call her Iemanjá each day you need her, but know she only demands you one day a year: the last day before January 1, in the last hours of the old year. She can protect you, but you must give Iemanjá what she needs. You must spread the decorative flowers atop the surf and let the water dissolve the wax candles for this ocean goddess to love.

Come around ten. Dress in white. Bring the sugarcane slush of your cachaça if it makes you more comfortable. Others will trace their signatures on the beach, will sprinkle their cherry perfumes on the skins of strangers. You will see altars erected and hear the incessant, maddening beat of the drums. Enjoy the carnival for a time—eye potential lovers, dance with your bare feet deep in the wet earth. But keep an eye on your watch. At midnight, when the moment shifts forward in its awkward, giant way, forget the fireworks, the crying, the caterwaul. Forget all and remember only that this is the moment Iemanjá wants you in her current, wants you to feel and taste and know the danger she steadies you from. Come unto her with your flowers and hopes and feel the waves grow strong. Watch your hands release your gifts, watch the water suck back the ribbons and hand mirrors and wine. Pray they aren't returned to you. If they are, Iemanjá has refused you blessing.

Only when the trinkets are on the horizon will you comprehend her gift. You will know that all identity is suspended from control. You will give in to the gurgle of the swells, and you will know it is Iemanjá who keeps the water from your lungs and from your nose. You will understand that this is the true mother's cradle, the womb of being that nurtures and disciplines all human life. You will wonder if this is what Gonzales Coelho felt that day he dropped to his knees in this water, centuries before the country had a name. He thought the bay was the mouth of a great river,

*the river of January. Is it an accident that he dropped to his knees here on
the first day of a new year, the morning after Iemanjá's voodoo blessing?*

*You will understand it doesn't matter that Iemanjá's name meant
nothing on that day in 1502. You will understand why Coelho felt pulled
upstream to that first division between prayer and slavery, death and heav-
en, daydream and freedom. You will understand that the river need not be
there to be there, that its truest headwaters are the imagination. You will
understand that we are all pulled back, against the current, from time's
commitment toward the preternatural nascence, this eternal January.*

After finishing the final sentence Eduardo cupped his chin
in a palm.

"You don't like it," the American said after a long silence.

"No, that's not true," Eduardo tried to assure him, although
his ambivalence was evident, even to himself. "Forgive me, my
English is good but not that good. Some things I may misunder-
stand at first reading."

"But still, you didn't like it."

The old doctor rubbed his temples, trying to muster a polite
smile. "It is very picturesque," he finally responded.

"That's not necessarily a compliment."

"Ah, so you want to be complimented. What you should
want, meu filho, is debate, a challenge to make you account for
your methods. But this is what I'd really be interested to know.
You speak here of imagination. What for you is the role of the
imagination?"

The American didn't hesitate. "I think imagination creates
a better reality," he said. It was the answer Eduardo expected.

"I suppose many artists would agree. And this is why the
laundress and her Macumba appeals to you. For her gods and the
everyday are indistinguishable. Iemanjá and Oxalá are as real to
her as this desk is to me. There's no distinction between the spirit and the world. And I guess you believe that as well—not, perhaps, in terms of deities and divinities or the occult, but in terms
of outlook. For you, divinity is just a matter of creativity and
ambition."

The American wasn't sure to what degree he'd been insult-
ed. "I take it you see differently."

Eduardo shrugged. "I'm a doctor. I've been trained to diagnose, not to invent, so that's why I strike you as a cynic. But do you know what the real difference is? The real implication of our differences, that is?"

"No," the younger man admitted.

"The implication is that every morning you awake you can face the day with the optimism that comes with knowing you need only come up with a better viewpoint. Whereas every day I awake, I face the knowledge of my own eventual defeat."

The American seemed to think hard for several seconds. "I don't understand you," he confessed.

"Death," the doctor said, impatiently. "In my occupation one is never not beaten by it."

Suddenly Eduardo feared he spoke with too much force.

"Let's try a different tack. You've read *The Plague*, by Camus?"

The American's eyes dropped to the tops of his tennis shoes. "Ainda não. But I want to."

"The next time you visit my home," Eduardo told him, "I will lend you a copy. I believe I have an extra. My wife will tell you that I've read it once too often. But from time to time I like to thumb through certain passages I've underlined. I would like you to read the book, with particular attention to those passages, and then I would enjoy hearing your opinion of them."

"I would like that, too. But maybe first you could tell me what you like about the book."

Eduardo reflected. "The simple answer is that it's told from the point of view of a doctor. You see, we each develop a way of looking at the world, and once we've committed to it, knowingly or not, we only seek out that which reinforces it. Little Conception, she is a spiritualist. You are a Romanticist. And I am a pragmatist. There are drawbacks to each, of course. I myself have only recently become aware of the pitfalls of the pragmatic. But we can talk about that some other time. As I say, I only read books in which there are doctors. And you being a writer, I'm sure you write only stories about writers."

A startled look crossed the American's face. It struck Eduardo as a mixture of surprise and guilt. "Funny you should say that," the young man said. "Because the other piece I brought for you to read, it's all about how this estrangeiro—well, maybe I should just let you look at it. Because I hate talking about what I write."

He rifled through the backpack again, retrieving several sheets of onionskin. Eduardo took possession of the pages, holding them flat in his palm as if his hand were a scale.

"Now the Rotary Club gets its money's worth," the doctor said with a grin. He laid the papers on his desk and then took the top one between his fingers. The first sentence went: *American music drifted toward the new American from a pair of loudspeakers that hung atop a nearby streetlight.*

As the American watched, Eduardo read the story by drawing his finger along the lines of type, sometimes smearing the ribbon ink. Two-thirds through the sheets, the old man without warning looked up at his guest, and the pair stared at each other for several seconds. The doctor seemed to have something to say, but instead of talking he scraped his tongue under his front teeth. Then he returned to the pages.

"Yes," he said some minutes later when he turned over the final one. "The Rotary Club will have gotten its money's worth from you come next August." He removed a pack of chewing gum from his desk and placed a stick behind his lips. "And I'll have to tell Luis Roberto to be more discrete when he's around you."

Then the doctor leaned forward, his eyes narrowed. "The only thing I'm left wanting is more detail about this shoeshine boy. He's a very sketchy presence to me. I'd like you to describe him a bit more. What he looked like, how he dressed, who was with him. Those sorts of things I find myself very curious about."

The request surprised the American. "What's on paper is pretty much what I remember. It was the texture of his hair that was most vivid. It was thick and rough. Uncombed."

Eduardo wiped the edges of his mustache again. "Yes, but what color was the hair? You don't ever say. Was it black, perhaps?"

"Yes, he was black-haired."

"And his skin—what color would you say it was?"

"That I know I say. He was brown."

"More precisely, please."

The American was nearly annoyed. "Café-au-lait brown."

"And nothing else? Are you sure, for instance, that he was alone? There wasn't perhaps someone with him, an older woman, maybe, whom you may have overlooked?"

"I don't remember anyone else. Do you know this boy? If there's something that would add another dimension to the story, I'd like to know it. I'd like to add it to the story."

"But why not rely on the imagination for that? No, no, that's not the question I wish to ask. My real concern is how close he came to you. And his actions—he didn't, for instance, cough?"

"No, I would've remembered that. As I say there, he stood beside me at the table. He touched my elbow. That was it."

Eduardo nodded. "Allow me to try my imagination now by proposing a simile: his breathing sounded like fingernails on an emery board. Would that be accurate?"

"Again, I don't remember. But why do I think there's something you're not telling me?"

"I'm just gauging your powers of observation. Isn't a writer supposed to be an observer?"

Before the American could answer, the doctor succumbed to a yawn.

"Forgive me," Eduardo told him. "I'm very tired. It's been a long day. I've not even dined yet. I'll probably sleep on an empty stomach. That's how tired I am." He lifted himself from his chair and made his way around the side of the desk. "I say we continue this conversation in a few days, when I've had the opportunity to rest."

The doctor patted the young man's arm, a gesture not of affection but of expedience: he was letting the American know their conversation was over and it was time for him to go. The young man stood and found himself, somewhat rudely he felt, led out the office door and into the hallway. The only additional sign of hospitality came when the men arrived at the hospital's main entry. Eduardo held the door open for his guest.

The doctor was aware he was being impolite. It embarrassed him. He thought he should apologize to the new American. He even considered thanking the young man, for Eduardo felt indebted to him. Earlier that night the weight of what had happened and what impended had the old man lamenting his age. That had been a moment of weakness, however, and it had passed. Now the doctor was certain he preferred to confront the future stooped by the years, not limber-limbed with the indemnity of youth. That he would leave to his foreign friends. But, of course, to explain such things to the American was to court further rudeness, and Eduardo prided himself on his and his city's hospitality. So by way of saying goodbye he told the young man something else instead.

"If my suspicions are correct," Eduardo said, "you'll soon have an interesting story to tell. I want you to come back in a few days so I can introduce you to its characters. The plot will unfold of its own accord. All you'll have to do is sit back and participate. And after your story is written, I will be interested to know whether the imagination for you still creates a better reality."

ALL APOLOGIES

"I only had three drinks."

He no sooner said the words than he wondered if they were truly his. For some weeks Guidry had felt a distance creeping between him and the talk that, for almost a year now since his parole, he'd been giving to any community group that would have him. In odd moments he felt as if he were a ventriloquist's dummy, his mouth made to pantomime someone else's sentiments. This particular afternoon he had a good excuse for his detachment: the cheap school-system P.A. broadcasting his speech wrenched his pitch into a high, unflattering register that didn't sound anything like him. Then there were the inhospitable acoustics of the gym. Guidry was accustomed to speaking in auditoriums and church fellowship halls, rooms with thick insulation and dimmed lights that lent an appropriate solemnity to his subject matter. But here, standing in front of a bleacher's worth of bored high-school students, his lectern set on the free-throw line so the net of a hoop dangled some feet behind his head, he felt insignificant and out of place. The sense of irrelevance made Guidry rush his opening statement; his well-rehearsed cadences skittered throughout the basketball court with all the grace of a Hail Mary shot. Despite the echo careening off the hardwood floors and tile walls, nothing in his preamble was reverberating—not for these kids, not for him.

Until that one statement. "I only had three drinks," he'd said. It stuck in his mind because it was a lie.

The night of the accident he'd actually downed a bottle of Beefeater, which was his going rate in merrier days. The cops who arrested him cracked jokes about how drunk he was. "Breathalyzer says you're hundred proof," one had said over and over. Each time the line was accented with just a little more exasperation, as if the cop couldn't believe it wasn't laugh-out-loud funny. Then there was the other officer: "I'd let you piss in the bushes, but you'd probably light them up, and we'd have to call the fire department."

It was strange because those strained attempts at humor were Guidry's only personal memories of the crash. He pretty much passed out as soon as he was handcuffed, and he learned the rest of the facts through the police reports and other discovery findings he studied with his lawyer during his trial. He'd been coached thoroughly on the details because the lawyer felt that only with a penitential command of the particulars could he earn a lesser sentence on the vehicular homicide charge. Guidry could thus recite the number of seconds the light he ran had been red, the number of inches into the intersection the car he hit had crept, the number of yards both vehicles skidded before slamming into a telephone pole. If pressed he could even reel off the number of minutes the other passenger lived before being pronounced dead: twenty-one. But Guidry was certain there was nothing about three drinks in all that documentation. He had no clue where that number came from.

Yet nobody in the bleachers caught the lie. The only visible confusion came from those wondering where the long pause that accompanied Guidry's thinking was leading.

"Three simple drinks, and look at me now," he went on. "You're probably thinking I just didn't know how to handle my liquor. Some of you probably figure you could drink me under the table and still make it home safely. But let me tell you, at that time nobody could keep a straighter face than me. If you'd met me then you'd never have guessed I was skunked—I felt so in control I didn't even believe I was drunk. So, you see, you should never try to measure your own impairment. You might think you can walk a straight line, that you can keep your nystagmus from jerking around. But then one night, like me, you'll get a rude awakening."

It was at this point in his speech that Guidry always doubled back and began his story over, this time filling in the outline of events with details that set the scene and created a sense of suspense. Earlier in his life—when he could afford to have a sense of humor about things—he'd had a talent for telling jokes, and he knew how to manipulate rhythms and pauses to enhance the drama of anything he said. Without any coaching he'd been able to ply a basic set of storytelling techniques to make his talk both engaging and affecting. He was adept at vivifying the automobile wreckage ("crumpled like an accordion"), appealing to the senses ("Burnt rubber–you wouldn't think it, but it smells a lot like burnt sugar, a horrible smell"), and forcing a certain empathy upon the audience through the use of the second person ("The first thing you'll probably do if you ever accidentally kill someone is throw up").

He wasn't using his abilities to get sympathy. If anything, the tone of his talk betrayed a certain self-loathing that was at its most evident when he summed up what it was like to live with the weight of remorse ("I wish I'd been the one to die. Trust me"). Nevertheless, the effect was usually the same: by the midpoint of his forthright admissions, his audiences would be rubbing their palms in discomfort, fidgeting in their seats. When he addressed women's groups, they dabbed their eyes with tissues or napkins to relieve the sting of his candor. Even here, facing high-school students who feted themselves on illusions of invincibility, it was beginning to work. He could see young women cup their jaws as they listened intently. Men were always more resistant, but now a few boys began to squirm, and Guidry saw them sit up stiffly and respectfully, as if called to attention. That sight alone was enough to help Guidry forget the awkwardness he felt just moments earlier as he tried to jumpstart his speech.

It was almost enough to make him forget the lie he'd told.

Depending on the group Guidry addressed, his talk ran varying lengths of time. Church congregations were the most patient, so when he stepped before a Wednesday night Bible study class, he could go for as long as forty-five minutes. Businessmen's associations were less tolerant. If he found himself the after-lunch speaker at a Rotary or Kiwanis Club meeting, Guidry did his best to be done in a half-hour. Any longer than that, and the blue-suited men would simply get up and walk out. Guidry had only spoken to one other group of teenagers, and they'd taught him that their attention span maxed out at twenty minutes. So by the time he found himself segueing into the climax of his talk, he was feeling as if he'd just begun. In many ways, though, it was a relief to reach this part of the speech because this was the point at which he could stop talking about himself. Guidry always ended his talk by telling his audiences about the person he wanted them to think of when he himself receded from their minds: the man he'd killed.

"Not a day goes by that I don't imagine where Gil Forrester would be if it weren't for what I did." That was the opening line of his ending. "He was seventy-seven years old, which is a lot of years to have lived, but it wasn't my right to say he didn't deserve more. Gil Forrester had four children and seven grandchildren. He was enjoying his pension. He had spent all his working life in the Saginaw auto plants, and he was only twelve years into retirement. He owned a trailer in Winter Park, Florida, where he and his wife would go every October to May. When he was here at home he served as a greeter at his church. Afterward, his children and their kids ate Sunday lunch with him. He spent a lot of time with those kids. He had a lot of things in his life to appreciate, and I took him away from them. Gil Forrester gave a great deal to his family and his community, and I took him away from them, too. I can say I'm sorry, but that never seems enough. I can never be sorry enough. Believe me, you don't want to have to live with never being able to be sorry enough."

And that was it: no humble thanks for the opportunity to speak, no prayer for those who might not heed the lesson he embodied. As he always did, Guidry stepped back from the lectern with a nod of the head and took a seat among a semi-circle of folding chairs. As the principal of the school leaned over to shake his hand, applause sounded from the bleachers. It wasn't the fervent kind of clapping he could elicit from a church audience, but it was good enough, especially coming from kids for whom he was nothing but a diversion on the way to football and band practice. Guidry never worried too much about how hard people applauded, anyway. He was too busy wondering if they clapped because of what he said or how well he said it.

Moments later he was in the school parking lot undoing the collar button that poked at his throat. The day was humid, so after making sure nobody was looking he wiped his forehead with the bottom wedge of his necktie. He had his car key in the driver's side lock when an unexpected voice interrupted his getaway.

"I just want you to know I don't believe for a minute that you're sorry."

When Guidry twisted around he discovered a woman staring at him from the curb. She was middle-aged and emaciated, her face sunken in a way that made her nose appear stretched into a fox-like snout. The woman looked as though she might have once been bigger but that something had come along to whittle most of her away.

"Excuse me?"

"You heard me. I said I don't think you've got a minute's regret in you."

"Do I know you?" Guidry asked with deliberate annoyance.

The woman crossed her arms over her chest. "You should. I'm one of those daughters you were talking about. Gil Forrester was my daddy."

Guidry had no way of knowing if this was true. He knew that Gil Forrester's family had attended his trial, but his lawyer instructed Guidry never to look at them, much less try to talk to them. "I'm sorry," Guidry said, automatically. It was all he knew to say.

"I've heard that from you for I don't know how long now. What does that really mean? You think you saying that gets you excused for what you did? Do you think a couple of words puts it all to rest?"

"I don't think anything." Guidry's back was up against the car door. He'd left the keys dangling from the lock, and one poked him in the spine. "I'm doing what I have to—you know that. It's part of my parole. I'm supposed to tell about the accident so others won't make the same mistake—so they won't be so careless, I mean. I . . . I don't know what you want from me."

The woman squinted hard. "What I want you can't give me. I want my father back. But that's not going to happen. So I want the next best thing. I want you to know I'm wise to you. I want you to know that every time you stand up to take a bow for coming into my life the way you have I'll be there to remind you you won't be getting off scot-free."

And with that her elbows dropped to her side and she stomped off. Guidry was afraid to move any part of himself other than his eyes; they followed the woman down the cracked pavement to a battered red truck. The woman got in the truck and roared away, leaving a hot trail of exhaust in her wake. Guidry remained pressed against the car. His ribs felt tight and he was short of breath. He was aware that he was sweating anew. When he was certain no one was looking, he took the tail of his tie and wiped his forehead again.

"She said she's going to follow you? She can't do that. I'd call the police if I were you. I think you've been threatened."

Guidry's girlfriend told him this later that night as they bathed together. The girlfriend's name was Tina. She was a romantic sort, so on the ten or so days a month when Guidry was scheduled to deliver his talk, she would fix him a nice meal and then they would retire to the tub, where she'd sit behind him in a foamy mountain of bubbles and knead the tension from his shoulders. Her massage was about the only luxury Guidry allowed himself since his release from prison.

"I can't call the police on her. Good God, I killed her father. She has a right to hate me."

He felt the hot bath water pour down his back and over his chest. Tina was rinsing him. She liked to watch the water cascade along his skin.

"She can hate you in the privacy of her own home. She can't confront you. Seriously, you need to do something. She may be so crazy with grief she'll come at you with a gun."

Guidry was shaking his head. The heat of the water brought a layer of perspiration to his temples and cheeks. Ever since the encounter with Forrester's daughter, he'd been wearing a thin film of moisture that made the day tediously uncomfortable. Even locked in the air-conditioned security of his apartment that afternoon, he'd been unable to relax because of the constant dampness that ringed his armpits and the waistband of his boxers. But bathtub sweating was different. It was relieving because it was purifying. Guidry tried to convince himself it was an appropriate form of penance.

"You want to know the crazy part?" he asked.

"Sure. Tell it to me."

"She could have nailed me today. I said something that wasn't true. I said I'd only had three drinks—that was a lie. But she didn't mention it. It went right over her head."

"You lied?" It must not have upset Tina too much because she didn't stop the rinsing. "Why would you do that?"

Guidry shrugged. "I don't know. I've talked about it for so long, I've told the story so many times that it seems just like that to me now, a story. Something that's not real. When I go to describe what happened, when I picture it in my mind, there's someone there who's supposed to be me, but I don't feel I'm that person." He craned his head around so he could face her. The tips of her hair were wet and the scented candles she lit while they undressed cast the blue shadow of a flicker across her exposed chest. "Does that make sense?"

"You've lost me on that one. But it's not like it was a big lie that you told. It's not like you stood up there and said the old man rode out in front of you. Who knows? Maybe it was a good lie. Maybe one or two of those kids will think you really did only have three drinks, and that'll scare them straight."

Guidry faced the faucet and handles at the head of the tub. He brought a handful of water to his face and became aware that, even though he'd shaved that morning, his jaw was rough and scratchy.

"I don't want to talk about it anymore," he said a second later. He pinched his nostrils to get rid of some foam that had gone up his nose. "I did it because I had to. It was the only way to get early parole. And I felt like it was the right thing. I felt I should have to be that ancient mariner guy, the one from the poem with the albatross around his neck who is condemned to go from place to place and recite his story. But now—I mean, what if that lie wasn't just a slip but some kind of rebellion I can't even admit to myself, some way of telling myself that I don't believe what comes out of my own mouth anymore? What happens when the day comes that I stand up and say I'm sorry but inside I'm not because I feel like I've done all the apologizing I can?"

Tina didn't answer for a while. When she did she asked a simple question: "How many more of these stupid speeches do you have to do, anyway?"

"I don't know. The parole officer keeps track of all that. He has to count it in community-service hours. There's some formula only he knows. It's like having a manager. I do my spiel when and where I'm told." He blew the air from his lungs with a loud sigh. "Christ, I really am in show business."

He felt Tina's arm glide around his waist as she pulled him, maternally, to her chest. "It can't be worse than picking trash up along the highway, can it? That's what I think of when I think of community service." She kissed his shoulder. "Don't worry about what's real and what's not—just close your eyes. Do it to get through it. That's my motto."

Guidry was wishing he'd taken that advice when, a half-week later as he prepared to address members of an AA chapter, he spotted Gil Forrester's daughter staring at him from the fifth row of a roomful of hardback chairs. She'd cut her hair since the afternoon at the high school. It was cropped so close to her skull that Guidry wondered if she weren't undergoing chemotherapy. He tried to ignore her but he found his eyes kept drifting back to where she sat. Whenever they locked gazes Guidry realized her expression wasn't going to change. She had fixed her face into such a tight, unrelenting scowl that her features seemed to flatten and stretch into a primitive tribal mask.

Guidry was so unsettled by the glare that he almost missed the new lie that slipped into his speech. "I was only going twenty-five when I ran the stoplight," he said.

The truth was he'd been pushing forty-five along a residential street when he'd missed the light and rammed the passenger side of Gil Forrester's Lincoln Continental. Guidry tried to compensate for the collision by swerving left, but his car was moving so fast that the only thing he succeeded in doing was to knock the Lincoln sideways into the telephone pole that killed the old man. The wrong speed could have been a simple slip of the tongue. It was easy to confuse numbers when there were so many to keep straight. Guidry not only had to remember the speed he'd been traveling, but also the length of the skid, the number of drinks he'd had, the number of minutes it had taken Gil Forrester to die. He'd done his best to memorize them all. During his trial he felt he had to master all those details. Going over the accident reports until he could recite them verbatim gave Guidry a means of displaying his remorse, if only to himself. It allowed him to square his need to admit his responsibility with the fact that he didn't want to go to jail. And then, after he *had* gone to jail, serving two years, remembering those numbers allowed him to believe that he deserved his parole.

Yet he told the audience that he was only going twenty-five. Guidry might have simply corrected himself, perhaps apologized for the mistake by chalking it up to nerves. But he didn't think of that. He'd said that number and saying it made it real, even if it wasn't true. Guidry felt he had no choice but to do what he'd done when he'd told the high-school kids he'd only had three drinks: embroider the lie.

"You wouldn't think that's fast, fast enough, at any rate, to do any damage, much less hurt anyone." Guidry's neck throbbed from twisting his head to the left half of the room. He was afraid to turn to the other side. He didn't want to see that look on Forrester's daughter's face. "But that's my point. When you're drinking and you're driving, you don't know what kind of damage you're capable of. . . ."

It was by far the worst performance he'd ever given. He never found the rhythm that gave his talk its usual disarming punch, and most of the details he so carefully described to make his meaning immediate washed away in a slur. At one point he lost track of where he was in his mental outline and he found himself too far ahead in the story; he'd skipped several important details, several dramatic moments. By the time he reached the climax he was sick of his voice—it sounded insincere, obligatory. Guidry even began to doubt the audience's interest in what he had to say. This was an AA meeting after all. What use did recovering alcoholics have for a morality tale about driving under the influence?

But that question was just a poor excuse for not confronting what really threw him off. When he finally looked to the center of the room, Guidry made sure not to focus on Forrester's daughter. She would be a blurred dot in his peripheral vision. Yet the more he talked the more he felt that blur grow bigger in his perception. He couldn't understand why, if she wanted to denounce him or berate him, she was remaining so silent and still. He realized that she was to blame for the syncopated chop of his delivery—he couldn't bring himself to commit to any cadence, any roll of the tongue, because he was anticipating when she'd interrupt him. But she never did.

When it was over Guidry did his best to slip away unobtrusively. He accepted a few perfunctory handshakes and pats on the back, nothing like the respectful and forgiving embraces typically accorded him. The AA group met in a basement room of the local community center. That meant that to steal to his car Guidry had to negotiate a long subterranean hallway. The hall was spookily empty. The only sounds he heard were voices that crept from out of the rooms where birthing classes and reading clubs met. What forced Guidry into an anxious shuffle was the fear that Forrester's daughter was hiding under every transom he passed, around every corner he turned.

But she never showed up. Guidry made it through the center's exit and then to his car without incident. Still, he felt anxious rather than relieved, and the trip back to his apartment was fueled by such urgency that he had to remind himself to slow down for yellow traffic lights and check both ways at four-way stops. When he was finally home the first thing he did was pull out the binder that held his trial transcript. He was going to make sure he didn't fudge any more facts.

By the time of his next scheduled talk he developed several surefire mnemonic devices to not confuse his figures. He was also fairly certain that Forrester's daughter wouldn't follow him to this presentation. He was speaking to a Methodist prayer circle, and prayer circles weren't open forums that just anyone could attend. His certainty seemed confirmed when he arrived at the church promptly at 6:30 A.M. to find himself greeted by a jolly minister offering a paper plate's worth of waffles and sausage. Guidry ate ravenously. The circle's members might think him rude for larding on the butter and syrup, but he couldn't help himself. All week he'd felt as if his abdomen was eating its way out of his body, and he was determined to glut its unruliness as soon as possible, even if that meant asking for a second helping.

Any satiety the gorging might have lent Guidry disappeared, however, when, barely two minutes into his introduction, the church's sanctuary door swung open and Forrester's daughter slid into a back pew. This time she leaned forward, heaping her atrophied arms on the seat in front of her, as if waiting for the cue to launch into the air, fox-like, and pounce. Guidry dropped his eyes to his shoes, pushed the hair back from his forehead. He felt the blood in his face drain away in a funnel of dizziness, and he had to clutch at the altar railing for support. He knew another lie was coming. He just didn't know when or where in his story it would happen.

So when it finally did happened, Guidry wasn't all surprised. What did shock him was how blatant this lie turned out to be.

"The man I killed," he told the prayer circle, "died instant-ly."

It wasn't true at all because Guidry knew the number of min-utes it'd taken Gil Forrester to die: twenty-one. He knew this number for a fact because that time span was recorded in the trial transcript. Also recorded there was how Guidry spent those min-utes. When the first police unit arrived on the scene—only four minutes after a nearby homeowner dialed 911—the cops found Guidry reaching into the driver's side window. He was shaking Gil Forrester's broken hand. The impact had sent Forrester's chin into the steering wheel, stoving it. Two teeth stuck in the upper arch of the wheel testified to the intensity of the crash. With blood pouring out his gums, his mandible snapped in half, Forrester couldn't begin to speak or scream. As the old man drift-ed off into shock, he was reduced to watching the drunk who'd killed him squeeze at his mashed hand as he, the drunk, kept say-ing, over and over, "Let me help you with that."

Guidry never included those details in his talk. It wasn't just that he was ashamed of what he'd done. The scene was too bizarre, too absurd. Narrating that part of the story would rob the dead man of even more dignity. In fact, when the policeman who first pulled Guidry away from the Lincoln testified at the trial, the judge had had to quiet courtroom observers. There'd been nervous laughter in the gallery when the officer described Guidry's drunken attempts to comfort Forrester.

Now Guidry felt as though he'd become his victim. Standing at the bottom step of the church altar, he found himself pushing air through his lips, his breath refusing to shape itself into a word. "I don't feel good," he mumbled after a moment of huffing. "I . . . I don't think I can talk anymore."

The minister rushed to his side to aid him to a seat, but the help came too late. By the time Guidry could relax on the cush-ioned pew, the breakfast he'd devoured lay in a pool at his feet.

To hide his embarrassment, he covered his face with his hands, but he could still hear the whispering that filled the sanctuary. As Guidry tried to wipe his soiled lips on his shirt cuff, he waited for one voice in particular to bore its way through the commotion. Yet the sound he expected never materialized. When the pastor and one of the church elders helped him up, promising to take him to a couch in an office anteroom where he could lie down, Guidry realized that Forrester's daughter had slipped away. There was nothing in the pew where she'd sat except an open hymnal.

Guidry's parole officer laughed when he heard the story.

"I'd have thought what with all the command performances you've done you'd be over the flop sweat by now," he said. The parole officer's name was Walker, but everything about him said he didn't stray too far from his chair anymore. He carried his burdens on his shoulders, which bowed from their weight, and his face was tight and pinched as if every word expected of him was an imposition. Except for the one arc of clear space where Walker rested his feet, his desktop was piled high with folders.

"I can't do it anymore," Guidry told him. He hadn't been scheduled to check in with his parole officer for another three weeks, but after the debacle at the church he'd telephoned to demand a meeting. "Don't you get it? This woman isn't going to be satisfied until I keel over. And that's not outside the realm of possibility. I don't care what I have to do to burn off these community-service hours. Give me anything. I'll swab a rest-stop toilet before I stand up and tell the story again."

Walker was leaning back in his chair, the springs groaning. His face hardened until his features grew as exaggerated as Forrester's daughter's. "Well?" Guidry finally said.

"I think you ought to quit your bitching."

"I'm telling you, that woman—"

"Do you know what a cushy deal you got? There's any number of parolees I deal with who'd dance a jig if all they had to do was deliver a talk a few times a week."

"Then let them do it! I'm telling you, I don't care what you assign me. I'll break rocks on a chain gang so long as I can keep her away from me."

Walker planted his feet on the floor as he sat up straight. "That's a no go. You've got a gift. That's pretty rare. I can't just send some inarticulate moron out to talk to these groups. The whole community-service program would be a laughingstock." He yanked a pen from his breast pocket and scratched at a doodle pad. "Here's your next show. I'm sure you'll wow them right out of their seats."

Guidry squinted at Walker's handwriting. "I can't do this— it's a damn victims' rights group!"

"Better to tell your story to them than a cell mate, don't you think?" A smile balled his cheeks into a pair of meaty lumps. He leaned back in his chair again, as if readying himself for a nap.

"It's you. You're telling her where to find me!"

"What?"

"How else could she know where I'm speaking? You're the only one who has that information! You've been setting me up."

Walker's smile faded, and a menacing tone thickened his voice. "Like I said, you should quit your bitching. If I could jerk your probation for whining, I'd do it in a minute. You really don't know how easy you've got it, do you? All you have to do is tell the story and say you're sorry. How hard is that?"

Condemned to telling his story, Guidry was intent on proving that it wasn't hard at all—and proving it as much to himself as to Walker. He was scheduled to address the victims rights group in two days, so that afternoon he sat at the secretary in Tina's guest room and wrote out his speech on a deck of index cards. By the time he was done–it took him several hours–the cards were as thick as his thumb, partly because he'd used a fat permanent marker, and partly because he made sure to include parenthetical cues to assist his delivery. It was easy to write *pause here* or *pick up pace* because he'd delivered the talk so many times its rhythm came naturally to him. The only cues he didn't spell out were the reminders to keep eye contact. In the past he'd made it a point to scan back and forth across his audience. But now there was a marginal note on every fourth or fifth card that read *Don't look up–don't!*

After he completed the cards he rehearsed his talk. This was something he'd never done before, not even for his debut performance. Guidry had been telling jokes all his life, after all, and he was at ease in front of an audience. With a minimal outline sketched in his head, he'd been able to pull together the facts and improvise a moving version of events that varied only in its length. But now he stood before the full-length mirror on the backside of Tina's guest-room door, and he read from his cards to make sure he could pass from one to another without losing his place. When he was satisfied with his new approach, he made Tina sit and listen.

"You want the truth?" she asked forty-five minutes later. It was the first time she'd ever heard his speech. Guidry had forbidden her from attending any of his performances.

"Yes—the truth."

Tina hesitated, then shrugged. "It seemed sort of stilted—stilted and remote. You need to come up for air once in a while. You've got your head buried in those 3x5s."

But as Guidry sat on the bed beside her, careful to lay his card stack on the night table, he wasn't at all disappointed by her response. "I want my head buried," he said, and to prove it, he buried it lovingly in her neck.

Given the effort that went into Guidry's rehearsals, it came as something of a letdown that Forrester's daughter was nowhere to be found when the victims rights group convened. Guidry wanted to show her that he couldn't be rattled, that he wasn't going to doubt the sincerity of his apology, even if it meant bleeding the drama from his delivery. Now, however, as he felt stood up by her, he wondered if she hadn't been a figment of his imagination. Maybe she was just the personification of his guilt, an image conjured out of conscience. Maybe she didn't show up because he didn't need her anymore. Thinking this way, Guidry was tempted to set his cards aside and return to his old manner of talking. But when he took to the lectern in the same community center where he'd met with the AA chapter, he felt too comfortable with his detachment to change his plan. He let his elbows rest on the lectern's edge so his hands were nearly level with his head, the cards obscuring his face. He scanned the crowd one last time, took a deep breath, and then plunged into his presentation.

As he read, his words meant nothing to him. They were merely a series of staccato consonants and airy vowels. Even the intonation he prided himself on was gone. Instead, he spoke in a rote drone. His voice was so monotone that within a short time he felt as if he sang himself a lullaby. Barely a third of the way into his talk, he was overcome by a pleasant sense of inoculation. Guidry liked the sensation because it made him feel removed from the moment.

When he finished he realized his audience shared that feeling. His concluding words were greeted with a brief, noncommittal round of applause. Most of the faces in the crowd were blank and remote. Guidry didn't care. As soon as the meeting adjourned, he stuffed his cards into his suit pocket and headed toward the parking lot.

"You're him then?"

Guidry had stopped at a lobby faucet for a quick drink. He was stooped over, his tongue licking at the shooting stream of water, when a gaunt man with a seed cap in one fist approached him.

"Excuse me?" Guidry straightened immediately, embarrassed to be caught with his tongue stuck so far out of his mouth.

"You're him, I gather," the man said once more. "I'm Marion's husband."

"Who?"

"Marion Gamble's husband. But maybe you didn't know that name. Her maiden name was Forrester. Her daddy—"

The name cracked something solid inside Guidry.

"What do you people want from me?" he demanded. His throat was hot with sudden indignity. "I can't apologize any more. Are you ever going to let me move on with my life?"

The man's eyes dropped to the floor. "I just thought you needed to know that Marion won't be bothering you no more. I knew what she was up to, following you around and such, and I didn't agree with it, not in the least." He finally looked up. "She had her a stroke this Tuesday last. The doc thinks she'll make it, but if she does it'll be a while before she's up and about."

Guidry slumped against the brick wall. "I'm sorry." Then a fear took hold of him, and before he thought better of it, his mouth was open. "You don't blame me for that, do you? I mean, I didn't know."

Gamble's mouth stiffened, and for the first time his diffidence evaporated. "I don't blame nobody for nothing. I don't see much use in holding to a grudge. I used to tell Marion that all the time, you know. But losing her daddy in the way she did, she couldn't get over it. I tried to tell her that bothering you wasn't going to get her what she wanted, but she wasn't one to listen to others' opinions."

He stopped for a second, occupied in thought.

"I 'spect her not being able to move on counts some for what's happened to her. As you can probably tell, mine's country people, and we used to have a saying. We used to say that having a stroke was like having a snake in you that's trying to lengthen out. That's what a stroke feels like, I mean. Well, I think Marion's snake got hold of her and took to stretching out something awful." He set the seed cap on the back of his head and with a short tug pulled the brim to his eyebrows. "I best go. Like I said, I just come to tell you that she won't be bothering you no more."

Gamble didn't wait for a goodbye. He crossed the lobby in a slow shuffle and pushed open the community center door so a thick light flooded the entryway. Guidry wiped a droplet of water from his chin. Then he went into a nearby restroom and combed his hair. As he tucked his comb into his pocket he felt his deck of index cards. He brought the 3x5s into the open air, bending them back and forth in his fingers as if preparing to shuffle a hand of poker. Before he realized what he'd done, he sent the cards flipping through the air, and the bathroom filled with a confetti shower. Guidry told himself that the cards no longer mattered. With Forrester's daughter incapacitated he had nothing to fear anymore, and he could deliver his talk the way he'd done for nearly a year now.

Seconds later, however, Guidry was on his hands and knees groping for the spilt bits. This business of being sorry, of displaying remorse—it was all too tricky, and if Guidry knew nothing else, he knew that he didn't want to be guilty of trickery. If he was going to have to spend another year or possibly two apologizing, he was going to do it in a way that to him was honest. He wouldn't care anymore if he didn't move audiences. He was going to stick to the facts recorded on his cards. That way, nobody could accuse him of lying or being insincere, least of all himself. With that thought in mind, he went about collating his 3x5s as quickly as he could, lest someone enter the bathroom and discover him on his hands and knees, dragging himself across a slick floor that soiled his palms and pant legs.

THE STORY
BEHIND THE
STORY
(Teenage Symphonies to God)

She settles deep in a cushioned chair in front of a video editing bay and watches as words slide sideways across a bank of monitors:

FAME SUCCESS GLORY FORTUNE PASSION
HEARTBREAK

Meanwhile, thanks to the stiff intonation of an accompanying voice-over, a buzz hums through the speakers that hang from the console corners:

"She was the pop princess whose cotton-candy anthems were a call to fun for a nation of disaffected teens. . . . A whirligig of adolescent enthusiasm whose bubble-gum hymns are the soundtrack to a lost age of innocence. . . . But then a sex scandal and a public break with the Svengali manager responsible for her ingénue image dethroned the reigning Queen of Teen. . . . Exiled from the music business, she was cast adrift on a sea of drink and drugs. . . . Until she found the strength to slay her personal demons and discover happiness in the family she never had. . . . Tonight on——, the story behind the story of Bethany Bardot. . . ."

She calls herself Beth now that she's thirty-three and a mother. One of her children, an infant with the antique name of Geneva, lies bundled on her lap. Her older daughter, the one who insists on being called Tori because Victoria sounds excessively old to five-year-old ears, pouts in a nearby chair, angry that

she must spend a good playground morning in this air-conditioned nightmare of an office. Because Beth is older, she no
longer resembles the face multiplied on the many screens staring
her down. That face is young and sweetly vacant as it lip-synchs
Valentine's Day verses about eternal love and devotion. This
one, the one that's hers now, is rounder and thickened by maternity pounds she can't seem to lose. The hair is different, too.
Since she married a few years back she's kept it short and its natural color—sandpaper taupe—even though, she realizes, the cut
is almost masculine compared to the mound of curls she once
sported. I looked a lot like a poodle back then, she tells herself.

But her thoughts are interrupted by the writer of the documentary about herself she's been invited to preview.

"The best thing about our show is that we oblige you to be
Aristotelian," he says. The writer is stick thin with an ostrich
neck and one of those insufferably intellectual goatees that are
trimmed to the width of a pencil stroke. With him sits the show's
director, a woman. She wears a cowl-neck sweater that's broad as
a bundt pan and color-coordinated to match her tortoise-shell
frames. For the entire five minutes the five of them have been
gathered in this room, the director has tweaked knob after knob
on the bay's control board, to no discernible effect.

Meanwhile, the writer continues:

"A life story isn't merely a life, you see. It's a story, and it
needs a plot. What's the most compelling kind of plot? Aristotle
says that it's the fall of flawed hero"—The director shoots him a
look—"or heroine, excuse me. Call it hamartia, call it hubris,
this fatal flaw is the essence of the human condition. It's one's
fate, one's kismet, the string along which the bead of existence
slides, inexorably, so you can't escape it. Now, how do you make
that fate dramatic? Well, you need a structure, and the best kind
of dramatic structure comes from that old standby, the Freytagian
pyramid, named in honor—no duh—of Gustav Freytag, the aes-
thetician who made a science out of the art of plot pacing. As
Freytag taught us, apropos of Aristotle, you must start off with a
conflict, build into rising action, ride it to the emotional climax,
and then descend with falling action. After that comes the
dénouement, whose promise of resolution enables our faith in
such principles as the probability and unity of events."

Because Beth's never heard of Freytag and knows nothing of Aristotle except his name, she pays little attention. But that doesn't bother the writer.

"If you don't tell your story according to these age-proven principles of dramatic tragedy, there's no momentum—and then what do you have? You've got an A&E *Biography*, that's what you have. Or one of those *Headliners and Legends* installments on MSNBC. Have you ever sat through one of those things? We're talking the basic-cable equivalent of a résumé. When you tell the story of a celebrity's life, it's got to add up to more than a mere sequence of occurrences. It's got to have the three C's—complication, crisis, closure. Otherwise, it's a flat line, and what's it mean if you flatline? It means you've died, that's what."

No one speaks for a moment, transfixed by the swirling visuals of the documentary's opening credits. Then the screens fade out and back in, immediately, revealing a lithesome seventeen-year-old in a cropped top and strategically torn jeans.

"Mommy, is that really you?" Tori asks. The teenager onscreen bounds in and out of camera range, squatting, kicking and bouncing, thrusting her hips and snapping her fingers, all the while training her eyes straight ahead so the viewer feels showered in the warmth of an attentive, teasing gaze.

"Is that me?" Beth answers, stalling. She's not sure how to respond. "I guess so. I mean, it was me. It's the me I used to be."

ACT ONE
(AGON, OR THE CONFLICT)

The voice-over resumes narrating:

"The music is a passport to a world of simple summer froth. It's a place where the ocean water's always warm and marshmallows are ripe for roasting. Where sunny days are made for milkshakes and volleyball games and frolicking with friends. It's the world of the teenager, and a little more than a decade and a half ago, no one made it more appealing than Bethany Bardot."

Onscreen the girl is now joined by a phalanx of teenagers. These kids clearly aren't pros, for their dancing is arrhythmic and out of synch. Even more obvious are the faces. They're a motley assortment. Some are acne-spackled, others are marred by bulbous noses, mongoloid eyes, double chins. One or two in the crowd smile to reveal the prison stripes of their corrective dental work. The girl at the center of attention works overtime to put her peers at ease, to loosen them up. She swishes from one to another, high-fiving girls while planting kisses on the cheeks of the boys. Still, the teenagers can't quite forgo their embarrassment.

"You look funny," Tori declares.

The writer and director laugh because it's true: the faked singing, the thigh-rubbing choreography, the lightly glistening swatches of skin that peek between rips in the singer's costume—they all add up to a spectacle that's undeniably, irredeemably, silly. As is the chorus of Bethany Bardot's signature song, which now pumps through the sound system. "Summer of Boys and Fun" it was called, and the words (Beth hasn't thought of them in years; she never plays her old music) return to her without the hard effort of trying to remember them, as if part of a long-forgotten catechism:

> *Take me to the beach*
> *And put me in the sun*
> *'Cause summer's here and the time's right*
> *For having boys and fun. . . .*

The part about "having boys" was just Lolita enough to create controversy. Church groups denounced Bethany Bardot for advocating premarital relations. Feminists adopted her as an icon of women's sexual empowerment. Meanwhile, her target market raced to the big retail chains.

"Five Number One hits," the voice-over announces. "Two multi-platinum CDs . . . hundreds of sold-out concerts . . . all in the dizzily short span of two years. . . . By her eighteenth birthday, Bethany Bardot had everything a teenage girl dreams of. . . . [Upbeat music fades; enter stark orchestration] And by twenty, she'd lost it all. . . ."

The shiny, happy faces disappear from the monitors, replaced by a series of blurry, black-and-white photos, all tinged in a nostalgic sepia tone. There's agitated Bethany waving a threatening fist at paparazzi; harried Bethany in dark sunglasses, a scarf shrouding her head. Broken-down Bethany on the lawn of a mental-health hospital, captured by a long-distance telephoto lens after the overdose death of her lover. Then there's a montage of tabloid headlines, the typefaces thick and dripping in exclamation points. The sort of style, Beth thinks, that should be reserved for weighty declarations like *War's Over!*, not *Bethany's Dark Secret, Revealed!* Thinking of what lies ahead in the show, Beth wonders if she shouldn't send Tori to another room.

On the screen,

CUT TO: HER, NOW: She looks tired, which she was, for the interview was taped just days after Geneva's birth. From her chair Beth watches herself saying, "I just sang about the stuff kids really like to do—roller skating, slumber parties, hanging out. The idea was to write a song for every teenage pastime so kids had an anthem for everything they did. A lot of people put me down, you know. (Pause). A lot of people. Like, if you're happy and you know it (wizened smile) you're an idiot."

Back to the voice-over: "To understand the Bethany Bardot phenomenon, you have to flashback more than a decade to a time of double-digit inflation, high unemployment, and entrenched public cynicism. Music was dominated by embittered, guitar-wielding college bands who raged about anger, uncertainty, anarchy. . . ."

CUT TO: A glib rock critic wearing John Lennon glasses. A long unlit cigarette slants from his hollowed face, which gleams with the cadaverous pallor of Keith Richards, circa 1975. Trimming the critic's chin as well is a goatee, apparently on loan from the writer. Soft red gels in the upper corners of the picture frame create an atmosphere of ponderous self-importance.

"What was the biggest hit before the Bethany era?" he asks. " 'I Don't Deserve to Live' by Fetal Position, that's what. You can't drop a bummer like that on the kids without begging for a backlash. The teenyboppers were tired of being down, that simple.

They wanted to escape, to feel good, to have some fun. Who can blame them? (Smug pause). You just wish it hadn't been mindless fun, you know?"

CUT TO: A pudgy, balding man in nylon running suit, his jacket zipper lowered to reveal a thick gold chain stranded among briary thatches of gray chest hair. A chyron in the lower left-hand corner of the screen identifies him as TYSON "TYC" DUMAS, FORMER MANAGER. Pronounced *tike*, Beth recalls, not *tick*. Short for Tycoon. Because that's what he always called himself. The Tycoon of Teen.

"I have a theory about adolescents," Tyc says. "When you work in the teen market, you're dealing with basic Velveeta emotions—I love you, I want you, you hurt me, I hurt you back. Pure cheese. Even so, that doesn't mean you can't aspire to high cheese. High cheese is what Brian Wilson used to call 'teenage symphonies to God.' Songs simple in sentiment, but grandiose, even operatic in production and delivery. Think the Beach Boys' 'Don't Worry, Baby,' Kim Wilde's 'Kids in America,' even 'Mmm Bop' by those cute Hanson sisters. But cheese alone is wimpy— witness Paul Anka in the days of 'Puppy Love' and 'Put Your Head on My Shoulder,' anything by the DeFranco Family featuring Tony DeFranco, Debby Boone and 'You Light Up My Life.' I would argue that your average one-hit wonder falls into obscurity precisely because his cheese lacks fiber. Where's that fiber come from? From hard candy, my friend. You need some sophisticated gloss, and gloss for kids means sex, simple enough. Nothing smutty—I'm talking wholesome sex. Straight-from-the-cow, three-glasses-a-day, bone-building sex.

"Bellybuttons, for instance. I take credit, you know, for making the midriff the accessory that no female between twelve and twenty leaves home unexposed. Bosoms are no good, though— they're dirty. They bring dirty things to mind. What I decided when I invented Bethany was that I'd dress her in a tight, collared T because a V-neck leads to décolletage, and plunging décolletage plunges you nowhere but into the dirty lowdown. (Wrinkles eyebrows, takes a deep breath) Those are the issues I had to grapple with, mind you. Everyone thinks being the puppet master is easy. But it's not—not at all. Being the idolmaker's much harder than being the idol."

The writer turns to the director. "I'm glad you left that monologue intact because it says it all. What he's just given us, in a nutshell, is the essence of the classic foil. Not an antagonist or enemy, but more like what used to be called the alazon, the fool whose buffoonery exaggerates the hero's fatal flaw to a comic extreme.

"It's good because the alazon is a vital staple of tragedy, including rock 'n' roll tragedy. Colonel Tom, who was he but Polonius in the Elvis production of *Hamlet*? And Suge Knight, wasn't he just Leporello to your average gangsta rapper's Don Giovanni? As supporting a player as the alazon is, though, he's vital to the coming crisis, for he's the one who proves the inadvertent agent of the hero's downfall. Something the alazon does brings on the nemesis."

The writer twists in his seat to address Beth. "I know you're probably thinking of nemesis as meaning villain, but that's a common misperception. Nemesis isn't actually a person but an action. It's what has to happen to restore the order of things. You see, a hero's most compelling attribute is his flaw, but that flaw's also a threat to the natural balance. The hero must fall, otherwise it's an offense to nature's way. We may wish it weren't so, but we want to see it happen because we know it's necessary. So a comic foil initiating that crisis is like a spoonful of sugar—it makes the inevitable go down easier."

It's at this moment that Geneva chooses to let out a conspicuous poot. The outburst explodes from under the folds of the swaddling blanket with a volcanic rumble that's entirely out of proportion to the child's size. The writer's lips curl downward until his goatee gathers around the edges of his mouth like iron filings drawn to a magnet. For a second he seems confused, as if he's not sure whether this indecorous interruption was meant as an editorial comment.

But Beth's too busy thinking of Tyc to take notice. He wasn't any of those things the writer said. She always felt sorry for him, in fact, because he was strictly a wannabe. Couldn't sing, couldn't dance, couldn't tell an octave from an octagon. Beth's glad she didn't tell the camera crew about the pre-show ritual in which Tyc would burrow his index finger deep in her navel to ensure that her diaphragm was tight. Or the night she headlined the Rock in Rio festival, when he suffered a nervous collapse after learning that a vengeful sound crew had broadcast his profane backstage rant over the stadium P.A., much to the shock of a hundred thousand pre-adolescent concertgoers. Later that night, curled on the couch in Bethany's hotel suite, Tyc cried himself to sleep claiming all he'd ever wanted out of life was unconditional love.

"Fasten your seatbelts," the writer announces, swiveling his chair back toward the monitors. "Here comes the rising action."

CUT TO: A montage of baby pictures and family photographs. Bethany, an only child, framed in an eerie halo of Kodachrome. Several snapshots feature a box-jawed father and his teenage bride, in addition to a Bible, which in every single image is displayed as if it were a second child.

"The Bethany Bardot story begins in an unlikely place—tiny Fairlane, Missouri, population 723," the voice-over says. (FADE TO: Shots of deserted streets, abandoned cars in front yards, paint-peeled facades). "A hotbed of Pentecostal fervor. . . ."

CUT TO: BETH: "My father was a minister, you see. I grew up spending hours praying, studying the Bible, speaking in tongues. I think that's how I decided I wanted to be an entertainer. Because speaking in tongues, if you do it long enough, really is a form of show business. Closer to vaudeville than pop music, maybe, but still, it's a performance—no kidding. I'm not saying it's dishonest, but you're definitely aware that you're putting on a show. Think about it: isn't channeling God's word just another type of lip-synching?"

CUT TO: HER FATHER. Beth's shocked. She hasn't heard from him in years, and the producers didn't tell her they located him. She's aware that the writer and director are stealing glances her way to gauge her reaction. She won't give them the satisfaction. Instead she focuses on the man's face, the face of her father. He looks older than he should. He'd only be fifty-five or fifty-six, she thinks. But here he is, white-haired, bespectacled, his body gaunt except for an incongruous wattle that ripples under his chin. Identified onscreen as PASTOR ROY BARTON, EVAN-GELIST, he flips open a copy of the Good Book before address-ing the camera.

"I raised my daughter to strengthen the vine, not to flop her toddies like a Babylonian strumpet. I suppose you'll be making fun of me for my beliefs, but the Bible's on my side: *The thoughts of the righteous are just; the counsels of the wicked are treacherous.* Now you chose wicked counsel, that's your business. The Lord made you free as a welfare dollar to put your lips to the Devil's tailpipe should you please. Just let me say this, though: I knew that girl had it in her to be good at singing. I'd heard God's voice in her voice all those years, after all. And in our own way we were stars. Sure. We'd get to a church to do some preaching and people would line up a dozen deep to get their pictures taken with us. If she'd stayed with me, we could've ended up a great father-daugh-ter duet. Just like those country singers—what was their names? The Cantons? Calhouns? No—the Kendalls, that was them. I always liked them. I always liked 'Heaven's Just a Sin Away,' too, despite the raunch implied by the title."

CUT TO: BETH'S MOTHER. Now Beth's beyond shocked. She remembers her mother only from photographs—a child her-self with a Dorothy Hamill hairdo and snaggletooth. Yet this woman's skin is so etched with age lines that her face could pass for a tick-tack-toe board.

"Let me just say loud and clear that I didn't abandon her," Beth's mother tells the camera. "I just couldn't stand her father. Really, the man thought he himself was called back from the dead, fresh unwrapped from a Turin shroud. The orders he gave—I had to keep my arms covered so no skin showed. (Shakes head) He would've killed me if I'd stayed. I wanted to take her, of course, but the man who promised to save me from Roy—well, in all sincerity, he wasn't much for kids. Turns out he wasn't all that different from Roy himself, but least he didn't pre-tend to be a holy roller."

CUT TO: HER FATHER: "The woman wasn't no good. She would've unlocked her legs for a one-eyed dwarf if one had asked.

There was no way she was taking my baby. I just did what any right-thinking man would've done."

MOTHER: "He stole her."

FATHER: "I saved her."

"There was a time"—the writer is telling the director— "when our idea of celebrity wouldn't accommodate this sort of storyline. Have you ever seen kinescopes of *This is Your Life?* Every voice from the past was one that contributed to the star's climb to fame. Eddie Cantor's high-school football coach taught him perseverance. Stan Laurel's grandmother encouraged his comedic inclinations. You know the wildest one? Frances Farmer. They actually brought on the doctor who did the lobotomy. It's such a bizarre sight, Franny sitting there thanking the man profusely for severing her frontal lobes, for discombobulating her so she might function in the real world. I'm telling you, Ralph Edwards must have had the balls of a mastodon to even try to pull that one off.

"And yet it works. You know why? Because stardom back then was all fate and forward motion. There was no such thing as undertow. But we don't find destiny credible anymore. Fame today's all about surviving and rising above, about making it in spite of obstacles. Can you name me one celebrity who hasn't had to transcend to triumph? That star doesn't exist in anybody's firmament."

Meanwhile, the voice-over continues: "In this cauldron of family dysfunction and Pentecostal repression, little Bethany daydreamed of life as a normal teenager. She fantasized about slumber parties, stuffed animals, and school dances. But the Rev. Roy had other plans. . . ."

FATHER: "We were on the road—I suppose it was four or five years. We'd travel from church to church, me preaching, her testifying. I reckon it was a good life. I kept her fed and she got her beauty sleep come nightfall. We stayed mostly at churches in west Missouri and east Kansas, sleeping in pews."

CUT TO: BETH, NOW: "We always slept on opposite sides of those sanctuaries. He had bad insomnia, you see, and something as simple as my turning over, my inhaling even, would drive him nuts. Once in a while I'd wake up and he'd be stooped over me going, 'Too loud! Too loud!' I remember the one time he actually sprang for a hotel room. I hadn't dozed off but ten minutes and he was shaking me: 'You're breathing! You're breathing!' Not snoring, mind you, but breathing. So he fixes me a pallet in the bathtub. I slept there with my big toe stuck up the spigot."

Onscreen, yet another montage: Bethany with microphone, one palm forward, eyes as big as rocks. And then: worshipers writhing on a wooden floor, tongues blooming out of their mouths. Beth winces. This is a part of her life she's managed to forget, a memory that's too amorphous to belong to her. But it's no good. She glances at Tori and recognizes Bethany Bardot's features among the girl's. And not just the features, but the expressions. Tori's eyes are big as rocks, too.

"Here I would have preferred a reenactment," the director declares. "They get to do those over at the E! *True Hollywood Story*, you know. The great thing is that the actors never look a bit like the people they're portraying. That's why they keep half the faces out of frame. Have you ever noticed that? They shoot those reenactments from the jaw line down. That's E!'s signature charm— they're pure cheese and proud of it. But the brass here won't let us stage simulations, so we're stuck with montage. It's unfortunate, because photographs, even in collage style, are flat and not at all symbolic. Too representational. With a reenactment, though, there's something almost . . . I don't know . . . metaphorical about it. That's the difference between the two forms. One's a still life, static, but the other's theatrical and therefore kinetic. It's got life. I'm telling you, a reenactment's pure kabuki."

VOICE-OVER: "As fate would have it, Bethany's salvation from this itinerant life came in the form of the very music that her own bubble-gum style would eventually replace. . . ."

CUT TO: HER FATHER: "The son of a bitch stole her from me, pure and simple. He stole my little girl."

CUT TO: TYC (grinning)**:** "I saved her. I did. Me, the idol-maker."
(Fade out).

ACT TWO
(SPARAGMOS, OR THE COMPLICATION)

VOICE-OVER: The future Bethany Bardot was a mere six-teen years old when a chance encounter at a Texaco station in Shawnee Hills, Missouri, changed her life. That was when she met the man who would light the fuse on her rocket ride to star-dom."

CUT TO: TYC: "I was road managing a series of navel-gaz-ers on the Midwest college-town circuit. Just the most dreadful of bands with the most puerile of names. We're talking Lubricated Gerbil, Cans of Piss, Pussyfinger. I ask you: in what parallel universe could you ever imagine Shadow Stevens or Rick Dees saying, 'Now, climbing two spaces on this week's chart, with our No. 6 hit, it's–*Pussyfinger'*?

"But these were trust-fund punks, you see. Half the lead singers were Ivy League dropouts. They could afford to be anar-chists. As they'd tell you until their jaws locked up, they weren't interested in making it big. Somehow I doubt today they find obscurity so fulfilling. I imagine them all sitting in offices some-where, daydreaming of a call from VH-1's *Where Are They Now?* when they should be writing software. But back then they took their cues from Fetal Position, who, of course, rode that anti-star bullshit right to the Hollywood Walk of Fame. Believe me, any kid who tells you he wants to be a musician and not a star is yanking your sack hairs. Nobody—and I do mean nobody—doesn't want to be a star."

The director is shaking her head.

"It's a shame we're going to have to bleep out portions of that," she says, to no one in particular. "Standards and Practices dictates that *pussy* can only be said on air if the shot contains an actual kitten. In other words, our freedom of speech continues to hide behind the skirt tails of double entendre. Personally, I long for the day when we can speak as real people speak, in bawdy Whitmanianisms in other words, without the false veneer of decency. I count it as a highlight of my career that I was present the first time *asshole* was ever said on basic cable. Before that we were bound to cheap and insincere synonyms: *a-hole*, *b-hole*, *pie hole*. It goes without saying that not a single one of them possesses the brute gravitas of *asshole*."

But Beth isn't listening. She's watching herself, back on the screen:

"Whenever my dad stopped for a leak at a gas station, I'd punch the seek button on the radio. You know, no matter where you are in America, there's always a hard rock station at 95.1 FM. That can be a very comforting thing. I was into the heavy stuff, you see, a huge Fetal Position fan. 'I Don't Deserve to Live'—that was how I felt. So I'm rocking out at the Texaco one day when there's a tap at the window. It's him, Tyc. Swear to God, he was the first person other than my dad I'd talked to in four years. So I roll the window down, and instead of hi or hello, he tells me to repeat whatever he says, to the letter. I'm thinking this is a practical joke, a *Candid Camera* deal, but then he goes, 'You're my little lovin' lollipop.' It sounded like the stupidest line on earth, but I did it. I told him he was my little lovin' lollipop."

CUT TO: TYC: "Sure, alliteration's a big part of the cheese. Think the Ronettes and 'Be My Baby.' Think Terry Jacks and 'Seasons in the Sun' or even 'Maggie May' by Rod Stewart. It has to be done with some restraint, of course. Little Jimmy Osmond's 'Long Haired Lover from Liverpool'—that one was way over the top, even for me. But there's no denying that alliteration is the hook and, in some instances, the line and sinker as well. It's writ deep in the very name of the genre: rock 'n' roll. Okay, so we were pop, not rock 'n' roll, but who cares? (Reflective pause, followed by nodding head) No, I would never actually make my girl

sing 'little lovin' lollipop.' It's far too 'Sugar, Sugar.' There's a reason the Archies were a cartoon, you know."

CUT TO: BETH: "I can't say why I agreed to go with him. I'd
kill any kid of mine that pulled such a stunt. But I guess I figured
nothing could be worse than sleeping in pews the rest of my life."

CUT TO: TYC: "I only had to hear that one phrase, to feel it
coming from her mouth (the tip of her tongue taking a trip of
three steps down the palate to tap at her teeth) to know, right then
and there, that the time had come to ditch the no-talents.

"The band I was shepherding around that day, for instance.
They had a name guaranteed to make a prepubescent feel as clever
as Noel Coward: Anal Saxon. I kept their gear stowed in a U-haul
I lugged behind my van. I just unhitched the U, and it was pure
Huckleberry Finn. Bethany and I lit out for the territory.
(Wistfully) Those were great times, just me and her and miles of
American highway. I knew a little spitshine was all she needed to
be a big hit. I just didn't know how fast she'd hit big. By the time
we got to L.A. she was famous. We didn't realize it, of course, but
the road out of that Texaco station was the road to stardom—literally."

CUT TO: FATHER: "I just come out of the john one day and,
wham bam, she's gone. First I think her mamma's come and got
her, but then I see these long-haired stringbeans loitering around,
claiming *they* been stranded. Let me tell you, it didn't take long to
tune the picture in. I had no choice but to go after them. God had
a plan for her, after all, and it didn't involve poking her babymak-
er in the world's face."

CUT TO: BETH: "All in all Tyc and I were nine months on
the road. We traveled from karaoke competition to karaoke competition. That was my education. At first he just chose what songs
I sang. But then he started shaping what he called my 'presence.'
That meant telling me how to hold the microphone, how to work
my hips, how many feet apart I should plant my legs.

"In the beginning I was terrified. Then I realized just how bad
the other contestants were. Frankly, when you're competing

against a Greek chorus of drunken frat rats doing 'A Country Boy Can Survive' it's hard *not* to win a karaoke jackpot. In-between gigs, while driving, he would teach me. He had a books-on-tape copy of *The Rolling Stone Illustrated History of Rock & Roll* that we went over and over until the cassette frayed. 'Bobbie Gentry good,' he'd say. 'Jeannie C. Riley bad.' I had no clue what he was talking about."

CUT TO: TYC: "Somebody had to teach her the difference between bubble *gum* and bubble *dumb*. She was so naive, taste-wise. She'd flip through a songbook and go, 'Dig this! Sheena Easton!' And I'm not talking *Come slip inside my sugar walls*, either. I'm talking (with perky finger naps), *My baby takes the morning train / He works from nine to five and then*—Jesus Christ! I'd have to grab the mike right out of her hand. I explained to her that hard candy requires at least a modicum of girl grit. 'Pat Benatar good,' I'd tell her. 'Laura Branigan bad.' One number I made her do over and over was Joan Jett: *Do you wanna touch? / Do you wanna touch?* (Sitting forward, he sings with clenched fist) *Do you wanna touch me there? Where? There!* Well, you can imagine how the yea-bobs in the bars took to that. 'Hell yes, I'd like to touch!' they'd scream back. (Nostalgic smile) That was the moment I knew she could coax the rowdy out of the crowd-y."

CUT TO: FATHER: "It's no easy thing being on somebody's tail when you got no clue where they're resting their feet. I must have pulled into every grease trap and tourist spittoon on I-70 West. I even kept count: 342 different piss joints and juke holes to be exact.

"It may've taken me some time, but I caught on that he was taunting me. His handwriting was a dead giveaway. I started seeing it everywhere I looked: in guest registers and on bulletin boards, on credit-card receipts that I fished out of trash bins piled high with ravioli, baked beans, fried eggs. I found out he was leaving me little coded messages in toilet stalls, smack dab in the middle of the dirty limericks and chicken-scratch peckers. He's got the penmanship of a seventh-grade girl—that's how I figured out it was him.

"That and the names. He assumed all manner of aliases that was his way of sticking it to me. One place I'd find him signing off as 'Buzz "Ted" Cherry, Bethany, Pa.' and not a mile down the road it'd be 'Hymen Bunstead, Southern Trespass, Al.' And then there were names I just didn't get: Victoria Darkbloom, that one turned up a lot, as did Humbert Haze and Clarence Quilty. Never have figured those out. But I sure understood his favorite: 'Mike Hunt, Minor Delight, Ne.' Now I know 'Mike Hunt.' I been in the army, see. Still, you can't imagine what kind of obscene things went floating through my nightmares when that 'Minor Delight' business showed itself."

CUT TO: BETH: "I didn't realize it, but I basically traded one controlling father for another. That's what Tyc became for me, a second father, but one whose authority I never thought to question because, well, he was fun. For God's sake, he'd take me shopping and actually enjoy it—more than me. We wouldn't get two feet into T.J. Maxx and he'd have an armful of miniskirts and Ts for me to try on. He was really into studded belts and knee-high boots. By the time we got to Denver I couldn't wear a pair of earrings without his approval. He'd always justify it by saying I was just acting out the image that he created.

"Like I said, I was too young to stand up for myself. But there were any number of little ways that I rebelled. For example, he'd give me twenty bucks and drop me off at Blockbuster to pick up The Bangles' *Greatest Hits*, but I'd come back with *Bricks Are Heavy* by L7. It absolutely drove him nuts that I liked Fetal Position. For a while I had a good fanzine stash, but he rifled my luggage and tossed them out. As punishment, he'd make me read aloud the chapter on Bob B. Soxx and the Blue Jeans in this book about girl groups he was always quoting."

This entire time the writer's been nodding.

"It's a telling remark," he says. "Not that last part about Bob B. Soxx, of course, but earlier, the thing about trading one father for another. It works well on many levels. Aesthetically, it's important because it's always better when the protagonist can articulate her own conflicts. That way, the drama's more organic. Believe it or not, some of the people we profile aren't the most self-aware or insightful, so we have to hammer home the plot points by dubbing in exposition, which can feel heavy-handed. Thematically what you say is good, too, for you're underscoring the basic object of your quest, which is the nurturing security of a stable home life.

"But what I most like here is the subtle structural commentary. Any viewer out there who made a C in Intro to Psych is going to hear that quote and go, 'Aha! I see where this is headed! It's just the same chapter in the Freudian book of the family romance, that old storyline, the father complex!' (Slightly annoyed) Everybody disses Freud for being reductive, you know, but the essence of his genius was to acknowledge that there are only so many storylines out there. More important than what you do, he said, is the compulsiveness with which you do it—or the compulsiveness with which you try not to do it. Either way, it's the very repetitiveness of an act that's key to decoding character.

"So I ask you: what's repetition but a pattern of behavior? And what is a pattern but a structure, the building block of form? Sure, Freud went a little waist-deep with the sex talk, but at the end of the day you've got to give him props. He understood just what Aristotle understood: 'All life is / is a search for form.' "

The writer peers toward the director, expecting validation for these insights, but she's too busy fixing a sloppy edit to offer much more than a perfunctory nod of agreement. When he subsequently looks back toward Beth for a response, all she knows to do is lift her eyebrows and smile. It takes the return of the voice-over to save her from his glare:

"It was during this time, as the self-proclaimed Tycoon of Teen groomed his future star, that inspiration led to yet another important stage in the blossoming legend of Bethany Bardot."

CUT TO: TYC: "All along I knew that the name had to go. There's not a hundred-watt station in the Dakota hinterlands that'll add you to its playlist if you're named Barton. I mean— c'mon! That's a name more apt to show up on a backwoods jug of hootch than on KROQ. So we weren't past Kansas City before I started toying with potential names.

"I had two criteria. Whatever it was, it had to be alliterative, for reasons already explained, and it had to be allusive—I wanted it to appear as if she'd sprung, pedigreed, right out the womb of pop-culture history. So I was thinking Bethany Brando or Bethany Bond. Then I thought maybe something more exotic and foreign was called for, and I came up with Bethany Beaucoup, Bethany Adieu, Bethany Bijou. And then suddenly those two strains came together: Bardot. Brigitte Bardot's an icon, and she's about as French a honey as you're apt to find. What's more, it sounded close to Barton, but it didn't sound hick, you know?"

CUT TO: BETH: "The new name? (Shrugs) Water off a duck's back. I never felt much connection to the old one, so severing myself from it wasn't an issue. I mean, I've met people whose entire sense of identity is rooted in their name. They're Rockefellers and Kennedys and Dylans and Jaggers—aristocracy, in other words. But when you're trying to kick your background to the background, an assumed name's no biggie. Really. Tyc could have called me Ringo or Ozzy and it wouldn't have made a difference. I was just ready to be somebody else. I didn't care who."

VOICE-OVER: "With a newly fashioned style and persona, Bethany Bardot and her manager found themselves lacking only one important element key to success. . . ."

CUT TO: TYC: "Material. We didn't have any. You can't very well record an album of covers learned on the karaoke circuit and expect to go multi-platinum. Just ask Leif Garrett. To break a new star you've got to have the song. What are those clichés rock critics always use to describe a classic? Infectious. Ineffable. A song that just insinuates itself in your mind and makes you feel as though you're getting an aural hummer.

"Now I knew we could sell the image, but we needed the song. Fortunately, I had an ace up my sleeve. My first job in the biz was as a piano tech for the band Tricky Alice. Tricky Alice is perhaps best remembered for its outrageous lead singer, who wore his leather pants so tight he was thought to be the only man in the entertainment industry with camel toes. Seriously! That guy's inseam was mesmerizing; he had a cleft chin for a crotch. That said,

Tricky Alice did enjoy a No. 2 smash with 'Dixie Itch.' It would've gone to No. 1 if it weren't for that travesty known as 'Hot Child in the City,' by the never-to-be-heard-from-again Nick Gilder. Working for Tricky Alice, I got to be pretty good friends with their keyboardist, mainly because I sent him the groupies too ugly for the singer. Throughout many tours, in fact, I was his designated trim coordinator. He'd landed pretty far afield from the music scene after Tricky Alice broke up, so I figured he'd be hungry for a new op. I knew if anybody could write to order, it'd be him."

CUT TO: A bald, bespectacled man sitting on a stool, one elbow tossed casually onto the keys of a sparkling grand piano. With his green cardigan and red turtleneck, he appears to be posing for a Christmas photograph, even though his interview was filmed just after Memorial Day. As the man speaks, a lonely strand of hair, barely visible, floats back and forth over his head, as if timed to the beat of a slow-moving metronome.

TUNESMITH: "No doubt many of my contemporaries wouldn't have taken kindly to receiving a request for the 'ultimate teen-summer pop song' accompanied by a 14-point checklist of criteria. But I looked upon it as a challenge. You see, after Tricky Alice, I did some doctoral work, which was when I was first acquainted with the oeuvre of the composer Terry Riley. Much of Riley's canon is a prolonged experiment in pastiche, which means he compiles familiar motifs and strains of musical styles to create a self-consciously sonic hodgepodge. The thought came to me: could one write a summer teen anthem utilizing the same approach, creating a song whose melody and lyric not only recalled but encapsulated the whole past of pop history, from 'There Goes My Baby' to Mungo Jerry's 'In the Summertime' to 'Wannabe'? That was the basic idea behind 'Summer of Boys and Fun.' "

The man twists sideways, away from the camera, and stretches his fingers across a width of keys. It takes Beth several measures to recognize the song she sang hundreds of times. The pulsing dance rhythm has slowed to a leisurely trot, and the chord progressions are clogged with unnecessary notes that seem more rococo than rock 'n' roll. Even worse is the singing; the songwriter lets loose with several trills that are unbearably pompous. The rendition reminds Beth of how rock bands will try to legitimate their music by commissioning philharmonic orchestras to perform symphonic versions of hit songs.

CUT TO: TYC: "It took hearing two seconds of his demo to know it was going to be a unit-shifter. It just smelled platinum."

CUT TO: BETH: "I can't say I thought it was all that great a song, but Tyc was in the driver's seat, so I just did what I was told. We didn't even re-record it. I just dubbed my voice over his on the demo. That's what the record is: one guy poking a synthesizer, and me. That's it. Hard to believe something so simple was ever so popular."

CUT TO: TYC: "I FedExed a copy to Juvenescence Records in L.A., and we cut a deal the next afternoon. Two months later, Bethany was No. 1, just like I'd told her she'd be. (Throwing up hands) What can I say? It was that easy. The hardest part was filling out the FedEx form. We didn't have a return address, after all. We were still living out of my van."

CUT TO: BETHANY: "It was fast, definitely. And as events would prove, it turned out to be too fast. It was like getting caught in a tidal wave. First it threw me up, and then it threw me down. What I guess I didn't realize is how fast it would throw me down. Or, for that matter, how far."

(Fade out.)

ACT THREE
(PATHOS, OR THE CATASTROPHE)

VOICE-OVER: "Under her manager's guidance, Bethany Bardot signed a contract with Juvenescence Records in April of

19–. By July 4th of that year, her debut single, 'Summer of Boys and Fun,' had topped the charts. But Bethany soon discovered that a sudden rise to fame can be as terrifying as it is exhilarating. . . ."

CUT TO: BETH: "When that song took off a funny thing happened. All of a sudden everybody, interviewers and execs alike, wanted to know where I saw myself going. It wasn't enough for them to give congratulations or say 'great job.' It was all 'What's next?' and 'Can you do it again? Can you top yourself?' I didn't understand that line of questioning for a long time. But then I got it. You see, nobody understands you when you're present tense. You only make sense from a retrospective point of view, when your story has a distinct beginning, middle, and end. When you get right down to it there are only two things people want to know about you: where to find the peak, where to find the plateau."

CUT TO: A jowly, unctuous man in a mauve suit and cherry-red tie whose hair is only a tad less oily than his skin. He sits at an immaculately organized desk in a deco-styled office. Behind him is a wall's worth of framed photos, their contents barely recognizable against the glare of the camera lights. There's one of this man shaking hands with Aretha Franklin; another of him kissing Stevie Nicks's cheek while giving Tom Petty a friendly slap to the back as Sheryl Crow smiles fetchingly to the side; even one of him giving a thumbs-up to an uncharacteristically uncapped Chuck D. It would take someone familiar with the history of Juvenescence Records, whose founder and C.E.O. this man is, to realize that not a single photo includes an artist signed to his roster.

The C.E.O. says, "As cutthroat as it might sound, our business strategy is founded upon the recognition that pop music is the quintessential expression of planned obsolescence. Or, if you prefer, natural selection. History has shown that most performers in this field, whether you belong to the Poppy or Partridge Family, whether you're a Cowsill or a Spice Girl, will follow the same career trajectory. There's a debut album that goes multiplatinum; a follow-up that does somewhere in the vicinity of forty percent of its predecessor's business (and thus, invariably, becomes known as the 'sophomore slump'); and finally, a third album, which we call 'The Bid' because it's a bid for critical acceptance—which is to say, it's an effort to secure at least a toe-hold on longevity by persuading reviewers you have something substantial to say. The Bid always proves the biggest failure of all, sometimes selling as little as one-tenth of the debut. But that's okay, because when you understand the trajectory, you as a businessman know how to hedge your investment, and you can pry at least a tiny return out of that last gasp by holding back on promotion.

"Now if you're lucky, you can come back anywhere from a year to ten years after The Bid with a greatest-hits package—a very low investment, I might add—which will ride a mild wave of nostalgia to produce additional revenue. But not everybody gets a *Greatest Hits*. Ever heard of *Steam's Greatest Hits*? Of course not! Most people couldn't even tell you it was Steam who sang 'Na Na Hey Hey Tell Him Goodbye.' But never fear. For those cases, we issue compilations that allow us to corral together our one-hit wonders. K-Tel put out oodles of popular compilations, as did Ronco, as do we at Juvenescence. Ours goes by the mildly clever title *You Hated 'Em Then, You Love 'Em Now*, which is a recognition that, whatever disdain consumers might foster for the pop hits of their youth, those hits when heard years later will elicit a certain . . . ironic adoration. That's because they're so—what's a good scientific word?—well, cheesy. We're currently on Vol. 8 in the series, and every one has done at least 250,000 units. So you see, there's no teen pop that can't be repackaged. You've just got to invent the right package."

CUT TO: TYC: "My strategy for breaking Bethany was a two-stepper. Step One: confound. Step Two: confuse. If one thing gets the opinion outlets going it's a star who is contradictory. The press can't stomach entertainers with more than one dimension to their personalities. Stars like that are too hard to understand, and who wants to waste a life wondering whether George Michael is brainier or Kenny Rogers sexier than they get credit for? Because the media will strive to reduce you to a single facet of an image, you're obliged to defy expectation, right on into perpetuity.

"That God stuff Bethany was always talking, for instance. In the beginning when it was just the two of us, that was all the hay she could make: God this, God that. It was annoying because, frankly, I was familiar with that word only in the adjectival form, as in *goddamn traffic, goddamn Kansas state troopers*. But then it hit me: what if we have a girl, one who's not quite a woman but is nevertheless dolled up to look like a rode-hard trollop, articulate her fiercely held religious convictions? A female star who teases both brain and prick? Why, it's not only odd, it's upsetting. And I therefore knew the press would flock to it like flies flock to shit. (Awkward pause) Not that Bethany was shit—not by any means."

CUT TO: BETH: "All I did was talk about what was important to me. I mean, I was—I am—religious. A Christian. There, I said it! And I don't apologize for it either. I said what I felt, which was that I believe in God. And all people could say back was, 'Oh, Please! Look at yourself! What a load! You can't be for real!' "

CUT TO: TYC: "We had another mindbender up our sleeves, too, one that had to do with that first video. Our song was all over the radio, see, but we didn't have a single frame of footage. Now the suits at the record company wanted a big production number with dancers, but I didn't trust the director they brought in. I'd seen his work. His idea of a teenager was a stripper shellacked in Estee Lauder to hide the stretch marks. My thought was that if critics were going to dismiss Bethany as a phony, why not stick something so unabashedly real under their noses that they couldn't help but feel the foundations of their reality undermined?

"So I took what little money I could scrounge up, and we made our own video. We rented a Howard Johnson's ballroom and installed a white backdrop. The kids in the supporting cast were actual kids; we brought them in straight from an eighth-grade dance and told them to be their own adorable selves. It was very guerrilla. The whole thing cost $600, not including the Dr.

Pepper and pretzels. As pretentious as it sounds, we did inaugurate a wave of do-it-yourself anti-videos. Six months later every alternative band in America was shooting itself in amateur style in a display of (with a roll of the eyes) credibility. But did we ever get credit for the cinema-verité vogue? Of course not! Godard could've cast Bethany Bardot in *Pierrot Le Fou* and still nobody would've taken her seriously."

CUT TO: BETH: "What is authenticity, anyway? There wasn't an actor within twenty miles of that video, and still, we were slammed as fakes. It'd take me an hour to recite all the synonyms of that insult the press employed: contrived, insincere, phony. 'Manufactured' popped up so often alongside my name that I thought it was my name—or part of it, anyway. The all-time worst, though, had to be when I was described as an 'integrity succubus.' You just knew that some writer somewhere had burned half a cerebellum's worth of synapses working up that killer-clever put down. Well, I hope he enjoyed the aneurysm. See, what I didn't grasp then is that when people speak of authentic or real, they're just talking fantasy—their fantasy. It's their fantasy of the perfect world that'd exist if everyone just had the good sense to share their good taste."

CUT TO: TYC: "Not only did we not have a video, we didn't have a CD per se. We had to commission more songs. That wasn't the problem that it might sound like, however. For one thing, I was intent on putting out a short CD. That's the downside of CD technology: you can fit eighty minutes worth of music on one, so artists feel compelled to come up with the aural equivalent of *The Brothers Karamazov*. You know my favorite record as a kid? *Meet the Beatles*. Twenty-nine minutes and out. (Droll smile) As my ex-wives will attest, that's always been my motto."

CUT TO: TUNESMITH: 'Summer of Boys and Fun' confirmed for me that I had indeed tapped a vein that was both creative and commercial. I thus set out to write eleven different songs, each of which would evoke an endless labyrinth of recognizable motifs and riffs from other songs—sort of a 'garden of forking paths' of musical notation.

"Take Bethany Bardot's second No. 1 single, 'The Hole in My Heart, The Heart in Your Hand.' Although I wrote it, I continue to find it one of the most profound ballads I've ever had the pleasure to hear. Part of the hook is the title. There's a little-appreciated genre in pop that I like to call the 'comma song.' I'm talking Tina Turner's 'River Deep, Mountain High,' Neil Diamond's 'I Am, I Said,' The Hollies' 'He Ain't Heavy, He's My Brother.' What makes those songs intriguing is the mysterious connection between the two parts of their titles. Such titles make use of an obscure grammatical device, parataxis, which is when the coordinating conjunction between phrases or clauses is deleted. Notice it's not 'River Deep *and* Mountain High,' or 'He Ain't Heavy *but* He's My Brother.'

"As a result of that missing conjunction, the relationship between the two terms is ambiguous, and ambiguity creates suspense. It's as though the song says to you (extending one palm), 'Look, I've got a hole in my heart. Meanwhile (extending the other) you've got a heart in your hand.' And the audience asks itself, 'How do those two facts jibe?' Of course, we can probably guess that there's some cause-and-effect relation, but we need the song to explain it. (Dropping hands to knees) I really do believe that parataxis played a large part in that song staying at No. 1 for fourteen straight weeks."

"I was tempted," the director says, "to cut that monologue. It reminds me too much of another documentary series we tried to launch a few years back. The idea was to trace the making of classic rock albums. We'd sit a musician down in front of a 64-track mixer and let them peel back the various sonic layers to talk about the instrumentation that goes into a great song. Unfortunately, there's just not a wide audience out there curious about the inspiration behind *Aqualung*'s flute solos or how Prince came up with the drum sound on 'When Doves Cry.' "

The writer nods in agreement: "I remember it well. It was a ratings debacle. We only made the corporation's investment back when we sold the unaired episodes to PBS. They give them away now during spring pledge drives. The sad truth, like the tune says, is, that: *It's the singer not the song / That makes the music move along.* Even here."

He turns to Beth. "You see, we must live with the reality that our viewership grows in inverse proportion to the musical value of our subjects. The fundamental law for us is that an hour on Donny Osmond will do better numbers than one on Dylan. Why? we used to ask ourselves. Why would the Carpenters generate more interest than the Clash? Why might New Kids on the Block out-rate Nirvana?"

The writer looks back to the monitors. "The reality is that while audiences might have loved what Kurt Cobain had to say, nobody wants to watch him die all over again. It's too painful. And yet everybody wants to know how nutted up that guy in Whitesnake was after the redheaded chick from the videos dumped him. That story's entertaining precisely because nobody's all that invested in it. I'm not knocking Whitesnake. I love a little 'Here I Go Again' as much as the next guy. But there's a big difference between the effect of that story and the one that arises from, say, the story of Lennon and Shakur getting murdered, or the death of Bob Marley. So we were truly baffled by our viewers' interests. Until, that is, we went back to the source. Back to Aristotle.

"You see, it's all about the catharsis. Aristotle's big question was, 'What's the purpose of tragic art? What's it supposed to do to us?' And the answer was simple: it should arouse our pity and fear. That's what he meant by that word *catharsis*. But to do that not only takes a certain plot but a certain type of protagonist, one that's neither too virtuous nor villainous but someone, rather, who's just like us. Just your average Joe who gets caught up in the throes of unmerited misfortune because of a frailty that the audience recognizes its susceptibility to.

"Now you take your average pop music star. He or she's usually someone who's nominally talented but who suddenly ascends to great heights of renown due to a fluke of a few hit songs. The unexpected change of fortune inevitably puffs the ego, and—this is the key—tempts the star into believing, 'I'm not disposable. I'm for the ages!' That right there is the frailty: we all want to believe we're gods, and we must live with the fact that we're probably not. We know how easily being a star would go to our head, how tempted we'd be to believe we were at least special if not immortal. And we're also aware of how hard it would be, in the aftermath, to live life as a has-been.

"That's the appeal, right there, of our show and shows like ours. We're a mirror of humility that lets the audience punish its tendency to vanity and self-importance, albeit vicariously. Sorry, Frankie Lymon, Buddy Knox, Bobby Vee, Johnny Preston, Gene Chandler, Bruce Channel, Bruce Hornsby, Blue Suede—you thought you were hot shit, but you weren't. Same to you, Paul and Paula, Dale and Grace, Santo and Johnny, Peaches and Herb, Joey Dee and the Starliters, Freddie and the Dreamers, Wayne Fontana and the Mindbenders, Bo Donaldson and the Heywoods, Jimmy Gilmer and the Fireballs. What's that, Richard Marx, Mary MacGregor, Eddie Money, Mr. Mister, Mike + the Mechanics, Hamilton, Joe Frank, and Reynolds, Kyu Sakamoto, Timmy T, Taste of Honey, Nino Tempo and April Stevens, Club Noveau, Klymaxx, Stevie B, C+C Music Factory, MFSB and the Three Degrees, EMF, SWV? You thought you had it made? Well, *foo you* for presuming.

"Yes, our condolences to Van McCoy, the McCoys, George McRae, Alan O'Day, Gilbert O'Sullivan, Paper Lace, Rhythm Heritage, Helen Reddy, Rose Royce, Leo Sayer, Seals & Crofts, Silk, Silver Convention, Will to Power, and the entire Williams family—Denise, Maurice, Roger, Vanessa, and Freedom, plus about one million others. It's time to humble up, Humble Pie. Too bad you were just human. But hey, at least you can rest assured that whoever's watching at home couldn't have handled fame any better. We, too, would've ended up drugged out, destitute, and venereally diseased.

"So that's why we tend to focus more on the cheese than the canapé. The audience identifies with cheese, but canapé is intimidating." He suddenly looks at Beth. "I hope you take it as a compliment when I say that we expect your episode to pull in some of our best ratings yet."

Before Beth can respond, however, there's a flash on the screen, and the picture cuts to Tyc, who's saying, "Once you've got the song on the radio, the video on cable, and the CD in the racks, it's time to tour. Now I had a strategy for that, too, which has since become the template for teen-pop success: I started Bethany performing in suburban shopping malls.

"Laugh if you like, but there's two things in malls that were integral to our success—teenagers and record stores. You should have seen the faces on the suits the first time I informed them that their newest star was booked to play the food court in the Twin Oakes Galleria in South Glendale. But I put her on a stage in between a Chick-Fil-A and a Moo-Goo-Gai-Pan Emporium, and there wasn't a Doubting Thomas in sight twenty minutes later when three hundred kids turned tail and headed straight to Sam Goody. (Smarmily flippant) Let me tell you, there was more elbow room in a Dachau boxcar than in that Sam Goody."

CUT TO: BETH: "I wasn't allowed to sing live. I don't know why—it was me on the CD, swear to God. But because I was lip-synching—I didn't even have a band up there with me—all these rumors started that my voice wasn't my voice. I wanted to take guitar lessons and do a number or two acoustically, just to disprove the naysayers. But Tyc said nobody cared whether it was true or not. He told me that there's no such thing as bad public-ity."

CUT TO: TYC: "Correction. What I said was the only pub-licity that could do us bad would revolve around her . . . how should I put this? . . . maidenhead. Because we kept putting it out there that . . . um . . . no farmer had yet been to the dell. It was a masterstroke on my part because all the talk about her chasti-ty inflamed both sides and left no room for ambivalence. We got the Puritans up in arms about her being too suggestive while the Bacchants soiled themselves dismissing her as contrived jailbait. Let me tell you, nothing's more entertaining than getting the blowhards to blow hard on something they don't know blow about. That was why I kept telling her, 'Whatever you do, don't let a canary in that coal mine!' Because I knew the minute that the Chevy made it to the levee, we could pack up and go home, plain and simple. And, as it turned out (Throws up hands) how right was I?"

CUT TO: A montage of the salad days. Here is grainy footage of a sweat-drenched Bethany Bardot prancing across stage in a white mini-skirt and tube top; Bethany rushing off-stage to collapse in the arms of handlers who wrap her, Tutankhamen-like, in towels; Bethany autographing CDs and record-store flats for excited fans, every one of whom is outfitted with a Bethany-inspired hair-do and Bethany-inspired wardrobe. An occasional sound bite from a wound-up adolescent testifies to how deeply invested those kids were in Bethany Bardot, at least for the two years she was popular. "Oh my gosh, oh my gosh," says one girl from beneath an explosion of permed curls. "She's just like so real and awesome. I mean, she's just so cool."

Some of the clips include the homemade placards the kids once made to wave at her tour bus as it roared by: *Bethany, We Love You! Bethany, U R 2 Cool! Bethany, Look at Me, Please!* Meanwhile, in the background, one can hear yet another Bethany Bardot hit, "I'm Throwing a Party (Be There, Be Squared)," whose staccato chorus goes something like this: *By gosh By gorry By jigger gee / I'm throwing a party / By golly By gall By gad By gum / I want you to come.* As the singer's trebled voice wails out these words, a parquetry of backup vocals chime in in agreement: *Be there*, they sing in aching stacks of digitally processed four-part harmony. *Or be squared.*

That song was never one of Beth's favorites. Even then she thought the message a little threadbare. She only agreed to sing it because back then she did what she was told.

As Beth watches random scenes from that part of her life unspool, she's aware of how disconnected from the past she's become. But it's not just the past—it's the present, too. For near-ly forty minutes now she's sat through this documentary feeling what she assumes is the chagrined amusement that seizes people when they leaf through old yearbooks. Beth never attended high school, of course, so she owns no yearbooks, but a few months ago she accompanied her husband to his twentieth class reunion, where she found herself envying his friends' casual disregard for their adolescence. Conjuring up forgotten names and trading antiquated gossip, they were able to laugh at the irrelevance of it all because the intervening years assured them that in the overall scheme of things, being a teenager had amounted to a big fat nothing. Youth had been just a sliver of time whose importance had long ago been overshadowed by the adult milestones of career, marriage, and kids.

And then one of the group brought up a varsity basketball star primed from childhood to expect collegiate and maybe even professional success, neither of which he'd managed to achieve.

"That guy," the friend had said, "peaked at eighteen."

It was a common putdown. You heard it about different people all the time. Yet Beth had been struck by how her husband stiffened and shot her a pleading look that said *Don't take that personally*. Beth hadn't taken it personally at all. She never thought of herself as having peaked young. But she was aware—and has always been aware—that that phrase can be found in any number of history books and pop magazines and on web sites galore, where it's used for one simple end: to dismiss her life.

It's a judgment that if she dwells on it too hard inevitably pisses her off, for the very idea that life can only shove forward toward a single climactic height ignores the mellower, more comforting rhythms that have come to constitute her days. As she's grown older, Beth's never asked herself where her life's headed or what stage of growth she may have reached. Instead, it's been the repetition that's been most gratifying. She likes the security that riding the circle's arch of a habit gives her. She likes knowing that 2 P.M. is gym time, that Wednesday's grocery day, that dental checkups come in February and August.

The more years her life coils around these routines, the more time itself begins to seem drugged, immobilized. So much so that Beth no longer experiences it as a straight line, a forced march through the hours. Time to her, rather, is a lazy Sunday nap that blends morning into afternoon. Is it really that hard to imagine, she wonders, that she doesn't dwell on the past, that she hasn't once regretted turning thirty, that she never resents seasons for passing? That, indeed, she looks forward to waking up next to her husband one middle-aged morning to realize that, despite the evaporating decades, the past and present aren't separated by anything thicker than the bed sheet that pools in the few spots where their bodies don't touch?

But now, watching a show that's supposedly a record of her life, she feels bound to a chain of events that's almost boorish in the way that it yanks itself forward. She shouldn't feel this uncomfortable, she thinks. Tori has dozed off, and Geneva is suckling contentedly at her mother's left nipple, so who is Beth worried about embarrassing?

Still, despite the indifference she tries to feign, she can't help but feel unsettled. Maybe it's because she's thinking about all the bits and pieces that aren't anywhere to be found in this documentary. Bits and pieces that have been left out, she realizes, because they don't advance the plot. If this were the true story of her life, it would have to acknowledge the things she learned during those years. It would have to list the books she read on the tour bus, the first books other than the Bible she'd ever read. Isn't it relevant to the person she's become that, to this day, she's a voracious reader who belongs to not one but two book clubs? And what about the museums she visited on the off-days, the ones that inspired the interest in art history that led her to enroll in the college-extension course that taught her words like *tromp l'oeil*, impressionism, and synthetic cubism? Aren't those things important?

But maybe most meaningful of all were the people she met. She never thought of them as fans, mainly because she could never stomach the sweeping disregard for individuality that pop stars betray when they speak of audiences en masse. It was fun to meet kids who liked her music, not because she was flattered by the way they gushed about her influence, but because it gave Beth an opportunity to imagine what a normal life might be like. The enthusiasm with which she'd ask about their pastimes would shock those teenagers; there were times that Beth knew she was coming off like a police investigator, she was so eager. Even this late in the game she remembers names: Alicia Jensen from Clear Point, Minnesota; Kelly Cone from Rushton, Indiana; Donna Hamburg from South Centerville, Tennessee. She told the interviewer about how she saved those letters. They were stuffed in an attic trunk, waiting for the day when her daughters were old enough to appreciate them. It would be Beth's way of saying to Tori and Geneva, "Look, whatever you're thinking, whatever you're feeling about being a teenager, it's nothing new and you're not alone."

Those were the words she'd always wanted to hear at any rate.

What had she learned by being Bethany Bardot? Simple enough: that there were things in the world more important than she was. More important than her ability to make money, her ability to get songs added in different radio formats and markets, her ability to hold her own on a list of the most intriguing celebrities of a certain year. It dawns on her now, though, that the things she described to the filmmakers, the things that went unused—might they have marked her need to shape a story that was maybe hers but was never hers to tell?

VOICE-OVER: "Despite Bethany Bardot's meteoric rise, signs on the horizon already hinted at the precipitous fall to come."

CUT TO: FATHER: "Well, by the 342nd time I found myself asking a salad-bar manager or busboy if he'd seen my daughter, I up and fell apart. It was in the lobby of a La Quinta Inn in Balderdash, New Mexico, and I went a little crazy after the night clerk told me to get lost when I asked if he'd ever heard of 'Mike Hunt.' For nothing more than putting my fist through a window, they carted me away to the nut barn. But I'm thankful, because it turned out to be a peaceful existence. Coffee in the morning, hot chocolate at night.

"And then one morning I'm sitting in the rec room nibbling my oatmeal when she shows up on the TV screen in nothing more than her birthday stitches. It drove me crazy. The camera kept zooming right up her skirt. I knew I couldn't stay and just enjoy my breakfast. I had to find her."

CUT TO: TYC: "That son of a bitch put the ooky in kooky. I had a private investigator keeping tabs full-time on him, so I knew he was coming our way even before he did. I couldn't very well have the old bastard turning up, now could I? We'd put it out there she was an orphan. I'd told *Rolling Stone* that I'd plucked her out of a state ward's home in Chillicothe."

CUT TO: FATHER: "Oh, sure, they had muscleheads galore to rough me up. But the beatings weren't ever more than what a lifetime could give me. Pretty soon I got smart enough to avoid the bodyguards. That's what getting waylaid in a laundry closet will do to you—make you smart. I realized that if I couldn't get at her, I could get to her, if you know what I mean."

CUT TO: BETH: "He started showing up in the audience, a paying customer. I'd be in the middle of a song and I'd look over to Section 232, Row M, and there he'd be, grim-faced and disapproving. But that wasn't half as bad as the signs he started waving around."

CUT TO: A still photograph of Rev. Roy amid a vast throng of teenagers, presumably gathered for a concert. Like many of the young women, he holds a placard. Theirs read *We Love You; You Rock; Rock On*. His reads *Bethany, Come Home or Go to Hell*.

CUT TO: BETH: "It was so embarrassing. I didn't understand why he wouldn't just let me be. I'd made it clear to him through my lawyers that I wanted nothing to do with him. That part of my life was over and done, forever. But then he went to the press, or the press went to him, I think, and it was all anyone could talk about. As a result, *Entertainment Tonight* ran a five-part series on child stars who hate their parents. Me and Gary Coleman, what company! And for the life of me, I'll never understand why *Vanity Fair* felt the need to devote 10,000 words to unraveling the story. This was back in the day, mind you, when the favorite adjective at *Vanity Fair* was 'Brobdingnagian.' Suddenly, I wasn't just a fake—I was a fake of Brobdingnagian proportions!"

VOICE-OVER: "Compounding Bethany's problems were creative battles over her sophomore effort, which was entitled—despite her objections—*Bethany Loves You*."

CUT TO: BETH: "No if's, and's, or but's, that second album sucked. I hated the songs. They were beyond childish. They were cynical, belligerent even, in their silliness. I tried to tell the execs that sixteen-year-olds weren't that frivolous, that they deserved to have their feelings taken seriously. What was their answer? 'Screw the sixteen-year-olds. The eleven-year-olds will lap it up.'

"You see, they had charts and pie graphs showing that more eleven-year-olds bought my first CD than any other age group. So I had no say in the matter. I just bit my lip and did my thing. And what happens? The first single sparks a lawsuit. I got in big trouble with the execs because in the deposition I said the writer probably spent more time defending that stupid song than composing it."

CUT TO: TUNESMITH (defensively): "You must understand my intentions. At the time I was intrigued with compressed modes of storytelling, ancient, classical forms such as the epigram, the haiku, the ghazal, the koan. And I asked myself: could the essence of adolescence be distilled into a few syllables so no extraneous word weighed down the rhythm? Could I produce a song that wasn't just a representation of teen life but was its embodiment, both in form and content? Honestly, that was the inspiration behind 'Gimme! Gimme! Gimme!' So you can understand why, to me, the lawsuit was frivolous."

Once again, he turns to his keyboard to begin an elaborate rendition of what should be a simple song. By the second verse the melody is so entangled in vocal frippery that Beth has a hard time making out the words: *Gimme gimme gimme your lu-huh-huv / Gimme gimme gimme that stu-huh-huff / Cause I just don't think I can get enu-uh-uh-huff.*

CUT TO: TYC (with a sigh): "I heard the first chord and I was singing *Yummy yummy yummy / I got love in my tummy.* I mean, it is the same tune—but so what? Everybody in pop cops their licks. It's tradition."

CUT TO: The ruddy skinned sexagenarian who nearly forty years earlier composed "Yummy Yummy Yummy." He's proud of the fact that he's lived off the royalties ever since. He's saying, "I knew we were headed for a big settlement the minute that girl's manager tried to brownnose me outside the deposition. He comes up and comes on, you know, telling me how much he loved my band, how he dug the album titles, *Skin Tight*, *Honey*, *Fire*. Then he gets onto the gatefold sleeves. 'How'd you get all those hot Nubian chicks to pose naked dipped in honey and jam?' he asks me. (With a shake of the head) I hated to break it to him that I was in the Ohio *Express*, not the Ohio *Players*."

CUT TO: BETH: "I'd never heard of the song or the band. How could people accuse me of ripping them off? The only thing that came to mind when I heard the melody was that old jingle—you know, *Libby's Libby's Libby's / on the label label label*. If somebody had a legitimate case for suing, it was the fruit company."

VOICE-OVER: "Family conflicts and legal problems were nothing, however, compared to what Bethany Bardot would confront when she met the man credited with derailing her career."

CUT TO: A clip of Fetal Position performing a feral rendition of its most famous song, "I Don't Deserve to Live." The singer in the center of the frame sports a shaved head and shaggy Van Dyke. The lead guitarist to his left also wears a Van Dyke, but his head is covered by a swooping, stiffened cowlick. Like the guitarist, the bass player is long haired but, unlike him, is clean-shaven. Meanwhile, the drummer, who's apparently still uncertain about his place among the other three, is so nondescript he could pass for a cell-phone salesman. The band chainsaws its way into the chorus, which goes *I don't deserve to live* (grunt!) / *I don't deserve to live* (grunt!) / *Got nothing to give* (ugh!) / *So I don't deserve to live*.

CUT TO: BETH: "Dick Clark introduced us. It was backstage at the American Music Awards. 'Bethany,' he said, 'this is Monk Spit, the brains behind Fetal Position.' It was strange because Dick was acting very formal and stately, as if he were introducing Gorbachev to Reagan at some arms summit.

"Of course, the moment was awkward, because it was rumored that Fetal Position had recorded a song attacking me.

That's a big alt-rock tradition, you know. All boho boys write songs about the private parts of mainstream girls they hope to humiliate. Mojo Nixon did it with 'Stuffin' Martha's Muffin,' which was about that MTV VJ. And years later Primus had a ditty called 'Winona's Big Brown Beaver,' although it was never determined whether it referred to Winona Ryder or Wynonna Judd. So the first thing I said to him was, 'If you're such a rebel, why are the ways in which you rebel entirely predictable? And if you're so punk, why does every single song of yours go *verse chorus verse chorus middle eight guitar solo chorus chorus fade?*'

"I think Monk was taken aback because nobody had the audacity to say these things to him. Certainly not somebody who was supposed to be the fakest thing this side of government cheese. After that night he refused to release the song, which created quite a rift in the band. To this day it's only available on Japanese bootlegs. He understood that nine-tenths of what he was doing wasn't provocative or thought provoking, just juvenile, and he was struggling to find some way to make punk intelligent without appearing pretentious.

"People don't want to believe this, but alt-rock is every bit as formulaic as teen pop. It's got its own set of rules, and they're just as prescriptive as those Tyc kept me to. For example, Monk recorded a cover of that old Bobby Vinton song 'Mr. Lonely.' You know (singing) *lonely . . . I'm Mr. Lonely.* . . . Fetal Position's management wouldn't let him put it out, though. They said it was 'insufficiently ironic.' So I'm sure he was attracted to Bethany Bardot in part because he knew it would tick off a lot of people. I was his *foo you* to the people boxing him in. Because our getting together really was the most rebellious thing he could do."

CUT TO: ROCK CRITIC (fingering his Lennon specs): "It was a rock 'n' roll Romeo and Juliet. So many people had so much to lose by them being together that you knew they were doomed. Think about what the fans must have felt when the news broke! If you were into Fetal Position, the very idea that the Voice of Your Generation, the Archduke of Disaffection, might be wooing the Symbol of Everything You Hate, the Queen Tease of Teen, with Godiva chocolates and ribbon-bound copies of *Griffin and Sabine*—why, it was blasphemous! The sense of betrayal alone! It was tantamount to Johnny Rotten getting caught in flagrante delicto with Bonnie 'Total Eclipse of the Heart' Tyler, or those two broads from Starland Vocal Band enjoying a little afternoon delight with Sid Vicious. And what about her? You can't very well be the celebrity spokesperson for Kids for a Drug-Free America and date a heroin addict, now can you?"

CUT TO: BETH: "It was very sweet and innocent. In effect, there were two Monks: the one that was for public consumption, and the one for those who were close to him. He was very businesslike about his teen angst, you know. He could turn it off when he wanted. The night we consummated the affair, for instance. He took me to a lovely dinner and we went skating at Rockefeller Plaza. And all this was not three hours after Fetal Position had been banned for life from network TV for showing up buck naked at the GRAMMYs. Except, of course, for the tin foil they'd wrapped around their genitals."

CUT TO: TYC: "I knew there'd come a day when she'd want a man—I just never thought she'd want one that was crusty and needle-pocked. But I blame the little cretin more than her. I tried to tell him to consider her image! But he'd just doze off into a smack funk. (Shaking head) One day he just up and did it— did *her*, that is. And poof! she was through. He couldn't resist, he said. They were in love, so he felt obliged. He had to.

"He had to go and lay the goose that laid the golden egg."
(Fade Out.)

ACT FOUR
(EXODUS, OR THE CONSEQUENCES)

VOICE-OVER: "Teen-pop sensation Bethany Bardot had reached the pinnacle of music-industry success when an ill-fated romance with punk-rock legend Monk Spit ignited a scandal that threatened both careers. Suddenly, tabloids competed to publish outrageous rumors . . . while editorialists dismissed the

relationship as a publicity stunt . . . while critics eagerly forecast-
ed the arrival of a musical fad that would replace both fading
stars with a new sound. . . ."

CUT TO: BETH: "I didn't understand how invested people
were in the image of Bethany Bardot. The letters they wrote me
after I took up with Monk! People who wouldn't lift a finger to
solve war or world hunger sat down and cranked out page after
page raking me over the coals for disappointing them. I mean,
please, get a life! One minister mailed me a sermon he'd written
about how girls should learn from my poor choices instead of
blindly emulating me. I was like, excuse me, isn't there an Old
Testament parable you could more profitably spend your time
studying?"

CUT TO: TYC: "Kids who liked Bethany suddenly not only
had to bite their lip but swallow their tongues, too. You'd have
thought the House Un-American Activities Committee had
been reconvened. You know, 'Are you or have you ever been a
Bethany Bardot fan?' In that environment of persecution, it was
inevitable that sales would suffer, that concert attendance would
fall. But it was much worse than I ever could've guessed. I mean,
the empty seats at those shows! It was as though the rapture had
arrived to yank kids right out of their shoes. That's how fast the
audience disappeared. It got to me, that and the wait. Wondering
when the news would break that Bethany was no longer a virgin
got my innards all knotty. I was constipated for three weeks
straight. It wasn't good for my health. I always told her, 'You
jump bones, I jump ship.' And so I did. I cut the ties."

CUT TO: BETH: "So one day he up and holds a press con-
ference to announce that he's firing me. *He s* firing *me*. My first
thought was, 'Who works for whom around here?' But that was
nothing compared to the story Tyc put out next. He told anyone
who'd listen that he was dumping me because I violated the
morals clause in my contract. What violation? I was in love! And
how can you contractually prohibit someone from sleeping with
somebody? And who cares? But the press lapped it up, them and
the lawyers. They all went to town."

CUT TO: TYC: "In retrospect it does seem a little tacky. But I honestly thought a morals clause was in her best interest. I loved her, you see. Why not? I invented her. I'm the idolmaker. And to have her stolen by a third-rate no-talent whose every other word was die and kill me—why, it was an insult!

(Wounded pause) "By the way, you think I did her dirty. What about him? I wasn't out of the picture a week before The Interview. You know the one, the one that textbooks still list as one of the Top 10 public-relations disasters of all time. What I did was nothing compared to that. What he did was nothing less than a murder-suicide, televised. Because he killed both of their careers."

CUT TO: ROCK CRITIC: "Obviously, Monk's coming on TV to explain the affair wasn't as epochal as Elvis on *Ed Sullivan*, or the Beatles on *Ed*, or even Michael Jackson introducing the moonwalk on 'Motown 25.' More like Lisa Marie trying to convince Diane Sawyer that she and Wacko Jacko were conjugant. Nevertheless, the sit-down made for cruel theater because, if you look at it, Monk's clearly riding bareback on a dose of runaway horse, if you catch my drift. The interviewer keeps asking if he's high, and the most discretion he can muster is to say, 'No more than usual'! It was certainly pathetic enough to be riveting."

CUT TO: An excerpt from said interview. Here is Monk Spit in a sweat-stained Fetal Position T-shirt. Two jagged strips of duct tape X-out the group's logo. This is Monk's *foo you* to his band, which, a week earlier, he disbanded in order to produce songs for Bethany Bardot's next CD. The interviewer, at the time herself a famous TV personality touted for her uncanny ability to coax intimate confessions from celebrities, is hunched forward, one elbow resting on a yellow legal pad as she taps a thumb to her cheek. "You admit you and Bethany Bardot are friends," she's saying. "How would you define friends? Would you call her a special friend? Is she more important to you than other friends? Would you say that she's a stay-the-night friend?"

Each question brings a soft grunt from the addled young man. Whether they're in response to the interviewer's prodding or whether Monk's entertaining some dream to which only he's privy is uncertain. The woman continues to press him. "Is this someone you'd take on a vacation? Is she someone with whom you could share a bottle of champagne in front of a soft fire on a snowy night?" Then, as Monk tries to lift his head to complete the upward swing of a nod, his chin snaps to a chest, and he seems to be out cold.

Undaunted, the interviewer pokes Monk's biceps. "Monk, are you and Bethany intimate?" One eye opens wide as a coin slot on a piggy bank. "Huh?" he says. The interviewer repeats the question. A long pause ensues as Monk tries to keep his eyelids from clapping back shut. When something audible finally bubbles from between his lips, it's not clear whether it's another *huh?* or a more declarative *uh-huh.* The interviewer doesn't let the uncertainty stand in her way.

"So Bethany is a stay-the-night friend?" she asks.

At this point, however, Monk's head tips to his shoulder, and the sudden weight on the side of his body upsets his balance so he slides sideways across the couch back. The fall stops only when his neck crashes into the armrest. The impact drops his mouth open, inspiring the interviewer to hunch forward even farther anticipating an answer. The only sound that makes it past the punk rocker's protruding tongue, however, is a throaty blast of a snore.

It was the morning after the interview's airing, Beth remembers, that she awoke to the headline *Bethany's Dark Secret, Revealed!* What was so dark about sex? And why were they calling it a secret? It was no secret, just her private business, hers and Monk's and nobody else's.

And yet the media grew so obsessed with the particulars of their sex life that she and Monk had had to hole up in the Hotel Chelsea to ride out the prying. Maybe the Chelsea was a mistake, because their stay there invited all manner of groundless Sid and Nancy comparisons. Maybe holing up at all was a mistake, for in the confines of a suite the fracas seemed all the more intense and suffocating. Phones rang constantly. Disc jockeys and TV personalities opined endlessly on the matter.

Then there were the intrusions—the reporters who posed as bellboys, the paparazzi who tried to pass themselves off as maid service. A half-open door led to an unauthorized photo spread in

Penthouse: Monk lounging in his boxers, scratching his nuts, Bethany in bed, a half-scoop of a breast exposed by a falling sheet. After that, the two of them posted guards at their doors. The guards would work a day and then disappear, never to be heard from again, until, that is, they were quoted as "anonymous sources" in the *Post*'s "Page Six" column, where they spoke of discarded needles poking up from the carpet and used prophylactics littering the trash cans.

It had taken Beth nearly two weeks to understand the obsession. The tone of the reporting finally gave it away. At first she'd been oblivious to the hints of contempt. Then the coverage grew mean and mocking, almost bitter. Strained humor crept into headlines—the front-page headline, for instance, that read *Monk to Bethany: Veni, Vedi, Vici Your Virginity*! Or the syndicated shock jock who spent four straight hours describing with Kama Sutra thoroughness the various ways he would "do" Bethany Bardot because "a hot piece of ass" like that deserved "to be boinked into oblivion by a real man, not some strung-out scuzz." Or the late-night talk-show host who peppered his monologues with Monk and Bethany references: "You know, of course, that Bethany Bardot and Monk Spit are having a wild affair. But the pop queen says she's not worried about getting pregnant. No, no, thanks to his heroin addiction, Monk apparently suffers from premature injection."

It didn't matter that the joke fell ten miles short of funny; the studio audience laughed anyway. Or maybe it was precisely because the wisecrack wasn't witty that people slapped their knees so hard. That the comedian hadn't bothered meant that Monk and Bethany weren't worth the bother. It was just further proof of the disdain that so much of the culture seemed to actively cultivate for them. It was as though the world around them said, "You've been brought to this place thinking you were adored and envied, but the joke's on you. You're merely here to amuse us. You're just an object of ridicule by which we bide our time."

That more than anything else, Beth has since realized, is the only explanation for stardom.

CUT TO: BETH: "People thought it was all hanky-panky and intravenous mainlining. But really, we were working. Monk taught me three chords, A, E, and D, and said, 'Now go start a band.' So I started writing my own stuff. I thought I had things to say. And writing was something Tyc never would've allowed. He didn't want me to grow up, you see. But I was determined that the next album was going to be all me. And it was. For better or worse, it was all about me."

CUT TO: TYC: "Oh, God, I used to beg her never to try to write. Not only is that the kiss of death—it's the clichéd kiss of death. You know, Peter Tork wrote one great song for the Monkees: 'For Pete's Sake,' song one, side two of *Headquarters*. But that was *a* song, and it never came close to cracking the Hot 100. I tried to tell her this, but what could I do? Her boyfriend, the Syringe Cushion, had her convinced she was the next Rickie Lee Jones. Let me tell you, she wasn't the next Melanie, much less the next Ricki Lee Jones."

CUT TO: C.E.O.: "Of course, we weren't surprised when Bethany announced that she would be writing and co-producing her third record. We fully expected it. Writing your own songs is part of The Bid, after all, and, like I said, The Bid's part of the trajectory. The fact that Monk Spit was working with her certainly made the situation more unusual than normal. The truth, however, was that the whole Fetal Position revolution was ancient history by that point.

"Why, Juvenescence Records had already marketed a teen-oriented punk knockoff, the Choad Stroking Zombies. You may remember their Top 10 hit, 'Sodomy, Sodomyou.' Yes, it was more juvenile than even we typically deal with, but that one song moved five million units, so who's to complain about taste? Still, by Bethany's third album, we were looking for a sound that was a little more . . . *fresh*. We were eager to invest in the next big thing. We just weren't sure what it was."

VOICE-OVER: "To make the intent behind her new album clear, Bethany named it *Declaration of Independence*. To most critics' ears, however, a more apt title would have been *Fall of an Empire*."

CUT TO: ROCK CRITIC: "You want me to read my review? (Obviously flattered) Okay. (Flips open tattered magazine) It goes (clears throat) 'This is bullshit.' (Closes magazine) That's it. In its entirety. It took me longer to finish than you might expect. You see, I wanted this review to stand as my homage to Greil Marcus, who once dismissed a none-too-good Bob Dylan album with the immortal line, 'What is this shit?' Mind you, I wanted to *evoke* Greil Marcus, not to plagiarize him, so I had to fiddle some with the syntax. It couldn't be 'What is this bullshit?' because, well, that would have been too obvious. So I took the line out of the interrogative mode and made it declarative: 'This *is* bullshit.' (Contented smile) They're the most famous words I've ever written."

CUT TO: BETH: "Not only did nobody take that album seriously, they went out of their way to ridicule it. It was weird. All along I'd been accused of being superficial, and now here I was denounced as presumptuous and pretentious. Not to speak ill of the dead, but I think it was Monk's fault. He kept pushing me to be . . . deep. I'd write a few lines of poetry and he'd say it wasn't dark enough. 'Gloom it up!' he'd tell me. 'Make the pain visceral!'

"It was him pushing me like that that inspired the song that caused the biggest fit, the one that was supposed to be the album's opus. It was called 'The Vietnam in Me.' Monk had me reading Sylvia Plath for inspiration, and I just loved those two poems 'Daddy' and 'Lady Lazarus.' She uses a lot of Holocaust imagery in them, so the persecution of the Jews becomes a metaphor for her personal alienation. I thought, hey, if she can get away with it, why not me?"

CUT TO: A close-up of the spinning spools of a cassette. As the slow, chiming tones of an acoustic guitar peal through the speakers, the lyrics to Bethany Bardot's bid for credibility scroll across the monitors:

> *From the north to the south to the east to the west*
> *A civil war brews in this breast*
> *From the air to the land to the unsettled sea*
> *A Vietnam's inside of me*

BACK TO: BETH (shrugging): "Listening to it now, I can see why people found it a little overwrought."

VOICE-OVER: "But Bethany barely had time to recover from the critical drubbing given *Declaration of Independence* when an even greater catastrophe struck."

CUT TO: ROCK CRITIC: "The death of Monk Spit: When it happened it came as a shock, even if it wasn't unanticipated. There were bookies in Vegas, after all, taking odds on when the fatal O.D. would occur. It was two-to-one that he wouldn't make it past Yom Kippur."

Meanwhile, the monitors blaze with footage of the spontaneous wakes that took place across America the week that Monk Spit died. Here are tearful Fetal Position fans gathering in public parks. Most appear college-aged; almost all are ear-, tongue-, or nose-pierced, and the more adventurous have tattoos crawling out their shirtsleeves and collars. It is a disconcerting sight, so many kids trying to look toughened and angry now reduced to sobs and gasps. To express their grief some light memorial candles and let the wax stream down their fists. Others clutch roses, the thorns burrowing in their palms as they rip petals from the stems. Strewn across the grounds are pictures of Monk. Most are torn from fan magazines, but a few appear to be original portraits done for a junior-high art class. The gatherings seem subdued and somber, except for the lone flash of anger that makes its way onscreen via a placard or lapel pin: *Bethany, You're to Blame.*

CUT TO: BETH: "The idea that it was my fault . . . I mean, I tried to save him. He used to tell me that I was the only thing that eased his pain. But then I started to realize that it wasn't me personally that they were indicting. It was the image of Bethany Bardot, what she represented. How did one obit put it? Oh, yes: Monk was 'a punk soul too sensitive to abide crass commercialism.' Don't think I didn't know the subtext of that statement. There was so much resentment against Bethany Bardot out there that I bought into it. How could I not? I symbolized everything that was cheap and plastic about American culture, or so I was told. What nobody was asking, though, was what I eventually had to ask myself: in falling in love with Monk, wasn't I again trading one father figure for another? In writing those songs the way he wanted them written, wasn't I just being the person he wanted me to be, the same way I'd done with my father and Tyc?

"But all that came later. Right after he died, I cracked up. They put me in a psychiatric hospital. That's where that famous picture of me was taken. The photographer climbed through the ventilation system of a nearby synagogue to snap it with a tele-photo lens. All the attention, all the blame—I started hating myself. I decided I didn't want to be Bethany Bardot anymore. Let them laugh at somebody else, I thought. I was only nineteen, and there are innumerable other people I could become in the years to come. Why not? I grabbed Monk's stash and split town. To disappear."

VOICE-OVER: "The death of Monk Spit marked the beginning of a long, dark night of the soul for the woman trying to escape the shadow of Bethany Bardot. . . . (Onscreen: B-roll of littered streets, loitering derelicts, pimps and whores). . . . Five years lost to a heroin haze. . . .Five years that saw a fortune squandered, a talent debased, a broken heart battered in the fisticuffs of depression and despair. . . ."

No, no, no, Beth is thinking. That's not the way it was at all. Yes, she dabbled with heroin for the better part of a half-decade, but was she truly addicted? She likes to tell herself she wasn't. Drugs were merely a way of hiding from reality. Besides, it wasn't as though she was incapacitated all that time. She read a lot of books, studied a lot, even: art, literature, the guitar. She got her GED. She also got to be pretty good on a twelve-string Ovation–until she realized that most contemporary music was starting to sound silly and adolescent.

As for life on the street, she couldn't say. She hadn't fallen that far. Yes, there was the perpetual downsizing, but no bums or hookers to bear witness to her dissolution. She sold her Hollywood bungalow to get out from under the attorneys' bills. It was the lawyers, more so than she, who burnt through her money. Then when the suite at the Chateau Marmont became prohibitive, it was off to a series of modest apartments and lofts. There was one point where a tabloid tracked her down to a mobile-home court in Bakersfield, but the reporter wouldn't believe her when she claimed she liked trailer life because she didn't have time for home maintenance. "You expect me to believe you're happy?" the man had said. "Please!" So she didn't argue.

And, yes, she had briefly been homeless, but it was only for a short period while she toyed with a move back to Missouri. She was thinking of going to journalism school in Columbia. She even bought a used van, a customized one, for the move. She ended up sleeping in it as she tried to work up the courage to apply to college. Was that so odd? Don't many young adults live out of a car at some point? Isn't that what being young's all about?

CUT TO: BETH'S HUSBAND. He's a moderately handsome man, older, with a bushy mustache that tries to balance out his receding hairline. He looks like someone who's never listened to music.

He's saying, "I was working as a drug-recovery counselor, and one day she just came into my office. I wouldn't say it was love at first sight. For one thing, I'm bound to professional codes of conduct that prohibit me from jumping into relationships with my patients. But I was struck by the way she described her desire to get clean: 'I'm bored.' That was it. I'm bored, not I need help, I feel awful, I don't want to die. I'd never heard anybody claim her addiction was tedious. And, no, I didn't know who she was. I don't have time to bother with entertainment news. One day she up and asked me: 'Don't you know who I used to be?' And I said, 'I'm more concerned with who you see yourself becoming.' (Shy smile) Two kids later, I think it's fair to say that was the line that hooked her. Wouldn't you agree?"

CUT TO: BETH: "I can't say why or how, but it just hit me one day: 'I want to be content.' I was tired of regretting what I'd lost, lamenting what might've been. Contentment gets a bad rap, you know. People equate it with settling down, and that becomes a synonym for settling for less. To be content implies that you've stopped searching, that you're no longer looking. It's the death of desire. And in America isn't it something just short of sinful to declare, 'I'm done. I'm not seeking anymore'?

"The older I get the more that becomes my definition of adulthood: when you no longer feel the need to look back—or, for that matter, forward. So that's my story. (Shrugging) Simple enough, I gave up being Bethany Bardot when I realized I'd rather be a grownup."

The line is Beth's favorite, the one that she feels should end the documentary. But, of course, it's not her call, and the writer and director feel no need to let things be.

VOICE-OVER: "But if Bethany Bardot is content to leave stardom behind, others touched by her story have had a tougher time letting go."

CUT TO: BETH S FATHER: "Sure, I was bitter for a lot of years. Here she sprung from my loins, and I wasn't good enough to get a little reflected glory? But you learn to cope in your own way. For me, that meant finding me a surrogate daughter. I was up in Fester County a few years back and came across this indigent family. I gave them a thousand dollars to take their three-year-old off their hands. Now she's twelve, and she's a better girl to me than that ingrate daughter of mine ever was. We even sing together. We've got us a little father-daughter duet we do. I may never hit the big time, but the last sanctuary we played, I signed twenty-two autographs."

CUT TO: TUNESMITH: "I'm really proud of the songs I wrote for Bethany Bardot. In fact, I think they're ripe for rediscovery. To that end I've been adapting them to a musical. It's about a teenage girl who becomes a pop star, only to fall back into obscurity. Sure, the story is a little contrived, but on an intellectual level it will ask some very profound questions: why does so much of American culture revile adulthood? How did we get to the point where we equate growing up with growing old?

(Excited) I've even written some new songs in the old Bethany style. Here let me play you one. . . ."

CUT TO: TYC: "My time with Bethany pretty much curbed my enthusiasm for the teen market. The shelf life's too short and the turnover's too great. I needed a slower pace; I couldn't take the constipation. So I went into managing comedians. Over the years I've cornered a very specific market: gay vaudeville. You wouldn't think it, but there's a big demand in homosexual night-clubs for comedy with gay themes.

"You've heard, no doubt, of the lesbian folk singer Phranc, whose name has long been rumored to be a playful pun on both *Frank*, as in Sinatra, and *frank*, as in speaking frankly. Well, my protégé at the moment is a young performer who calls herself Bhing, and, yes, the name's designed to not only suggest the King of Crooners but also the existential condition of *being*, as in the Heideggerian notion of *being-in-the-world*. Pretty artsy-fartsy, in other words. My Bhing's a sort of Ani DiFranco type, but early Ani DiFranco, back when she was sexually ambiguous. Bhing has a great joke I've just got to share: 'Did you hear about the pornographer who got fired for being too avant-garde? He didn't know he wasn't supposed to think outside the box!' (Laughs until eyes must be wiped) You've got to agree that's funny—goddamn funny. . . ."

CUT TO: ROCK CRITIC: "People who came of age back then want to know: what was the significance of Bethany Bardot's music? The answer is (contemplatively) none. There wasn't any, not that I can see. Both she and her songs came and went the way pop stars have for more than fifty years. That's what's ultimately great about American popular culture. It's a self-cleaning oven.

"To me what's a more interesting question is: what's become of all those eleven-year-olds who adored her, who wanted to be her? They're twenty-five now. They're women. Some of them never grew up. They still sleep with stuffed animals and use words like 'icky.' Then there are the ones eager to prove that they're grownups. Their adolescence embarrasses them, so to make themselves feel better they indulge in a little revisionist history. They assure themselves that they were never into Bethany Bardot at all but were instead disciples of Hüsker Dü, Black Flag, the Replacements, and, yes, even Fetal Position. (With contempt) They're the posers.

"Then there are the ones I find the most intriguing. They're the ones who outgrew music. At some point in their lives they just lost interest and stopped listening. Maybe it's when they started worrying about grades. Maybe it wasn't until they got married to make babies. Whatever the age, their complete disinterest in the things that once impassioned them baffles me. All that energy, all that investment and identification, and . . . it doesn't mean shit to them now. It makes me wonder what they say to themselves on those days when they're riding in their SUV's, chauffeuring sons to trombone and tuba lessons, and without warning the seek dial on the radio lands them on a string of words that they once held as dear as a mantra: *Summer's here and the time's right / For having boys and fun.* I can hear them: 'I suppose it was important to me once, but no more. For when I was a child I played with childish things.' Yes, I imagine them thinking about how, from the far side of thirty, those lyrics and that tune seem just a wee bit . . . cheesy.

(Nodding head) "Maybe that's what it means to be an adult. To accept that the foundations of adulthood stand upon a whole hell of a lot of cheesy detritus" (smiles and shrugs).

CUT TO: Shots of Beth and her family, setting the dining table, washing dishes, taking a long stroll through a local park.

The voice-over says, "Today, the former Bethany Bardot is a wife and mother happy to stay home. Long ago she resigned herself to life outside the limelight. And even though it's been more than a decade since she reigned over the pop charts, not even time can take away the memories of being an idol to millions of her peers, a symbol of the giddy, awkward joy of being a teenager."

CUT TO: BETH (reading a question from a Trivial Pursuit game card): "Name the teen pop star known for her hit 'Summer

of Boys and Fun' who caused a scandal by losing her virginity."
(Flips card; is silent for a moment) "Well, what do you know? It's
me. The me I used to be. (Lays card on table and then stiffens)
Yes, my life makes for good trivia. But that doesn't mean it's been
trivial."

(Fade out to the strains of the last great Bethany Bardot hit,
"Atomic Youth," whose anthemic chorus warbles away to a
bleating synthesizer riff: *Atomic youth / We're the future and the
future's proof / Atomic youth / Yeah, yeah, uh-huh, oh yeah.* Roll closing credits).

As soon as the monitors go blank, the writer and director
swivel their chairs to face Beth. "Well, what do you think?" one
of them asks.

That was my life, she wants to tell them. But it wasn't all of
my life.

She doubts they would understand, however, and explaining
would take more time and energy than she cares to spend. So she
lies. "I liked it. It flows. It's just . . . I don't know . . . the ending
seems a bit odd. The tone's not quite right. I come off sort
of . . . snippy."

The writer and director exchange glances, then smile slyly in
mutual agreement. "We're glad you mentioned that," the writer
tells her. "Because it brings up a point we need to discuss."

DÉNOUEMENT

(ANAGNORISIS, OR THE RECOGNITION)

"You see," he goes on, "we've found that the audience really
likes it when our show ends on a note of what Aristotle called
peripeteia, or the reversal of fortune. For an hour we've seen the
hero"—The director shoots him a look—"or heroine, excuse me,
soar and fall and then crash and burn. . . . And yet, despite the
inevitability of this fate, viewers still want to believe in his or her
essential goodness. The reversal of fortune allows for that. It's a
way of rehabilitating the main protagonist, of reminding us why

we identified with that person's story in the first place. In our case, the best kind of peripeteia is when the hero shows he's game for a second shot at stardom. We're talking, in other words, about the comeback."

The director chimes in. "Believe it or not, viewers take comfort in knowing that somewhere out there on the darkling plain Quiet Riot's ready to crank it, that Bobby Goldsboro's just a hair's breath away from his umpteenth rendition of 'Honey.' It's somehow reassuring. And without that attempted return to the glory days, the story feels only four-fifths complete."

The writer's been nodding throughout the entire pitch. "It wouldn't be too difficult to set up," he adds. "Nor would it take too much of your time. We can get you a pickup band to work out a modern arrangement of 'Summer of Boys and Fun.' We'll put you on a club stage in front of a sympathetic audience."

And, again, from the director: "You don't even have to do a whole show. We only need sixty seconds of footage. Really, it wouldn't be any hassle at all. It'd give your family an opportunity to see you live."

"They see me live everyday," Beth says.

She's smiling because this isn't the first time the offer's been made. From the moment the producers approached her about her participation in the show, there was talk of resuscitating Bethany Bardot. A new *Best of* CD would be released, replete not only with all digitally remastered tracks but alternative takes and studio oddities. Beth would be invited to guest on another of the channel's hit shows, *Behind the Magic 8 Ball*, a round robin in which stars from yesteryear forecast the future of contemporary teen sensations. There was even talk of Bethany Bardot returning to the stage as part of a touring revue based on the documentary series. She'd get to sing her hits in a forty-five minute showcase set bookended by The Jets and El DeBarge. "We can get you a gig at the Beau Rivage in Biloxi," they assured her. "Rick Springfield tore the ass out of that place last summer. You can even do your Vietnam song if you want."

But Beth turned them down then, just as she turns them down now.

"It's flattering, very flattering. But I just can't go there."

The writer and director try (but not too hard) to mask their disappointment. Aware that she's letting them down, Beth decides the time's right to leave. She gives Tori a shake. The girl bursts alive, confused. When she realizes she's dozed through most of the preview, her face twists. "I missed it!" she yells in a voice that her mother knows as a presage to a temper tantrum. Dreading a crying spell, Beth gives the girl a shush. The director, feeling a twinge of unfulfilled maternity, assures Tori that there'll be plenty more opportunities to see the show. The documentary will air twenty times over the next month, after all. That news calms the child long enough for Beth to gather Geneva and her diaper bag. Then it's up and away from the editing station into the hallway that will direct her and her children back to normalcy.

"Just one more thing, Bethany."

It's the director again. She's standing along a corridor wall that's decorated with a tall reproduction of the show's logo. Surrounding the painted letters are autographs, most of which are accompanied by some variation of *You Rock* and *You're Awesome.*

"Would you sign our Wall of Fame for us? Everybody we've profiled has."

Beth forces a smile to her lips as she trades Geneva for a black Sharpie. The baby's no sooner in the director's arms than she squalls and whines at being cradled by a stranger. Beth presses the Sharpie's tip to the wall and starts scrawling her name. Only, for a second, she can't decide which name to sign. But the choice isn't really hers, is it? Who ever heard of Mrs. Beth Gregorowicz? So she scribbles a signature she hasn't written in years in as illegible a hand as she can muster.

As an afterthought, she adds a short epigram: *Nostalgia's just a dead man's way / to say "Give me money."* Beth wonders how long it'll take the staff to recall the source of that line—an old Fetal Position song, words and music by Monk Spit.

She's re-exchanging the marker for her baby when Tori pipes up, "Can I write my name?"

The director's lips tighten with a condescending smile as she pats the child's head. "I'm sorry, sweetie. But the Wall's only for people like your mommy—famous people."

"Tell you what," Beth comforts the girl. "We get home, we'll tape construction paper to our own wall, and you can sign away your soul."

And with that, the family makes its way down the hall, past a glass partition and sentried front door to the busy street outside. The pedestrian traffic is thick, so Beth clutches Tori's hand and presses Geneva tighter to her breast. It's two blocks to the city garage where their mini-van is parked. After only a few steps, though, the strap of the diaper bag slips off Beth's shoulder, catching her in the bend of her arm. She's hesitant to let go of Tori, who has proved adept at slipping from her mother's side, so she allows the bag to dangle for several steps. But then its weight proves too cumbersome, and so Beth must stop to yank it back into place.

When they resume walking Tori insists on playing a game she's fond of. She'll skip out in front of her mother until Beth's arm is jerked straight and Beth finds herself bobbing along in the girl's wake. Then, without warning, Tori will plant her feet and drop back until Beth's arm is fully extended behind her body. Sometimes the girl will refuse to walk and Beth must drag her by the wrist. Other times she'll draw her knees to her stomach with a kick and swing forward, aiming for her mother's side. Either way, Beth finds it annoying. She doesn't say anything, though, because she figures a game like this is what being a kid's all about.

After a few paces they come to the crosswalk at the block's end. Toward the middle of the intersection Tori goes for another swing. Only this time as she's dropping her shoes to the pavement she misjudges the height of the curb and trips, nearly spilling Beth and Geneva on top of her. Beth catches her balance and reprimands Tori with a brusque tug. But it doesn't do a whole lot of good. A few yards farther on and the girl is back to having her fun again, as if the risk of a tumble is something that doesn't exist in her world.

As Beth tries to leverage her weight to prevent another fall she's aware of how literally her responsibilities pull her in different directions. She also knows her trundling isn't exactly graceful or poised. Her pace speeds and slows to compensate for Tori; every third or fourth step requires a half-hop to keep the child in line. Beth imagines what a lumbering sight she must be in the eyes of fellow pedestrians. But that's the true rhythm of living, she figures: not a determined stride along a straight line, but the awkward step, the unsure footing. She thinks again of the documentary, of how its sequenced events advanced like an invading column of soldiers, how those events were presented as so resolutely linked as to have their own logic, their own inevitability. There was no room for accident, for any fortuitous incident to occur outside the causal chain.

Her life's never felt that neat or that arranged. Maybe that's why the telling of her story, of what was supposed to be Beth's story anyway, struck her as superficial, as artificial even. Because once you accept the essential ungainliness of life, its flatfooted indirection, there's no more believing in form. The drama of accumulating days doesn't add up to an outline that's linear or pyramidal or circular even. Time merely unfolds in a shape that's . . . well . . . misshapen. Or maybe, Beth decides, shapeless. Yes. The shape of life is shapelessness itself.

So be it, she thinks. Right now she's where she wants to be. What else is there?

Meanwhile, she moves ahead slowly, a half step back for every four steps forward, into the sprawl of what's to come.